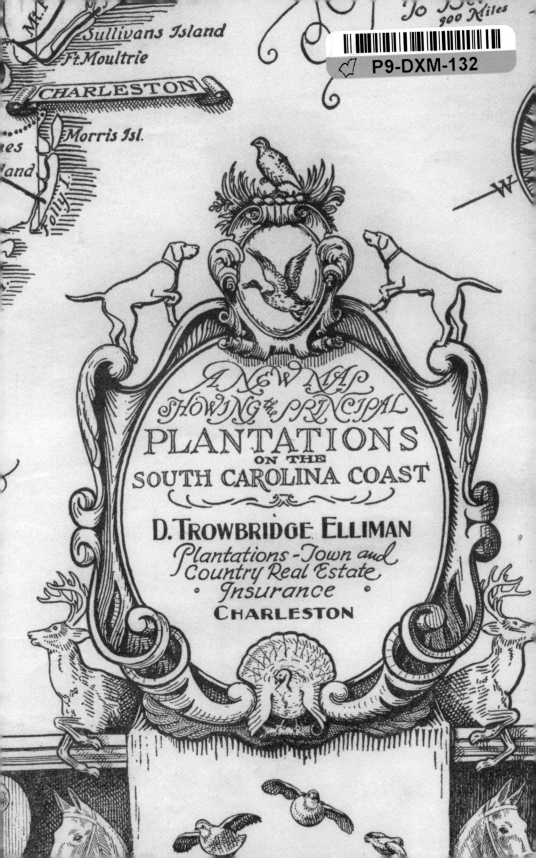

Sullivans Island
Ft. Moultrie
CHARLESTON
Morris Isl.

A NEW MAP
SHOWING the PRINCIPAL
PLANTATIONS
ON THE
SOUTH CAROLINA COAST

D. TROWBRIDGE ELLIMAN
Plantations - Town and
Country Real Estate
Insurance
CHARLESTON

Lowcountry Summer

DOROTHEA
BENTON
FRANK

Lowcountry
Summer

wm

WILLIAM MORROW

An Imprint of HarperCollins*Publishers*

Grateful acknowledgment is made to the South Carolina Historical Society to reprint the endpaper maps. Used with permission.

HarperCollins books may be purchased for educational, business, or sales promotional use. For information please write: Special Markets Department, HarperCollins Publishers, 10 East 53rd Street, New York, NY 10022.

FIRST EDITION

Library of Congress Cataloging-in-Publication Data has been applied for.

ISBN 978-0-06-196117-5

10 11 12 13 14   OV/RRD   10 9 8 7 6 5 4 3 2 1

In loving memory of
my sweet brother, Billy

CONTENTS

1

Welcome Back to Tall Pines

I T IS A GENERALLY ACCEPTED fact that at some point during your birthday, you will reassess your life. When you are young, and by "young" I mean the sum of your years is under twenty, your whole life is still in front of you. Your un-jaundiced eyes are sunlit and wide. Your lungs rise and fall with breathless optimism. Whom will you marry? Who will you become? Will you be blessed with good children? Live in China? Climb Everest? Visit the Casbah? Sail the Amazon? Will the riches of the world find their way to your door? The details of your future life are still shrouded in the opaque mists of time's crystal ball and you, the anxious and impetuous young you, hopping from one foot to the other, cannot wait to get there.

But, darlin', when your years creep north of thirty, your assessing eye blinks, drifts to the past to scan your scorecard because your future is pretty much a foregone conclusion. Or is it? Surely by forty, you *should* know who you are and how well you are doing with your life. At least you hope you'll have life under control by then.

At least that's what I was thinking about on that Sunday afternoon, the fifteenth of April, 2007, when most of my family gathered at Tall Pines. They were there to toast the culmination of my forty-six years and wish me well as I embarked on my forty-seventh. None of us knew about the disasters to come that would change me and everyone around me forever.

Had I not learned a thing? Apparently not. It was God's grace that my mother, Miss Lavinia, was gone to glory or she would have slapped me silly while whispering in an even jasmine tone her deepest disappointment in my judgment. Mother had taught me better. She stopped any nonsense before it could gain steam. But where was she when I needed her? Gone. Yes, I still suffered over my mother's death for many reasons, not the least of which was that as soon as we were reunited in life, she slipped through my fingers and died. It was completely devastating and very, very unfair. And, how would you like to have the job of filling Lavinia Boswell Wimbley's shoes? You would not. Never mind she literally had hundreds of pairs, one size smaller than my foot.

I looked around. Rusty and my brother, Trip, still together after all these years despite all the interference, were in the living room and as always the heat between them was excruciating. I often wondered if what mischief they had with each other between the sheets was as provocative as their behavior in the company of others. As he handed her a plate of food, any fool could see his other hand traveling to her lap for a tickle. So silly.

I wondered what my mother's friends Miss Sweetie and Miss Nancy thought about them, not that Rusty or Trip would have been even slightly wounded for one second to learn that they had embarrassed their elders. They were oblivious. The old crows, knowing them, probably found the lovebirds' croon to be titillating. Why, they still fooled around in chat rooms for singles, pretending to be college coeds! They thought it was hilarious! I guess it's fair to say that out here in plantation country, your social life was really truly only ever going to be what you made of it. And available men of their age were almost all gone, meaning deceased. Any old coots who were still on the prowl wanted young girls, younger than me, something that made me feel uncomfortable.

And you might know, Trip was still campaigning for Frances Mae to sign new separation papers that she had no intention of signing. Perhaps it was the fact that Rusty and Trip could not marry that kept their fires burning. We always crave what we cannot possess, do we not?

And Millie and Mr. Jenkins? They had enough going on between them to produce smoldering embers in every fireplace at Tall Pines Plantation, but they would never admit it and we rarely caught a glimpse of it. They were old-school, discreet and modest. Ah, discretion! I admired them for those qualities, although discretion seemed to be difficult for me to embrace. Let's be honest. When a suitable man came into my life, Miss Lavinia's blood coursed through my veins like the fast train from Dijon to Saint-Tropez.

Speaking of "all aboard the TGV"? My current beau was a wonderful guy named Bobby Mack. Bobby was a little bit shorter than I am and sort of stocky. But he was a willing fellow who was passionate about everything, including me. There were many reasons why we were not likely to marry, but the main one was that he was an unreliable companion. Every weekend and holiday and even today was spent working. Bobby raised pastured Heirloom pork to the music of Chopin, but every time I turned around, he was throwing a pig pull for a hundred people or climbing on a truck to personally deliver a carcass to Daniel Boulud in New York. It was annoying. And the other reason was that he always smelled like traces of the literal pits—deeply smoky and a little greasy—an occupational hazard which could not be washed away by any soap yet produced on earth. But when we'd argue and I would decide it was time to say good-bye forever, he would show up at my door with five pounds of bacon. That was about all it took to sustain us for another month or so. I'm a fool for pork. And to be honest, I liked the way he smelled, but when we were around other people, I would see them sniffing.

My handsome son, Eric, now a freshman at the University of South Carolina, was there also. He had come home for the day with Trip and Frances Mae's oldest daughter, Amelia, who was a junior at the university, majoring in American history. Yes, it was true. Amelia, who had sprung from the fiery womb of Satan's favorite hellcat, had become lovelier to behold with each passing year. Except for her unfortunate hair, poor thing—that endless tangle of black strings was all twisted up on her head and held with combs and rubber bands. But her eyes were nice, bright blue like Trip's, with thick lashes. Millie and I often wondered why Amelia chose to major in American history. Maybe the poor dear thought that if she scoured our country's past with enough diligence, she could find a reasonable explanation for the piss-poor protoplasm of her mother's genetic code. Who's knows? Thank God Amelia was more like Trip.

But my Eric? It's incredible to say this but all of his learning-style differences seemed to have practically disappeared or else he had developed such strong study skills and compensating skills from years of Rusty's tutelage that it seemed that way. In any case, he had blossomed under Trip's attention and my flawless mothering. Do I hear a groan from the peanut gallery? Okay, here's the truth. Between Millie, Rusty and me, Trip and Mr. Jenkins, Eric had enough parents for ten boys. And of course, when Miss Lavinia was alive she doted on her only grandson.

And Richard, my ex? Eric's father? That British slime of the earth with his postured accent? The not-such-a-genius psychotherapist/

psychiatrist? His contact with all of us had dwindled to a bare minimum and that suited us just fine. Eric was already in college, practically grown, and the last decade of his life had played out with only Richard's slightest presence or interest. Richard's loss, not ours.

The university was under an hour's drive from Tall Pines, but to Amelia and Eric, it was light-years away. Freeing Amelia of her chaotic life in Walterboro and moving Eric away from the plantation had brought about all the changes in them you would expect as children finally come of age. Independence! They were learning how to inhabit the adult world and to draw their own conclusions about worldly matters. They stood taller, and without prompting, even self-corrected their student slouch from time to time. They were less rowdy and more considerate of others. I looked around to see my Eric leaning forward, listening in earnest to Miss Sweetie as she piffled on and on about my recent purchase of a portion of her strawberry business.

I think Miss Sweetie was happy about it. She had no children to inherit and she had always been like an aunt to me. We finally agreed after a lot of discussion that she should remain on as the spokesperson for the company, the president emeritus, traveling to state fairs and appearing on the Food Network as our ambassador, judging cakes, pies, tarts, and breads made with our jams, and salads made with our pickles, and giving small scholarships to worthy students. My job was to oversee the management of the business, which required very little time as it wasn't overly complicated and she already had great managers in place. We changed the name of the business to Sweetie's, much simpler all around than the confection formerly known as TBDJOTP, The Best Damn Jelly On The Planet. She had wanted to retire, but I assured her that if she did, she would be as dead as Kelsey's cow in six months, whoever Kelsey was. Even Millie got in on the conversation that took place on the veranda last fall.

"What you gone do with yourself if you retire, Miss Sweetie? You gone dry-rot! That's what! Retire? That's some fool, 'eah?"

We giggled and it came to me that Miss Sweetie just wanted to be assured that she wouldn't be in the way and that her expertise was truly wanted and valued. Tears came to my eyes thinking of my mother then. Older people are terrified of outliving their usefulness and I would never let Miss Sweetie feel that way. Miss Sweetie was loving her new role and I was staying busy when I wanted to be.

My old career was packed up in boxes. After all, the Lowcountry didn't need another interior decorator, especially when the nearby population who actually *used* a decorator only did so every hundred years or so. We loved our threadbare Aubussons and Niens and petit point curtains about which we could brag Sherman had overlooked in his infamous march, attempting to burn the Carolinas all the way to hell. We cherished every nick and dent in our great-grandmother's four-poster bed and every hidden compartment in our great-grandfather's secretary. Ancient coin silver candelabras were irreplaceable; mint-julep cups were closely guarded. Napkin rings were still in use, even for kitchen meals. Okay, maybe not for kitchen meals, but you know what I mean when I say that we were trying to sustain a certain way of life. Besides all that, Eric was gone off to find his future and what was I supposed to do with myself? So it was me, strawberries, and the pig farmer. Until my birthday of that year.

We were enjoying each other's company and sharing a late afternoon buffet lunch. Millie had prepared chicken Pirlau, a salad of asparagus and orange wedges with avocado in a citrus vinaigrette, and, of course, steaming-hot biscuits so light they literally collapsed and melted in our mouths like a soufflé. Miss Nancy brought the dessert fresh from her oven. It was a hummingbird cake. The smells of sugar and spice taunted us like a whispering siren from its spot on the buffet. And Miss Sweetie made a strawberry trifle with whipped cream, my ultimate favorite.

There had always been something charmed about the personality of Mother's dining room. Food tasted better there. When we gave a party of any sort, the room seemed to sing with its own pleasure of playing hostess and I always half expected Mother to pop out from behind the curtains, announcing her own miraculous resurrection.

The day was warm and we were serving ourselves in the dining room and finding a place to sit in the living room. All the doors were open and spring was in full bloom.

I was telling Miss Sweetie, Miss Nancy, and the others about a dream I'd had last night.

"I was on the veranda and I can't remember what I was wearing but I think it was a dress, a long one, some gauzy combination of nightgown and beach cover-up. I'm not sure. Mother suddenly came out through the French doors and oh! She was radiant! Absolutely radiant! And, here's the thing, y'all! She looked to me to be about my own age."

"Your mother was one of the most beautiful women I have ever known," Miss Sweetie said, choking up. "Lord! I miss her so! It squeezes my heart every time I think about her!"

"*Moi aussi!*" said Miss Nancy. "There was no one like our Lavinia." She handed Miss Sweetie a tissue from the pocket of her expensive cardigan, French in origin, I had no doubt. "Take hold of yourself," she whispered to Sweetie.

"I'm perfectly fine," Sweetie whispered back, slightly insulted, taking the tissue and blotting the corners of her eyes.

"Boy, is that the truth," I said, glossing over Miss Sweetie's fragile emotions, hoping that telling the rest of the story would hold them in check. "Miss Lavinia was one of a kind! Anyway, Mother took me by the hand and the next thing I knew we were flying all over the Lowcountry. We flew over the Edisto, the Ashepoo, and the Combahee rivers and down to Charleston, over St. Michael's Church and the custom house. We were so excited looking at all the houses on

South Battery. Then we came down and walked along the seawall, arm in arm. And I think she said something like 'Look! Look at all the happiness!' Suddenly we were on Church Street or maybe it was Tradd, looking in the windows. Every living room was filled with pink and white balloons and people laughing, having fun."

"*What?* Mom?" All the color drained from Eric's face. "That is a very strange dream," he said.

"No, it isn't," I said. "I dream about my mother all the time."

"No, Mom, it's bizarre."

"Really? Tell me why, Dr. Jung. Are you going to interpret my dream for us like your daddy used to do?" I was just teasing my adorable boy and reached out to ruffle his carefully combed mop of strategically placed locks that nearly covered his eyes. "Hey, are you okay?"

"No, uh, where's Amelia?"

"I'm right here," she said, walking across the rug and eating at the same time, a habit I detested. "Aunt Caroline, this is the best meal I've had in ages! I sure hope you're enjoying your birth—"

I forgave her on the spot.

"Amelia!"

"What, Eric? What's the matter with you?"

"Uh, we forgot something in the car. Be right back." Eric put his plate on the table and took Amelia's arm. "Come on."

"Right!" Amelia said. "OMG! How stupid are we?"

Amelia shook her head and they hurried from the room.

"What in the world?" Miss Sweetie said.

"Who knows?" Miss Nancy said.

"Humph," said Millie. "I got my own suspicions."

Millie knew about things before they came to pass, which could be useful, worrisome, or highly irritating.

"Kids!" I said. "Anyway, I kept thinking she was trying to tell me something."

"Maybe she was telling you to have some more fun," Miss Nancy said. "All work and no play? Should be the other way around once in a while. *N'est-ce pas?* That's why I'm off for France! What was she wearing?"

"Bon voyage!" said Miss Sweetie, still slightly bent out of shape.

"I think she was—no, wait . . . I can't remember!"

My back was to the door but I could see the sudden changes in Miss Nancy's expression and then Miss Sweetie's, and there was never a woman who could shoot her eyebrows to the stratosphere so quickly or grin as widely as Millie Smoak.

"What?" I said.

"Turn around," they said together.

There in the doorway to the outside stood Eric and Amelia holding bouquets of balloons. Pink and white. I nearly fainted. Miss Sweetie sank into a club chair with her hand over her mouth and Miss Nancy patted her on the arm. They both had tears in their eyes.

Rusty said, "Is this a joke?" She rubbed her arms as though she'd caught a sudden chill.

"No, darlin', it's just a little birthday greeting from our mother," Trip said, and chuckled.

"It was my idea but I don't know where the idea came from," Amelia said. "You never said anything about liking balloons before."

"Well, I adore them!" I said, and took the ribbons into my hand. "I really do!"

"Yeah," Eric said. "Amelia asked me what to buy you for a gift and I said you didn't need anything. So she said what about balloons?"

"It's so perfect, you just don't know!" I said, gave them a kiss on their cheeks, and turned to Millie. She was giggling like a schoolgirl and I joined her in a burst of laughter. Then I looked around the room at my slack-jawed gathering. "Oh, come on! You know Mother! Isn't this the grandest feat?"

"Freaky," Eric said.

"Completely weird," Rusty said.

"For once I agree with her," Amelia said, and hooked her thumb in Rusty's direction.

"Thanks," Rusty said.

"Well, I think it's completely wonderful," Miss Sweetie said. "Completely wonderful."

"I think so, too . . . is that the kitchen doorbell?" I said.

"I think that door is locked up," Millie said.

"Finally!" Trip said. "Probably my dear estranged wife with my daughters . . ."

I saw Amelia cut her eye at Rusty in disgust as though Rusty were the living embodiment of Hester Primm. I was glad Rusty had missed it because I didn't want there to be trouble and why insult her? Like most people, bad manners made me uneasy.

"I'll see about it," Mr. Jenkins said, making his way toward the dining room.

It buzzed and buzzed with such persistence that Millie and I and then Trip followed. What we found was a horror show. There in the doorway was off-the-wagon Frances Mae, gathered upright by the muscular arms of Matthew Strickland, the sheriff of Colleton County. On his other side stood Chloe, crying like a baby. Her forehead was cut and there was blood all over her. She was entirely disheveled, and Frances Mae, for once in her slovenly, drunken, miserable life, appeared to be penitent—that is, if her silence could be translated into regret.

"Oh Lord!" Millie cried, and hurried to the sink to wet a clean dishcloth.

"Daddy! Oh, Daddy!" Chloe had begun great gulping sobs. She was traveling toward hysteria and I didn't blame her. Who wouldn't be hysterical?

What had Frances Mae done now?

Trip swooped up his pudgy seven-year-old Chloe and sat her on the kitchen counter like a rag doll. Millie moved in and gently applied pressure to the wound, handing Trip a second cloth to wipe the rest of the blood away.

"It's all right, baby," she said to Chloe in the sweetest voice she had. "It's just a little bitty cut. You're not even gonna need stitches."

"Head wounds bleed a lot. Should I bring this one into the kitchen?" Matthew Strickland said, bringing our attention back to my low-life sister-in-law.

"Good grief!" I said. "Well? Let's see if you can park old Hollow Leg at the table. I'll make some coffee." I reached into the refrigerator for the coffee and into the cabinet for a filter.

Matthew poured Frances Mae into a chair and she put her head down on her folded arms and appeared to pass out. I began filling the coffeepot with water.

"It's all right now, sweetheart," Trip said to Chloe, and then asked, "So, what happened, Matthew?"

"I saw her Expedition swerving a little going down Highway 17, so I followed her. I knew it was Frances Mae because of the bumper stickers. So I figured she was liquored up. Then, no surprise, she turned on Parker's Ferry and I kept on behind her. When she went to turn into Tall Pines, she bounced off the gate and then slid into the ditch. So I picked them both up and brought them to you."

"Nice," I said, and flipped the switch on the coffeemaker. "God in heaven, Matthew, and that's a prayer of thanksgiving. What in the world would we do without you?"

"Well, you might be spending some more time in the court-house. That's for sure." Matthew smiled at me and I remembered what it was like to fool around with him not so long ago. God, he was hot. Probably inappropriate for me, but white-hot, honey. By the look in his eyes I could see that he was still interested. I blushed. Okay, I didn't blush. I twitched in the South.

"Frances Mae?" Trip shook her shoulder. His voice was filled with disgust. "Frances Mae?" There was no response. The fumes coming from her were powerful enough to cure a string of bass. "She's as drunk as a goat. Out cold."

"Obviously," I said.

"The SUV is still in the ditch," Matthew said. "Fender's messed up."

"I'll call a tow truck directly," Mr. Jenkins said, and opened the cabinet where we kept the phone book. "Won't be the first time. Won't be the last."

"Jenkins?" Millie said. "Don't you be scratching they mad place!"

"Humph," Mr. Jenkins said. "My age? Say what I please."

At that precise moment, Eric and Amelia appeared at the kitchen door.

"Do you want us to light the candles on your cake, Mom?"

"Yeah, Eric's eating all the icing around the edges with his finger, Aunt Caroline."

"Gross, Eric!"

"You do it, too, Mom!" he said.

"Mother would never do something so vile, son," I said with a wink, and handed him a pack of matches from the drawer.

"Yeah, right," he said, and then he added, "Hey! What happened here?"

"Aunt Frances Mae wasn't feeling very well and she accidentally ran off the road into a ditch," I said, without missing a beat. After all, we had become accustomed to spinning this sort of *situation* into some reasonable explanation over the past few years.

"Mom!" Amelia called out.

Frances Mae raised her head and opened her eyes. "Yewr sisters are li'l bitches. Woulna drive Chloe," she said, and once again, her head went down and her lights went out.

She referred to her other daughters—my namesake Caroline, known as Linnie, and Isabelle, called Belle, as in southern, and she was anything but.

"Holy shit!"

"Eric!"

"Sorry! But she's baked!"

"In the parlance of the young people? Duh," I said, and gave Chloe a kiss on the hand. Poor thing. "Tell Miss Sweetie and Miss Nancy I'll be right out. The Wimbleys were never ones to let a *situation* ruin a party."

"A party?" Matthew said.

"Another birthday," I said, and put the back of my hand over my forehead, feigning the next step to a swoon.

"Well, I should be moving on, then," he said.

"Heavens no!" I said, and took him by the hand. "Come have a slice of cake!"

Matthew smiled. "Well, thanks! Don't mind if I do."

His entire six-foot-two frame just radiated testosterone. What was I thinking? Hmm, maybe he'd like to play with the birthday girl later on? I know, shame on me.

"Tell Rusty I've got my hands full here," Trip said.

"Oh, now. You go on out and sing for your sister's cake," Millie said, attaching a Band-Aid to Chloe's forehead. "Mr. Jenkins and I have this all under control."

"I want cake!" Chloe whimpered. "Can I please?"

"Of course! Just wash your hands and skedaddle!" Millie smiled and helped Chloe jump to the floor.

The candles were lit and everyone sang, wishing me a happy birthday. Happy birthday? My pig-farmer boyfriend was in absentia, the county sheriff was the current cause of some very naughty thoughts, my drunk sister-in-law was passed out at my kitchen table, and my dead mother had sent me balloons. What else could a girl want?

2

Excess

Do not think for one minute that I was going to let Frances Mae Litchfield's—okay, Frances Mae Litchfield *Wimbley's*—self-indulgent escapade ruin my birthday party. As you might remember, I simply left her in the kitchen with Millie and Mr. Jenkins. But it was a little bit of divine justice for that day to have been the occasion on which Frances Mae would once again show her true colors. I know it doesn't sound nice for me to take any kind of delight in the weakness of others, but you don't know what a detestable witch of a sister-in-law she has been to me. So, in the cosmic sense, I had my cake and ate it, too.

Eventually Frances Mae sobered up, and Amelia, who was beside herself with embarrassment, drove her and Chloe home to Walterboro and then she and Eric continued on back to school. All glibness aside, the whole incident was deeply upsetting because of what happened to

Chloe. But instead of raising hell in the moment, I took a cool step back because number one, it was Trip's place to do the hell-raising. And second, I didn't want to rile Matthew and have him feel an urgent obligation to arrest Frances Mae. But unfortunately Trip did not step in except to soothe Chloe. Maybe he was so shocked that he didn't react. Maybe he would react later.

There would be an aftermath because there was always an aftermath. It began when Mr. Jenkins had Frances Mae's SUV hauled out of the ditch and sent it off to the body shop. He said it had a dozen empty water bottles, apparently thrown in the back along with assorted fast-food wrappers and old magazines. And in an uncharacteristic piece of criticism, he remarked that the interior of the car had a rank smell. If Mr. Jenkins was reporting *this,* then her SUV must have been absolutely disgusting. Then he said that Trip, whose veins occasionally pumped the holy blood of saints, had rented a veritable tank for her to drive in the meanwhile.

It was expensive for Trip to have an estranged wife like Frances Mae because you could neither rent her a tuna-can car nor could you rent a car based on some algorithm that determined her worth as a citizen of the world. According to Mr. Jenkins, Trip kept saying that she was still the mother of his children and drove three of their four daughters all over the place and that their safety was paramount to him. I couldn't have agreed more on that point.

But any way you shake it up, the fact that Chloe had been hurt while in the car with her mother was a *huge* warning sign to all of us, gnawing away at my normal reserve and desire to mind my own business. Okay, maybe I didn't always mind my own business and Chloe's precarious *situation* was way over the limit of what I was willing to silently endure as the child's aunt. Frances Mae was flat-out dangerous.

On Monday, Millie and I discussed the *situation* all morning while sitting in the kitchen, going over invoices and considering some new labels for Sweetie's. Every time I bumped into her during the day, the discussion continued, growing into a simmering stew. Well into the afternoon she brought me a pile of checks to sign that one of Miss Sweetie's minions had delivered to Rosario, our housekeeper. By then we were in agreement that something had to be done. She stood by the sink, rinsing a glass and talking to me in that tone of voice that all family members knew meant "you had better listen to what I'm saying."

"All I did last night was fret over that child, 'eah? I couldn't sleep for beans! And all day long I can't even eat. This is a terrible thing going on and it's gotta be stopped. Frances Mae's getting drunk up and running the road can't continue."

"Oh, Millie. You're right. I'm sick with worry, too. But you know, this is Pandora's box. If we get involved, I can smell huge drama."

Millie looked at me with her most serious Mount Rushmore expression.

"Gone be worse drama iffin we find ourselves standing over that baby's grave. That chile was all kinda shook up and so was I. So wrong. Jenkins was so mad I thought he was gonna bust. What you gone do?"

"Me?"

"Yes, ma'am! *You!* What? You think if Miss Lavinia was alive she wouldn't do something?"

"Oh Lord, Millie. I know, but I'm not Trip's mother."

"You the eldest? You need to have a little 'come-to-Jesus meeting' with him."

"Fine. Oh, fine. You're right."

I called Trip and asked him to stop by for a glass of tea on the way home from his office. It was around six when he came in through the kitchen door looking like utter hell. Signs of stress were digging narrow gullies all around his eyes.

"Hey there, brother of mine! How was your day?" I stood on my tiptoes and gave the poor rascal a smooch on the cheek.

"Mondays have a reputation for a reason."

"You're telling me? Good day, huh?

"Yeah, great. So, what's going on?"

"Nothing. I just wanted to talk to you. That's all."

Trip stared at me as he loosened his tie, pulled it off, wound it around his fist, and dropped it into the pocket of his jacket. He knew me so well that sometimes it was frightening. Trip looked really exhausted, something I had not seen on his face in a long time.

"Want to walk down by the river?" he said, sensing that this conversation could wander into serious territory.

"Yeah. That sounds good." I handed him a frosty traveling mug of iced sweet tea and filled one for myself, casually screwing on the tops after I tossed in some sprigs of mint from Millie's garden.

"I can't stay long. Rusty's cooking fish."

"What kind?"

"Frozen." He looked at me and smiled. "Some salmon from Nova Scotia I caught a while back."

"Sounds too good to miss! So, let's go."

As we had done probably a thousand times in our lives, we ambled across the grass, down the sloping lawn toward the dock. There was a nice breeze, and suddenly, as though we had been folded into some invisible gauze of magic, we were children again, brother and sister surrounded by all the music and smells of the magnificent Edisto River. In the distance, a scattering of great blue herons flew overhead, gliding on the airstreams, resembling creatures from the days of dinosaurs. This place, these acres, were the center of my universe. And Trip's.

The river often summoned a part of us that it seemed to own, especially in times of trouble. We approached the water as though drawn by a beckoning finger, stopping to lean against the rails on the platform that led to the floating dock below. It was the same spot where we always stood to adjust our bearings when a shift in our world was happening.

Now there was the addition of Eric's boat in the landscape, hanging above the water in dry dock. It was a blue-and-white Sea-Pro with

a seventy-five-horsepower engine. Trip chose it for him as a graduation gift from all of us last summer, a little runabout that didn't
give me a nervous breakdown when Eric took it out alone. Eric had
become quite the accomplished river rat, thanks to the patience and
gracious attentions of my brother. Once again I was reminded of the
many loving ways that Trip had filled in for Richard.

We never said this out loud but it was obvious to everyone that
Trip couldn't handle his daughters and had all but thrown them into
Frances Mae's lap. He was naturally drawn to Eric because Trip was
a man who should've had sons.

Richard, on the other hand, couldn't have put a boat in the water
if his life depended on it, even to escape a global nuclear attack from
the Klingons. And yes, mentally castrating Richard was one of the
ways I released the contempt I felt as the years went by and he continued to treat Eric so poorly. Richard's day of reckoning would come
and there would be a hefty price to pay. I believed in karmic justice.

But for today, I was down by the river with my brother trying to
tactfully broach the subject of his daughters' safety.

"I didn't sleep all night," he said.

"That explains why you look like you been rode so hard. And
FYI, who slept?"

"Truly."

"So, did you talk to Frances Mae today?" I said.

"No. Hell no!" Trip cut his eyes at me and then took a long drink
of tea. "Why would she call me?"

"Well, I was thinking she might call to say thanks for the rental
car. Or maybe to apologize? And say that what happened yesterday
would never happen again or something to that effect. Although we
all know it could happen again this afternoon."

"You think she's gonna drive drunk again? After what happened
yesterday? Is she that stupid?"

"Well, let's see. She's drunk all the time, so if she wants to go somewhere, and she's gonna drive there, chances are about one hundred percent that she's gonna be driving drunk, right?"

"Her butt is gonna wind up in jail. I mean, she can't expect the police to overlook her problems forever."

"Yeah. It's true. Matthew's a great friend, but the law's the law. And yesterday he rescued Chloe while she was bleeding from the head."

"It was just a little scrape," Trip said.

I squinted my eyes and tightened my jaw. "A little scrape. Trip? Are you serious? You've got a big problem here, bubba."

"Yeah? What's that?"

"The kids shouldn't be in the car with Frances Mae. Period! And let's face it. Belle can't be expected to run car pool for Linnie and Chloe, and Amelia's off at college."

"So? That's Frances Mae's inconvenience, not mine."

Sometimes Trip could be exasperating.

"Actually, you are technically correct. But if something happens to your girls at the hands of Frances Mae, when you know she's perfectly fine with getting behind the wheel of a car drunk as a dog, you'll never forgive yourself. And that's where she's headed. She's the proverbial disaster waiting to happen."

"Shit. Great. Fine!" Trip looked at the floorboards of the deck and then out across the water. "So what are you suggesting I do?"

"Somehow you've got to get the girls out of harm's way. You have to!"

"Aw, God! Come on, Caroline! What are you trying to say?"

"I'm saying that as long as those girls remain with Frances Mae? They're in danger, Trip. You know it and I know it."

Trip turned his attention back to the breadth and length of the river, watching for the nearly imperceptible movements of the placid water. Even the tiniest bug gliding over its surface caused ripples, seismic echoes that extended out a thousandfold from the epicenter, a Lowcountry reminder that one decision could have a disastrous impact that lasted forever.

My brother was not a stupid man. Even though Rusty managed the most minute details of his daily life, from what he would enjoy most for entertainment to which necktie would intimidate the defendant's attorney in the courtroom, Trip would acknowledge that he had and would always have a tremendous obligation to his daughters. But, like people say, talk was cheap.

So, as Millie and I had planned, I planted the seed and watered it. I hoped I wouldn't have to wait long to hear him say that he understood and agreed. I didn't know how much time was on the side of the girls' safety, but I knew the odds did not weigh in their favor.

"Well," Trip said, with a loud sigh, "there's rehab. But we've already tried that four times."

"Alcoholism is a fiendish disease, an absolute monster."

"And you know she blames Rusty for her drinking. She blames Rusty for everything."

"Look, Trip, there's enough blame to go around for everyone to choke on it, but at the end of the day somebody has to be the parent here and I'm afraid that's you, big brother."

"You're older."

"A minor detail."

"Humph. So, let's slice this mess as thin as we can. You think I need to take custody of the girls, somehow, and send Frances Mae to a rehab program that will work, somehow. Is that about it?"

"Basically, yeah."

"Yeah right! I can see this now. Let's say they all say *okay,* which they won't. I move them over here, right? After Belle and Linnie wreak complete havoc at every blessed turn, Chloe turns into a thumb-sucking bed wetter, shrieking through the night. Then Rusty can't take it anymore and leaves me forever." Trip's arms were flailing in the air and his face was getting redder by the second. "Forget it. I'm not doing it."

"Trip? Have you checked your blood pressure in a while?"

"The answer is N-O!"

"Oh, Trip. I'm gonna agree that it wouldn't be the easiest of situations from the get-go, but don't you think they'd come around?"

"Those scheming, manipulating, lying troublemakers?"

"Trip! These are your daughters! Come on. I mean, Rusty is a sweetheart! She adores children!"

"Yeah. Yeah, she does. And they adore her! But my children? My lovely girls are the only ones in the world who despise Rusty. I mean despise! They think the sole reason their mom and dad aren't together is because Rusty is the tramp who stole their old man."

"Well, that's just ridiculous."

"Maybe. Maybe not. Sometimes I don't know what's true and what isn't. You know what I mean? I was perfectly miserable in my marriage but I was functioning well enough. Well, not really. My life was actually a sham. I was drinking and gambling . . ."

"I remember it well. The glory days."

"Very funny. But look, I was functioning. Then I got bailed out, thanks to Mother, got myself reasonably together, and somewhere in the process I met Rusty. Nothing else has mattered since then but her. She changed my whole world! Now I'm a model citizen—well, sort of—but my career is going gangbusters because she brings all this peace—yes, *peace* and stability to my life. And such happiness! For the first time in my entire life, I'm actually happy! Can my girls see this? Don't they realize that Rusty, not that shit-bird mother of theirs, is the reason my life is back on track? Hell no! My girls are plenty old enough to care about my happiness but they don't."

Although he was right, Trip's words were confirmation that all men are big fat idiots when it comes to understanding the thought processes of hormonal teenage girls.

"Come on now. No teenage girls care about their parents' happiness if it interferes with their own world. It wouldn't be normal."

"But I should jeopardize the only personal happiness I've ever known to take on a bunch of ingrates/borderline thugs?"

"It's true. They're a rough bunch. It's not fair but this is the downside of parenting. You have to change their tunes, Trip. You don't want them to grow up and keep on acting like they do now anyway, do you?"

"Of course not."

"Amelia is coming along, don't you think? At least she was smart enough yesterday to be totally mortified by her mother's, um, condition. And she's smart enough to understand the risk Frances Mae took with her little sister."

"Yeah, Amelia is the pick of our litter."

We were quiet then for a few more minutes, Trip undoubtedly feeling the weight of a thousand pounds on his conscience and me unsure of what to say next. All I could do was think about how Belle and Linnie had been suspended from school for bringing liquor to ball games and taken to the police station for using fake IDs to get into local bars and then getting so drunk that they peed in public. (Peeing in the wrong place came from their mother's side of the family.) Their behavior had to be such a slap in the face to Trip, and I thanked God that our mother had not lived to see his hooligans in action. Finally, Trip spoke.

"Aw, crap."

"You always were the eloquent one, Trip."

"Thanks. Look. Let's be serious here. Rusty's going to flip if I decide to take the kids. And don't forget the main burden of their care would fall to her. I'm home for meals and to sleep and that's about it. Besides it would be an open invitation for them to mutilate our lives. It's not gonna work."

"You have to discuss it with Rusty, Trip. These are your kids! Just talk to her and see what she says."

Trip looked at me and pulled the corner of his mouth up in a grimace, shaking his head. "I gotta get going. I'm already late. It's almost dark."

"Okay. Call me if you need me, okay?"

"Right. Oh, and by the way?"

"What?"

"Thanks for the pep talk."

"You'll thank me when they all live long enough to give you gorgeous grandchildren!" I called after him. He kept walking.

"Without criminal records!" I called again.

He shot me the finger without missing a step. It made me smile, which says a lot about how our relationship had matured.

I watched him walk toward his car, thinking his shoulders were broad enough to handle anything, but this was not going to be pretty.

3

About Amelia

Later that evening, after supper was cleared away and Millie had gone home for the night, I was still in the kitchen, channel-surfing, looking for something to watch to kill time before crawling upstairs. Four hundred channels and nothing to hold my interest for more than thirty seconds. But then, relative to the drama in my real life lately, how could I expect the worlds of network and cable to concoct something as compelling? I decided to take a walk outside and see what wonders were on display in the night sky.

The stars were just coming out, littering the heavens with glistening crystals and slivers of diamonds. The longer I stood and watched, the more tiny lights flickered their hellos from high up in the skies. I thought of my father then, James Nevil Wimbley, III, known to all as Nevil. He had known how to find many of the constellations and would point them out to Trip and me. When I was a very young girl, weeping inconsolably from a terrifying dream, he would perch me on his hip, take me outside, and tell me to look up. "Have you ever seen anything more beautiful, more peaceful?" he would say. I would shake my head, unable to tear my eyes away from all the marvelous stars winking against the vast navy-blue sky. "Let's count them," he'd say, and the next thing I knew I was falling back into a peaceful sleep.

Clear quiet nights and star-strewn skies were reassuring about order in the universe. Standing there in the side yard, I could feel my pulse slow down. I meandered toward the cluster of Adirondack chairs, situated for years between the live oaks like old friends, inviting me to sit and visit. At last I breathed more naturally. There was nothing like a Lowcountry night to put life in perspective. Moments like this made me believe for that fleeting moment that there was a real possibility for peace on earth. Why not?

The trials and tribulations of Frances Mae and Trip were frightening and the new battle lines had yet to be drawn. I was wondering and then desperately hoping that Trip would have the chutzpah to stand up to Frances Mae and that he would use his talents of persuasion to make Rusty understand the urgency of acting now. I was pretty confident, because she was a very generous and sensible woman, that Rusty's cooperation would be easily gained. Frances Mae's alcoholism, which had made her so deadly unpredictable, and the risky situation in which she had placed Chloe made me absolutely ill. Frances Mae would do it again and again until someone made her stop. I knew it and it terrified me.

I was on my way back inside when I heard the phone ringing. I rushed to grab it before it went to voice mail. It was Eric calling from school.

"Hey, Mom! What's up?"

"I don't know, sweetheart. You called me, remember?"

Some of the current phone manners were bewildering to me, never mind tweeting with Twitter, texting, and whatever the new deal was. Maybe I was just too literal in the way I processed language.

"You sound out of breath."

"I was outside looking at the stars. Pretty gorgeous out there tonight."

"Yeah. I'm sure. So, I was just wondering if there was any more news on Aunt Frances Mae?"

"No. Nothing new to my knowledge. Why? Did Amelia say something?"

"Amelia? Amelia said plenty! From the time we dropped Aunt Fan and Chloe off in Walterboro until we parked the car in Columbia, Amelia was ragging on her mother nonstop. I mean, you wouldn't believe some of the stuff I heard. She really hates her mother's guts."

"Ah, come on now. Nobody hates their mother's guts. And Frances Mae can't help herself. She's sick, Eric. Amelia is old enough to understand that."

"Yeah, well, both of us got that but we had a hard time understanding what she was doing driving drunk with Chloe."

"I'll give you that one." I pulled a half-full bottle of wine from the refrigerator, twisted out the cork, and poured myself a glass.

"We went in the house when we got to Walterboro, right? And Amelia basically ripped Belle and Linnie a new one for letting Chloe get in the car with Aunt Fan being all wasted."

"Yeah, but here's the thing. Those girls shouldn't have to police their mother. Why didn't one of them drive Chloe over?"

"They didn't want to have to see Rusty and they probably didn't realize how in the bag old Fan was."

"Maybe. Anyway, Frances Mae is a lucky woman that nothing worse happened, but this whole business of vilifying Rusty with every second breath is just stupid."

"I think Amelia knows that. Sort of. But it's hard for her to take the other side. I mean, her mom and sisters run a pretty wicked campaign against Rusty."

"Listen to me, Eric: I think that at this point I am way more concerned about the girls' safety than I am about Frances Mae's ridiculous pride. And y'all should be, too."

"You've never really liked her, have you?"

"Me not like Frances Mae?"

"Yeah. I mean, like the world doesn't know it."

"Oh, Eric, it's so complicated."

I became uncomfortable whenever anyone brought up my personal feelings about Frances Mae. It wasn't that I didn't like her because she was a low-class redneck slut from nowhere. I didn't like her because she was greedy, jealous, small-minded, petty, and mean-spirited. But try explaining that to your nineteen-year-old son who still lives in a world of thought where things were either black or white. He thought families should stick together. Period. No exceptions. That opinion fueled *his* rage against his father and his half brother, although he rarely showed those feelings. Besides, Frances Mae was not and would never be blood. I didn't have to love her.

"I know it's complicated."

"Eric. Look, son. This isn't about me being critical of Frances Mae."

"Whatever. Anyway, Amelia is just totally frustrated with her mother. She's worried about her, about what she might do next. That wreck scared the living hell out of her. But she's stuck in Columbia, you know?"

"I know. The wreck scared me, too. What about Belle and Linnie? What did they have to say?"

"Well, Belle is just like counting the days until she gets out of high school and leaves Walterboro in the rearview mirror. She feels bad about leaving Chloe behind but not bad enough to stick around. She ain't ever coming back. And Linnie? Linnie cares about Linnie. That one's a short story. The end."

"So you don't think that either one of those girls is particularly interested in running interference for Chloe, like to take over driving her where she needs to go and so forth?"

"Pretty much, and that makes Amelia even more frustrated."

"I'm sure it does. Poor child."

"Which one?"

"All of them."

"Yeah. But what can you do?"

"Well, I sure can't stand around and watch Frances Mae drink herself to death and maybe maim, disfigure, or, God forbid, and that's a prayer, kill her daughters in the process."

"Yeah, but you, me . . . we're not in charge of Aunt Fan. No one is."

"Well, there's Trip. Technically."

"Right. I keep forgetting they're not divorced. But what can he do?"

"I think he's considering his options as we speak."

"Like what? Rehab again?"

"Yeah, probably . . ." My voice drifted off and I knew Eric sensed that I had not revealed all that I knew.

"So are you gonna tell me what's really going on or what?"

"I can't say, honey, because I don't know. That's for Uncle Trip to figure out. And Rusty."

"I guess."

"Rusty. You know, she's actually a really nice lady. It's too bad the girls can't see it, because then things could be a lot easier for everyone."

"Right, I know what you mean. Logistics and all. Well, all I can tell you is that Amelia is freaking . . ."

"I'll call her."

"That might be a good idea but don't tell her what I said, okay?"

"I'm the Great Sphinx, baby, and you know it."

I told Eric that I loved him and he said that he loved me, too. We said good-bye, and even after I hung up, I stood there with my hand on the receiver. I already missed him. He would call me later in the week, he had said. He had a paper due on Wednesday and an important test on Friday. And no, there was no young woman in his life and if there was I would undoubtedly be the last person to hear of it. As far as I knew, he was living in the stacks. But then, why *wouldn't* a handsome young man like Eric have someone? Ever since when? Yes, it was Christmas. That was the last time I heard him talk about a girl. It didn't make sense. Maybe he did have someone and he just didn't want me to know. Maybe he thought I wouldn't approve.

For years now, Eric and I had shared observations about family matters and other things that were more mature in nature than I suspected other parents enjoyed with their young sons. But then perhaps it was more typical for single parents to discuss grave adult matters with their children because there was no spouse on the scene. Eric was certainly more mature than most of the boys his age. No doubt this was part of the reason why. We used to joke that Eric had been born a little old man. I wished that Belle and Linnie were less self-centered and even just slightly more maternally inclined toward Chloe. It would have given me greater peace of mind to know they were focused on their little sister's safety. But those girls? They were Frances Mae's clones. Chasing boys and "getting around" had earned them some very sullied reputations. It was deeply embarrassing to know this. They were not embarrassed about it one iota.

On the other hand, even though they were Lolitas, shouldn't they be allowed to pass their teenage years unencumbered by the unfortunate problems of their mother? Yes, they should. In an ideal situation. Who among us had ever enjoyed a completely idyllic childhood? But maybe if those girls were forced to assume some extra responsibility, they might not have the time, energy, or inclination to take down the entire defensive football team of Colleton High School every weekend. They would never cooperate. I hoped they knew all about birth control and sexually transmitted diseases. I made a mental note to gently inquire the next time I got them in private. They could probably give *me* an education. Very little surprised me anymore.

My mother crossed my mind. For at least the fifth time that week, I thought it was a good thing she had not lived to witness all of this because it would've killed her. What would she have said? I knew then that Millie was absolutely right. Miss Lavinia would've called Trip on the carpet and insisted that he get his wife the necessary help and that his daughters learn a little something about discretion. "In my day," she would have said, "tramps sneaked around and they lied about their sexual exploits!" She would have told Belle and Linnie that one boy at a time should have been sufficient for them at their age. Although one was never enough for Mother after Daddy died, but then Mother was much older than the girls.

I should have been more insistent with Trip. I would call him again in the morning. I would call him and tell him that he simply must do something immediately.

I decided to call Amelia. She might tell me something that could prove to be helpful to push Trip into action before it was too late. I got her voice mail. In a clever moment, I didn't leave a message because I knew she wouldn't call me back if I did. If she saw a missed call, she would be more likely to become curious or worried and actually call me back right away. See that? I was still onto the ways of our youth-obsessed culture. In less time than it took me to turn off the lights in the back of the house, the phone was ringing again.

"Aunt Caroline? Is everything okay?"

It was Amelia. Ah, I loved it when I was right. It didn't happen nearly often enough.

"Yes, of course! I just wanted to thank you again for the fabulous balloons! Made me feel like a kid! Can you believe that crazy dream I had?"

"Spooky, if you ask me. I mean, seriously!"

"Well, it just goes to show you that this is a crazy world."

"Yeah, and that Grandmother Lavinia is still hanging around."

"And thank goodness she is! Anyway, sweetheart, thanks for coming and bringing my boy home. I loved seeing y'all. I always do."

"Aunt Caroline, I should look so good when I'm as old as you! Seriously!"

Mentally, I gave her a good slap right across the face.

"Thanks, hon. So, Amelia?"

"Hmm?"

In my mind's eye I could see her multitasking, probably looking something up on the Internet or playing on that infernal Facebook, which I had to admit was very handy when researching the lives of old boyfriends, finding out who was single again and so forth.

"Was everything okay driving your mom home? And was it okay when you got there? Where were your sisters?" Did that sound too nosy? Probably.

There was a distinct pause. I could hear the opening and closing of a door and assumed she was going somewhere more private. Her roommates were probably home.

"Oh, Aunt Caroline. What are we going to do about Mom? I mean, I can't be there all the time and Belle and Linnie are practically useless. I made them swear not to let Chloe in the car with her if they thought she was, well, you know. But I can't depend on them. They're completely unreliable, as we all know. Sometimes I feel like the only grown-up in my whole family."

Her remark wasn't too far off from the truth.

"Well, I had a talk with your father today and we all agree it's time to take steps again. My problem is the same as yours. I'm worried, very worried in fact, about the safety of all of your sisters. What happened yesterday was inexcusable. It really was."

"What can I do? I mean, I have a year left of school! I'm up to my ears in papers and all kinds of crap!"

I hated the word *crap*. It was so common. I cleared my throat, a signal of my displeasure, and I could hear her sigh. When I was her age we never used that kind of language in front of adults.

"Well, maybe you can talk to your sisters about Rusty."

"And do what? Help them hire an *F*-ing hit man?"

F-ing was worse. But then she had learned to express herself at the knee of a dairy cow.

"No. Please! Don't be ridiculous. But here's the *situation*. If your mother goes to Promises again or the Betty, somebody's gonna have to care for Chloe, you know? Bath, supper, homework, bedtime."

"We hired a housekeeper last time."

"And last time your two younger sisters got arrested for engaging in lewd acts in public, which nearly killed your father."

"He got them out of it . . ." Her voice trailed off in weariness.

"Yes, but we don't want a repeat of that performance, do we? They were caught without panties! Do you remember that?"

"God. They are such little idiots."

"No, they're really quite clever, and well, they just have their priorities out of whack and they make some very bad choices."

She groaned loudly. "Oh! Why is this happening to me? I am the good girl! I never did anything! Why can't I have a normal life? God! I hate them!"

In the next instant, I could hear Amelia's voice start to crack and I didn't want to be responsible for making her cry. This was no time for tears. I had not called her to upset her. The poor girl!

"Well, Amelia? Honey? Listen to me right now. This isn't your fault. You know that."

"I know. But I don't need this!"

"Who does? I think you'd rest a lot easier—we all would in fact—if someone who really cared about the welfare of children was around if and when your mother agrees to take a break from, well, polite society for a stretch of time."

"Polite society?" Amelia was mounting her high horse and was about to unleash the part of her social conscience that dealt with class struggle.

"What would *you* call it?"

"I don't know. But calling it taking a break from polite society? It makes you sound like such a . . . well, you sound like a little bit of a snob, Aunt Caroline. I'm sorry."

I knew that she thought I was a snob. Her whole family thought I was a snob. So what? Well, maybe I was. But not all the time. Really.

"If not coming right out and announcing that *rehab* is imminent for a family member for the *fifth* time makes me a snob, then so be it. I'll be a snob."

Honestly, my niece would go a lot further in this world if she softened her language and could remember not to correct her elders. But at that moment I guessed that in some way she was trying to defend her mother, the low-rent drunk who nearly killed her sister. And I was fully aware that alcoholism was a progressive disease and that Frances Mae was firmly in its clutches and being eaten alive by it. It was all deeply upsetting, and when I was upset I did indeed have the capacity to get bitchy. Unapologetically so. I'm way far from perfect.

"Sorry," she said. "Oh Lord! Let me think about this. You're right. We would all be totally insane to leave Linnie and Belle in charge of the house and Chloe."

"My point exactly."

"So what are we going to do? Wait and see what Dad says? I guess."

"I'm just saying that if your sisters would consider the fact that maybe Rusty isn't the Antichrist, maybe there could be a possibility for an easy and workable solution. Do you see what I mean?"

"Yeah, sure I do." She sighed deeply. "Look, I think Rusty is okay. In fact, I think if I had met her under different circumstances, I'd probably really like her. But I don't care what any of us say, you know how Mom feels. Mom says she's a home wrecker and that's pretty much about it."

"Well, she might be, from Frances Mae's point of view, but she's got time on her hands and it's not like you can commute from Columbia. And I have a business to run."

"Right. What about Millie? Couldn't she come and stay with them?"

"Millie? Humph. She's got a job, and besides, there would be a bigger revolt than if Rusty was there! Millie has no patience for nonsense. Zero tolerance. Anyway, Trip has to work this out. I'm just an aunt. He's y'all's parent. And here we are planning your mother's absence when I don't even know if Trip has talked to her about it."

"Well, there's really no option but rehab, is there, Aunt Caroline?"

"None that I know of, honey. I wish there was a pill."

"Well, actually, there is one. It's called Antabuse, I think. All I know is if you take the pill and drink booze, you puke your guts out and you could die."

Puke was such a repulsive word and *guts* was better used in conversation between men regarding the eviscerating of deer and fish and animals they caught in the woods. Antabuse was it?

"Good Lord! *That's* pretty powerful."

"Yeah. It is. In fact, you can't give it to somebody with heart trouble or any kind of vascular weakness because they really could drop dead."

"Is this what they teach you in college these days?"

"No. I found it on the Internet. It's been around since the 1950s, believe it or not. I was trying to find a solution for Mom. You know. She's my mother, right? I worry about her morning, noon, and night."

"I'm sure you do, honey. I'm sure you do. But, sweetheart?" The poor child. She needed to study, not to fear for her sister's life. "Listen, I don't want you to worry anymore. Let us old fogies do the worrying for a while, okay? Why don't you see if you can soften your sisters' hearts and I'll keep you in the loop on everything. Is that a deal?"

"Sure. I'll try. But they're pretty convinced of the party line, you know."

"Yes, I know that. Listen, Amelia, on another topic?"

"Sure, what?"

"Do you think Eric is seeing someone?"

There was silence.

"Are you there, Amelia?"

"Yes, I, um, don't know. Maybe you should ask him?"

"Oh! I didn't mean to pry, I mean . . . of course, you're right!"

We said good night and I felt like I had failed miserably in trying to console her. But I had let her know that she wasn't alone. Poor girl. Not even twenty-one years old and she was like Atlas trying to hold up the globe on her back. And to make matters worse, I asked her to betray some sort of confidence by prying into Eric's business. Of course I was prying! He was my son! I was his mother! So, if she didn't want to tell me, she must know something. I'd find out.

I put my wineglass in the sink and decided to forgo the grapes for a while—at least until Frances Mae went away.

I went to the front of the house to turn out the rest of the lights and saw familiar headlights at the end of our avenue of oaks. I blinked the porch lights to signal that it was not too late to approach. Was it Trip? No, it was a patrol car driven by my friend Matthew. Matthew was coming by to check on me. That cheered me on the spot. I watched as he pulled up our long road. I ran my hand through my hair to smooth it. And I bit my lips to give them some color, hoping I didn't look like a hag. He got out of his car and turned to look at me standing there in the doorway. Good grief, he was so appealing. Was it the uniform?

"Can I help you, Officer?" I said, teasing him in my best slow Scarlett drawl.

"Yes, ma'am, I reckon you can." He said this with a smile but his eyes were telling me another story.

"Would you like to come in?" I leaned against the doorjamb and he stood very close to me, leaned down, and smelled the side of my neck, giving me chills.

"Yes, ma'am, I reckon I would."

"Do you want to pull your car around back for the sake of the neighbors?" It appeared I was to have company at least for a few hours.

"If you think I should, then I will. But there's nobody out here tonight. I checked. A couple of opossums and some bears."

"Bears?" He was kidding, of course, but I pretended to be alarmed. "Oh my!"

"Yes, big black bears. Hungry ones. I just wanted to make sure you were safe."

It should be noted here that I had not slept with Matthew in decades. Okay, it was last week but there was no sleeping. I was unsure of how to proceed. No, I wasn't. I mean, was it all right to just sleep with him without some sort of goal on the relationship beyond the obvious? Of course it was. We were consenting adults, after all. So much for moral dilemmas. Problem solved.

"Are you hungry, Officer?"

"Yeah. Do you have something you might offer a starving servant of the people?"

I thought of offering him a roll in bed with honey, but instead I said, "That depends on what you're starving for. Why don't we go inside and see what we can find?"

Our words were corny and silly but intellectual debate on the true meaning of life was not on the agenda. I led him through the hall and up the stairs to my room. Now, may I just mention that the kindest thing ever invented by mankind is the dimmer switch? I slipped into the bathroom to change into something ooh-la-la, and there was my tub, filled with hot water while camellias and gardenias floated on the surface. I stopped for a moment and then I realized. Miss Lavinia approved.

4

Spring Forward

I T WAS BARELY EIGHT-THIRTY IN the morning but Millie and I had already been talking for almost an hour. I woke up with the birds and could not get the image of Chloe's bleeding head out of my mind. I was still worried sick and called Millie as soon as I saw the lights on at her house. So over a pot of coffee, Millie and I cooked up a plan that we hoped might convince Frances Mae to go to rehab, sign new separation papers, and give the children to Trip for an unspecified period of time.

"Get your brother on the phone and tell him to get himself over here," she said. "I'm making biscuits."

I looked up at the cuckoo clock on the wall, its hands permanently stuck at 11:11 and wondered why we didn't fix it or pitch it. It hadn't worked since I was a child. But I hated moving or changing anything that Miss Lavinia had put in place.

Thirty minutes later, Trip walked in the back door, his hair still wet from his shower but combed perfectly in place. He dropped the morning newspapers on the table and Millie picked up *The State*.

"Morning!" he said, and gave me a hug. "I saw Matthew Strickland's car here last night. Everything okay?"

"I thought I saw a bear," I said without missing a beat.

"Really?" Trip said in all innocence. "We haven't had bears around here in ages!"

Millie, whom I had always believed had a third eye hidden in the thick braid that encircled her head, had somehow missed Matthew's arrival and departure. She shot me a look of surprise and then she sighed, with a pretty good idea of what had transpired last night.

"A bear," she said, seeing right through me. "Girl, you are Miss Lavinia, more and more each day."

"I'll take that as a compliment," I said.

"What am I missing here?" Trip poured himself a mug of coffee and ignored the possibility that I might have a romantic life. "Do you have any cream?"

"Nothing," Millie said, shaking her head. "Second shelf on the left. You ain't missing nothing." The timer pinged. She put the newspaper down, grabbed an oven mitt, and pulled a sheet of biscuits from the oven, smiling because they were perfectly browned on top. With the deftness of a professional chef, she swept them into a linen napkin folded inside a sweetgrass basket and placed them on the table in front of Trip. "Just try to resist," she said.

"Ah, Millie! You're going to ruin my waistline."

"Please. So what's up with you today?" I said. I put a jar of strawberry jam and another of elderberry jam on the table with a plate of butter. "Do you want juice?"

"No, thanks. My day? Well, let's see. This morning I'm going down to Beaufort to take a deposition at noon. Seems some stupid sumbitch, let's call him Mr. Jones, thought his wife was screwing a friend of his, Mr. Smith. Turns out Mrs. Jones was just watering his plants, feeding his cat, and picking up Mr. Smith's mail while he was away at a Bible camp trying to get over the fact that he had discovered his wife in flagrante with another woman, with whom she then ran off with to Calistoga, way out there in California. When Mr. Smith came home from Bible camp, Mr. Jones went over there to the house and shot him in the leg, only he missed, nearly amputating Mr. Smith's jones, if you get my drift. Now Mrs. Jones wants a divorce and it's pretty obvious to all parties involved that she actually did drink the Kool-Aid for Mr. Smith, but I hear tell Mr. Smith thinks she's not Christian enough and he's not interested in jeopardizing his ticket to the Pearly Gates. And Mrs. Jones is quite the delectable little morsel, so go figure. So that's my day."

"I'm a little confused over here," I said.

"Me, too," Millie said. "What kinda fool thing is all that?"

"There's big money to be made when you mix up jealousy, infidelity, and guns. People are unbelievably stupid. So what's on your agenda?" He stuffed a whole biscuit into his mouth, dripping butter down his chin.

"Gross." I handed him a napkin. "The usual. But we're looking at a deal with a big yogurt producer to provide their fruit, so we'll see. It's a private-label deal for Wal-Mart and Sam's Club. Miss Sweetie is all excited. It would be Sweetie's Yogurt and she'd have her face on the label."

"Cool."

"Very. So tell it, little brother. Did you talk to Rusty last night about taking the kids?"

"Of course I did."

"And?"

"What do you think? I almost had to use the paddles on her."

"Paddles? What are you saying?" Millie asked.

"He means heart-attack resuscitation paddles, right, genius?"

"Yeah. Millie? We got any eggs in the house?"

Millie, who was now perusing the obituaries, pushed her reading glasses down her nose and looked at him.

"You want scrambled, fried, or sunny-side up?"

"Any way you feel like making 'em. Thanks!"

"So, Millie and I have been trying to figure out a way to help you out of this *situation* and we've got an idea."

"I'm sure," he said with a trace of sarcasm.

His sarcasm was a sign to me that Trip was prepared to be annoyed over the meddling of two well-meaning women, but sarcasm and annoyance had no impact on his appetite as he buttered up his fourth biscuit and shoved it in his face. He continued.

"Look, I appreciate y'all's concern, but Rusty ain't having none of it. Okay? I take the kids, I lose Rusty. It's a lose-lose. Not happening."

"But what if you could get Frances Mae to sign new separation papers and you were free to marry Rusty within a year?"

Millie slipped a plate of scrambled eggs in front of him and he immediately took two huge bites.

"Thanks, Millie. These eggs are so pretty they ought to be on the cover of *Southern Living* magazine!"

"You're right," Millie said.

Trip turned his attention back to me. "Oh, sure. And how are we going to accomplish that? Should I put a pistol to her head and just tell her to sign on the dotted line?"

"No. And please don't talk when you have a mouth full of food."

"Thanks, Lavinia."

"That's *Miss* Lavinia to you."

"Right. Well, let's hear your brilliant idea because no tactic I've tried in all these years has worked."

"You're gonna use the old tried-and-true method. M-O-N-E-Y. Open your wallet, Trip. Money works every time."

Trip may have been a great guy in many ways, but he was very, very tight with a dollar. In my opinion, there is very little more offensive than a cheap man.

Trip sighed deeply. "Did you hear that, Millie? My lovely sister wants me to spend even *more* money on Frances Mae's shenanigans!"

"Yes, sir! I hear her giving you what for and I'm saying we don't think you can afford *not* to pay for her nonsense."

"Humph," Trip said.

So far, Trip was unimpressed with our point of view.

"Listen, you're going to give her that house in Walterboro and you're going to give her a generous alimony settlement. And you're going to tell her that she can have the girls back when she's been sober for some period of time, which you'll figure out. Then you tell Rusty to start planning a wedding."

"I already give Frances Mae everything I can. And you forget I have a new swimming pool to pay for. And the landscaping. And the lighting. And the irrigation. And the outdoor grill and all that. And since my investments aren't earning what they were, I'm taking every case that's out there to keep the *Enterprise* afloat. I'm not made out of money, you know."

"Who is? But what if you *stop* paying her? Just don't give her another dime? She'll listen then. What if—no wait—what happens *when* she gets caught driving drunk and goes to jail? And she *will* drive drunk again and she *will* get caught. And they have to put her in jail! It's mandatory! All I have to do is make one phone call. Then you'll get full custody anyway and she gets nothing. Not one dime! Zero! Bubkes! So, just tell her it's all or nothing. Then we stage an intervention and off she goes to rehab, which I'll research, and this time you lay down the law with her."

Trip looked at me with the most incredulous expression I had ever seen on his face.

"What?" I said.

"Why didn't I think of this?"

"Good question."

"And you really think Rusty will go along with this?"

"Of course she will. She adores you. I think she will really try with the girls. Besides, she'll be busy planning a wedding. All females love weddings and your girls will probably want to help. Well, they might."

Trip still looked very uncertain.

"Trip, listen to me. This is the best of all possible worlds. The girls will be safe and out of danger. Frances Mae will no longer be a threat and she'll get the help she needs. And Rusty, bless her heart, gets you, till death do y'all part. Now, why she thinks you're such a prize is anyone's guess . . ."

"Oh, thanks. And you'll call Matthew Strickland?"

"It will be my pleasure!"

"This might actually work. Anyway, it's sure worth trying. The one thing that has Rusty deeply concerned is the safety of the girls. I mean, if we take them and they don't behave, there's always boarding school."

"That's the spirit. I actually heard about a boarding school in Georgia where they make the kids dig up onions when they get into trouble and they have to recite Bible verses before they're allowed to eat their dinner."

"That could be just the ticket for my little scamps."

"So you'll talk to Frances Mae, then?"

Trip wiped his mouth with his napkin and stood. "Yes, I promise." He gave me a kiss on the cheek and kissed the back of Millie's hand.

"Ladies? I'm off to further the cause of justice. Thank you for breakfast, Mrs. Smoak, and thank you both for your excellent counsel." He saluted us and left, slamming the door behind him.

"He's such an ass," I said to Millie, and picked up a piece of Trip's fifth biscuit, popping it into my mouth. "Why he ever tore up those separation papers is anybody's guess. He must've been crazy."

"Humph. Call Rusty and invite her over here for lunch," Millie said.

I looked at Millie's face. Her eyes were in a tight squint and her jaw was clenched like a steel trap. "What's wrong?"

"Something he said didn't set right with me."

"What?"

"I don't know. But if he's worried about losing her because of taking custody of his own flesh and blood, then as sure as my name is Millie Smoak, he shouldn't be marrying her."

"Lord in heaven! Millie, you're absolutely right."

"Humph. Usually I am." She opened the refrigerator door and looked inside, taking inventory. She pulled out the remains of a roasted chicken. "How's chicken salad?"

"Great. Waldorf salad?"

She nodded. "Sure enough, if I can find me a decent apple in this wasteland. When's the last time we went to the grocery store?"

"I can go this morning. I was actually going over to Miss Sweet-ie's anyway. I can stop at the Bi-Lo. It's no problem."

"You don't worry; just go call Rusty. I'll call our Mr. Jenkins and tell him to shake a leg. We both need a change of scenery. Too nice a day to be inside."

Millie was getting about the business of reducing the chicken to bones and I went upstairs to my office.

Around the time Eric went off to college and I was thinking about what to do with myself, I redecorated a guest room that hadn't seen a coat of paint or a new throw pillow in years. In between the windows, I put in built-in cabinets with glass doors across the top and shelves across the bottom. I still had not installed the lighting inside the cabinets but I would get around to it. I sighed, remembering the precious contractor who did all the work. He was Irish, complete with blue eyes the color of the sky and a brogue so thick he was almost impossible to understand. Michael was his name and we didn't do a whole lot of talking anyway. Lord, he was amazing! I finally stopped seeing him because it was getting too serious and the last thing I wanted was another husband.

I decided to call him and see if he had a good electrician who could get the kind of lighting I wanted. I couldn't remember his last name, so I wound up going through my files and found it right where I had left it, stapled to the folder that held all the invoices of the renovation. Michael Sullivan. How could I forget a name like that? It seemed that lately I was forgetting things all the time. It was probably nerves. Maybe a reunion with the contractor would be what I needed to put me back on track. I hesitated, knowing that the phone call would lead to "why don't we get together" and I put the folder back, not wanting to reopen that can of worms. When a love affair was over, it was over.

I called Rusty.

"Caroline?"

"Hey, girl! Want to have lunch today? Millie's making her fabulous Waldorf salad."

"Absolutely! I've been working in the yard since the crack of dawn, hacking away at the bamboo with a machete like Indiana Jones. I'll tell you what. Once bamboo gets going, it takes over."

"I hear you! I've got to get on Mother's roses, too. They're a mess. If it's not black spot, it's aphids."

"Maintaining a garden is never ending, isn't it? What time?"

"How's noon?"

"Great! I'll hop in the shower and see you soon!"

I hung up and thought what in the world was wrong with Trip's girls that they couldn't see with their own eyes just how wonderful Rusty was? Didn't they know by now that it was Rusty who bought every card and gift they received from their father? Didn't they know that it was Rusty who made sure that every parents' night, play, and recital they had was on Trip's calendar in red letters? Hadn't Rusty chosen Amelia's and Isabelle's cars? And arranged their insurance, all of their tuition payments, and everything else? She did all this, operating quietly in the background, not asking for or expecting a single word of thanks from them. Whenever we talked about the animosity of the girls, she always said that she took it in stride because she understood how problematic her relationship with Trip was for them to understand and reconcile. No, by anyone's measure, Rusty was a wonderful woman whose sole purpose in life had become seeing about my brother's happiness and well-being. He was lucky to have her and his hardheaded quartet of ignoramuses was lucky to have her working on their behalf.

It wasn't long before we were outside on the portico, clinking our glasses of tea and remarking on the weather. What a day it was! Millie was right. It was too beautiful to stay indoors all day long. Wonderful breezes were coming off the river. They carried the salty, addictive smells of mud banks and mollusks, spun together and laced with the smells of pinesap and all the robust and earthy fragrances of the woods. Enormous cumulus clouds floated across the brilliant blue sky, igniting gratitude in my heart that I had not felt in a long while for the gift of my life and for being in this glorious place.

"I love this time of year," I said. "Mother Nature is like a giant dose of Prozac."

Rusty giggled. "Prozac. You are too much. But it's true. Everywhere you turn, something is coming into bloom."

"I love it."

"Me, too. Trip and I love to eat outside. Somehow everything tastes more flavorful. You have to come over and see the new grill. It was just installed. Trip is dying to have a barbecue."

"I'll bet so. I'll get Bobby Mack on the phone and get him to bring us something. You know, I saw Trip this morning."

"Oh? I knew he was in a hurry to get somewhere! That man does love his sister!"

"Well, I love him, too, but I think he hurried over because Millie was making biscuits."

"Then who could blame him? I wish she would show me how she does it. She flat-out makes the lightest biscuits on the planet."

"Oh, I'm sure she would teach you. And it's the truth. I'd rather have one hot biscuit from her than a dozen glazed Krispy Kreme donuts."

"Amen. So what's going on?"

"Nothing. Just the usual. You know."

"Caroline?"

"Okay. Look, Rusty, we've known each other for years and I love you like a sister. You know that, right?"

"Of course! What's wrong?"

"Aside from the herd of elephants in the room? Millie and I are scared to death that if Trip doesn't get those girls away from Frances Mae, something terrible is going to happen."

"I couldn't agree with you more! I told Trip just last night that he needed to take custody and get Frances Mae into rehab PDQ or she was going to wind up with her car wrapped around a tree!"

"You did?"

"Look. I can drive Chloe where she needs to go, back and forth to school and all that. Linnie and Belle have a car to drive. It wouldn't be forever, would it?"

"You mean you would bring them here? Knowing how they feel about you?"

"Caroline? Don't you think enough is enough? I don't want to be their mother. They've already got one. I just want to help them get through a difficult and complicated time."

"You told Trip this?"

"Of course I did! Why? What did he tell you I said?"

I put my fork down. Somebody was lying. I knew then that my brother had sold Rusty up the river so he wouldn't have to take responsibility. Trip was in deep trouble with me.

5

Graffiti

BEFORE I CALLED TRIP AND kicked his bahunkus into the next century, I decided to talk to Millie. I surely didn't want to start trouble between Rusty and Trip, so I made not one peep about Trip's big fat lie, telling me of her insistent refusal to consider my nieces living with them. I simply soft-pedaled during the rest of the lunch, emphasizing instead how willing I was to help her. I told her I would be happy to stay with the girls if she had to go somewhere or just have a weekend away for a break. I would do all I could to help her and she appreciated it. Overall, I thought if Trip and Rusty had the girls, it would be a great opportunity to try to imbue the little strumpets with a healthy dose of Wimbley cachet, meaning basic civilized behavior, and then, if they could manage it, a dollop of refinement. Frankly, I couldn't wait to get my hands on them. They really were a disaster. Rusty agreed.

So, it was late in the afternoon and I was in the kitchen with Millie, giving her the rundown of my conversation over lunch with Rusty.

"Do you think I should get Trip over here and just straight up call him a liar? Millie, you know how I absolutely lose complete faith in someone when they lie to me. I just can't believe that Trip would be so deceitful!"

"Caroline? I think before you go off all half-cocked and crazy on him, we should try and figure out *why* he would lie. He hasn't lied to any of us in ages! Ever since his rough patch, that is."

"Rough patch. Humph. I don't know why he would say such a thing about Rusty, but he did and it's very disappointing. That's all. I put up with enough deceit from my ridiculous ex-husband! Trip's supposed to be focused on all the things we talked about this morning!"

"Well, why don't you give him a chance? Don't you think Rusty is going to tell him what y'all talked about?"

"Maybe you're right. But I've got my eye on him! Both of them, in fact!"

"Caroline? You did what you can do. Trip is a grown man."

"I know. You're right, of course. I should wait and see. I don't feel like having a big confrontation with Trip. I *hate* conflict! Truly, I do. Well, usually."

Millie arched an eyebrow.

"Well, okay, maybe I like to stir the pot sometimes. Anyway, as you said, I just want him to do the right thing. Really. I do."

Millie smiled at me and said, "Honey, quit pushing so hard! You've got to let him do it in his own time and in his own way."

"I guess, but isn't there some urgency here?"

"Don't you think he knows that? He ain't stupid."

"I hope! At least now we know the truth about Rusty. I was having some dark thoughts about her."

"You see? Look at you. Don't be so easily swayed. I always knew she was a nice woman from the minute she walked in this house. When your brother started all that foolishness, hanging his coat on her nail, I knew something was fishy! Didn't I tell you what?"

"Yes, you did. And you know what? I would much rather find out that Trip told a whopper than that Rusty didn't want to take care of his children."

"Humph! I'm gone save you a lot of time and trouble and tell you what an old woman knows. Your brother is scared out of his wits to take over his girls. This ain't nothing but plain old fear. You blame him?"

"No. I really don't. They scare me, too. Listen, there's something else."

"What?"

"I think Eric has a girlfriend."

"What's wrong with that?"

"Something. Because when I asked Amelia if he did? She told me to ask Eric."

"Well, did you?"

"No. Not yet."

"You want me to consult my orisha?"

"Would you?"

"Only because it's Eric. Don't want no fool woman messing him up, 'eah?"

"Me either!"

Millie's gods and goddesses were called orisha and Millie was the high priestess of her Ifa religion and I'll tell you all about that in due time. But for the moment you have to know that she was connected to the other world in ways Microsoft and Apple had yet to imagine!

It wasn't until very late that night when I was trying to sleep that I realized something else about Trip and about me. We had barely known the value of having a father because ours died when we were so young. So what role model did Trip have to become a father himself? None but the succession of eager boyfriends Mother had paraded through our young lives. Most of the memories we had of our father were really mine, stories rearranged and retold over the years until we created our own truth, one we agreed on together. The life-changing sorrow and trauma of losing our father in that horrible plane crash was only compounded by our mother's frosty behavior toward us in the following years. We were just children who needed reassurance that the world around us was safe. But instead, Miss Lavinia became the Ice Queen and only began to come around and show affection for us as she approached the end of her own life. It was no wonder that Trip was so reluctant to just barge in and assume the reins. He didn't have the first clue about what to do or how he was supposed to feel.

I had probably become the opposite kind of parent from Trip. I was married to an older man who, as it turned out, was so judgmental and dictatorial that it became unbearable. It began on our wedding night, if you can envision such a thing, when Richard made it plain he thought fidelity was a bore. Can you imagine how I felt? When I was in labor, Millie and I found out that Richard was in London, shacked up with his ex-wife, Lois, the trashy thing with the nasal accent that gave certain Yankees their questionable reputation south of the Mason-Dixon Line. His infidelity stung then, still stung now, and probably always would. But the worst insult was to know he preferred Harry, his obnoxious son born during his marriage to Lois. That made me hyperprotective of Eric. His criticisms of Eric made me actually want to do him physical harm. Some days I wished I had.

I looked at the alarm clock. It was just after midnight and I knew I wasn't going to be able to sleep anytime soon. Thinking about Richard's attitude and behavior had infuriated me as though these things had just happened hours ago instead of years. I got up, threw on my old jeans and a chambray shirt, and drove over to Trip's. His kitchen lights were still on and the side of his house that faced the river was all wide open. I got out and gave my eyes a moment to adjust to the darkness. I couldn't see him or Rusty through the windows, but when I turned to go back to my car to grab my cell phone, I spotted him down on his dock. He was alone, leaning on the rail, standing in the same position as we always did on my dock. His posture said he was deep in thought. I called out to him from about fifty feet away. I was convinced that I could help him sort out this problem.

"Hey! Want some company?"

He turned to face me, and even in the darkness I could sense the depth of his somber mood.

"Hey. Sure. What are you doing up so late?"

"Bear hunt. But it looks like it was called off."

"Right. Me, too."

"Couldn't sleep."

"Me either."

The Edisto moved ever so quietly beneath us, tiny laps against the pilings like whispers, waltzing its way in slow motion and with a lyrical determination toward the Atlantic. The river was lit by a sliver of the moon and countless stars, but in its center it appeared to be bottomless and menacing. All around its edges the water held the silhouettes of trees—loblollies, palmettos, and live oaks to assure us. We could see ourselves reflected in it. In that moment the Edisto knew all there was to know about us.

"So what are you thinking about?" I said.

"My life as I knew it has come to an end."

"Oh, good grief, Trip. Isn't that a little melodramatic?"

"Nope. It's over. Done. Finished."

"Well, then maybe that's a good thing."

"Maybe. I had one of my associates start drawing up separation papers today. Should be done by day after tomorrow."

"Good. Did you get all the stuff I e-mailed you on Promises Rehab in Malibu?"

"Yeah. It's no bargain."

Why was it always about money with him?

"No, it's not, but they say they can show that people who go through rehab in a residential environment instead of a hospital have a higher chance of staying clean and sober. And to be honest, what's money for anyway?"

"I'd just like to see a return on my investment this time. She is still the mother of my children."

"Yes, that she is."

"I keep telling myself that." He was quiet again. "Can I just say something terrible and you won't hold it against me?"

I could see that Trip was getting worked up because now he was standing up straight and had jammed his hands deep into his pockets.

"Of course!"

"Why didn't Mother stop me from marrying her? Why couldn't she have done that one thing for me?"

"Frances Mae was as pregnant as a Christmas tree, you might recall, and you were hell-bent and determined to make her your wife."

"Yeah, but couldn't Millie have mixed up some potion and slipped it in her tea to, you know . . ."

"Cause her to lose the baby? You're kidding, right?"

"No, I'm not kidding."

"You've heard the expression 'water over the dam'? I mean, I do remember Mother considering killing Frances Mae with her bare hands now and then, but none of us would ever do anything to harm an unborn child. Not even Mother, and especially not Millie. Anyway, what's the point of thinking about that now, four children and twenty years later?"

"Because that one decision, that one lousy decision to marry her and bring Amelia into the world, led to this moment."

"I happen to be a fan of Amelia," I said.

"Oh, no! So am I! Aw, hell! Maybe I was never the right person for Frances Mae."

"Back then, you thought you were in love with her, but now? You have to wonder who *would be* the right person for Frances Mae."

"Truly. But I thought I loved her. You're right about that."

As it turned out, Trip had actually done all the things we talked about, down to the last letter. At least he made a noble attempt. He informed Frances Mae that she had to go to Promises immediately. He also told her that she must accept the separation agreement he was offering her and give him full custody of the girls, and that she would be well advised not to drive her car. Trip told her the highway patrol of the entire state of South Carolina was on the lookout for her Expedition, which he had paid to repair to the tune of five thousand dollars.

He said, "And oh, by the way, you don't sign the papers and give me the girls? No more money. You can go get a job."

She called him every name in the book and slammed the phone in his ear. He called her back a million times, and each time, his hearing was compromised by more screaming and another slam.

"So you want to know what really kills me? I mean, this is the great-granddaddy booger of 'em all."

"Let's hear it!"

"So the phone was quiet for about ten minutes and then she called me back. She said, 'Trip? Whether you like it or not we are still a family. I'm signing nothing! The girls can go stay with you and your whore and I'll consider going to rehab and if I go I'll try. Really try. But when I come home I want you to come back to me or I will come to you and I want that whore out of our house!' I was like, you're kidding, right? *Our* house? This is some bullshit, right? And guess what?"

"What?"

"She's not kidding."

"Holy God, and that's a prayer. She's delusional. She's completely crazy."

"Crazy like a fox. She just wants to ruin my life. She can't stand to see me happy."

"Who knows what goes on in some people's heads, you know? Maybe she does still love you, Trip. Maybe she does."

"Hard to fathom."

"Listen, girls are much harder to raise than boys. But you have me, you have Rusty, and guess what? You have Eric, too. Trip, engage all the children. You know what I mean? This is a family problem and we should all take a part in the process."

"Well, at least summer is almost here and we do have the pool. That should appeal to them."

"Exactly! Go hire a housekeeper who can drive! She can take the girls back and forth to classes for the next few weeks and then school will be out. We'll get Chloe organized with a summer camp that picks her up and drops her off every day. And I'll help Rusty figure out what to do with Belle and Linnie. Amelia's probably going to work. Don't worry! In the end I think you'll see that it was worth all the effort. I really do, Trip. And it's the right thing to do."

"So you think that if I just throw money and more money at this, it will solve the problem?"

"No, I think that if you involve yourself in their lives a little more during this unfortunate time, they will love you for it."

Trip looked at me finally with his lopsided grin and said, "Okay, Miss Lavinia, got it!"

Maybe truth had soaked through the granite of his thick skull.

The next morning before eight, I was greeted by Matthew Strickland, not off duty and looking very stern.

"Matthew! What a surprise to see you so early in the morning. Come in, come in. Would you like coffee? Is everything all right?"

"Coffee would be great," he said, and stepped into the kitchen. "I'm afraid I've got some bad news for your family and especially for your brother."

"What? Are the girls okay?"

"Oh, yeah, they're fine. But I'm gonna have to lock up Frances Mae this time for sure."

"Oh, dear God! What has she done?"

"Well, you're not going to believe this and I'm not rightly sure how she managed it, but she got herself a ladder and some spray paint and went about defacing private property. You know that spot up on 17 South where you make the left to go on down to Savannah?"

"Come on, Matthew. I'm aging here! Give me the details. And how are you sure it's her?"

"Because she wrote all over the billboards at the 17 cutoff. Right up there as pretty as can be she wrote, 'Tell Trip Wimbley to go home to his family!' And on another one about one hundred feet down the road she wrote, 'Rusty is a f-ing whore!' Big red letters . . ."

I stood there holding his mug, trying to suppress some massive giggles and thinking as fast as I could.

"Wow. And that's it, I hope? Do you take cream?"

"Yeah, just a little. That's it so far. Who knows what the day will bring? Listen, Caroline, you know how I feel about you and your family, but we just can't let this woman go running wild all over the countryside."

"Don't worry!" I said. "She's all done."

I told Matthew that we actually had a plan in place and that if Frances Mae went to the pokey at this point, it would throw a considerable wrench in the works. He listened carefully and then he smiled at me.

"Caroline? It seems to me that y'all could take care of this unfortunate incident if Trip will pay for the cleanup and if y'all get her out of town in the next couple of days. I don't like the idea of locking up Frances Mae. It's ugly and it's embarrassing."

"You darling man! Are you hungry?"

"I'm always hungry when I'm around you."

"Jeez, Matthew! I meant, would you like some toast? I was going to make some for myself."

"That would be good, too."

So Matthew consumed four pieces of lightly browned toast with a mighty gusto, spread with butter and a new mixed-berry jam that Miss Sweetie was thinking we should produce.

"I like this," he said. "It reminds me of something my grand-mother used to make."

"Ah, Matthew! Why can't all men be like you?"

The minute Matthew was out of the door I dialed Trip's cell and told him what Frances Mae had done.

"That's it! That's the final straw!"

Five minutes later he called me back.

"Okay, are you playing bridge this afternoon? What I mean is this: Is it okay for me to have a meeting with Frances Mae and my lawyer in the living room around four? I'll have the papers."

"Of course. I'll bake a cake."

"Very funny."

Millie arrived to find me doubled over in laughter. She closed the door behind her and said, "All right now. Tell me what's so funny."

"Oh, my! Guess what my sister-in-law did now?"

I told her and Millie's eyes grew wide. She began to laugh with such abandon that she bent over and slapped her thighs.

"She did *what* now?"

"Oh! Can't you see her up on a ladder with her big fat butt hang-ing out of some tacky little dress?"

"Oh, Lawsamercy! This ain't funny! This is terrible!"

"I know!"

And then we laughed all over again until tears spilled down our cheeks.

"I told Trip I'd bake a cake."

"Shoot! I'll make that cake. This might be your house, but this is my kitchen!"

I knew at once that Millie was going to reach into her bag of tricks and throw a little voodoo in the pans.

"Millie? What are you planning on?"

"Let's just say that my pound cake will make Frances Mae agreeable. Look, I want that woman on a plane to California today! Don't you?"

"I'll say!"

"And I had a little session with Oya last night."

Oya was her favorite goddess.

"And?"

"And I think our Eric got himself a woman."

"Is this a good thing?"

"He ain't gone marry her."

"Then I shouldn't be concerned about somebody stealing my baby's heart?"

"Nope. Not unless you think you got some other cause for worry."

That satisfied me for the time being. I would simply ask Eric and I would see what he said. He'd had lots of girlfriends before and they were uniformly benign. But he was my only child and I wanted to know what kind of company he was keeping.

"Well, thanks, Millie. I feel much better. I gotta go see Miss Sweetie for a couple of hours. I'll be on my cell."

"Humph. Go do what you have to do. I'll call you if I need you."

"Okay."

I took my purse and left. Then I took ten steps, turned around, came back, and opened the door. Millie was standing there.

"What?"

"I *still* can't believe Frances Mae really did that!"

Millie was shaking her head and grinning as wide as she could. "Gone out of here, girl! I got work to do!"

Miss Sweetie's plantation wasn't too far from ours, just up the road near Green Pond. Her house was even older than ours and her land had been in her deceased husband's family since the mideighteenth century. Unlike our family, who bequeathed Tall Pines to women in the family, hers was passed down through the male line. I often wondered if other members of her family would want it when Miss Sweetie went home to heaven, but a thousand acres wasn't something you just took on without a lot of thought. The maintenance alone required very deep pockets and an excellent sense of humor. The bad news was that like Tall Pines, Magnolia Point was a money pit. The good news was that Magnolia Point smelled like heaven when the strawberries were in bloom. As you might guess, instead of an avenue of oaks, Miss Sweetie had an avenue of one hundred or more enormous magnolias that led up to the front of her astoundingly beautiful and historic Georgian home, whose scale was nothing if not grand.

Black-lacquered shutters were hung all across the front portico, ready to close and latch in case of a hurricane. The massive ancient walls were constructed of small handmade bricks and ranged in color from the palest pink to deep maroon, flecked from time and moss. The large thick panes of glass were warped with age, filled with tiny bubbles and halos. While I suspected they were not original, they looked as old as anything I had ever seen in downtown Charleston. Glass had always been interesting to me, the way it continued to shift and reshape as it aged. Richard and I had owned a small collection of handblown vases and objects. I always loved the idea that they might be alive in some way because they literally held the breath of the artist and because they were always moving and changing. I had left them all with him, and looking at Miss Sweetie's windows reminded me that I missed them. And then it hit me. Life had become a continuum of leaving people, innocence, and belongings behind and moving on to something new that wasn't always necessarily better. First, it was my father, then it was my childhood, a childhood shrouded in grief, propped up in the company of strangers in a boarding school. Then I left Charleston, Mother, and Trip to find New York and Richard and to bring Eric to the world stage, only to renounce Richard and the life we had there to come back to find Mother and Trip and to stand by him while we said good-bye to Mother, and then Frances Mae began her wretched downward spiral. And here I stood at Miss Sweetie's door, reaching out for the door handle, feeling suddenly blue, wondering how many more exits were in my future.

"Snap out of it, Caroline!" I said to myself out loud, and decided instead of just walking in, I would ring the doorbell.

6

Miss Sweetie

"CHILD? LOOK AT YOU! COME on in and let me fix you something cool to drink!"

After a prolonged wait, to my great surprise, Miss Sweetie answered her own door. This was unusual. She had a houseman, Clyde, who had worked for her from the days before she had married Mr. Moultrie, who had long since gone to that great big strawberry field forever. Clyde was almost completely deaf, as old as Methuselah, crooked with age, and, more often than not, could be found somewhere nodding off in a chair.

"Thanks! Where's Clyde?"

"Law! He's gonna have his ninety-sixth birthday this weekend! Isn't that just marvelous?"

"Wow. Ninety-six. How do you celebrate that?"

"All his children, grandchildren, and great-grandchildren are coming to see him from all over the country. They're going to have a big family reunion."

"Is he working today? I'd like to wish him a happy birthday."

"Is he working? Well, he's working but not with the same fervor he had even last week," Miss Sweetie said, and then whispered, "I'm glad his family's coming. He's really slowing down. You know . . ."

"This could be the last live performance?"

"Hush! Slow or not slow, he's been a part of this place for so long, I don't know what I'd do without him! Follow me. He's in the butler's pantry polishing silver. That's about all he can do these days besides answer the door, and that's only when he can hear it, poor thing."

Mr. Clyde's length of employment was not unusual. All across the South, old plantations and large properties were peppered with an ancient population tending the gardens, feeding the animals, ironing flat linens like napkins and pillowcases, and, like Mr. Clyde, polishing silver. Historically, these small armies of men and women had worked for cash, so that when retirement age rolled around, the Social Security money they could collect was not enough to sustain even a marginal lifestyle. So they continued to work as long as life and limb cooperated, insisting that work guaranteed their longevity. Families like ours and like Miss Sweetie's never downsized and moved to condos in Boca. Sell the blood-soaked land our ancestors had died to protect? Never in a million years! We stayed where we were born until we drew our last breath, making sure that our heirs swore the same fealty to the cause.

Mr. Clyde looked up from the sink when I entered the pantry and he smiled to see me. Amazingly, he still had a full head of white curly hair, which he wore cut close to his scalp. Because silver polish was deadly to remove from clothing, he wore old-fashioned, blue cotton sleeve protectors that covered his arms from his biceps to his wrists. A black canvas apron covered the front of his shirt, tie, and trousers. His wing tips shone like melting licorice and his black-striped necktie was knotted in a full Windsor. I had never seen him without a tie in all my entire life. Mr. Clyde was buffing a small silver tray with an unhurried vengeance and a chamois cloth.

"Well, good morning, Miss Caroline! How are you this fine day?"

"Mr. Clyde? I just had to come in here and wish you all the best for your birthday! Miss Sweetie told me you had a big one coming up this weekend!"

"Well, at my age they all big ones. But I'm still on the right side of the grass and thanking God every day. My daddy? He live to see one hundred and seven years!"

"My goodness!" I said. "What's the secret to such a long life?"

"What's the secret? Well, I reckon it's staying busy so you don't lose your beans, eatin' right—always have my daily dose of greens, you know—and being happy. Yes, ma'am! Stay happy 'cause it makes your heart want to keep ticking!"

"I'll bet you're right! And that's it?"

"Well, before bed I always take me a little nip of Oh Be Joyful to ease my aching bones, but that's more medicinal than recreational."

"And just how many doses does it take to ease your bones?" I giggled and so did Miss Sweetie.

"Well, now that depends on the ache! Yes, ma'am! That depends on the ache."

Mr. Clyde, pleased that his clever remark had amused us, returned his attention to his work and we went on into the kitchen after I wished him well again.

"He is the dearest man on earth," Miss Sweetie said, peering into the refrigerator. "Oh, me. Sometimes I stare inside this thing half expecting something to talk to me! *Drink me!*"

"I know just what you mean. Iced water is fine for me. Really."

"All right, but I can make us some tea in five minutes."

"No. Don't trouble yourself. Water's fine. You know, I think all that caffeine can't be good for me."

"Oh, pish! These darned doctors and all their advice! They'd like us all to weigh one hundred pounds and never eat a blessed thing except unsalted oatmeal with no butter. They like to scare us into going to them every time you turn around."

"Yeah. If you're sick, they make money. If you're not, they don't."

"Glory! You're right! Everything's a racket these days, isn't it?"

She took two tumblers from a cabinet and filled them with ice and water.

I looked around her pristine white kitchen with all the red accents and smiled to myself. She had certainly cornered the market on strawberry accoutrements. There were dishes, mugs, canisters, dish towels—you name it—all of them had strawberries on them somewhere. She even had a red Viking range with eight burners and two ovens. It looked like a big valentine centered on the back wall. In fact the entire kitchen was a kind of valentine, a love letter showing how important her kitchen was to her. I agreed with that position because I had always felt that as much as I enjoyed the drama of a gorgeous living room or the glamour of a beautiful dining room, the kitchen was the heart of a home.

Her kitchen was where we usually worked, all of our papers spread across her oversize trestle table. It was still early in the day and sunlight was pouring through the windows. I noticed a grouping of bird feeders outside on black wrought-iron shepherd hooks and I thought how nice it must be for her to sit across from the windows and watch the migrating birds come and go.

"That's new, isn't it? The bird feeders, I mean."

"Yes! It is. Isn't it just the perfect thing to keep me company? After Jake died last year, I decided I was too old for another dog and then I saw these on the Internet and thought, well? Why not?"

"Why not indeed? Now, let's talk about inventory. It's planned for next week . . ."

We talked about shrinkage due to expiration dates, breakage, and how much we had to write down for taxes for 2006.

"It'll be a cold day in you know where before I insist on producing strawberry-pomegranate jam again. Remember how we thought all those little seeds would be a surprising burst of flavor? All those antioxidants? All people did was run to the dentist and write me letters of complaint."

"Yeah. Way worse than raspberries. We couldn't give it away. How much do we own?"

"I'm afraid to tell you," Miss Sweetie said. We stared at each other for a few seconds and then she said, "Okay. Four hundred cases. That's forty-eight hundred jars."

"Holy smoke. That's a lot. Maybe I can give them to Bobby Mack at a big discount and he can use it as a marinade?"

"Maybe we should try it as a marinade first?"

"I'll ask him to send me a pork shoulder and I'll try it tonight. Is that the worst problem we've got?"

"Yes, I'm happy to say. Other than this, it's strawberry chiffon heaven around here! And, by the way, we're very close to landing the Sara Lee account as well. Did I tell you about this?"

"No! Oh, Miss Sweetie, that's wonderful!"

"Yes, it is! Even though I am supposed to be just a spokesperson, our head of sales drags me into everything. Anyway, they have a whole new line of low-fat muffins and our strawberries . . ."

Her eyes twinkled and she became very animated as she told me how Sara Lee proposed to market the muffins and how much revenue we stood to gain if we acquired the account. For all of her complaints about how it was time for her to retire, it was obvious that Sweetie's was keeping her going.

"And, Caroline? I had a call from Nancy this morning about our bridge game this week. She was headed to Beaufort for a breakfast and she saw the billboards. Do you want to tell me what's going on? Mother McCree! We had no idea Frances Mae was so, well . . ."

"Crazy?"

I felt the back of my neck ignite and my face was in flames.

"Oh, come on now." She reached across the table and patted the back of my hand. "I know it's none of my business, but if I can help in any way, you know how much I loved your mother and—"

"Miss Sweetie? Frances Mae is no Picasso and she's always up to something awful, isn't she? Such an embarrassment. But this time? She's all done."

"Whatever do you mean, dear?"

"That Trip is finally, pardon my language, beyond the fury of every devil in hell."

Miss Sweetie gasped in false shock and said, "Well, it's high time! I know this is none of my business but I have to tell you, your mother would not have liked this one bit. Nice people don't hang their dirty laundry out in public."

"No, you're right. And I don't like it either."

On the way back to Tall Pines, my trunk loaded up with four cases of strawberry-pomegranate jam, my cell rang out with the theme song to *Goldfinger*. It was the music designated for only Bobby Mack and don't ask why. I had not heard from him in ten days and the way my life went? Anything could happen in ten days.

"Princess!"

"I was just going to call you! Where've you been hiding, darlin'? I've been missing you," I said, thinking now here he is and what am I to do with Matthew Strickland? Hide him in the closet?

"Just working like a fiend, that's all. I was up in Hyde Park, New York, teaching a bunch of Yankee chef wannabe kids at the CIA how to make sausage and, of course, the most efficient way to finish a hog."

"You mean, finish him off for good?"

"Ah, come on, pussycat. That sounds so harsh."

"Boooooobbeeeee?"

"Hmm?"

"Can you have someone bring me a shoulder of pork? Pleeeeease?"

"I can have someone bring you a shoulder of pork, and later on, I'll bring another shoulder for you to lean on and cry about how you been missing your man. How's seven?"

"Oh, Bobby! That would be so wonderful! I can't wait to see you!"

We hung up and I prayed, Oh dear Lord, please help us get Frances Mae on a plane to California and Trip back to his house with Rusty and Matthew Strickland on duty at the other end of the county by six forty-five. Thank you Lord, Amen. P.S. Oh, and also with my hair blown out, necessary places shaved and moisturized, and Millie tucked away somewhere out of sight with Mr. Jenkins. Amen and thanks, again.

It didn't seem like a lot to ask for from heaven given all the pious things I had done lately. Okay, perhaps I'm not exactly pious, but I had certainly given Trip's kids lots of well-intentioned thought. I hoped that counted for something.

Trip arrived at three-thirty with his lawyer, who was a precious thing named Oscar Rosen. I saw no evidence of a wedding ring and filed that detail away for later, should Bobby and Matthew exhaust their talents or pitch their tents elsewhere. What was the matter with me, always planning my next liaison? Nothing. Because if I didn't, who would?

By ten minutes to four, Millie's mystery cake was on Mother's buffet with plates, forks, and small linen napkins, and the silver tea service was ready to go.

"What's in the cake?" I asked Millie in a whisper. "Can I eat it?"

"It's a chocolate pound cake and you'd better have some! I've been baking all day!"

"But what's in it?" Millie narrowed her eyes at me and I narrowed mine right back. "Besides chocolate, I mean."

"You don't be worrying yourself about that, 'eah? Just serve everybody a nice fat slice."

Trip was pacing like an animal. The tension was building. Even Millie was nervous. Frances Mae was predictably late. The doorbell rang.

"Who the hell is that?" Trip said. "Coming to the *front* door? Who comes to the *front* door?"

"Religious and environmental fanatics. And on occasion, the authorities. I'll answer it," I said.

"Hold yourself together," Millie said, and picked up the intercom and asked who it was.

"Mack Farms! Got a delivery for Miss Caroline!"

"It's my pork shoulder. I'll go get it."

"What? You're having a pork shoulder delivered?" Trip said. *"Today?"*

"Yeah, we got pig coming and going today," I said, hoping a little levity might lighten Trip's anxiety.

It did not.

At first Trip said to Oscar, "Stay with me, okay?" And then a minute later he said, "Why don't you all wait here in the kitchen with Millie and I'll call you when I need you?"

"Fine with me," I said, trying to strike a sultry chord with Oscar and an acquiescent one with Trip. I unwrapped the roast and looked at it, plumping it with my hands like clay that would become a sculpture. Why I did this I have no idea, except to me, there was nothing more beautiful in the world than a pork shoulder. I dumped a bottle of the wicked strawberry-pomegranate jelly in a saucepan with some mustard, cloves, and brown sugar and turned the heat to low and the oven to 250 degrees. "But I think we should serve cake first, you know, so it doesn't appear to be some kind of ambush, don't you?"

"You're probably right. Okay, then. Oscar? Change of plan. We'll all be in the dining room when she arrives. I just hope she doesn't expect me to be nice to her. It's costing me another five thousand dollars to clean up her mess from this morning. There's paint all over the damn place."

It was twenty minutes after three when Frances Mae's SUV rolled into the side yard at last. She got out, smoothed her shirt and hair, and moved toward the kitchen door, wobbling a bit.

"She's in the bag," I said to Millie, who stood by me as we both peeked through the kitchen window, standing just off to the side so that she couldn't see us.

"Good," Millie said. "That'll make it easier for Trip to stand his ground."

"You're right. Lord, I hope he doesn't lose his nerve."

"Humph. What in the *world* has that woman got on her back today?"

The door opened and the room was filled with Frances Mae. There she was, inappropriately dressed in what appeared to be one of her daughters' short skirts and a knit top. On a skinny teenager it would have been fine, but on her matronly figure it was too revealing and downright ridiculous. Millie's eyes took a roll and so did mine.

"Hi, y'all," she said.

"Hi, Frances Mae," I said. "Trip's in the dining room."

"Okay," she said, and left the room so quickly she could have been walking across hot coals.

"Her breath is a freaking fire hazard," I said.

"Poor thing," Millie said.

"You think so, huh?" I stirred my marinade, basted the pork, and put the roasting pan in the oven.

"Shush! I wouldn't want to be her, would you?"

"No, ma'am, but you and I would never be her. Not for all the money in this world."

I gave them a few minutes and then went to the dining room to cut and serve the cake. When I got there, Frances Mae was already eating an enormous slice in large bites, probably in an attempt to disguise the alcohol on her breath. For Frances Mae to make herself at home annoyed me beyond words, but then it wasn't unusual for Frances Mae to break rank and assume the cake was hers to cut. She had all the manners of a goat.

"What were you thinking, Frances Mae?" Trip's voice was drenched with irritation and he struggled to maintain a civil tone.

"What?" she said.

"Defacing public and private property?"

"What did the messages say on the billboards, Trip?"

"For *me* to come back to *you* and that *my* gorgeous Rusty is an F-ing whore."

Suddenly Frances Mae's face changed and she began to weep, not sobbing, but tears poured out of her eyes like someone flipped on a faucet. I was stunned. I looked at Oscar, who quickly offered her his handkerchief—I loved men who carried linen handkerchiefs—which she took and used to blot her face. What was in the cake?

Trip's mood had suddenly changed, too, and he said in a softer tone, "Look, Frances Mae. You need serious help."

"No, I do not."

"You've been drinking today, haven't you?"

"No."

I couldn't believe what happened next, but Trip produced a Breathalyzer from his jacket. "Then you won't mind breathing into this little tube?"

"What? Why should I do that? And what are you doing with that thing anyway? Are you the police now?"

"Nope. But you're an alcoholic and we all know it. Frances Mae? You've got to go into a long-term in-patient rehab program or you will never get off the booze. Like I told you yesterday, I'll pay for the whole thing. All the arrangements are made. There are two nice male nurses parked in the van out back and they are going to take you there straight from this house. And just so you know, I could've had you committed to the psych ward at MUSC but I didn't. You're going to sunny California instead."

She had some fight left in her.

"Screw you, Trip Wimbley. I ain't going nowhere."

"Yes. You *are* going, Frances Mae. In the meanwhile, I'm taking full custody of the girls and I'll take total care of them. But here's the deal: I want you to sign the divorce papers. I am willing to give you the house in Walterboro and this much money . . ."

Trip showed her the number on the paper, and by the look on Frances Mae's face, she was immediately sobered.

Frances Mae straightened up and put on her best voice of self-righteous indignation. "I will never give up my children, not even for twice that much money."

Trip was stunned. Frances Mae had been married to him for long enough to know that the first offer was a lowball.

"I'll just be in the kitchen," I said, and no one noticed as I left.

I mean, honest to God, I had no business being there in the dining room. So I stood with Millie on the other side of the swinging door, after almost knocking her out cold when I went in.

"Sorry!" I whispered.

"Where'd you think I'd be?" Millie whispered back. "Now, shush!"

We heard Trip say, "Oh yes you will because another DUI is going to put your butt in the hoosegow for a mandatory five days, maybe up to a year, and maybe up to three."

Frances Mae must have turned her face to Oscar.

"And, excuse me, but just who in the hell are you?"

"I'm representing Mr. Wimbley."

"Well, screw you, too, because I ain't signing nothing!"

"Frances Mae? It's rehab or jail. In either setting you can't care for the kids. And you'll lose custody anyway, so why can't we just be civilized about this?"

In my mind I had already said more "holy shits" than I could count and Millie's eyebrows were dusting the ceiling. I cussed in my head all the time. And sometimes out loud, but hopefully not too much.

But Frances Mae, whether she saw the soundness of Trip's argument or not, was still having no part of his plan.

"Civilized? You call yourself civilized? I'd call you a snob maybe, a self-centered momma's-boy philanderer living with a tramp, maybe. But civilized? No, I don't think it's civilized to offer me money to sell my children."

"I'm trying to help you, Frances Mae. I'm trying to be generous here."

And this was when the halfway coherent sister-in-law became possessed by the redneck from hell.

"Generous? Yew spent more money on all yewr dogs 'en guns 'en boats 'en who knows what in one month than you ever spent on me in all our years together!"

"It may seem that way to you, but let me assure you that I am not talking about just money here, Frances Mae. I don't have to give you anything. I could let you just get another DUI and sue you for custody, which I would win in any courtroom in the land. It would be all over the papers and the girls would be mortified one more time. Is that what you really want? To mortify your children?"

A seeming eternity passed before we heard Frances Mae answer. "No."

"So, what I'm doing here is trying to handle this with a little compassion for you to get you the help you need and to help you avoid any more humiliation. You must admit that the things you have done were absolutely irresponsible. And to be honest, *criminal*, Frances Mae."

"Humph. Well, that's just fine because I don't need no man to be reminding me for one more second that I'm not good enough for this stuck-up family of yewrs. I'll go to rehab and I'll get sober, but when I come back, I want my girls."

"Frances Mae?" Trip said. "Let's cross that bridge when we come to it. So far there's no evidence of your ability to stay off the bottle. Don't you think you've embarrassed the children enough? Us *all* enough?"

What happened next was almost unbearable. Her waterworks went into overdrive and she began to wail.

"Oh God, *why*? You know I *love* yew, Trip. I love yew with *all* my heart and I'm gonna up and *die* without yew. *Please!* Won't you come back home? Let's try again, Trip. For the kids? *Please* give me another chance. I love yew *so much*. I'll never drink another drop! All I ever wanted was to marry yew and have a family with yew . . . that's all I ever wanted in my whole life . . . my whole life is yew and our kids. It is."

"I know, I know," we heard Trip say. "But it's no good anymore, Frances Mae, and we both know it."

I looked at Millie and she looked at me. We were both in tears hearing Frances Mae's anguish and feeling how completely chopped to pieces her heart was. It was just awful.

"That cake ain't working right," Millie said. "St. John's wort don't agree with her."

"Evidently," I whispered. "Is she gonna be okay?"

"Oh, yeah. A few hours from now it'll work its way out of her system."

"Oh God! Please no!" Frances Mae cried, and then her sobbing began in earnest.

"I'm sure glad Mother didn't live to see this either," I said in a low voice.

"We're saying that too often around here," Millie said. "We need this *situation* fixed! Awful to hear and painful to witness, I know, but things got to change."

Frances Mae must have signed the papers because about five minutes later we could hear Oscar say, "Okay. I think that does it."

We moved away from the door as quickly as we could and tried to look busy. Sure enough, in seconds Frances Mae came sailing through with Trip.

She looked at me and said what she had probably longed to say for years.

"You know what? This house was supposed to be *mine*. But noooo. Your life was supposed to be mine! But noooo. When *your* marriage didn't work out with that ugly nasty Jew shrink—big surprise, city girl—you came running home to your crazy-ass bitch momma with your tail between your skinny legs and y'all both ruined my whole life. Well, guess what? You ain't seen the last of me, Caroline Laveen! No, you have not."

"You'd better watch your mouth, Frances Mae."

I was boiling mad and knew I shouldn't have said a word, but anti-Semitism was something I could not and would not abide. And nobody, but *nobody,* was calling Miss Lavinia names.

"Come on, Frances Mae, let's go," Trip said.

"Good luck, Frances Mae." I was shaking with anger as my adrenaline pumped its way through my veins. I wanted to stab her but instead I said, "Get out of my house and don't ever come back."

"We'll just see about that, won't we, missy?"

"Humph," Millie said when they were out of the door, making their way toward the van that had indeed arrived during the time we were listening at the door.

"I really don't like her," I said.

Millie looked at me and nodded. "Right now? There ain't much to like."

7

Chaos

H E CAME BACK INSIDE THE house and we looked at each other, Millie, Trip, and I, dizzied by the shock of Frances Mae's hysterics. Her fury was still whirling around the room like hundreds of tiny poltergeists, slamming from wall to wall and floor to ceiling. My throat quivered from the struggle to find words to accurately describe how I felt.

"Oh my God, Trip! She's completely insane!" I knew I was on the border of hysterics of my own. "Let's start with her false sense of entitlement and work our way around the barn. She still thinks she's supposed to have my inheritance!" I tried to calm down. What was the point of getting so upset?

"Well, she's not going to have it and you know it. So let's move past that now."

"You're right, of course, but do you know how it feels to have someone insist that your home is theirs?"

"You're talking about the ranting of a drunk. It's craziness, so forget it! I just hope this place she's going works on craziness, too."

"So does the rest of the world." I took a deep breath.

"Great God. I really, really hope this works." There was a well of sadness in his voice as though he believed the cause of Frances Mae's problems really could be laid at his feet.

"It can't hurt," I said.

"I've never seen her cry like that. I mean, she was wailing!"

Trip was obviously profoundly moved by Frances Mae's passionate grief and that squelched my annoyance considerably. Because the truth was that I wasn't in my state because I was insulted. Who cared about her ridiculous outburst anyway? Okay, me, but just a tad. No, our concern was quickly redirected to Trip's crumbling status quo, to his conscience and the fervent desire that Frances Mae's horrible alcoholism would finally come to an end.

"I'm gone pray for her," Millie said, and that meant she would be praying like no other woman I had ever known.

This episode was a dark chapter in our family's history. We had hung our share of drunks in the family tree but they had been all male. We'd suffered a fair number of philanderers and ne'er-do-wells like every other family but they were men, too. Nothing compared to the controversy and disgrace Frances Mae and her two middle daughters had brought into our lives. Maybe I cared more about that than I should have but I still hated it. No doubt Frances Mae's departure would be grist for the gossipmongers, and Lowcountry tongues would wave like flags in a squall on the Fourth of July.

But Frances Mae was gone and this terrible chapter was in the past. We had to pick ourselves up and go on to the other issues racing to the forefront. Rusty. The girls.

Suddenly, as though the universe sensed we needed a momentary distraction, the rich and savory smells of the roast filled the air. It still had hours to cook, but if it tasted like anything close to its perfume, I might have found a use for the strawberry-pomegranate jam after all. A small blessing in a day of deep potholes but I would take it and be glad for it.

"Where's Oscar?" Trip said.

"Oh!" I said, not having given Oscar's whereabouts a single thought since Frances Mae's arrival. Precious Oscar! "What kind of a hostess am I?"

"It's not as if we were giving a tea party here, sister. I'll go get him."

Trip left the room and Millie leaned back against the sink and sighed loudly.

"This is some day, ain't it?"

"You can say that again. I was just thinking, Millie . . ."

Trip came through the swinging door with Oscar the Possibility on his heels.

"So, in just a few months I'm a free man," Trip said, managing to just barely smile.

"Congratulations. So, Einstein? Have you worked out the details of this colossal change with the kids?" I said. "And Rusty?"

"Nope. It was enough to organize an intervention and tell Belle to bring Chloe home from school. What's in the oven? Pork?"

Had he heard and processed what I said? Well, if he didn't want to elaborate I wasn't pushing the issue. Yet.

"Fifteen pounds of paradise. Bobby Mack's coming for dinner and I'm trying to unload a quantity of jam impersonating a marinade. It's just a business dinner."

"Oh," said Trip.

"Right," said Millie, who knew better.

"It smells great," Oscar the Pelvis said.

"It is great," I said, and winked at him, which I knew was very cheesy but no one saw me do it. Out here in the country, a single woman had to maximize every potential. It wasn't like I spent my day tripping over the bodies of available men.

"'Eah, Mr. Oscar, come see." Millie opened the oven door and pulled the rack out to show off the meat. "That, sir, is a roast!" Then she turned her attention to Trip. "So, tell me something. Who's gonna make them girls dinner?" She closed the oven door and stood up straight with her hands in the small of her back. "And see about their homework and all that?"

"Well, I guess Rusty and I are gonna take over and figure that out as we go."

"Humph," said Millie, rinsing the basting brush and knocking the water from it on the side of the sink.

"That 'humph' from Millie means you're being naive, Trip," I said as politely as I could.

"In fact, I'm gonna go pick Rusty up now and get over to Walterboro. I think the thing to do is sit them all down and talk to them."

"Yeah, but what are you going to say?" I said.

"I'm gonna tell them to start packing. They're moving in with us."

I began to panic. "Wait a minute. Do you really want Belle driving your girls back and forth to school in Walterboro? That road is only two lanes with deep ditches on both sides and there are eighteen-wheelers all over the place going a million miles an hour! And, it's too far!"

"Then we'll stay in Walterboro and bring them here on the weekends."

"Trip? Have you taken leave of your senses?" I said. "Do you really think Rusty is going to sleep in Frances Mae's cootie bed? Are you crazy or what?"

"She won't care. We'll take our own sheets. Whatever. Anyway, the kids are out of school at the end of May. Belle graduates and then they move in here with us."

"I love you, Trip, but I think you're dreaming. Seriously."

"We'll see. This is my responsibility now."

Oscar the Pelvis was standing by the door, ready to leave.

"It was very nice to meet you," he said, moving his nose from side to side like a small rabbit that had just hopped out from a thicket.

Why hadn't I noticed this annoying twitch before? It was clearly not allergies. Well, he would still suffice in a drought, but that twitching nose thing would have to stop. It was very distracting. And to be perfectly blunt, I preferred my seismic activities to occur in the south, if you know what I mean.

"It was lovely to have met you, too," I said, and held out my hand to him. He took it into his like a rare jungle gardenia and gave it a gentle squeeze. "I hope we'll meet again!" I forced my eyes to smile at him as he and his twitch backed their way out of the house, grinning at me, at Millie, and yes, even at Trip.

"Lawsamercy, girl!" Millie said when Trip and Oscar were out of the house. "Of all the things you had to inherit from your mother! You cast a spell on that poor little man like the voodoo queen from the bayous of Louisiana!"

"Oh, come on, Millie! I was just having a little fun with him."

"Humph!"

"Look! It's slim pickings out here in the woods! You sure are harrumphing a lot today! What are you thinking?"

"I'm thinking you scare me you're so much like you know who! Girl? Where's your mind? Don't you know your telephone is gonna be ringing off the hook for the next week or who knows how long? Them girls ain't gonna do what Trip says just because he's their daddy. Daddy? Daddy? So what? They's teenage girls who don't listen to nobody on a good day! All hell's about to bust loose and I don't mean maybe."

"Oh Lord. You're right. Maybe we should try to give them a little heads up. I mean, maybe we should tell Amelia what's happening so that if the girls go running to her she'll already be in our court. What do you think?"

"Call her. Call her right this minute."

I dialed Amelia's number and the call went to voice mail. I waited until the recorded voice gave me an opportunity to leave a message and then I hung up.

"You ain't leaving no message?" Millie said.

"Nope! She'll call back twice as fast. Watch!"

Within three minutes Handel's *Water Music* filled the air, one of my favorite ring tones. The one I had designated for Amelia. Ah, memories. I answered the phone, and indeed, it was Amelia.

"Aunt Caroline? Is everything okay?"

Worked like a charm every single time.

"Amelia? Do you have a moment, sweetheart?"

"Yeah, sure! What's going on?"

"Well, this morning there was an unfortunate incident involving your mother and several cans of spray paint . . ."

I went on to tell her all the details and of course she became angry and finally she began to cry.

"*Why* does she do these things? Why can't I have a normal family?"

"Define 'normal,'" I said. "No one has a normal family. Maybe the Cleavers were, but how boring were they? I'm just so sorry this has happened, but I'll tell you, this was inevitable."

"Well, thank God Mom's finally getting some help, even if it is her ninth attempt. Maybe it will work this time."

"Fifth. And we're lucky it was nothing worse. I mean, at least she didn't hit a tree with Chloe in the car."

Amelia was very quiet then, probably envisioning her little sister's lifeless body lying in a gutter like the literal one in which she was born and how a real tragedy may have been averted by her father stepping in.

"Listen, Amelia, here's the thing . . ."

We talked about the geographical, emotional, and psychological challenges of the girls coming to live with Rusty and Trip at Tall

Pines and the commuting issue. Amelia agreed that Rusty would never and should never stay in their house in Walterboro, even if it were just for a short period of time.

"They hate her guts, Aunt Caroline. They're so stupid they'd probably kill her in her sleep and think they were doing Mom a favor."

Guts again. I really didn't like to hear that word coming from her mouth.

"That's pretty extreme."

"I know but I wouldn't put anything past them, would you?"

"I . . . I don't know."

"Do you think I should come home and take care of them?"

"Absolutely not."

One thing was certain. Amelia had grown to be such a promising young woman in so many ways. I didn't want the tawdry habits of her gum-chewing, body-pierced, Goth-haired sisters to hold her back one inch from wherever she was headed.

"Amelia, I think it's best for you to stay in school right where you are. In fact, I am certain of it. Your dad's on the way there now with Rusty. We have to let them figure this out. After all, they're the adults."

"Go tell that to Belle and Linnie. Chloe? Sure, she'll do whatever they tell her to, but not Belle and Linnie."

"Well, listen, if they call you, and I'm sure they will, please ask them to go along with your father for now and to go easy on Rusty. This has been a terrible day for everyone."

"Sure, I can do that, but I can't swear they'll listen to me. Eric and I are having supper together tonight. Do you want me to tell him about all this?"

"Please. It's probably best that he knows, in case they show up at his dorm or something crazy like that."

"Right. Okay, then . . ."

"And tell him anytime he wants to talk to me about his girlfriend, I'm happy to listen."

I heard her gasp before she said okay and good-bye and it left me to wonder what was it about this one that was so different?

I hung up and Millie was standing close by waiting to hear what Amelia had had to say.

"Nothing earth-shattering," I said, because she could tell enough from my side of the conversation that it wasn't worth repeating it all.

"I'll set the table for you," she said.

"Thanks, Millie."

"For your *business* dinner . . ."

Millie knew I meant monkey business.

Oh, shoot. I felt my heart being pulled in fifty directions and I felt sorry for everyone. Was it true that Frances Mae was still in love with Trip? Maybe. And did she really feel low class and unwanted because of Mother's snobbish attitude? Probably. And was it because of Trip's place in Mother's heart that they had driven her to drink, to become an alcoholic, to take incredible risks with her children? It was conceivable. And how much of the guilt rested on my shoulders? A healthy percentage. And now that Mother was gone, had she transferred all that hatred and resentment to me? It seemed so. I probably deserved a lot of what Frances Mae felt toward me, though I was loath to admit it. But did she have one iota of understanding of what it was like for us to have someone like her in the family?

From the very first moment Mother and I laid eyes on Frances Mae, she was completely inappropriate. There she was in a tube top, jeans and high heels, and bleached hair, grinding her well-used pelvis into Trip's on the fender of Trip's car right in front of our house. And she had plumped-up slick red lips just like a bigmouth bass. Heavenly days. I would carry the memory of Mother's slack-jawed profile into my dotage as well as the image seared into my mind of Frances Mae eyeballing the house, calculating its worth. I watched with fascination over the next few years as she inventoried our home and its contents and as she began her crusade to acquire it all by producing babies, an unproven method if ever there was one.

I never really cared when Frances Mae went on the occasional bender. She usually did it at home and no one knew except her children and us. Everyone knows, except illiterate families who never watch *Dr. Phil,* that alcoholism affects the entire family and makes them all liars. Everyone becomes a part of a conspiracy to protect the drunk. Belle and Linnie might have been mean and rotten little stinkers, but even they would experience a sense of relief that they would have a reprieve from their mother's drama when they learned their mother was going to be gone for sixty days. Sixty days was not a long time, but maybe that relief would bring them to the negotiating table in better humor. Although Belle was eighteen, which I assumed was the legal age of consent for everything except marrying your first cousin, did she really want the responsibility of Chloe and Linnie and the house? Did she want to go to the grocery store and prepare meals? I didn't think so. Surely Belle would realize this would bring her an enormous amount of additional aggravation and responsibility when she needed to be focused on finals and where she was going to college in the fall, a detail that still hung in the air, although Carolina seemed willing to have her with some academic stipulations. That was probably where she would go, since Eric and Amelia were there.

It was almost six o'clock. I took a wedge of cheese from the refrigerator and some green grapes and put them on a platter to let them come to room temperature. Bobby Mack was going to arrive within the hour. I basted the meat again, threw some potatoes, onions, and carrots in the pan to roast, and said good night to Millie.

"Don't you want me to stay and help you with dinner? I don't mind, you know," she offered, knowing my answer before I could speak.

"Oh, Millie, it's been such a trying day. Thanks, but I can handle this myself."

"I have no doubt about that!" she said, and shook her head.

When she left, the house seemed surprisingly quiet. It was finally mine again. I passed through the dining room and turned on some music that I bought from Williams-Sonoma. Love songs from Brazil filled the air and I was filled with excitement. The roast wouldn't be ready for at least another two hours. What would I do to entertain Bobby Mack until dinner was ready? Talk about a rhetorical question? I raced upstairs to shower and change, leaving the front door unlocked.

It wasn't long until I heard Bobby Mack's car door close. I had just slipped one of my mother's wilder animal-print caftans over my head and was debating the matching turban, finally deciding to leave my hair loose around my shoulders. I gave myself generous spritzes of Joy in all the important places.

"Caroline?"

"I'll be right there, darlin'!"

I took a slow walk down the stairs toward where he stood in the foyer. He seemed heavier and I wondered if he was aware that he was gaining weight. His face was turning red, which I took as flattery.

"Look at you, pussycat," he said in a sort of breathless tone.

"Meow," I said.

He swept me right into such a muscular embrace that my C-three and C-four disks clicked with a crunch, relieving the tension that had been hidden there for days. Bobby Mack's hug was more potent than an orthopedic specialist.

"I'm so glad to see you!" I whispered in his ear.

"And I'm so glad to see you!" he said while his lips hopscotched my neck and throat.

"Would you like some champagne?"

"Whatever you want, I want!"

"Oh, Bobby!"

"What's that I smell?"

"Come see, baby boy."

I took him by the hand and led him into the kitchen. The air was thick with the smell we both adored—roasting pork. I opened the oven door.

"What do you think?" I said, slicing off a tip from the end and feeding him with my fingers. He, of course, pretended that he was going to suck my fingers right off my hand. Men are so silly.

"I think you know how to drive me wild, Miss Caroline."

"You open the champagne. This baby won't be ready until eight-thirty or so. It seems that I have forgotten to wear panties, so I'll just slip upstairs and—"

"I'll just be right behind you!"

Well, he was. Figuratively and literally. This boy had spent a little too much time in the barnyard, but I wasn't complaining. Sometimes I felt like a foreign heathen with all the missionaries I had known. So there we were, doing the wild thing, I was feeling very wanton and wayward, and Bobby was breathing very hard. The next thing I knew there was a deep groan, a massive thrust, and he collapsed on the side of my bed. He was out cold.

"My God! Are you all right? Bobby Mack! Answer me!"

I checked for a pulse and there was none. Quickly, I called 911, thinking I would then dress him and start CPR.

"Nine-one-one. What's your emergency?"

"My friend appears to have had a heart attack! He's not breathing! Please hurry! Oh my God!"

"Just calm down, ma'am. Tell me your address."

"I'm at the end of Parker's Ferry Road—Tall Pines Plantation! Hurry! Please!"

"I've just dispatched an ambulance to your house. Now, have you ever done CPR?"

"Yes, but not since I was in my twenties! Oh God! What if he dies?"

"Okay, here's what I want you to do . . ."

Forgetting about everything except saving Bobby Mack's life, I put the emergency aide on speakerphone and followed his instructions. It wasn't easy to haul Bobby to the floor. His deadweight felt like a thousand pounds. Deadweight! What was I saying?

"Bobby Mack! Wake up! Oh God! Please wake up!"

I tilted his head back, pinched his nose, and covered his mouth with mine, blowing with all my might. His chest rose and fell and I repeated this several times. Then I placed the heel of my hand in the middle of his chest and pressed down with every bit of strength I could summon. I kept repeating the two actions until I thought I heard him start breathing. When I was sure he wasn't dead, I sat back on my heels and began to cry.

"Oh, Bobby! I was so frightened!" I took his hand and squeezed it.

Bobby was disoriented and unsure of what had happened. I heard people coming up the stairs calling out "Hello, hello!"

"We're up here! Right in here!"

I stood up to grab my caftan and I threw it over my head just as I saw the medical workers rolling the stretcher into the room. When the silk of the hem hit my feet, I looked up into the eyes of Matthew Strickland.

"Um," he said in a very quiet voice. "I heard the call and just wanted to make sure you were all right."

Oh. My. God, I thought. But I said, composing myself as my mother would have done and this was definitely a WWLD moment (What Would Lavinia Do), "Matthew, this is precisely why I love you so much! Wait just a minute, okay?" As calmly as I could, I picked up the telephone to speak to the 911 operator. "Help has arrived," I said. "Thank you so, so much for all your help. I think we saved a life tonight. Yes. Of course. Thank you again. Good night."

I scooped up Bobby Mack's belongings and placed them on top of his belly on the stretcher.

"Where are you taking him?" I said, ignoring Matthew for the moment.

"Medical University in Charleston. Look's like he's had a massive heart attack. But since he's stable now, we think it's safe enough to transport him to Charleston."

"Yeah, we're halfway there and Charleston's closer and better equipped than anything else around here," said the other attendant.

"I can't thank you all enough. Here, I'll come out with you." We proceeded across the upstairs balcony and down the front stairs. "Now you need to know that this man is a very important man . . ." I ranted on about Bobby Mack's stature in the world, a little nervously perhaps. When they closed the back of the ambulance, not before I had kissed Bobby's forehead of course, I was satisfied that he was in good hands. Just as I came back into the house, the telephone was ringing and the kitchen door slammed on its hinges. In seconds Millie and Mr. Jenkins were there, all fluster and concern.

"Everything's fine!" I said, and rushed by them to grab the phone on the hall table. It was Trip.

"Caroline? I've got a big problem here! Can you drive out to Walterboro and talk some sense into these girls of mine?"

"Trip? Any other time, I'd be honored, but tonight it seems I have a little *situation* of my own." I told him an abbreviated version. He whistled long and low.

"Gotta love this family. We'll talk tomorrow," he said, and hung up.

I placed the phone back in the receiver and turned to face Millie, Mr. Jenkins, and Matthew Strickland. "The Girl from Ipanema" was streaming from the living room and everyone except me had already noticed that I had Mother's caftan on inside out.

As though everything was perfectly normal, I said, "Have y'all had dinner?"

8

The Girls

I<small>T WAS A MINOR STROKE</small> of genius that Trip and Rusty drove to Walterboro in separate cars. Trip stayed there overnight. Rusty most assuredly did not. In fact, the great-hall clock had just struck seven-thirty the next morning and there she was on my kitchen steps like Marley's ghost. I was upstairs, finishing dressing, when I heard the bong from downstairs and the slam of her car door. I hurried to unlock the kitchen door and let her in. Rusty, whose appearance was always a redheaded Grace Kelly circa 1950 perfect, looked like she'd just run through a wind tunnel.

"Good heavens! Girl? Did you sleep at all last night? You look like who did it and ran! You want coffee?"

"You would, too! I'll help myself." She took a mug from the cabinet and filled it. "Come to think of it, you had a heck of a night yourself! Trip told me what happened. Awful."

"Well, obviously the worst part is Bobby Mack's heart attack, not my personal embarrassment. I mean, who cares about that? Needless to say, I am worried sick about him. I'm headed down to Charleston to see him."

"Is he going to be all right?"

"I think so. I mean, the EMTs said he was stable when they took him away."

"Good grief! And Matthew was there, too?"

"Yeah. Matthew is so sweet. He understands everything. I think everyone except Trip knows that Matthew and I have a funny little thing going on sometimes that isn't so serious, so it *was* an awkward moment. The thing I love about Matthew is that he always makes me feel like everything is going to be okay, you know what I mean? Oh God, why am I running my mouth about this? Tell me what happened with the girls last night! I'm dying to hear!"

"What happened? What happened? I don't even know where to start!"

"Do you want breakfast?"

"Heavens no, but thanks. I couldn't eat a thing!"

"Me either. So, you got there and what?"

"We got there right before six last night. Trip went in the front door and the three girls were in the family room, draped all over the furniture like big old yard dogs. Schoolbooks were everywhere but they were watching some loud reality television program instead of doing homework, which annoyed Trip to no end. To make matters worse, there was a pizza box full of uneaten crust on the coffee table and a giant bottle of Diet Coke. Dirty glasses everywhere."

"Nice touch."

"Right? So Trip says, 'Girls? Turn off that television. We need to talk.' They looked up to him, said nothing, probably because they were stunned to see him there in the first place. Then they looked over to me and said, 'What's she doing here?'"

"And you said, 'Oh, I'm here to bake cookies?' "

"Are you kidding me? I didn't say one word. I stood there and let Trip do all the talking. So when they didn't turn off the television, he just picked up the remote and turned it off himself. They started moaning, even Chloe joined in like a choir member, and I was counting on her to cooperate. No such luck. Trip said something like, 'Let's all go in the dining room. Now!' "

"And they said, 'Oh, yes, Father dear! Whatever you want!' "

"Not quite. The groaning continued until finally they got up, went to the dining room, and took a chair. Trip sat at one end of the table, which is where I guess he used to sit. He told them that Frances Mae was gone to California and wouldn't be back for at least eight weeks but it could be longer."

"How'd they take that?"

"They just got quiet. Then Belle realized that her mother was going to miss her high school graduation. She became furious. I mean, she didn't start complaining because it was a fait accompli but the disappointment was all over her face. All she said was, 'My graduation! There it goes, y'all! Poof!' And she snapped her fingers in the air."

"Poor child. But on the bright side, maybe she will be spared an embarrassing scene. Old F.M. could've shown up blitzed and passed out flat on her face or something."

"True. Anyway, after it was all said and done, they finally agreed on a plan of sorts."

"Which is?"

"That we'll hire a housekeeper to live in and who drives and who will stay with them five days a week. She'll manage Chloe's life and the house, and the girls will clean up after themselves. We hope. Linnie and Belle can drive themselves to school, but they all have to spend the weekends with us out here."

"I'll bet that plan's got about enough of a chance of survival as a snowball in hell."

"Why do you say that?"

"Weekends, honey. What about prom? What about ball games and other things like dates? Sleepovers? I mean, these girls have a weekend life, don't they?"

"Well, thankfully at that moment the girls' attitudes were tempered by the news about Frances Mae, but they asked the same questions you just did. Trip, bless his heart, said, 'Look, we'll handle each event on a case-by-case basis.'"

"Case by case. You just can't take the lawyer out of the boy, can you?"

"Guess not. Anyway, this weekend will be my first weekend with them and I gotta find a housekeeper on the double!"

"Didn't Frances Mae have someone helping her out a couple of days a week?"

"Yeah, but she quit. No surprise there. I've got her number and thought I'd start with her anyway."

"Well, the country's suffering from a lot of unemployment, so there's probably a lot of talent out there."

"I sure hope so."

"I'll ask Miss Sweetie and Millie if they know anyone looking for work."

"Thanks. I'd appreciate that."

"And if it gets too hairy with them this weekend, you can always escape over here. So, are you sure you don't want some breakfast?"

"No, thanks. I'm okay. Don't have much of an appetite anyway."

"Me either. So, Rusty? Who's helping out over there until you find someone?"

"Trip. He'll be there every night. He stayed last night."

I looked at her and shook my head. My left arm was across my chest, the elbow of my right arm rested on it. The fingers of my right hand strummed my lips.

"You look like Jack Benny when you do that," Rusty said.

"Oh, thanks. Jack Benny. We're supposed to be too young to know who he is. I'm just wondering how in the world this is really going to work."

"I don't know but it seems like a reasonable plan, doesn't it?"

"It seems to me that you and Trip are overlooking the fact that the girls resent you like Tibetans resent the Chinese. I mean, Rusty, don't you know they're going to make your life miserable?"

"Caroline? They will. I'm certain of that. But I don't have any alternative here but to try and make this work. Even the girls finally admitted that leaving them there on their own wasn't the best idea."

"Come on. Did they think that they could handle everything by themselves?"

"Of course! Belle kept saying, 'But I'm eighteen!' And Trip would say; 'Yes, you are, but for the sake of your own safety and your reputation, you still need adult supervision in the house.' They must've thrashed that argument out about twenty times. It was exhausting."

"I'm sure. But it sounds like you came away reasonably unscathed."

"Oh no I didn't. Linnie called me a *F*-ing bitch under her breath and gave me the finger, twisting her hand in front of her face that had a pretty ugly expression going on."

"What? What are you telling me? That little witch!"

"Too bad for her Trip saw it all and heard her."

"Oh Lord! What did he do?"

"He said, 'Girls? If you want continued financial support for all of you, you will show Rusty all the respect I show her. Understood?'"

"Go, Trip! Go right for the wallet! That man could make a buffalo scream!" I threw a fist into the air. "I didn't know he had it in him!"

"Frankly? Me either! I don't know what happened to him but, boy, is he on a mission!"

I glanced at the wall clock, the one that worked. It was after eight and I knew I needed to get going. With the morning traffic it would still take almost an hour to get to Charleston and to find Bobby Mack's room at the Medical University. Parking was guaranteed to be a nightmare.

"Good, right? It's about time he got on a mission!"

"I guess it's time for me to get moving. Give Bobby Mack my best. Poor thing."

"Yeah, I think it really scared him. But then if having a heart attack doesn't put the fear of God in you, what will?"

"Linnie and Belle. They could frighten the devil himself," Rusty said with a laugh as she got up. She put her mug in the sink and filled it with water. "I have to keep telling myself that they're just girls and not so scary. Really."

"I'm sure you're right, but remember, I'm happy to be the port in the storm."

"I'll remember that."

I watched Rusty back out of my yard thinking how glad I was for her optimism and for her dedication to Trip because Trip never could have handled his three girls by himself. Not in a million years.

Just as I was leaving the house, Millie was coming in.

"Morning!" I said. "I'm going down to Charleston. I'll see you this afternoon. Can I get anything for you?"

"Caroline? Before you go running off, I'd like to have a word with you."

I could feel it coming. I knew Millie was upset about last night. And thoroughly embarrassed. Once the ambulance left, she and Mr. Jenkins had gone home as quickly as they could and left me there with Matthew. Honestly, I knew Matthew couldn't have been too happy with me either. I mean, it had to have been uncomfortable on some level for him to witness everything, but thank the Lord, he was hungry. Saved by the stomach. I fed him the dinner I had prepared for Bobby and me. The whole time he ate I was waiting for some kind of rebuke and I wondered again how I would unload all that jelly. The rebuke never came from Matthew. However, now it was the light of day, Millie was here and she still had that look on her face—the resolute steel jaw and steaming hairy eyeball—the ultimate combination.

"Sure. What's up?"

"You're going to see Bobby Mack, I assume?"

"Of course!"

"Now you listen to me. What happened here last night was not your fault."

"Shoot, Millie! I know that!" Thank God she thinks that, I thought.

"Just the same. I want you to be a little more careful. You hear me? That man has too much fat all 'round his belly and that's an invitation for heart trouble, 'eah?"

"Well, you're right, of course. So I should just go after skinny men?"

"That's up to you, but it ain't fittin' for the EMS to be coming 'eah in the night and hauling off naked little fat men, 'eah? Your momma? She spinning in she grave today! And you gone tell me that your Matthew wasn't so embarrassed, too? Nice as he is to you and all this crazy family?"

"He was actually fine with it."

"Humph. Maybe 'cause with Bobby Mack out of the picture, that clears the coast for him?"

"Oh, come on! We're just friends!"

"Is that what they call friends today? Humph! That's some fool, 'eah?"

Millie knew that Matthew had a part-time residence beneath my duvet, but in the interest of decorum, we never discussed it. I picked up my handbag, checked to make sure I had my cell phone, which I did, and I opened the back door.

"I'll be back by two. Call me if you need me, okay? Oh, by the way, big news flash. Trip needs a housekeeper to live in five days a week until Frances Mae comes home. ASAP. Do you know anyone who's masochistic enough to consider it?"

"Anyone I'd send into *that* hornet's nest? No, ma'am."

"Well, maybe an enemy?"

"I'll think on it. Maybe Rosario knows someone."

Rosario had been our housekeeper for ages. She spoke almost no English and just came, did her job, and left. We loved her.

"Thanks."

I left Millie and tried to put Trip's problems out of my mind for the ride to Charleston. It was a gorgeous day to take a drive. The sky was that crazy impossible blue found only in the Lowcountry of South Carolina. Crayola should've made a crayon and named the color of it just that—Lowcountry blue. Like French-blue cotton shirts or navy-blue wool uniforms. The sky was bluer than a robin's egg, more blue than cornflowers or all the bluebonnets in Texas. And when you stood on the shores of Sullivans Island or Edisto Beach and looked out over the endless ripples in the sparkling water to where the horizon met the sky, it was simply breathtaking. All that blue! It made you want to fly or to sing or to fall to your knees in thanksgiving.

I was feeling pretty lucky then, to be surrounded by such great beauty, to have a little time for myself away from everyone and the insanity of the past few days. So Millie was upset with me for dating someone who was a walking heart attack? Baloney. She could say that but I knew she was more concerned with propriety than anything else. What did I care about propriety? Who was there to judge me? The squirrels? And if others did judge me, what did I care about their opinion of my behavior? Very little. I mean, I was living an authentic life, doing what I wanted. I tried very hard not to embarrass Eric, and I thought I did a pretty good job at that. The truth was that I was bored to death living out in the country, selling truckloads of strawberries and fooling around with a pig farmer here and an officer of the law there. I was so bored I had even momentarily considered the assets of a man whose nose twitched like something feral.

Maybe I needed to think about a condo in Charleston. Perhaps I could find a new social life in downtown, become a volunteer for the museum or the symphony. I could raise money, run a gala, do some good in the world. Or I could get involved with the university in Columbia. Surely they had organizations for parents who were sort of miserable?

What was the matter with me? Some days there weren't enough hours to do half of what I intended to do and on others, like this one, I was like a rudderless boat floating down the river to nowhere. Oh, yes, I was going to see Bobby, but I also knew that his heart attack marked the end of our affair. It could be years before Bobby would have the courage to have sex again. Don't ask me how I know this. Let's just say that I do. In a few weeks we would have dinner. He would be apologetic after dessert and say that he's sleeping more lately, since his incident, and that his doctor said he should take it easy, you know, not to do anything too athletic. But I knew that his doctor would have advised him to resume his life and not to worry. No matter. It was human nature to worry that if your heart had betrayed you once, it could do it again. So, if the choice was life without sex versus sex and possible death? No decision. I'd let him think it was his choice to end things, that he had fallen out of love with me rather than the horrible truth that he was frightened by his mortality.

When I finally arrived at Bobby Mack's bedside with an over-priced bouquet of flowers in a cheap glass vase and the *New York Times* tucked under my arm, the scene was exactly what I expected it would be. A couple of fellows from his business were there, standing up, getting ready to leave, when I pushed opened the door. There was my sweet guy propped up on pillows with an IV in his arm. His friends nodded politely and knowingly to me as they passed. I knew they would snicker like schoolboys once they were out of earshot. Did I care? Um, no.

My spirits sank as Bobby's eyes met mine. They said it all.

"How are you, darlin'?" I said.

"I cheated death, Caroline. For a man who cheated death, I reckon I'm doing fair to partly cloudy."

I put the vase of flowers and the newspaper on his bedside table and kissed his forehead.

"Well, you look wonderful," I said, and thought, Damn, I'm gonna miss this man.

9

Weekend Warriors

WHEN FRIDAY ROLLED AROUND, RUSTY and Trip had yet to locate a willing victim to serve as housekeeper for the Walterboro residence. Neither Millie, Rosario, nor I had any leads either.

"Maybe you're not exactly offering an irresistible deal," I suggested ever so gently to Trip over the phone.

"You serious? I'm offering two hundred and fifty dollars a week, health-care benefits after six months, and a paid two-week vacation! That's a bloody fortune just to keep house and fix dinner for a bunch of girls!"

"What? No. It's not a fortune. It's right at minimum wage. Granted the health benefits are nice if she's not suicidal in six months, but a two-week vacation is very standard stuff, Trip."

"Really? What's minimum wage these days?"

"Not much. Five dollars and eighty-five cents an hour. I think."

I heard Trip whistle, low and long. "Wow."

"Not wow. Miss Sweetie pays eight dollars an hour to our most menial laborers. A gallon of milk is like four dollars or something. You can't believe what it costs to live these days."

"Five eighty-five? Still seems like a lot to me. I think I made two bucks an hour or less when I was in college."

"Um, m'dear? College was a long time ago, Mr. Wimbley. I think if you want anyone to take that job, you're going to have to sweeten the deal by a lot."

"Maybe you're right."

"Ain't no maybe about it," I said.

"Well, I'll be bringing Chloe out after school this afternoon and I thought it might be nice for you to come over and barbecue with us. The girls are coming, too. I'm gonna break in the grill! Her maiden voyage! Rusty's got steaks marinating and I've got some Wahoo thawing. And as King of the Grill, I'll even make you a julep. The julep of your life!"

"Now you're talking. What time?"

"How's six?"

"See ya!"

King of the Grill indeed.

All week long, Rusty had entertained the United Nations of candidates in her kitchen and mine. In addition to leaving a dozen messages for Frances Mae's old housekeeper, she'd spoken to women from Chile, Guatemala, Belize, Brazil, Portugal, Ghana, and even some from Romania and Croatia. It wasn't like she wasn't trying. Most of them only spoke a few words of English and none of them had legal papers for working in the United States. The one woman who was barely fluent only had to say, "Girls make too much laundry, too much hair in the sink," and that instantly soured her interview.

Rusty called and said, "I'm interviewing right here. I can't be driving all the whole way out to Walterboro to show the house until I find someone who at least looks like a possibility. Do you blame me?"

"No, of course not. Chances are you'd run into one of my darling nieces at home playing hooky anyway! I mean, who knows what they're up to when Trip leaves in the morning?"

"Not even an hour ago, Trip said the same exact thing to me. Frankly, I don't like to think about it."

"Me either," I said.

"It makes my stomach hurt to know how vulnerable these girls are. I mean, I really hate to criticize, but they wouldn't have such bad attitudes if anyone had ever been vigilant enough, meaning Frances Mae. A little guidance wouldn't kill them."

"Well, Trip did have to show up at his office and make a living like most men do. And you know the old Chinese saying, right? Fish stink from the head down? They're just like their mother. Well, not Amelia so much anymore or Chloe yet."

"This is our big chance, Caroline. You know, to undo some of the madness and show them how to behave."

"Oh my God! Does this mean I have to set a good example? I hate that!"

We had a good laugh and I told her I'd see her at six.

But as the afternoon wore on I had a growing anxiety that steadily crept toward a full-blown bummer. Frances Mae was gone away and their girls were coming here. I thought about my childhood and compared it with theirs. Maybe Trip had left their family household, and maybe he had a live-in girlfriend, but he wasn't dead. Dead was final in a way those girls had yet to understand. Frances Mae's nasty relatives went to the cooler on a regular basis, but they came back. And would any of them help Trip now? They barely spoke to each other! They had yet to find common ground.

Her girls were clueless about the reality of growing up wondering what your father would have thought of you—would he have been proud? Would he have cried like a sentimental fool at your graduations, wedding, and when you put your first child into his arms? And did they know what was it like to live your whole life trying to please and to win the approval of a parent whose spouse's accidental death shattered your world and the heart of your family into so many pieces that there was no repair?

No. They did not. I did. But they did not.

I tried to concentrate on going over sales projections for my strawberry fields for-fucking-ever business and finally admitted to myself for the first time that I didn't give two shits about strawberries. I was feeling particularly uncharitable when the thought crossed my mind that Miss Sweetie's longevity wasn't my responsibility either. I got up from my chair about every ten minutes and walked around my desk. Why had I committed myself to this business in the first place? I knew that on some level of my subconscious mind I was trying to replace my mother with Miss Sweetie, but I also realized that was just impossible because there would always be only one Lavinia Boswell Wimbley. Ever. As much as Millie or Trip might rail that I was becoming her, I knew that I was a weak imitation and always would be.

On the other hand, which would be the good-girl side of me, I did love Miss Sweetie. She was a dear lady. She had given my mother the benefit of her great friendship all her life and so much comfort in the end. I owed her something, but I didn't owe her the rest of my life. Solving berry blight or mold problems wasn't the thing on which I dreamed of hanging my life's reputation. And when Miss Sweetie went to glory, did I want to spend the rest of my life worrying about jam and Sara Lee and breads and pies? No, I needed something larger and more important. I needed to live up to Mother's reputation, to be truly bold and original. And how was I going to do that?

The minute I began flogging myself, there came a rush of justifications for my present state and an appraisal of its worthiness. Holding together Tall Pines was a noble endeavor. I was carrying on a tradition that had begun in my family generations ago and there was nothing that exceeded the importance of tradition in the Lowcountry. And overseeing the berry business wasn't really a bad thing either. It anchored me to Tall Pines and gave some structure to my day. I was able to honor my mother's memory by becoming meaningful and more relevant to her closest friend. To be perfectly honest, in some odd way, just seeing Miss Sweetie's face lessened the loss we both felt without Miss Lavinia and kept her alive at the same time. That did give me a certain amount of genuine satisfaction. Maybe I would get the girls to help me over the summer. Belle and Linnie especially. Maybe having some purpose would help them mature in the right direction. I didn't know, but I did know that I was sliding into a lousy mood.

I was missing my Eric then, and just as his face came to the forefront of my mind, the phone rang. It was him. The only thing, and I mean the *only* thing, that my ex-husband, Richard Levine, had ever been right about in his whole miserable insignificant life was Jung's theory about the collective unconscious. Somehow Eric heard my heart pining for him.

"Darlin'? Are you all right?"

"Yeah, sure. Why?"

"Well, rare is the occasion when you call me during the afternoon."

"It's 'rare is the occasion' now? Mom? Are you channeling your mother again?"

"Perhaps."

"Mom? You sound totally bugged. What's up?"

"Well, lots of stuff. Uh, nothing. I'm not bugged. Actually, I'm fine. I'm a little concerned about the girls spending the weekend with Rusty and Trip, but other than worrying about their personal safety, you know, things like the house burning down or a knife fight with mortal wounds resulting in death, or some kind of terrorist explosion, I'm really fine."

"See ya in two hours," he said.

"Oh, no! Honey, that's okay! I'm—we're fine! It's just like having Osama bin Laden for the weekend and worrying if loud noise might set him off, that's all. I don't want to mess up your weekend."

"Yeah, okay. See you in a few. Love you!"

So that was it. Eric was coming to watch over my nervous system, which, even I had to admit, was growing a new network of tentacles complete with suction cups. Maybe it was a good thing, that he was coming home, I mean. Gosh, I surely was feeling goofed up. I decided to take a shower and blow out my hair. That always made me feel normal again. And I would find an opening in the conversation to ask him about his new woman!

I went down to the kitchen for a bottle of water and there was Millie baking something and humming one of her gospel tunes of ancient Gullah origins.

"Smells like sugar. You're baking?" I said.

"Yes, ma'am! Making oatmeal-raisin cookies for them girls. You know, a little something to welcome them."

"Humph. Should've made a devil's food cake!"

"You're bad, 'eah?"

"That's why you love me!"

I could tell she was smiling without her even facing me just by the way she shook her head.

"And, I'm making chocolate-chip cookies for Eric."

"How'd you know he was coming home?"

"Humph," she said.

Because Millie just knew, that's how.

It was almost four in the afternoon when I heard Trip's big SUV roaring across the property. I wondered if he had Chloe with him and what kind of a mood she was in. Had she packed pajamas, play clothes, and toys? What if she didn't have anything to occupy her time? Why hadn't I thought to run to the drugstore and buy her some coloring books or something? A Barbie? I was a terrible, thoughtless aunt and I made a mental note to correct that.

"Millie? What did we do with Eric's toys—you know, the ones he played with when we first got here?"

"It's all up in the attic. Don't you remember? We threw out the LEGOs and all the paper stuff like craft books. And we saved all the comics, them crazy Transformers, and his storybooks."

"I'll be right back."

Because it was too warm that afternoon for a search through the attic, the first place I went was Eric's room. A dozen or so model planes he had built from kits were suspended from the ceiling by invisible wires. His collection of remote-control cars was lined up on top of his bookcases, each car parked neatly at an angle like a miniature showroom of an exotic car dealership. My father's field binoculars hung crookedly in their cracked leather case on the wall by the window, and Eric's student telescope stood nearby. There was a Garfield piggy bank filled with pennies that served as a bookend to dozens of science-fiction paperback books from high school. He adored Robert Jordan and had read and reread every single word he wrote. Action figures, arms and legs askew in rigor mortis, reminded me of Eric as my little boy, so anxious to grow up and be somebody's hero.

Well, he was more than my hero; in fact he was my raison d'être! And he always would be. I had a thought then about how powerful the role a birth father figured in a child's mental health and how that relationship or the lack of that relationship traveled with us all through our adult life. Eric had a father who couldn't be pleased. If Little Harry Shit Bird aced his SATs, it was because he was a natural genius. If Eric aced his SATs, which he did, Richard would've accused me of spending a fortune on tutors. Some loving father he was.

I had scant memories of my own father but I clung to them like a starving beggar. It seemed I was doomed to one unhealthy or compromised relationship after another because, and I would never admit this to a soul, I wanted what no one could give me. I wanted that bottomless empty place in me to be filled. That longing, that endless longing, to be quieted and soothed.

And little Chloe had a father who no longer loved her mother. At all. In fact, her father loved someone *else* with such passion there was no cunja magic on the planet that could ever undo the spell. Nice variation on the refrain. How were those little childhood nuggets going to impact this poor girl as time went on? We all understood why Trip's marriage to Frances Mae was intolerable to him. It had been intolerable to *us*! So, to make matters worse, Chloe probably suspected that there was something enormously unacceptable about her mother besides her raging alcoholism. Like what if her daddy left because he didn't love her or her sisters, too? Father loves someone else; mother is a reject and so are the children. It was a nasty soup to place before a little girl and then to expect her to happily swallow it.

Sometimes something else would emerge to save the self-image of many children with problematic backgrounds. Like a musical talent, a gift for science or math. Perhaps they would be fortunate to possess extraordinary good looks. Chloe could lay claim to no such thing. That poor frizzy-headed cinder-block-shaped chubby body of a little girl was as homely as a mud fence. In addition, she had a surly disposition and no particular gifts to recommend her. Worse, she was a whiner, which to my mind was the most obnoxious habit a child could develop. What would we do about her? This would require serious consultation with Millie and new combinations of her herbs.

In the meantime, there were others besides Chloe to consider. There was Belle and Linnie, and although Amelia seemed to have made great strides in college, all four girls were going to need vigilance and care. I needed to win their confidence! Yes, that would be the first step! I needed to teach them about what mattered to Wimbley women and to women all over the Lowcountry and to women of stature all over the world! Tradition! By golly! I would join forces with Rusty and Millie and together we would raise the sights of these young women, raise them to look at things they had never considered. I would open their eyes!

I had no idea of how to begin, but without that consultation with Millie, I took my father's binoculars and threw the strap over my shoulder. Chloe might get a kick out of learning about birds. Okay. Birding was a bit nerdy, but I also knew that knowledge was power. The first step to empowering Chloe would be to teach her about the natural world around her. She could ignore me, but she would learn all the same. Osmosis would rule.

I dressed for Trip's barbecue, deciding this was definitely not a caftan occasion but rather a time for casual, nonthreatening attire. The night might get chilly and no doubt dusk would bring out hordes of bugs. Bugs were the one drawback of living on or near the Edisto. Or anywhere in the Lowcountry for that matter because water was all around us. My mother used to say, where water is found, bugs abound. She was right. I sprayed my ankles and the back of my neck and hands with Skin So Soft. The advantage of Skin So Soft is that it actually worked and it didn't reek like other regulation insect repellents loaded with DEET, which gave me a toxic rash. I chose a plain pair of beige trousers and a lightweight rose-colored cotton sweater set. I put Mother's pearls around my neck and then took them off, deciding they might trigger an unpleasant memory for the girls. Hadn't Frances Mae just about had a nervous breakdown when she saw me wearing them the day Mother died? Didn't they represent the matriarchy? Yes, they did and it didn't seem the appropriate moment to flaunt any kind of authority from my camp.

"Mom?"

Eric was home.

"I'm up here, baby! We're supposed to be at Trip's by six. I'll be right down!"

"No worries! Amelia just dropped me off. She's already there!"

"Good!"

So, Amelia had come, too! Well, of course she had. How else would he have come? I was completely befuddled then, but Amelia's coming was an important step in the right direction. The next generation was stepping in to run interference against the infidels. My chest expanded with a long-overdue sigh. I did a quick mental review of the morals and ethics I wanted to impart to the girls and took a last glance at myself in the mirror.

"Aunt Caroline?" I said aloud. "Brace yourself."

Somehow I knew because, like Millie, I knew things. Before we arrived at Trip and Rusty's with Millie's cookies, stacked and resting in a cheerful covered tin on the seat between us, before we saw the long red-and-blue flames leaping from the barbecue and Trip screaming "Stand back!" and spraying the fire extinguisher like a madman sending foam everywhere, before we saw Belle and Linnie perched on opposite sides of the picnic table, carefully and deliberately positioned out of Trip's line of vision, arms draped around the necks of two unknown swarthy young men with visible tattoos, all of them engaged in some serious and frantic tickling of the tonsils, and even before we saw Chloe spinning alone, looking up at the sky to make herself dizzy, and yes, before she threw up all over her dress, I knew. The enemy was all around us and we were headed for a revolutionary war.

10

Etiquette Unchained

H OLY SHIT, MOM! WHAT THE . . . ?"
    "Please! Do not use vulgar language in front of your mother! Isn't this enough to deal with?" I swept my arm across the scene before us. Did anyone have a sense of decorum anymore? Apparently not. This insufferable and flagrant nonsense had to stop immediately and never happen again! In front of me, anyway. Or innocent little children especially. I didn't know where Rusty was at that moment, but she certainly would not have approved of what Belle and Linnie were doing in public or in private. In fact, if they behaved this way in public, what *did* they do in private? The audacity! Five generations of Wimbleys had to be spinning in their graves at warp speed. Pearls or no pearls, I was going to step in and assume the matriarchal position.

    "Take Chloe in the house right now to get her cleaned up, will you? Please?" Eric seemed rooted to the place where he stood, his jaw hanging open like a nineteen-year-old bloodhound. "Eric? Are you with me?"

"Yeah. Sorry. Jeez. Y'all ought to get a room," he mumbled as he passed Linnie and Belle and walked toward Chloe. "Grooooss."

They ought to get *two* rooms, I thought, and took a deep breath. Eric's comment to them had done nothing to cause a pause in the action. I walked right up to Belle and poked her hard on the shoulder with my index finger. Startled, she pulled away from the young man and looked up. In the passing of less than two seconds, I noticed that her beau had thick black eyelashes and brazen onyx-colored eyes, a wide mouth with full lips, and more teeth than Farrah Fawcett. I wondered momentarily if he resembled his daddy and if his mother was in good health. Hmm. But I had a job to do and it was not the best time to inquire.

"Excuse me? Just what do you two think you're doing? And who are these two young men? Who invited them?"

"Oh, Aunt Caroline! Lighten up! This is my friend Juan."

My thermostat readjusted itself to boil. My jaw was clenched like a sprung bear trap yet I managed to speak.

"I don't think you just told your aunt to lighten up, did you, dear? And another thing, we don't behave this way in front of your little sister. Or your father, is that understood? It's vulgar and crass. So! Now! Let's start again, shall we?" I took a deep breath and looked from Belle's face to her friend's. "Hello, young man. I am Isabelle's aunt Caroline Levine." I began to extend my hand for him to shake, then thought better of it and quickly pulled it back and ran my fingers through my hair. From the looks of him, I was suddenly fully aware that his hand may have traveled to parts unknown without the benefit of soap and water afterward.

"*Buenas tardes, señora.*"

Great. No hablo the mother tongue.

"Will you be staying for dinner?"

"I thought you said they weren't invited," piped in Linnie, who now stood away from her "friend," hands on her hips, head to the side with a sullen, defiant expression.

"Watch your mouth, young lady. You can behave yourself or your friends can leave at once. So what's it going to be?"

Linnie shrugged her shoulders and whispered something in her "friend's" ear.

"It's impolite to whisper," I said.

"Cut the crap," Belle said to her. "Don't make trouble."

"Language?" I said.

"Whatever. This is Antonio. Antonio, this is my aunt Caroline. She's in charge of the world."

"Nice to meet you," he said.

Well, I thought, at least he took an ESL course or something. And that he looked uncomfortable gave me some relief that at least he had the decency to understand that cavorting around with my niece in broad daylight was not exactly kosher. How old was he anyway? He looked way too old for high school. I was certain of that.

"Thank you. Now! I am going to excuse myself and see if I can help my brother rescue dinner."

I walked across the lawn to the barbecue area Trip had built at the end of the pool. And most important I traveled in a stride of certain purpose to show those young fools what poise and dignity looked like.

"Trip! Hey! Oh, my! What happened?"

"I know! *Look* at this mess!"

There lay the steaks, gorgeous thick rib eyes, covered in the icky chemical bath of the fire extinguisher. The King of the Grill did not show well as king. King's executioner perhaps, but not king.

"Bummer! Too bad," I said. "I'll take that julep now."

"I think maybe it was the oil in the marinade that caused the sudden burst of flames. Think I can hose them off? I mean, do you know how much money steaks cost?"

I just looked at him like the lunatic I knew he was. Money, money, money.

"Yes, I do know how much steaks cost, and no, you cannot hose them off and eat them because you will be poisoned and die. In fact, we will all die a miserable and painful writhing death of gastro-intestinal nightmarish proportions that you can only even imagine!"

There was a pregnant pause in our conversation as Trip accepted the fact that the steaks were indeed beyond salvage and consumption.

"You sound pretty sure about that."

"I am. Now. Where's the fish? And. I'm parched."

"How am I going to clean this grill? This is completely disgusting!"

"Trip? Throw the steaks in the garbage, close the lid of the grill, and let's go inside. Somebody's thirsty?"

"This is very disappointing," he said.

"To say the very least."

Sometimes Trip could be maddening.

"How's your friend Bobby?"

I was surprised that he remembered to ask. Maybe he did have a sensitive bone after all.

"Bobby's happy to be alive and probably out of commission for a while."

"That's too bad."

"You're telling me? Now, who are the young men with my nieces?"

"Landscapers."

"Great." Poor fellows, I thought.

It wasn't my place to make a judgment. Indeed, most Mexican families I had ever met had better family values, stronger loyalties to each other, better work ethics, and a greater sense of dignity and respect for others than most of the rednecks in the Southeast. It was the landscapers who were at risk. They could do so much better.

Inside, Rusty was brushing Chloe's hair up into a ponytail and

Eric and Amelia were moving around chairs to set the table on the adjacent screened porch.

"Hey, Caroline!" Rusty said. "Trip? I thought we should eat on the porch. Too many bugs outside."

"That's fine with me but the steaks have entered into family lore," he said.

"I threw up," Chloe said to me for reasons unknown.

In my world, the subject of vomit and other foul bodily functions that spew, emit, or blast forth are usually better left untold when in polite company.

"Yes, you did," I said, when I wanted to say, *You made yourself throw up, you silly little girl,* but because she was only seven years old and because part of me felt genuine empathy for her that because of her boozehound mother, she was trapped in her unfortunate situation, I did not. "Chloe, dear? If you get invited to Buckingham Palace, don't tell that to the queen, okay?"

"Okay," she said, and scampered off to the den to watch television.

"We need paper towels and a spray cleaner," Eric said.

"There's pollen everywhere," said Amelia. "Look." She held up a yellow finger.

"Yuck. Under the sink," Trip said. "Longest pollen season in the history of the world."

"Messy stuff. So, Trip? What happened to the steaks?" Rusty said.

"Torched them," Trip said, and then added in a theatrical voice worthy of Richard Burton's Hamlet, "The mighty flames gave me the opportunity to check out the reliability of the fire extinguisher."

"Yikes. I'm assuming it worked?" Rusty asked.

"Worked great but I may have totaled my new grill."

Rusty giggled.

"Darling? Don't you worry about your new baby. I'll have Gloria shining, good as new, by tomorrow," Rusty said. "Meanwhile, we're ten for dinner and I don't think there's enough fish to go around."

"Gloria? As in Gloria the Grill?" Amelia said, and she could not restrain the giggle that came bursting through her clenched teeth. "That is so lame!"

"Amelia?" Rusty said with a warm smile that glowed all over everyone. "Any grill that costs that much should have its own name. So, it's not just any grill, you see. It's *Gloria*."

"Not to be confused with Henry the Hibachi?" Eric said.

"Yep. Or Vinnie the Viking!" I said, referencing their kitchen appliances. "Although a hibachi grill is a poor relative next to Gloria out there. Now, then. Dinner?"

"No worries," Eric said. "I'll get pizzas for us. They can have them here in thirty minutes!"

"Eric? Darlin'? Pizza's okay, but I think this may be what the world's currently calling 'a teachable moment.' Rusty? What do you think?"

"I'm not sure what you're talking about."

"Well, I'm thinking there are probably at least three entrées we can pull together and we can teach all the girls what you do when there's a kitchen disaster. Eric? Go get all your other cousins and their boyfriends. The boys will clean up the porch and all the women will help put together a meal. Tonight is the opening of the Wimbley Diner! Chloe can design the menu."

Over the next fifteen minutes or so, after Trip finally poured Rusty and me a glass of wine, we got the complaining mostly out of the way, and finally we were beginning to reach an understanding— they had to help if they wanted to eat—and get organized. After all, Trip, Rusty, and Aunt Caroline only have so much patience, kiddies.

But like many things, life had become instantly different in many ways for my nieces and for my brother and Rusty. All these untried arrangements required some thought and trials. So, I assembled them all and gave them the plan for the evening, which was met with less enthusiasm than I had hoped. The young men weren't the problem. They took rolls of paper towels and Windex and out the door they went to tackle the layer of pollen. It was the girls.

"I'm not even that hungry," Linnie grumbled.

"Me either," Belle said.

"Of course y'all aren't starving!" I said with a smile. "But the men have to be fed!"

"Why?" Chloe said. "Why can't they feed themselves?"

Actually, I thought, that's a good question. Rusty must have thought so, too, because when I looked over at her, she had stretched her eyes wide and was nodding at no one in particular.

"Because they're babies," I said. "We're the nurturers—such as we are, that is."

Rusty spoke up. "And because if men don't eat they get cranky. Maybe it's blood sugar or something, but they get cranky like old dogs! Isn't that right, Caroline?"

"Yep! So why don't you girls dig through the cabinets, the fridge, and the freezer and see what you can find."

"You mean, like it was our house?" Chloe asked in all innocence.

"Well, yes, and it is your house, Chloe," Rusty said. "Now you have two houses."

"Wow. *Two* houses," Belle said with sarcasm, and opened the freezer. "Well, there's ravioli in here that doesn't look too bad."

I ignored the remark and Rusty sighed.

"I just bought it last week," Rusty said. "There's garlic bread in there somewhere, too."

"I could go for a grilled cheese or some mac and cheese," Linnie said, holding up a block of good-quality Cheddar cheese and a box of Chef Boyardee macaroni and cheese.

"You eat that stuff?" I said to Rusty.

"Trip buys it at Costco. By the case. He loves it."

"Linnie?" I said. "Why don't we make it from scratch and let's make the instant one, too, and we can see which one we really like? You know, like a food challenge?"

"Because I don't know *how* to make it from scratch?" Linnie said, without a shred of charm.

"Ah! But I do! I used to make it for Eric all the time! I'll show you how. No biggie. And there are some sausages in there from Bobby that we can fry up with the mac and cheese."

"How is Bobby?" Rusty said.

"We're on hiatus."

"What's I-ate-us?" Chloe said.

"High-a-tuss," I said, and smiled at her. "It means my boyfriend and I are giving our relationship a little time off."

"Why? Did you have a big fight?"

"No, honey. We're still great friends. It's okay."

"Oh. Okay, if you say so. So what's going on this menu?" Chloe asked. "Fish and salad? Grilled cheese sandwiches? Mac and cheese with sausage? How do you spell *sausage?*"

"*S-a-u-s-a-g-e.* And ravioli," Belle said, and still staring into the freezer, she pulled out a foil bag of garlic bread. "Here! Got it."

We put it all on the counter and everyone chose which entrée they would make. Belle grated Parmesan and Cheddar cheese while Linnie chopped onions.

"I'll make salad," Rusty said.

"I'll boil water," I said, and began to fill a pot. They all stopped and looked at me. "Oh, come on! I have a sense of humor, too, you know? How about if I get on that mac and cheese? Darlin'? Grate us two cups of Cheddar, okay?"

"Sure," Belle said.

"Thanks, precious." I winked at her and she rolled her eyes. "Linnie, when you're done . . . hey! Where'd you learn to chop like that?"

Her knife moved across the cutting board so quickly I was astounded.

"Food Network. I'm like OCD for it."

"Wow. You might be the new president of the slice-and-dice club!"

"Thanks," she said, and unintentionally released the tiniest of smiles.

"Well, when you're done, why don't you take Chloe to the den and show her how to make a menu with the computer."

"Hello? I'm almost eight! I think I can do it myself."

"Yeah, really, Caroline! What *are* you thinking?" Rusty said, teasing. "She's probably more nimble with a computer than we are."

Chloe gave us a very self-satisfied bounce of her unfortunate square head and flounced away to the den.

Maybe there's hope, I thought. Well, a glimmer of it anyway.

Orders were taken and eventually we sat down to what could be characterized as a hurricane meal, which would be one prepared with whatever could be found but with no electricity or water, having boiled the pasta in Evian on a charcoal grill or whatever we had on hand, although Trip would have been apoplectic if we had used bottled water to cook. The cost, you know. From my vantage point—that is, over my plate of macaroni and cheese and a glass of white wine—it appeared that the evening was progressing smoothly. Rusty was telling a story about Owen, her little brother whom she adored, who was a veterinarian and loved animals as much as people. Chloe remarked that she'd like to have a puppy. Despite her few years on earth, Chloe was smart enough to realize that this was a prime opportunity to lobby for a pet. Everyone hesitated. How Rusty would respond could have a great impact on how all the girls would feel about her. At first Trip objected, saying that they had plenty of dogs around that she could play with, but then Rusty said, "No, Trip, I understand what Chloe feels. She wants her own dog to love."

"Chloe's right, Uncle Trip," Eric said. "She's a kid. Kids need to raise their own pets. You know, a pet that's loyal to them."

"Maybe," Trip said.

"I'll see what Owen thinks. Personally, I'd love to see a puppy around here. Dogs are good for people." Rusty smiled at each girl and they actually smiled back at her. Sort of.

This was headway, not much, but Rusty and I were glad to have found something, anything, to build on with Amelia, Belle, Linnie, and Chloe.

I was congratulating myself on the success of the evening when our new young friends from Guadalajara began a sidebar conversation.

"*Esto sabe a mierda,*" Juan said. *This tastes like shit.*

"*Ni le daria de comer esto a mi perro,*" Antonio added. *I wouldn't feed this to my dog.*

The girls and Eric, who all spoke some basic Spanish, exchanged looks and snickers.

Rusty gave the guests a frosty smile "Okay *¡Por favor! No hablen de la comida de esa manera. ¡Nos tomo mucho trabajo para prepararla!*"

The girls' eyes got wide and Juan and Antonio gulped. Properly chastened, they quickly replied, "*Lo siento mucho, señora.*"

We all knew what *that* meant, just by the expression on their faces.

"Señorita," she corrected them gently.

"Not for long," Trip said pleasantly.

A mushroom-cloud silence blanketed the table immediately and completely. In fact, the silence was so profound that it seemed the crickets ceased to chirp, the birds stilled in the trees, not one more leaf rustled, and all the way down in the Edisto, the fish failed to jump and flop. All ears, perked like bird dogs', awaited an explanation for Trip's remark. There was a long pause until Amelia spoke up.

"What's that supposed to mean?" she said.

"Exactly what I said," he said. "You girls are old enough to understand, aren't you? When my divorce is final, I intend to take Rusty down the aisle and marry her."

Now the silence that continued was greatly intensified, so much so that I could almost hear the girls' hearts slam against their ribs as panic set in. Glasses returned to the table with muffled thuds, forks and knives clinked against plates, and they became quiet. Amelia, Linnie, Belle, and Chloe looked from one face to another for some support or a cue on how to respond.

"Look," Rusty said, being magnanimous and sensing trouble, "a year is a long time. A lot can happen."

"Momma's gonna die," Amelia said.

The world of Frances Mae's girls was rocked once again. First, their father had left them. Then their mother left them, and although it was temporary, she was still gone. And now, puppy or no puppy, there was a stepmother in their probable and close future. The news understandably deflated whatever sense there was of hopefulness around the table, and personally, I thought Trip had revealed his intentions way too soon. It was very insensitive to me that he had not waited awhile for the girls to get their bearings. He had not waited for Rusty to find a groove with them, something easy and quantifiable that they could all depend on. Maybe his nerves were frazzled and he just blurted it out, assuming they had probably guessed his intentions ages ago. But they had not. It was obvious, to me anyway, that Amelia had not thought about it beyond the pain it would bring Frances Mae. Belle and Linnie were so self-involved that they probably only thought of Trip actually marrying Rusty in terms of accepting that they had better somehow find a way to deal with their new reality, as this was, in fact, *their new reality*. But Chloe was visibly upset. Later on, as I tucked her in for the night while Trip and Rusty were closing up the kitchen, she seemed particularly quiet and uncertain about how to express her unhappiness.

I said, "What's bothering you, sweetheart?"

"Nothing."

"Come on now. Tell your aunt Caroline."

She turned her face into her pillow and wouldn't look at me.

"What is it?" I said again.

"Tell Rusty . . . tell her I don't need her stupid puppy anymore. I don't want it."

"Oh Lord. Darling? Let's say your prayers like a good girl and let's see what tomorrow brings, shall we?" I kissed the back of her head and promised to make her pancakes in the morning. This child, this poor child, was killing me. She was fast asleep before I closed the door, and if not, at least her breathing was even.

A short while later I was back at home. I walked down to the dock before going inside. I was not quite ready to turn in for the night. Eric had stayed behind with the older kids to watch something on television. So, I stood there alone, leaning over the weathered rails, watching the water moving along beneath me. As my eyes adjusted to the night, hundreds of stars began to come into view. I couldn't get poor Chloe off my mind. What had transpired over dinner, the news of Trip's intended marriage, that is, marked another step toward the loss of her innocence. Her words wrenched my heart. *Tell her I don't need her stupid puppy anymore.* The poor child. She needed a puppy to love more than anyone on earth.

I had to help Trip and Rusty make the girls thoroughly comprehend that choosing to get along with Rusty did not mean they were rejecting their own mother. It did not mean that at all. And I had to make Trip consider that just because the girls appeared to have every benefit that wealth, health, and youth could offer, it didn't mean they were not vulnerable to other sinister forces like drugs, alcohol, or depression. Not to mention the temptations of promiscuity. A change in a parent's marital status could trigger any of those things.

Amelia, Isabelle, Caroline, Chloe, and Eric's generation was vastly different from mine or Trip's. Our childhood was hugely complicated and fraught with other kinds of issues that led to some bizarre choices in our personal lives when we were young adults. But we weren't caught in between our parents, wishing with all of our hearts that they would reconcile or that somehow they could just go back to the life they had when they were all under one roof, living as a family. We had no guilt about our reality. It just was. Trip's girls were left to wonder if and how much their shenanigans had contributed to the problems of their parents, resulting in their separation and now there would be a divorce. How much of a burden did they carry in their hearts? And I always wondered if Eric suffered because of Richard's preference for Harry. Of course he must. But Eric knew that I would see Richard dead, buried, and gone to hell before I would excuse him for it. The difference between my divorce and Trip's was that Richard was just wrong. In Trip's case, he had married the wrong person, stuck with her as long as he could, and when he couldn't take it anymore, he bolted. Come to think of it, hadn't I done the same? The one difference there, however, was that Trip bolted to Rusty's arms a little too soon for societal convention to give the happy couple a smile of approval. I just came home to Mother.

Miss Lavinia may have been crazy and eccentric, but life at Tall Pines had given a solid rhythm to all our days. Our rules were not exactly carved in stone but at least the adults exercised some discretion when our moral compass took that occasional spin counterclockwise. In any and all cases, there were expectations. Lines drawn. An observance of certain proprieties. A rigid adherence to specific traditions and manners. And when I came back to Tall Pines with Eric, there was plenty of warmth and love to go around, especially from Mother, who was making up for the lost years. But while she heaped her affection on Trip, Eric, and me, everyone knew there was no love lost between Mother and Frances Mae and, by extension, her daughters.

That was what the girls lacked. Love. Guidance. Structure with some flexibility in its parameters. And some major oversight. They needed to learn that disappointments, even catastrophic ones, were inevitable but bearable when you had someone to whom you could turn who would carry you through whatever darkness had the better of you at that moment. Frances Mae could not possibly have had the first clue on how to raise her girls as young ladies. That was where I would come in, beginning with Amelia. As the reigning queen of Tall Pines, it was my right to insist on the continuance of certain ways of life. As though an evangelical healing was taking place in me, I could feel a transformation rising in my veins. All at once the vision became clear. This December, Amelia Wimbley would take her rightful place in Lowcountry society. Trip and I would present her at a lavish Christmas cotillion. With my help, a lot of coaching, and the right dress, she would set a new tone. One of dignity and higher ideals. When their time came, her mealymouthed, uncivilized little sisters would clamor to follow in her footsteps. Somehow I would bring this all to pass. The queen would make ladies of them all. God Save the Queen.

11

More Dirty Laundry

MORNING SEEMED TO ARRIVE EARLY, the first glints of sun sighing, breathing between the slats of the blinds, forerunners of light that eventually spilled all over my bedcovers at angles hued a soft silver blue. Of course morning *always* arrived early, except during the dead of winter when heavy mist rolled in from the Edisto. Fog blanketed Tall Pines with clouds so thick you would strain to see halfway down the avenue of oaks before the midday sun melted it away. Those winter dawns, when day seemed indefinable, I became the consummate slugabed, cocooned under blankets with pillows over my eyes to block the light. I could not rise. I would lie there and dream back in time, sometimes envisioning myself in the 1860s, an observer of the Civil War battles that had taken place all around our property. Yankee soldiers, in their bedraggled uniforms raced toward our house on horseback. I could nearly hear the approaching thunder of hooves, louder and louder, until the soldiers finally stopped in the front of our house, dismounting and firing their guns into the air to frighten us, to let us know our freedom was at an end.

Their diabolical intention was to throw all my family out, seize all our possessions for their own use, turn our home into a hospital or a covert meeting place where they would plan the slaughter of more dissenters and devour our food, leaving us to starve on the side of the road. My mother used to recount these stories to me and Trip as her mother had told them to her and her mother before her. These were the family myths, remembered so vividly and massaged, exaggerated, and stretched as the mood saw fit. I loved them all.

"They did not know that we had hidden all our silver and jewels in barrels that were buried safely belowground in the icehouse. That's why we still have so many beautiful things that you'll inherit one day!"

I didn't care about inheriting anything when I was six years old. Inheritance meant my family had to die and I could not bring myself to consider that.

"And they never expected us to sneak into their rooms as they slept and slip our butcher knives between their ribs, killing them one and all. But we did. We knew the secret passageways through the chimneys and walls. It was awful, I'm sure it was awful, but it was the only way to save Tall Pines from ruination! Of course we threw their nasty traitorous corpses right into the Edisto to feed the gators and posted cholera and smallpox signs all around the property. 'Warning! Keep out!' That held those Yankees back! By golly! We surely did. We saved the day, didn't we?"

Mother told us those stories in such a dramatic way that she might have been hallucinating the memories of her ancestors. Her eyes grew large and she waved her arms. Sometimes she whispered so low that Trip and I had to lean in to hear what she was saying.

Then she would stand and shout so loud that Trip and I would get overexcited and couldn't sleep that night. We'd ask her a thousand questions, begging for more details, and she would always comply, right down to descriptions of what the ladies were wearing, how they manipulated the bricks to reveal the hidden tunnels, what day of the week it was, what they said to each other . . . In retrospect, I'm sure the stories were mostly fabricated because no one loved a good yarn like our Miss Lavinia. There were many diaries, stored for safekeeping since Mother's death, in the attic trunks. I'm sure Mother read them all, and most likely, they were the source for her stories. One of these days I would open the old trunks and have a look. When I found the time . . . In any case, I had always been wildly proud of my ancestors' resolute bravery and cunning. Those were the qualities that my mother always emphasized to us when she told the stories. For years I had dressed as a colonial dame on Halloween and sometimes on Thanksgiving. When I was feeling confident that Trip wouldn't tease me to death, I would wear the outfit all day.

"The Wimbleys are made of mighty strong stuff!"

I could hear my Miss Lavinia's voice in my head just like it was yesterday.

But this particular Lowcountry morning was deep into spring and it was also the stuff of dreams and great imaginings. The temperature was perfect, somewhere around sixty. The linens on my bed were cool to the touch. I plumped my pillows, fell back into them, and stretched. Somewhere in the distance a few birds were singing for their breakfast and a woodpecker was at work on a dead tree limb. It felt like six o'clock and I rolled over to check my alarm clock to confirm it. It was exactly five minutes before six. Wasn't it a marvel how the body perfectly sensed that for which the mind demanded proof?

It was going to take some of the Wimbley bravery and cunning to weather the coming weeks. I wondered if Amelia and her sisters had ever even heard the stories of Henry Heywood Wright IV and his stalwart wife, Elizabeth? Would Trip have told them? Maybe bits and pieces, but all the family portraits still hung on the walls of this house, not his. And the artifacts were here, too. Frances Mae would have resisted hearing our history because it would have intimidated her. I was sure of that. How stupid! Perhaps if Frances Mae realized that our family's place in South Carolina's history books was not bought but hard earned, she might have been inspired to rise instead of fall. Now, there's a thought.

Perhaps a little family education would help to bring the girls around. As soon as the hour permitted, I would get them all over to my house for a big fattening breakfast—eggs, bacon, grits, and genealogy with fresh-squeezed juice.

I showered, dressed, and looked in on Eric, taking a deep breath. There is nothing more intoxicating than the smell of your own child. And even though he was nearly a man, he was sleeping like a sweet angel. He was still and always would be mine. I decided to leave him alone, to let him snooze a little longer.

I rang Millie at eight to see if she felt like helping with breakfast. It was really her biscuits I was after, which I'm sure she knew. My stomach rumbled at the thought of them.

"Mornin'! You up?"

"What do you think, chile?"

Millie had a long-established habit of starting her day before early birds even thought about worms. She got up to read her Bible and to work her garden before the sun was too high in the sky.

"Well, I'm calling Trip to bring the brood over here for some eggs and to fertilize the family tree, Lavinia style."

"I ain't missing this! I'll be right over!"

"Great!"

Then I called Trip. He was up all right. He'd already been up and down the Edisto, dropped the papers on our back steps, and exercised his dogs. He was on his second pot of coffee he said and hankering for Millie's biscuits, too.

"We'll be there at nine-fifteen! Thanks!"

I decided that breakfast in the dining room was in order. We were going to start the day in a dignified way with a beautiful meal. I opened the silver chest, deciding to use the family's oldest flatware and most intricate linens to set the table. I removed the napkins from the linen press and counted out eight. They were always wrapped in acid-free tissue to prevent those nasty little brown spots Miss Lavinia treasured as symbols of the history of the linens. These were gorgeous old Irish linen, softened from innumerable launderings, with hand-tatted lace borders attached all around by tiny even stitches. The lace was so light and I fingered it gently. I remembered the story that told how my grandmother Amelia had made them as a gift for her mother's birthday when she was a young girl. It must have taken her forever because they didn't have electricity in those days. I wondered if she sat in the living room or her own bedroom and worked by the light of gasoliers or candlelight. But then I remembered that needlework would be done in the daytime using natural light. Whatever the circumstances, I could not have tatted lace like that if my life depended on it.

There were many surviving remnants of my grandmother's needlework, all of them beautiful—pillowcases with lace insets, hand-embroidered monogrammed handkerchiefs, and so on. But their age and fragile state had relegated them to the special-occasion category of usage. I had done some fine needle crochet work in my time, but that had been years ago, when I was a mere girl. In the rat race of New York City living, I had never even considered seeking out a crochet needle or an embroidery hoop. Richard would have laughed in my face, saying how silly I was to compromise my eyesight and why didn't I just trot myself over to Bergdorf's and buy what I wanted? The skills and refinements that were once a lady's great pride were lost to the past; that was for sure.

As I snapped a snowy damask cloth in the air to settle it over the dining-room table, it occurred to me that all these things should fall into conversations with Trip's girls. Even if they had no interest in learning about them, they should know that all embroidery and lace was not born in some steaming sweatshop in a remote village in China, created by some poor peasant woman with her only child strapped to her back while she squatted near her small Buddhist altar, burning incense and sipping cold weak tea. Right? It was possible to surround yourself with gentility for very little money. It was all about how you spent your time. A young lady could either waste her life away with pursuits like Guitar Hero, singing god-awful karaoke like a braying mule, or she could opt for something more useful.

Lord! Have mercy on my body and soul! I sounded more like my mother with each passing hour. Well, that wasn't the worst thing, was it?

I was folding the last of the napkins, carefully placing them on the left of the forks, when I heard the back door open and close.

"Millie? Is that you?"

"Nope! It's me, Rusty!"

I swung around the far end of the table, smoothing the cloth as she stepped into the dining room. She had the most peculiar look on her face.

"Hey! Good morning! What's wrong?" ·

She sighed with a gush of air I could feel from five feet away.

"It seems our camellias are in bloom again."

"What? They bloomed in January, didn't they?"

"Yeah, but now we're growing actual bloomers."

She held up two very skimpy-looking pairs of thong underpants on her index fingers. I gasped. She cocked her head to one side.

"Nice. Don't you think?"

"My God!"

My mind began to race. Rusty had found these on the camellias.

Their provenance was unmistakable. The intention was insulting. The girls were screwing the gardeners or landscapers or whatever it was those young men from last night did for gainful employment. It was an in-your-face vulgar gesture that I, in the wildest moment of my life, would not have deemed appropriate under any circumstances except an 8.9 earthquake, a circumstance when you had to abandon all propriety and your clothes and run for your life. Perhaps the girls' earth had moved, but they had done this to be deliberately disrespectful to Rusty and Trip and to let them know they intended to do as they pleased.

"Throw them in the garbage before Millie gets here and don't give the nasty little tramps the satisfaction of grossing you out. We're going to ignore this."

"Is this an outrage or what? What do you think?"

"I think those young men could do so much better. My nieces are a disgrace. That's what I think. Now hurry. She'll be walking in the door any second." I heard the back door open and close again. "No! Wait! She's here! Hide them."

Rusty threw the panties in the open door of the linen press and slammed it shut.

"Not on my grandmother's linens! Mother of God!" I hissed.

As fast as a bolt of lightning could scorch the earth, I opened the front windows and dropped the offending garments behind the boxwoods. At least they were out of the house. I would put on gloves and maybe a Hazmat suit and dispose of them later. To be honest, I felt a little faint. I closed the window and turned to see Millie standing there with that knowing look on her face.

"Don't make me go scrying in my bowl this morning, you 'eah me? What's going on 'round 'eah?"

"Scrying?" Rusty said.

"The art of predicting the future by staring into water. Nostradamus did it all the time. Very handy for predicting the end of time and all that," I said. "You don't want to know, Millie. Let's get some sausage going in the pan. They'll be here soon."

"Humph. Suit yourself. You don't have to tell me what I already know," she said with some annoyance in her voice. "I'll be in the kitchen kneading dough."

We followed her and I realized that keeping secrets from Millie was a worthless pursuit on many fronts. She was my finest ally and siding with Rusty over her would offend her. So as always, I came clean.

"It's Belle and Linnie," I said.

"Playing with them man-boys I saw?" she said.

"More than playing," Rusty said.

"The vulgar little wenches left their thong bikini underwear in Rusty's camellia bushes last night."

"*What?* What kinda fool nonsense you telling me?" Millie's eyes narrowed and she put her hands on her hips.

"Bloomers. They probably thought it was funny," I said. "Hold on! Rusty? You'd better check their rooms for pot. That's stoner humor."

"Good grief," Rusty said, sounding defeated before the next battle had even begun.

The dining-room door swung open and there stood Eric with bed hair, drawstring pants drooping, and a wrinkled T-shirt, stretching, looking much like a yawning Statue of Liberty.

"Morning, Mom!" he said. "Hey, Rusty. Hey, Millie. 'S'up?"

"Hey, baby!" I gave him a hug and ruffled his hair. "I'm glad you got up. Go make yourself presentable. Everyone's coming for breakfast and they'll be here anytime now."

"'Kay," Eric said, and did an about-face. "Biscuits. Sweet," I heard him say behind the muffled wood of the swinging door.

"If kids couldn't say 'sweet,' 'excellent,' or 'awesome,' I wonder how they'd communicate," Rusty commented.

"Not as well," I said. "And that's the pitiful truth."

Rusty squeezed five pounds of oranges for juice. Millie made dozens of biscuits and stirred a huge pot of grits. I hauled out my largest cast-iron skillet and fried up tons of Bobby Mack's apple-wood-smoked pork-sausage patties while I scrambled a dozen eggs in butter in another. The kitchen smelled like paradise. Breakfast was and would always be my very favorite meal.

My grandmother's old Sheffield silver warming dishes, gleaming like mirrors, were soon filled. We were just placing pats of butter and jelly dishes on both ends of the table as Trip and the girls arrived. Speaking of Bobby Mack and jelly, I still needed to unload all that inventory. I made a mental note to call him.

"Mornin,' y'all! I'm starving," Trip announced.

"What else is new?" I said.

He gave me a smooch on the cheek and tried to pour himself a mug of coffee. The pot was empty.

"Morning, Aunt Caroline!" Amelia said. "Can I help with anything?"

"Morning, sweetheart! Thanks, but breakfast is all ready and in the dining room. Girls? Why don't y'all wash your hands and let's go to the table."

Linnie and Belle rolled their eyes and went to the sink.

"I already washed them this morning." Chloe held out her hands for inspection. Clearly, she had missed a few places. "Guess I'll just wash them again anyway." She was still wounded from the night before. At least she seemed sullen and I knew Rusty's impending marriage to Trip was still the reason.

"Can't hurt." I smiled at her with all the warmth I could muster. "But hurry now before it all gets cold! Nothing worse than cold grits!"

"Ew!" she said, and literally hopped to the powder room like a bunny.

Poor little cabbage, I thought, she can't even wash her hands right.

I sat at one end of the table, the one closest to the kitchen, where Miss Lavinia used to sit. Trip took the other end, where, yes, our father sat when he was alive. It was always a little unbelievable to me that we were now the rightful owners of those places at the table unless I married again, which, as we all knew, was not very likely. But there we were. I was in Mother's chair; Trip was in Daddy's. I loved sitting in Mother's chair and I hated it, too. Trip probably felt the same way about Daddy's.

Rusty was seated on Trip's right, with Eric and Chloe on my left, and Amelia was seated to my right, with Belle and then Linnie on the end. The whole family minus Frances Mae. It wasn't that Frances Mae's absence went unnoticed; it was that Rusty's presence and new status were so much more immediate. I became nervous suddenly because I wanted everything to go well and I knew it might not.

Trip offered a blessing that went on for so long it would soon be lunchtime if he didn't wrap it up. I swear, ever since he stopped drinking and gambling, it was obvious that he had lost a big chunk of his brains. I cleared my throat.

"Ahem, ahem!"

Everyone giggled. Even Trip broke into a grin.

"All right. All right," he said. "Thank you, Lord, amen."

"Whew!" I said. "Moses, Trip! Is there anyone left to pray for or to thank? Come, let's fill our plates. Chloe, why don't you help yourself first since you're the youngest."

Well, don't you know, little Chloe, who was never first for anything (except to be in line to get beat up with the ugly stick), sprang from her chair with her plate, rushing to the buffet.

"Wait, honey, let me help you," I said, intending to remove the lids of the warming dishes. I knew they would be hot to the touch.

But no; hell, no. There was not a stitch of obedience in that child's makeup, no urgency to heed the words of an elder, and no sooner had she lifted the top of the dish than she immediately burned her hand, and the whole business, the lid of my grandmother's antique silver dish, came crashing to the floor with a spoonful of eggs.

It all landed on the Nien rug that had graced the floor since John C. Calhoun came here to duck-hunt. Okay, maybe that's not quite accurate, but didn't I tell that child to wait?

Rusty jumped up from her seat and rushed to Chloe, who was screaming from pain whose severity was highly exaggerated, let me assure you.

"Let me see your hand, sweetheart," she said.

Rusty said it so sweetly that Chloe's howl was instantly reduced to a whimper and she unfurled her fingers. This was momentous. Rusty had soothed the little beast. For the moment.

The dining-room door swung open and Millie whooshed in.

"What happened?"

"It's all right, Millie," Rusty said. "I think Chloe was surprised by the heat of the lid; but it's all right. She's not burned. But let's put some ice on it anyway, okay?"

Rusty said this to Chloe, who nodded. Millie picked up the lid, placed it by the side of the dish, scooped up the eggs in her hand, and took the spoon to rinse it. The three of them disappeared into the kitchen to administer some TLC, making me slightly ashamed of my judgmental self, that part I had obviously inherited from Mother. It was genetic, you see, not my fault.

"Well, I could eat a horse," Eric said. "Mind if I serve myself?"

"Of course not, darling! Help yourself! Girls? Y'all, too! Let's not let one little snag ruin the whole meal. Chloe's fine!" I smiled at them all, hoping I sounded like a loving caring aunt, knowing I was a disingenuous, judgmental stinker of a witch who only wanted to slap Linnie and Belle across their silly faces for what they had done to insult my brother and Rusty, who would be a much better stepmother than either of them deserved.

Everyone fixed a plate of food for themselves and I waited until last, hoping Rusty and Chloe would rejoin the table, but they did not. I decided not to remark on this but fervently hoped in the other side of my heart—that part that was not the judgmental stinker of a witch—that Rusty was in the kitchen making some headway with Chloe. Life would be so much sweeter if we could only just get along. And if everyone would just behave themselves. The way I wanted them to.

Finally, I took my place, spread my napkin across my lap, and lifted my fork. Linnie and Belle had not waited for me and in their haste they were already scraping up the last bits of grits and eggs from their plates. Trip cleared his throat, which was his way of letting his two middle daughters know their poor manners were a disappointment to him. They didn't even give Trip's disapproval a moment's notice.

Amelia said, taking her first bite, "Don't mind them, Aunt Caroline. They can't help it."

"Well, dear, hopefully we can teach them some manners by Christmas," I said.

"What's happening Christmas? Mom, this is so good. Can somebody pass the biscuits down here?" Eric said.

"Well, I haven't had the chance to discuss it with my brother yet, but I'd like to give a ball in Amelia's honor."

"What? Why?" Amelia said.

"To present you to our friends as a young lady, a young woman ready to take her place in Lowcountry society."

"I'm gonna *F*-ing puke," Linnie whispered to Belle, and they both giggled.

"I heard that," I said. "If you need to excuse yourself, you may."

To my utter surprise, Linnie and Belle actually straightened up. I guessed I had a formidable way every now and then.

"I don't know if I'm up for all that," Amelia said. "I don't even have a boyfriend to take me. Who would I dance with?"

"Nonsense," I said. "You'll dance with Eric. And your father."

Belle and Linnie were about to fall from their chairs in laughter and from elbowing each other.

"I'm sure you think this is all a riot," I said, "but let me tell you, it will be a gorgeous night and we'll all have lots of fun."

"Basically," Eric said, "it's just a dinner dance. It's fun. I went to Miss Nancy's granddaughter's deb ball last year. She came out with St. Cecilia's in Charleston. Now, that was an anthropology experiment."

"If she doesn't want to . . ." Trip said. "Besides, I never joined St. Cecilia's you know."

"What? What's the matter with you, Trip Wimbley? Every woman in this family for the last hundred years has been a debutante! Except me because I was in New York with Richard that year. I'm aware you never joined and I think we all know why." The minute the words were said I regretted them.

Trip looked at me in a burst of anger. For the first time in a long while he was deeply provoked with me. I had stepped over a line I was not entitled to cross. We could rag on Frances Mae all we wanted to in private, but it was never all right to put her down in front of his girls. The truth was that Trip was entitled to be a candidate for the St. Cecilia's Society but he had never tried to join because Frances Mae Litchfield was so unsuitable. In all likelihood, he would have been rejected, Mother would have been mortified, and the whole thing would have had disastrous repercussions for the next hundred years. And I also knew he was about an inch from reminding me that I had been living with Richard and intended to marry a Jewish man nearly twice my age and that was the real reason I had skipped the deb experience with the Charleston crowd.

"Caroline?"

"I'm sorry, Trip. Let's just say it wasn't right for us at the time."

"That's more like it."

"Anyway, all that was aeons ago and who cares? We don't need St. Cecilia's. I can rent the ballroom at the Francis Marion Hotel. I'll invite everyone, we can have a beautiful dinner and fabulous music, and we'll all have a marvelous time! Don't you think it sounds like fun, Amelia?"

Amelia. Poor Amelia. She might as well have had a target painted on her forehead once she was in my sights. I was already redesigning her appearance, promising myself to be subtle about it, remembering how fragile a girl's confidence could be at her age. I couldn't imagine her thoughts and I wanted to give her some time to see the wisdom of my proposal, knowing she'd come around. As we know, of all of them, Trip's whole brood of Halloween-scary offspring, she was the one for whom I had the highest hopes of making a suitable marriage and a successful life.

"Um. Sure. Probably," she said. "I mean, it's awfully nice of you to think of doing something like that for me. Really it is."

"Well, you'd meet lots of nice young people your age and that can't hurt. Maybe we'll fly to New York for a dress. How does that sound?"

Amelia was very surprised by even the mention of something in her honor, much less a trip to New York.

"Shoot, I'll go with you, Amelia," Eric said. "I can go see Dad and my half brother." I gasped a little and Eric laughed. "I haven't seen him in two years, Mom. Might be nice to check in? You know, see if Harry has won a Nobel Prize yet?"

"We'll see," I said.

"I've never been to New York," Amelia said. "Could we go to Radio City and see the Rockettes?"

Amelia was interested and I was so glad! Whoever knew that she had the slightest desire to see the Rockettes? And if Eric went along, it would be more fun for her. Most important, what other dreams did Amelia have?

"Absolutely! And we can go to the Metropolitan Museum of Art and the Guggenheim, and hear an opera and see a ballet . . . why don't you go online when you have some time and do a little research. You tell me what you'd like to do and I'll try to make it happen."

"Wait a minute," Belle said. "Wait just a minute! How come she gets to do all this stuff and we don't?"

"Do you really want me to answer that question in front of your father?" I said with my sweetest smile.

Trip ignored me but the air became suddenly heavy, as though devils were rising from between the planks of flooring and oozing from the corners of the walls.

"Maybe not, Belle," Linnie said, giving Belle big eyes and a push on her arm.

"I think I'm gonna get some more grits, if that's okay. How about you, Mom? Can I get you something?"

"No, thank you, sweetheart," I said, and then looked back at Belle and Linnie, giving them the flambé hairy eyeball, a variation which I had just learned from Millie.

Just then the door opened and Rusty and Chloe were back to rejoin the table. Chloe had three large Band-Aids across her palm. She plunked herself in her seat and whispered to me with her eyes stretched as big and wide as two saucers.

"I'm really getting a puppy, Aunt Caroline! Don't tell, okay?"

"Okay!" I winked at Rusty, who winked back at me and smiled. With her other hand, Chloe continued eating a biscuit Millie must've given her.

"What'd we miss? Is there anything left for us?" Rusty said.

"You didn't miss a thing," I said, "and there's enough left for Beauregard's army!" It was then I remembered to do what I had intended to do in the first place. "Linnie? Belle? Amelia? And you, too, Chloe . . . did your daddy ever tell you about the time that some of Sherman's army, who were obviously lost, came to this house during the War Between the States?"

"*What?*" they all said together.

"She means the Civil War," Trip said with a laugh.

"*She* is the cat's mother and I mean the War of Yankee Aggression! Well, here's what happened and every word is true. Every single word!" Okay, maybe not.

12

Settling Down

WE WERE IN THE KITCHEN, just Eric and I, packing a small cooler of leftovers for him to take back to school. Somehow we all made it to Sunday afternoon without bloodshed and only minor squabbles. Tomorrow would mark Frances Mae's absence as one week. We had only seven weeks left to shape up Trip's girls. I shuddered at the thought of her return.

I told Eric that after yesterday's breakfast and today's dinner, I imagined that staying with Rusty suddenly held more appeal for the girls than enduring an endless history lecture from me. He did not disagree.

"You went on for like an hour, Mom."

"I did? Yeah, I suppose I did. But you know the details of our past are very important. It's essential for those girls to understand who they are and where they come from. Otherwise, how can they plan some kind of a future for themselves, you know, give themselves something to aim for? I'm just trying to expand their horizons."

"Right. Actually, Mom, Linnie and Belle are thinking of majoring in political science and then joining the diplomatic corps when they graduate. Belle thinks she wants to be an ambassador to somewhere in South America; Peru, I think. I heard them talking about it."

"Heavens! I hope you're kidding!"

"I am."

"Well, that's a relief."

I heard him chuckle.

"Very funny," I said, smiling to myself.

"Can you imagine those two running embassies?"

"No. I cannot fathom."

"Man, I used to think that I had a lot of growing up to do, but those two?"

"Baby, my mother used to always say that every flower blooms in its own time."

"Weird."

I smiled and glanced at Eric's grinning profile and thought about how close he was to adulthood. The outside world was beginning to close ranks around him bit by bit. It wouldn't be too many years before I would need him more than he would need me, but I was very determined never to be a burden to him or anyone. That much was certain. Was it his youth that made me think about my own advancing years? I wasn't that old. I wasn't washed up yet. I was still in the game. Wasn't I? And who was his girlfriend?

Amelia was coming to pick up Eric soon. He'd be back in his dormitory at Carolina that night and I wouldn't see him again for a week or so, which at that moment seemed like an unforgivable amount of time. How often during his life had I wished I could just freeze-frame us just as we were? How the years raced by like a thief, stealing my son's youth. The first thing to go were his little-boy freckles. They had all but vanished, erased by the sun's bronze patina on his cheeks and nose. The next thing I knew, he sounded like a man. "Mom?" became "Mom," that one syllable resonating with a base thud. Then I turned around one day and saw that he had grown peach fuzz above his lip and on the sides of his face. On and on it went until he towered over me and melted my heart every time I heard his man voice say, "I love you, Mom."

"I just hate for you to leave, Eric." I couldn't help pouting.

"Yeah, me, too. But you know I'll be back as soon as I run out of clean socks."

"All over the world, mothers depend on that."

He could not read my mind or know the exact thoughts I had at the moment, but Eric knew my heart better than anyone ever had. He didn't even have to look at me to know that I hated his leaving. Intellectually, I knew he had to go back to school. Of course I knew that. But every time he left, I suffered a kind of emptiness that I could physically feel from the back of my throat to the middle of my chest. His leaving made me feel a trace of panic for no discernible or sensible reason. Maternal pangs, I guess. And not to be a big old worrywart, but I wouldn't stop praying for his safety until I heard his voice telling me he was back, safe in his dorm. Then I could flip that mental switch and start stressing over things like his being mugged walking to the library at night or that some little conniving trollop was going to break his heart and I would have to kill her with my reasonably new German knives, hacking her apart, limb by limb, and gouging her eyes out. I considered my paranoia to be well within the range of normal.

"So? Are you going to tell me about her?"

"Who?" he said.

"Your new girlfriend, Eric! What's her name?"

"Oh, great. Who told you?"

"I just knew, that's all. Look! If you don't want to tell me, that's okay. I mean, I thought we could talk about anything . . ."

"Oh, okay. But it's nothing, really. I just go over to her place for dinner, that's all."

Oh. My. God. He was having sex. My son was having sex!

"Oh? Is she a good cook?" She had better *not* be a good cook.

"Yeah, not as good as you or Millie. But she's a pretty good cook."

"What does she make?" I hated her.

"You know, the usual stuff. Meat loaf. Mashed potatoes. Chicken fingers, stuffing, carrots."

"That's kid food." My alarms started ringing all over my brain. "Eric? Does this young lady have a child?" Was that possible?

"She's not that young, really."

"Really? How old is she?"

"I think she's like twenty-seven or maybe she's twenty-eight? Anyway, she's got this really cute kid named Larry. He's two. What?"

I must have looked faint and then I realized I was gripping the counter. If my son married this damn fool, I'd be a grandmother! Well, a grandmother-in-law.

"Nothing, sweetheart. What's her name?" Fainting was a real possibility.

"Erica. Erica Swink."

"Oh? Eric and Erica?" Maybe it would be a step-grandmother? I was feeling very nauseated. I reached in the cabinet for a box of Club crackers and started eating them to soak up the bile I could feel rising in my throat.

"Yeah! Isn't that weird?"

"Yeah. Weird. Well, look, Eric. I trust you to do the right thing, you know that right? I'm sure she's a lovely girl."

"Yeah. If this thing lasts, and I sure hope it will, I'll bring her home to meet you soon. You'll like her."

"I'm sure I will, darlin'! And is she a student?" I was dying inside. *Dying!*

"Oh, no. She works at the campus bookstore."

"Oh! Well, that's good. She has a job and all." Minimum wage.

We looked out the kitchen window to see Amelia walking toward the door.

"I'll go get my stuff," Eric said, and I nodded.

In the past, Amelia simply would have pulled up in the yard and leaned on her horn. Had the transformation begun? Was dignity making a comeback? Had we ceased to blare our horns like bad-boy bubbas at a tractor pull? It was another small beginning, infinitesimal really, but I would take it. Take it, relish it, and add to it. And I would say nothing about Erica Swink to a living soul. No one!

I opened the door for Amelia.

"Amelia, sweetheart!" I gave her a breezy hug with a pat on her back. "I'm just packing a cooler for Eric. Can I give you anything to take back to school? I have at least ten pounds of ham here, and Lord knows, Millie made enough cookies and brownies to last until Christmas . . ." The Academy was going to swing down to the Lowcountry, arriving any minute now to give me my Oscar for Best Actress.

"Sure!" she said. "Contributions of any kind of food are always welcome. My roommates hate to cook but we all love to eat!"

"Hand me the Ziplocs, okay?" I took the box from her and began to fill a bag with ham slices. "Well, let them have the sweets, darling! We want you to look good in that dress in December, don't we?"

"I guess so. Gosh," she said.

For someone poised on the threshold of a world of great beauty, holding a passport to elegance, she looked mighty glum.

"What's wrong?" I asked.

"Nothing! I mean, well, I'm a little worried, that's all."

Poor thing. She should only know how my insides were convulsing at the thought of some wretched girl with a baby touching mine. That was something to *really* worry about!

"What's bothering you, Amelia? Tell your auntie so I can help you feel better."

"I don't know, Aunt Caroline. I mean, I can't dance. I'm a total klutz and everyone knows it. I haven't worn a pair of high heels since I don't know when, and who's going to come to this thing anyway? I mean, it's not like I have a ton of friends who would even get it or any relatives besides my dad and you and Eric who know how to behave. My stupid sisters will probably suck up everyone's cocktails and who knows with them? They're totally trouble. And it's just that——"

"Darling child. Hush now! You're just nervous. Now, take this food, go call Eric, and tell him it's time to hustle his buns! You go back to school, make all A's, and let me worry about all that other stuff!"

"And you know Belle's graduation is like in a few weeks. Shouldn't we be doing something for that?"

Like what? I thought. Send her to a convent in Patagonia run by German nuns who use corporal punishment to motivate good behavior? Like bamboo under the fingernails? The old-fashioned rack?

"You're right! What did you have in mind?" I said as sweetly as I could.

"I'm clueless. Maybe we should ask her?"

"I'll call Belle tonight. Is Trip taking the girls back to Walterboro?"

"Yeah. As far as I know."

"There's been no word from your mother, I guess?"

"Nada. Zilch. Silent like the tomb. But she's not allowed to contact us."

"Right. I had forgotten that. Well, let's assume no news is good news."

"Jeez, I sure hope so."

"We all hope so," I said, and wondered if I really meant it.

When Amelia and Eric were gone, I sank into a chair at the kitchen table. I was putting Erica Swink out of my mind and not thinking about her again that night. I had bigger, smellier fish to fry. Erica would probably fade into the sunset before Memorial Day. I hoped.

Amelia was right. How had I continued to ignore the fact that our social world of acceptable guests was truly so minuscule? In all the time I had been back in the Lowcountry, I *still* had not connected with the downtown Charleston crowd, the hunt-club crowd, the golfing crowd, the arts crowd, the political crowd, or any crowd for that matter. Not even a book club! Well, surely Trip had an address book filled with satisfied clients. And I would simply have to prevail on Miss Sweetie and Miss Nancy to funnel a guest list in our direction and I knew they would. I didn't want Amelia to be embarrassed by a thin turnout. It seemed to me that any crowd under one hundred people would leave us all with a red face. I would pull off a grand occasion if it was the last thing I did.

And what about Belle's graduation? I know this probably sounds a little harsh, but did that miserable unrepentant tramp really think she was entitled to a party in her honor? In my book, she still deserved a good slap across her insolent face. She and Linnie had behaved abominably all weekend, right up to dinner earlier today, when they finally began to simmer down after Trip corrected them about a dozen times.

Wait! Let me backtrack for a minute. For dinner today, Millie had baked a fruited ham and made red rice, deviled eggs, green-bean salad, a zillion biscuits, and brownies that were so rich and chocolaty they made you literally drool for another cold glass of milk. They ate like horses and then they calmed down. They became pretty reasonable by the end of dinner. What kind of nutritional habits did they have? They probably drank triple espressos for breakfast and caffeine sodas all day long. Maybe that was how they stayed so skinny and why their behavior was so frenetic. That was it! They were overcaffeinated and overstimulated! I was a regular Sherlock Holmes, by golly.

I dialed Trip's cell phone.

"Hey, where are you?"

"In the car driving the girls back. Why?"

"Well, I just had a thought and I wanted you to look into it."

"Sure. What?"

I could hear the girls talking to each other.

"Am I on speakerphone? You know I can't bear that." Modern technology made me grind my teeth and the girls didn't need to hear what I was going to say, did they?

"Well, I've got my hands kind of full here. Why don't I just call you when I get to the house."

"Fine. That's fine. Fine."

My thoughts were drifting to the next logical step, which would be for me to go to the Walterboro house. I could see myself pulling a garbage can up to the refrigerator and throwing out all the junk. Then I would go through all the cabinets and do the same thing. Lastly, I would go to that Piggly Wiggly out on Bells Highway and restock the house with healthy food—whole-grain everything—and maybe I would even bake my little miseries a chicken.

I called Rusty.

"You okay?" I asked. "You have to be wiped out."

"I'm totally and completely exhausted."

"I'm sure! Listen, I have a new theory . . ."

I gave her the gist of my bad-nutrition idea and she agreed with me.

"You are one hundred percent right, Caroline. Of *course* what you eat affects your moods. Food affects everything!"

"Why didn't I think of this before?"

"Who knows? Why didn't I? Listen, when I was working with all those LD kids, the minute I could get their families to get the kids off refined sugar and caffeinated drinks, there was an immediate, I mean, *immediate* improvement in their ability to focus on whatever we were studying."

"Big surprise, now that I think about it."

"And you think there's no relationship between sugar and ADHD?"

"Obviously there is! And I think the same thing goes for carbs, right?"

"Yeah, no doubt about it. They metabolize as sugar and store as fat. Bad news. So let me ask you something, Dr. Atkins."

We both giggled.

"What?"

"Exactly how do you plan to rectify this?"

There was only one choice, one clear path of action.

"I'm getting in my car and driving over there right now."

"You are? Well, good luck!"

"*Vaya con Dios,* right?"

"Sí! Caroline? Call me if you need reinforcements."

"And you'd come?"

"What? Heck no! I've seen enough of them today! I'd send Millie!"

"Wish me double good luck."

What to wear to a search-and-destroy mission? I decided to go just as I was. It was not a Miss Lavinia caftan event.

If Trip tried to call me while I was driving there, I didn't know it. That stretch of highway was a dead zone for cell-phone reception. I rolled into Walterboro right around six and pulled into their yard on Lynnwood Drive minutes later. There was a moment of doubt while I debated ringing the front doorbell or to go in the back like a family member, deciding the back porch was a better choice. Strangers and company used the front door. After all, Auntie Caroline didn't want anyone to be suspicious. They were all in the breakfast room finishing up supper.

Trip stood when he saw me coming and opened the door for me.

"Hey!" he said, wiping his mouth with a paper towel. "What a surprise! What's up? Bears on the loose again?"

"Just this momma bear. Can I have a word with you?"

"Sure. You hungry? There's plenty of . . ."

We looked at the table, where my nieces were winding up their feast of canned soup and grilled rubber cheese sandwiches. Uneaten burned crusts were tossed on a central plate and splattered broth made little puddles on the table. An open pickle jar stood by Trip's plate with a large fork sticking out of it. It could have been Neptune's trident. A bomb-shelter-size bag of potato chips was open, waiting for the next greasy hand to find its way inside. Seldom had a meal been so easy to resist.

"Nah, I'm fine. Thanks. Ate before I left."

"Doesn't look so great, does it?"

"Actually, that's why I'm here."

We walked into the den, out of earshot. I started telling Trip that I had come to the conclusion that Linnie and Belle were caffeine slash sugar junkies, which was why they were so rude and jittery all the time, and that all the sodium wasn't doing Chloe any good either. Just as I was about to wind it up, and it should be noted that in typical man fashion he was rolling his eyes and shifting his weight from foot to foot with complete disinterest, his cell phone rang. He took the call and walked away from me toward the living room. I followed him and stood there by the entrance waiting for him.

"Who? Yeah, hey. What can I do you for?" Pause. "What's the charge? Aw, Gawd, Bubba! Did they give you a pair of pants at least? Jeesch! What's bail?"

Some Bubba who needed pants was in trouble. Man with no pants? My curiosity was on high alert. Who was he talking to? There were at least twenty-two gazillion Bubbas in the Carolina Lowcountry and they were not necessarily of the Crimson Collar tribe. It could have been anyone. And why do southerners call some perfectly manly and refined men Bubba? Well, Bubba is usually a term of endearment, easily pronounced, and slapped on little tykes in their early years by their mothers so that the younger siblings can call their Big Bubba by a squishy nonthreatening name. Mommas also call their sons Bubba because they're frequently named for their fathers to honor them. In Trip's case, he was named for his father and grandfather, so he was a third, and the nickname is short for the triple III at the end of his name on his birth certificate. Fascinating, right? Probably not. Anyway, he sure was taking a long time on the phone.

I looked at him in concern, silently mouthing *what?* He gave me the two-minute signal with his fingers, indicating he would be off the phone momentarily. I nodded and kept quiet.

"Okay, okay. No, don't worry. You can pay me back. I'll be right there." He closed his phone and looked at me. "What a world. Good thing I keep some cash in the house."

"What happened?"

"That was Bubba Poole who just called. He was over at his girl-friend's house when her husband came home and he had to jump out of the bedroom window in his altogether. He ran home through the woods with it swinging in the breeze and somehow, by the grace of God, no one saw him. But when he got to his house, his wife, Nancy, was standing on the back porch without her sense of humor. A disagreement ensued and then there was some altercation including some threats that were made against his manhood with a very scary large pair of garden shears, during which time he took flight once again and got picked up by Walterboro's finest."

"You couldn't make this stuff up. But why is he calling you? You're a matrimonial lawyer."

"Poor Nancy. Nancy Poole's one terrific lady. Pretty as a picture and sweet as pie. An unbelievable gardener, in fact. Hence the shears, I guess. Why is he calling me? Because this wasn't Bubba's first time up at bat and I can smell divorce in a gale wind the same way women can smell a shoe sale from fifty miles away. Besides all that, Bubba's got more money than Croesus and a taste for danger. It will be lucrative as well as interesting."

"Okay. Got it. So what about my nutritional thoughts? Can I go in there and do something drastic?"

"Caroline? You go in there and do whatever the hell you want in that kitchen. I couldn't care less. Just remember those are my girls. I gotta go rescue Bubba."

Trip was gone in minutes and I went into the kitchen to assess the battlefield. In the first place, the garbage cans were full. Dishes that had to have been from last week were stacked in the sink. The dishwasher was full but had not been run. There was grease all over the stove from the frying pans they had used to make their grilled cheese sandwiches. The more I looked, the more appalling the details became.

"Pretty messy, huh?"

I looked around to see Chloe with two plates in her hands. I took them from her but was hard-pressed to locate a spot to put them down. The countertops were covered with various open cartons, empty cans, balled-up paper towels . . . need I say more? It was probably the most disgusting kitchen I had ever seen, and if Frances Mae saw it in this condition, she'd go on a binge for sure. Say what you want about Frances Mae Litchfield, but she kept her house in pretty good shape, considering she had spent years living with young terrorists and an overgrown baby boy. I finally just put the plates on top of the refrigerator and sighed.

"Chloe? Do you want to help Aunt Caroline perform a miracle?"

"Sure!"

"Where does your momma keep the dishwasher detergent?"

She bustled around me and produced a box of Cascade from under the sink.

"This stuff?"

"Yep! That'll do her!"

I filled the soap wells, closed the door, and turned on the dishwasher. It was so jammed full it could not have held another tea-spoon. Then with Chloe's help I pulled the plastic bags from the trash cans and tied off the tops. Some container had broken through the bags and leaked into the cans, which now smelled like something had died in there. As quickly as I could, I double-bagged them. This job was going to make me retch. I was sure of it.

"Can you put those on the back porch, sweetheart?"

"I can take them all the way out to the big cans, if you want."

"Lord love ya, darlin'!" She was an ugly little duck to be sure, but her heart was in the right place. "Linnie? Belle? Where are you? Can you girls come to the kitchen now and give me a hand?"

Belle appeared with her dirty dishes in hand and Linnie was right behind her.

"What now?" Belle said, and handed me her plate and bowl as though I was the new housekeeper.

I reached out for Linnie's dishes, stacked them on Belle's, and shoved them into a spot on the counter.

"I want y'all to take these trash cans outside and rinse them out good with the hose and some big squirts of this." I handed her a bottle of liquid detergent.

"Why me?" Belle said. "I've got homework to do."

"So do I. Tons of it," Linnie said. "Besides, that's not our job."

"Really? Whose job is it? Take a whiff," I said.

They leaned over the rubber can, inhaled ever so slightly, and gagged.

"It's unsanitary. Y'all made this mess, so let's get busy and clean it up."

They stood there and looked at each other and then back to me as though I had just crawled down the ladder of an alien spacecraft, deciding if it was worth it to defy me. They made a poor choice.

"Sorry," Belle said, "I've got to go write a paper. Get Dad to do it when he comes home."

"Yeah," Linnie said. "Get Dad to do it."

I was aghast. If I had ever spoken that way to Lavinia Boswell Wimbley, she would have blistered my bottom. But these two? Did they care? They spun around on their heels and started to leave the room.

"I don't think so," I said in my imperial-bitch voice. "Y'all stop right where you are and listen to me." They stopped but did not turn to face me. "Turn around, please."

They turned and looked at me with the most hateful faces I had ever seen on them. My heart was pounding in my ears. I was furious.

"Some things are about to change around here. First of all, we're going to use some manners and have some respect for each other and show some respect for this home. If you continue to live in this squalor, you're going to give yourselves E. coli. Nice people don't live like this. Animals live like this. When I leave, this house is going to be clean, neat, and orderly. And you want me to tell your father to do it? Are you girls serious?"

"Um . . ." they said.

"He even works on a *Sunday night* so that you girls can have a nice house and all the blessings you have and that's how you would treat him? He should come home and wash trash cans?"

"Um . . ."

Um, indeed, I thought.

"I think it's time y'all started taking some responsibility around here. So either you can decide between yourselves who's taking what job or I'll decide for you. Do you understand me?"

"I was going to do the dishes later," Belle said. "It's no big deal."

"Yeah, seriously!" Linnie said. "Why are you making such a big deal out of this? It's just a couple of days' worth of stuff."

"How about this? I don't like your attitude. You both have some nerve. And you know what? Your mother would pass out on the floor if she could see this place and hear the way you talk."

I surprised myself at what I had just said. But it was true. Frances Mae may have been an insufferable gold digger, but it seemed we shared an affection for neatness and order.

Well, the mere mention of their mother struck the lightning rod of their guilt nerve. I could see an immediate change in their faces and in their body language. We went from arms crossed over the chest "Aunt Caroline is a coldhearted witch from the seventh circle of hell" to arms hanging like old baguettes "Aunt Caroline is probably right." It was interesting that pushing the Frances Mae button had such a profound impact on them. Or maybe they had not thought I was serious at first, or they couldn't envision me with a sponge, getting my hands dirty, doing real work.

"Okay, okay. Let's go do the cans together and then you wash and I'll dry," Belle said to Linnie.

"Well, the dishwasher is still running, so why don't we check out your laundry situation. After the cans are rinsed?" I suggested, and then realized they had no intention of moving beyond the kitchen. "You know, Rusty is looking for a housekeeper for y'all, but so far there are no takers. I'm thinking you girls will be out of underwear in a few days, so why not just take care of it now?"

"She's right," Linnie said to Belle as though I was invisible.

I *was* going to point out that it was impolite to refer to another in the room as he or she. It was right on the tip of my tongue. But you couldn't make a silk purse from a sow's ear in one day, so I let it slide. They were poisonous enough as it was.

"Tell you what," I said. "Do the delicate load first and then hang everything on hangers, regular clothes next, then sheets, and we'll do towels last. How does that sound?"

"It sounds like four loads of laundry," Belle said. "I'll never get my paper written!"

I looked at my watch and saw it was almost seven o'clock. She was right. The wonderful thing about the approach of summer was that our part of the world enjoyed longer days, but more daylight was also easily translated into longer workdays.

"Okay, then just wash clothes tonight and we'll do the sheets and towels another day."

"Okay," they said, and disappeared to throw their things, their dainty little thong bikinis that made me nauseous to look at them, into the washer.

"And the garbage cans," I called out.

They returned, took the cans, and went outside to deal with them.

I immediately pulled another garbage can up to the refrigerator, opened the door, and gasped. What I found there is difficult to describe except to say that nothing, not one article in a bag, bowl, or container of any type would ever find its way to my table. They had yogurt so far beyond its expiration date it had reincarnated into another life. A milk carton on the second shelf in the back had chunks in it. The cheese had green patches. The bologna had turned white. The celery was limp. Here was evidence of Frances Mae's illness galore. And, lo and behold, what do you think was stuck in between the ketchup, pickles, and mayonnaise on the shelves of the door? Red Bull. There had to be at least two dozen cans of the supercaffeinated energy drink derived from a lab. It had absolutely no nutritional value and it was on its way down the drain.

I stood there, snapping open the cans and pouring out their contents, when suddenly Chloe reappeared.

"Whatcha doing?" she asked.

"Cleaning out the fridge. What are you doing?"

"Linnie and Belle are gonna scream their heads off at you."

"No. They're not." I paused for a moment, thinking of what to do if they did. "Why would they do that?"

"Because they drink that stuff morning, noon, and night."

"Well, I think it's very bad for people to ingest something like this and I want to keep them healthy, so I'm throwing out all the junk food and old stuff. Wanna help?"

"Nope. I don't wanna get killed. I'll be back."

She skipped away. I knew at once she was going to find her big sisters and rat me out. I was right. Just as I had pitched the last package of greasy processed meat, it was pandemonium.

I could not tell you exactly who started the screaming, but I just stood there while my two nieces, whom I now believed to be in desperate need of a psychiatric evaluation, yelled and called me terrible names at the top of their lungs while Chloe covered her ears and ran out of the house.

"Momma's coming back and she'll fix you good!" Belle screamed.

"Momma's gonna cut your stuck-up ass!" Linnie said.

"Your mother will do no such thing!!" I picked up my purse, looked at them calmly, and said, "Are you finished, ladies?"

They made some demonic guttural sounds and then gurgled to a close.

"Okay, here's the deal. Your father and I strongly believe that eating processed food isn't good for your hyperactive bodies, your wretched dispositions, or your mediocre academic performance. Red Bull does nothing positive to enhance those things either. It's not even food."

"But I need it!" Belle wailed.

"I'm sure. Addictive personalities run in families, you know. That should give you pause, kiddo."

"You can't stop us from drinking Red Bull!" Linnie said.

"With your father's cooperation, we can minimize its use. At least in this house."

"Great. Now the food police are here," Belle said.

"No, I'm not the food police. I'm your aunt who is trying to help you girls understand that taking care of your body is something to be taken very seriously."

"You think we don't know that? You think we're stupid?" Linnie said.

Lord above, and that's a prayer, this child had the sassiest mouth I had ever heard.

"No. I do not think you're stupid. I think you are both exceptionally bright young women with marginal ambition and questionable ethics. How's that? The good and the bad. It is my intention to teach you about integrity and the great happiness that can come from living a more organized and healthier life. And a little gentility wouldn't kill you either."

"Oh, great," Belle said. "Are you going to try and make debs out of us, too?"

"No, not today. Today I am going to the grocery store. My intention is to fill this house with healthy choices for your meals and to reestablish some kind of order in your lives. And when I come back, which will be in about an hour, I expect to find this kitchen cleaned, the refrigerator wiped down, and all the trash outside where it belongs."

They just stared at me as though no one had ever tried to give them any boundaries or instructions.

"And the clothes washer humming away."

The stare continued.

"Okay, then," I said, and walked from the house to my car with a stride that meant all business. I backed out of the yard, turned onto the street, and drove to the stop sign.

"Oh, dear God!" I rested my head on my arms on the steering wheel and prayed. "This is much harder than I thought it would be. What am I going to do with those girls? Plan a party for Belle? *And just who in the hell is Erica Swink?*"

13

Miss Lavinia in the Garden

TWO WEEKS PASSED, STILL NO housekeeper, and the running back and forth between Tall Pines and Walterboro was putting a strain on Rusty's and Trip's nerves. As each week went by and we got closer to Belle's graduation, we also got closer to the return of Frances Mae, which Trip, Rusty, and I were dreading more and more. How would she be? Sober, of course. But would she try to weasel her way back into Trip's heart with some insane dramatic fight? I hoped not. The girls didn't need any more turmoil. None of us did.

Speaking of the sweetie pies, Trip's girls were tolerating Rusty better than they were tolerating me, as I was obviously driving them to the limits of what they could endure. She was the devil they preferred. At least that was what they told Amelia, who told Eric, who repeated the story to me. Eric's report, and there was no mention of Erica and no inquiry from me, had its surprises, as Amelia said that Linnie and Belle were actually grateful for the kindness with which Rusty treated Chloe. Even though Linnie and Belle would have loved for the world to perceive them as tough cookies who didn't care one whit for the rules of the game, they were still sensitive enough to recognize that their baby sister had been the most damaged by the weaknesses and personal failings of their parents. Or perhaps they were just beginning to accept the inevitable—that Rusty was going to be in their lives whether they liked it or not. In any case, they appeared to be less combative when Rusty showed up at their Walterboro door. At least that's what she and I surmised since they didn't make guttural noises or hiss in her face.

When they saw me on the other side of the door, they rolled their eyes and made some unflattering remarks like "Aunt Nazi is here," and there was no smile as they said it. They didn't exactly have Stockholm syndrome. But I still considered this to be an improvement.

We always arrived unexpected, thinking that element of the unknown would put them constantly on their guard, and hopefully make them worry about being caught doing something they should not have been doing. So far, try as we did, we had not been able to nail the little darlings, which surprised me, as I knew they were naked all the time and snorting the fumes of every product under the kitchen sink. Rusty thought I was being unduly harsh. I knew better. I knew it in my bones.

Rusty always brought them thoughtful food like a decorated carrot cake, blueberry muffins with perfectly glazed crunchy tops, a roasted chicken still warm from the oven, or organic eggs that had just been laid that morning. I brought cleaning supplies, a healthy lecture, and a surreptitious inspection of their rooms, the refrigerator, and the levels of dust throughout the house. Maybe that had something to do with their noticeable lack of enthusiasm for me.

It was Wednesday morning and I was talking to Rusty on the phone.

"I still can't believe Belle skipped her prom," Rusty said.

"Honey, that girl? She's way too cool for something so traditional."

"Maybe, but if I had missed my prom I would've been suicidal."

"Me, too. So the girls get out of school two weeks from Thursday and Belle graduates on Saturday morning. How are the plans for the party coming along?"

Rusty and Trip had taken on the planning of a barbecue and swim party for Belle's entire class. Belle had a thousand objections to that because she felt the plantation was too far away from Walterboro and no one would come. The invitations went out over the weekend and Belle was proven wrong.

"The phone's been ringing off the hook all morning. I guess the invitations must have arrived and were intercepted by the parents. They all want to know if there will be adult supervision and a lifeguard and all that. They are especially concerned about alcohol."

"Alcohol is always a worry. Drugs, too."

"Well, I just told them all that they're welcome to come and help chaperone."

"And?"

"And I'll bet you dollars to donuts that not one of them shows up. But you know what? I'm going to make some adult food, like maybe some marinated chicken or something, and have enough to serve just in case. I mean, it's their child's graduation, too? Maybe they want to take pictures or something?"

"I'll bet you're right. So what can I do to help?"

"Let's see. The food's covered and I've ordered tons of balloons and I got a pile of those foam-rubber noodle things that work like rafts."

"Kids love those things."

"Yep. And I found great beach towels on sale, so I bought two dozen. We can always use them, right? Gee, maybe I should have bought more. What do you think?"

"I think a lot of kids will bring their own. Don't worry."

"You're probably right. So I got the cutest plates and napkins and I was thinking about getting a DJ? What do you think?"

"Nah. Let the girls make their own mix and blast it from your sound system. You have outdoor speakers, don't you?"

"Yes. Yes we do! Great idea! In fact we just got them—they're fake rocks and they're wireless."

"Good call. We don't want anyone getting electrocuted. That would ruin the whole day." I was completely deadpan, entertaining the vision, knowing there wasn't enough current in little speakers to cause a catastrophe.

"Right! God, you're so bad." Rusty giggled. "And then I was thinking about getting banners made, you know 'Congratulations, Graduates!' Or something like that. Or a bubble machine? Or a Sno-Kone machine? What do you think?"

I giggled then, too. Rusty was going to break the bank and Trip would have a full-blown conniption fit and die gasping for air.

"Um, I think somebody's spending too much time on the Internet? This isn't a wedding, girl!"

Rusty laughed and agreed with me.

"You're right, you're right. Gosh, can you imagine if I had my own children how spoiled rotten they'd be?"

"They'd be rotten from head to toe. Now tell me: What I can do?"

"Well, I was thinking that maybe Matthew knows some young policemen who could work as lifeguards?"

"I'm sure he does. I'll call him right away."

We hung up and I stared at the phone for a few minutes. Rusty had to be one of the most considerate and generous people I had ever known. She was using her time to plan every conceivable detail of this very nice party for Trip's daughter who would just as soon spit in her eye as say thank you. All she wanted to do was make Belle know that she and Trip cared about her graduation day and that they wanted it to be as happy and memorable as possible. Just as I was musing away on the positive qualities of Rusty, there came across my internal monitor a mental image of Frances Mae. I could see her just gnashing her teeth and wallowing in misery over missing her daughter's graduation. But truth be told, it was better to miss it from the confines of a rehab center in sunny California, where she could do yoga and meditate, than from some dismal jail cell where she had to wear an orange jumpsuit that flattered no body part. If Frances Mae had not gone away to Promises, she would surely be a guest of the state by now. Poor thing.

I called Matthew.

"Darlin' man? You busy tonight?"

"Why, no, ma'am. What's going on?"

"Well, I was thinking about making a fabulous dinner for you around seven?"

"Just us?"

"Why not?"

"What's the occasion?"

"Hunger."

"Hunger? Hmm. What are you hungry for?"

"Oh, Matthew. You know me. I'm hungry for everything."

"I'll see you at seven."

I was in an Italian mood. Everyone loved Italian food, Italian wine, Andrea Bocelli, and those three young tenors. Didn't they? It wasn't quite eleven. I still had ample room on the clock to make a round-trip to Charleston and be home in plenty of time to put together something that would thrill him.

I picked up seven pieces of veal shank at the New York Butcher in Mount Pleasant to make osso buco, figuring Millie and I could eat the leftovers the next day. Tomorrow the meat would be married to all the flavors and absolutely mouthwateringly delicious. As usual, I got into a conversation with Bill the owner, who was the coolest guy around.

"You making brown gravy with this?" he said.

"You know it. I like to use the gravy on risotto."

"Me, too. You having a party?"

"Nah, just cooking for a friend."

"Uh-huh."

"Well, actually, a man friend."

"Aha! I knew it! Nobody comes all the way here from Timbuktu to cook for an old aunt or something. Am I right?"

"Oh, Bill! Yeah, he's . . . well, he's . . ."

"Got it." He raised one eyebrow and gave me a smile. In general, Bill was a serious fellow, but when it came to matters of the heart, he softened. "I'm gonna give you a quarter pound of pancetta, too. Dice it and sauté it with the meat to give it a trace of smoke."

"Sounds great," I said, and actually blushed, something I rarely do.

He handed me the package. "My mother always said, love makes the world go 'round."

"Mothers always say things like that, don't they?"

"Yeah, and she was right, okay? My mother was always right."

"Mine, too," I said to be agreeable, knowing that my mother did so many things wrong it was just ridiculous.

As my heels crunched along the gravel in his parking lot, I suddenly remembered making veal chops for Richard years ago when I was young and in the business of serious seduction. It was that butcher at Zabar's in New York, Abe was his name, I think, who made me realize that I could bring a man to his knees with the right cut of meat. For a while I drifted from broiling everything to concocting pastas and stews. But ever since Bobby Mack had come into my life, I became a roasting and braising fool. Low and slow was how you turned meat into butter. There was something very satisfying about cooking a meal for someone, especially if it was good, and if they appreciated the effort. Matthew always did.

I stopped at Whole Foods for cheeses, olives, and a fresh baguette, and in a moment of weakness I picked up a quarter of a seedless watermelon to cube and serve over vanilla sorbet with champagne. Watermelon was just about my favorite fruit in the world—besides strawberries, of course. I hoped Matthew would think that champagne in his dessert was a little exotic. Even though my relationship with Matthew didn't quite qualify as a serious love affair, somewhere between the butcher shop and passing Rantowle Creek, I decided it wasn't nice to just treat him like a friend with benefits. Mother might not have minded if we fooled around, but I didn't think she'd be quite so sanguine if I wanted to marry him. If I intended to continue on with him, it would seem that I should give the long-term possibilities a real shake. It was a good thing my mother was dead. Well, she was dead but only technically. Still, there was only so much she could do to interfere. I hoped.

When I got home I dropped all the groceries in the kitchen, grabbed my clippers, filled a bucket halfway up its sides with warm water, and went out with the intention of cutting roses to make a huge bouquet for the living room and to fill the vases on the dining-room table.

Even though the afternoon sun had traveled across much of the sky, steam was still rising from the lawn. Heat owned the Lowcountry from May until well into October. It was almost like watching a time-lapse photography documentary on something like the evolution of the earth because every day you could count on something new emerging, being born and reborn. By small degrees, the temperature would rise each day. Leaves reappeared on shrubs and trees, quietly unfurling to show their pale green bottoms and shiny green leather tops. Flowers bloomed each week, tiny buds at first then growing in profusion and enough sweet fragrance to drive you mad. By May, the Lowcountry was more alive than ever, dressing herself for the annual parade of admirers who would arrive from Ohio and Pennsylvania to take pictures and say oh how magical it all was just to be here, even if only for a few days. Of course, while all these lovely tourists filled the coffers of various businesses around Charleston various species of bugs multiplied by the millions after each rainfall, eating everyone to pieces as the months rolled forward.

You see, this was the most addictive thing about living in the Lowcountry. It made me aware—aware of nature's doings and aware of the passing of time. The geography and all of its trappings were as alive as I could imagine the world to be. I liked the fact that the sun warmed me through and through and I didn't even mind the beads of perspiration that cropped up across my upper lip and the back of my neck. It meant I was alive, too.

I worked my way through Mother's rose garden, thinking of her while I clipped flowers for the house and deadheaded the spent blooms. After all, these roses were a part of her legacy, as they would be of mine someday. What would she have said about the state of her garden? She might have been pleased to see it thriving. She would have been thrilled to know that a photographer from *Southern Living* magazine was coming out in a few weeks to take pictures of the roses. But what would she say about our family? Probably plenty. She would have been relieved to know that Frances Mae was safely on the other side of the country but she would not have liked the way her granddaughters were behaving. That much was certain. I thought then that she would have told me I was doing the right thing to be stern with them. She would have said in her royal voice that children needed discipline and to set goals to achieve their own levels of personal excellence. And while she whispered all that from the Great Beyond, there were gusty winds and dark clouds gathering in my mental harbor. I was remembering how, when our father died, she deposited Trip and me into boarding schools so fast it made heads spin. Millie had objected strongly then, but Mother wanted us out of the way. It was so awful.

Our structure had been bought and paid for, not provided in a loving way from a loving mother. Old anger resurfaced immediately, but it was quickly eclipsed by the longing I felt to be with her once more. Even five minutes with her would have brought me unimaginable joy. It was a terrible day, a mighty and terrible heart-wrenching sorrow, when a child buried her mother. Yes, it was. And the pain of it never left you. You just somehow limped along through life having become used to a terrible emotional disability. I sighed so hard then, I was sure the branches swayed.

I wondered then if she ached to be with me from wherever her spirit had flown. Now and then she would send me a sign that she had not evaporated, but where was she the rest of the time? Did she somehow watch me as I went about my daily life? For all our differences, it was her eyes in her final days that swallowed me whole as though she couldn't get enough of my face to take away to eternity. No one ever adored me as my mother had at that time. I thought then that perhaps one reason she had sent Trip and me away to school was that she was afraid, maybe even terrified, of her capacity to love us and the risk it carried. So she just simply held back? That wasn't right. But maybe the reason she was so cold to us was that the enormous feelings she had for our father had nearly crushed her when she lost him. Maybe her mourning was too much for her to bear, and if she had some distance from us she might have been more easily healed and then buoyed again with enough loft to eventually reel us back into her orbit. At least it had played out in that order, but I would never fully know the truth. It seemed then that, like every other sorry human being whose heart had been ripped open by loss, I would rewrite that story until I found a truth I could accept as plausible, one that made me feel all right about my mother and about myself. She was my mother, after all.

I began to envision her working alongside me as we used to do so often before she so quickly and unfairly declined. For some crazy reason I told myself that if I concentrated hard enough I could bring her back to life and place her right there with me in the garden. So I thought of her in her big hats and gloves leaning through the bushes, pinching back buds and chatting away, until I could almost feel her breath moving the flowers.

I felt an urgency to tell her everything I was holding back. *I'm lonely, Mother.* What would she have said about me sleeping with Matthew? *He's so nice to me.* I knew once again she would have said to go and have my fun for now, but that he was not an appropriate choice for a spouse. Real or imagined, I found that opinion to be unacceptable. Who was she to say what was appropriate and what was not? Had she not slept with the UPS man and then Raoul, her gardener? Who knew what other men had made their way to her sheets? Probably scores of them. Well, it did me no good whatsoever to waste much time pondering Mother's escapades because it didn't matter anymore, and besides, Matthew had not presented himself as anything but a dear and caring friend.

Ah, Matthew. Every woman should have a man in her life like my Matthew. He was masculine but sensitive enough, confident but not too arrogant, handsome not pretty like a momma's boy, and very easy to be with. We had many things in common, most of all a shared passion for the Lowcountry. Above all, Matthew had integrity and compassion, two qualities in short supply among men *and* women these days. He certainly could have thrown Frances Mae in the pokey on many occasions, but his compassion for the family overruled the law of the land. And Matthew's main rationalization for not locking her up was that he didn't really believe the state could solve her personal problems. It was up to the family to keep her off the road and to get her into treatment. We had done that and he was satisfied. Besides, in our neck of the woods, the population of our internment center was composed of those who manufactured pharmaceutical products for self-medication and recreational purposes—read: meth-lab junkies who settled their differences with guns and knives. Even Frances Mae had no business in a jail like that.

I started getting excited about spending the evening with him, and who knew what the end of the evening might bring? Was it a Lavinia caftan night? Ooh la la! Yes! Wait! No! God help me, I was so stupid sometimes! Had Matthew not seen me in a caftan, one that was inside out, on that unfortunate night when Bobby Mack almost went to the light? Um, yeah. Jesus, I thought, get it together, Caroline. Nonetheless, I would wear something provocative. I gathered up my pail of roses and went back to the house, leaving the ghost of Lavinia tangled in the thorns, right where she belonged, with those highfalutin Lady Astor opinions of hers. Indeed.

While the osso buco simmered, I showered and dressed, spraying perfume in all the important nooks and crannies. After I pulled ten different outfits from my closet, I finally decided to let shoes rule the night and took out my crazy Pucci wedges that were a pink-and-purple paisley silk. Nothing in the universe matched them, so I decided on white tissue crepe pajama pants with a coordinating big shirt of the same fabric. And, of course, Mother's South Sea pearls. Given my mileage? I was pleased with my appearance.

The whole house smelled delicious from the pungent fragrances of sautéed rosemary and pancetta combined with the wafting steam of wine and chicken stock. I basted the meat every ten minutes or so and in between I minced shallots for the risotto and set the table with Mother's favorite china—the Victoria pattern from Herend. The roses I had cut filled two gleaming Chinese export silver vases on the dining-room table. I filled another tall vase that was so old it had probably belonged to Robert E. Lee's godmother's aunt. Well,

Robert E. Lee's mother's contemporary, okay? It was loaded with blooms and stood on an end table in the living room. Needless to say, the veritable mountain of assembled roses smelled like you might think heaven would.

As I flitted around the house attending to all the details that come with making dinner for a guest, my mind hopscotched over such earth-shattering topics as whether or not it was gauche to put paper hand towels in the guest powder room and what cooks did before the advent of paper towels or canned chicken broth. I mean, I could make stock with the best of them, but to be honest, I thought some brands were as good if not better than anything that ever came out of my pots. I had used nearly two quarts with the meat and I would use another one with the risotto. I figured at least six chickens met their demise so Matthew and I could enjoy moist veal and plump kernels of Italian rice. Well, chickens are stupid anyway, but I tried not to think about the poor little cow. All kidding aside, the rumors of how they were slaughtered were deeply disturbing. Much worse than pigs, according to Bobby Mack. Maybe someday I would give up meat altogether. But not now. No, no. Not that night. Was I getting nervous?

It was six-thirty and Matthew would be arriving soon. I filled the ice bucket, checked the white wine to be sure it was chilled to the right temperature, and pressed the remote control to get the music going. The stage was set for a beautiful evening. I stopped in front of the hall mirror and gave myself one last honest critique. I looked positively virginal. Okay, maybe not. But I could still pass for thirty-five. Okay, thirty-seven.

"Oh, just forget it!" I said out loud to no one. "I look good for my age and that's what matters."

Minutes later the doorbell rang and there stood Matthew, leaning on the threshold looking less like an officer of the law than ever, holding a bottle of good red wine. He was wearing a black textured linen shirt and his khaki gabardine trousers hung from his hips the whole way down to his (mock?) alligator loafers just as they should. The man smelled divine, as tempting as a Hollywood tabloid packed with scandalous sin of the carnal variety. He was as fine a specimen as ever that walked up to my front door. Ever. I was a little weak.

"You look absolutely gorgeous," he said.

"I know," I said, and giggled. "So do you."

Eventually, after a glass of wine and enough sexual innuendo in the hold to sink the *QE2*, we finally sat down in the dining room. Dinner was delicious and passed at a slow and leisurely pace because what was the rush?

"I need to ask you for a small favor, Matthew," I said.

"Anything," he replied.

I told him about the pool party and our concern for the kids' safety. He started to laugh.

"Are you asking me if the young guys on the force want to come over here and supervise a bunch of eighteen-year-old girls in bikinis? Are you kidding? How much do they have to pay you?"

We had a good laugh at that and I was assured it would be no problem at all.

"And I had some shocking news this week."

"You wouldn't be a Wimbley if you didn't. Tell me."

"My son has a new girlfriend."

"You don't look very happy about that."

"She's twenty-seven and has a two-year-old baby. Her name is Erica."

"Eric and Erica? You're kidding, right?"

"I only wish."

"It won't last."

"Your mouth, God's ears. I mean, I'm not naive, you know. I know he's at the age to be sexually active and all that. But she's too old! What does a girl her age want with a young boy like Eric?"

"Well, let's think about this for a minute. Maybe she's lonely?"

"Maybe. Maybe she's broke? I know she works at the university bookstore. Can't pay much."

"I have some friends in Columbia. Want me to check her out?"

"Nah. Not yet. If Eric found out I was snooping around into his personal life, he'd never forgive me."

"Yeah, but if this was twenty years ago and y'all lived in a small town, you'd all know each other. Know what I mean?"

"This wouldn't be going on if we all knew each other and that's what bothers me. I'd know her momma and the girl would've been Eric's babysitter. Taking down the kid you babysit for is gross."

"Caroline? I love you to death but sometimes you can be so—I don't know—*prim*? Is that the word? If that's what's happening, there's not a man in this world who would tell him it's wrong."

"Or a woman who would say it's right."

"Stop worrying. Let him have his fun."

"You're right. I'm a prude. Well, where my son is concerned anyway."

Shaking his head and smiling, Matthew reached up to the roses, fingered a petal, marveling at its suede finish, and then he stood, inhaling the center of one, and just shook his head as though he had never smelled a rose before.

"These flowers are unbelievable," he said. "How do you find time to do all this? I mean, run a business? Manage this whole property? Obsess about Eric? And raise roses like these? My God, they smell like I don't know what!" He sat again, taking a long sip of his wine and then wiping his mouth with his napkin.

"It's the dirt, darlin', it's always about the dirt. And a little time management. Plus I do have Millie and Mr. Jenkins."

"I guess. Amazing you don't cut up your hands, though. You know, the thorns and all that."

He reached across the table and took my right hand in his. The next thing I knew he was standing again, now behind my chair, moving my hair aside and running his mouth across the back of my neck. Then he pulled my chair away from the table, and it should be noted that what was to unfold occurred with zero argument from me, and pulled me up into his arms and you can imagine where it was all headed. Dinner was ended and dessert was transforming into something infinitely more urgent and specific. The watermelon could wait.

"I'm all done playing with you, Caroline."

"I've been thinking the same thing about you," I said, and felt something like a twinge—no, more like a cramp—deep and low in my abdomen. This had only happened once before in my life, when I was about to sleep with Richard for the first time. My body already knew what my mind was just beginning to grasp. Matthew meant business.

I guess it was around three in the morning when I woke up—or regained consciousness, to be perfectly honest—and my bedroom was ransacked like the scene of a crime. All the pillows were on the floor, the sheets were tangled, and I was lying there in the crook of Matthew's arm with my head on his shoulder. Our heads were at the foot of the bed. I slipped away from him and went to the bathroom to find my robe. Looking in the mirror was a little shocking, to tell you the truth. My lips were swollen and slightly bruised, my mascara was smudged all under my eyes, and my hair was a rat's nest of snarls. My body ached all over from sheer exhaustion. I smelled like his sweat.

Whew, I thought, remembering slowly what had transpired. If this isn't love, it's close enough for me.

My mother, Lavinia, came to mind, uninvited and insistent. I could hear the tinkle of her laughter.

14

The Deep End

A s I STOOD WITH ALL the family watching Belle's graduation procession file into the gymnasium in alphabetical order, I have to confess that there was a tiny sting of discomfort to be reminded that Belle's moment, her whole life in fact, was on the rise and the converse was true for me. My estrogen tank was spitting dust balls. I was the old divorced aunt, cranky and demanding, perhaps because my literal finale was somewhere nearby, just lurking in the shadows around a few more corners. Soon I would grow hairy moles and a mustache, and liver spots would show up all over my hands. I'd be wearing baggy acrylic cardigans with wadded tissues stuffed up my sleeve. I would . . . wait! *Like hell I would!* If and when I reached the cardigan stages of life, I would damn well drape myself in a good quality three-ply fully fashioned cashmere with knitted-in pockets.

And if I grew anything gross on my body, I knew how to find a dermatologist, didn't I? Good grief! Snap out of it, Caroline! But how old would I be when Chloe graduated? Oh, who cares?

At least I had Matthew. But I really shouldn't say "at least" because the truth was that he was anything but the least. Still, these hallmark events were exactly all that, days when the young flew around on an adrenaline high and their elders looked on, remembering the high-flying days of their own youth.

High school graduation meant you were leaving a chunk of your life behind and beginning the deadly serious business of becoming who you wanted to become. Who would Belle become? Had I become who I wanted to be? Good grief, I thought. Maybe there were ten milligrams of something floating around in my purse that would brighten my mood. I dug around, and nothing. Not even a piece of chocolate. But! Take heart, Caroline! There was a peppermint! (This should tell you everything about my state of mind if I was getting jacked up over finding an old mint of unknown origins in the bottom of my bag.) I popped it into my mouth. Chloe was watching me with the keen eye of a turkey buzzard.

"Do you have any more?" she whispered.

"No. Sorry." *You don't need another thing to go in your mouth today,* I wanted to say, but did not.

She looked at me sullenly, as though I had denied her the very air she breathed, but she was quickly distracted by her sister passing our row.

"Belle! Belle!" she said, a little too loudly.

"Shhh! Hush, honey," I said, turning my focus to Belle in her cap and gown.

Belle passed, gave an overt wave and a wink, beaming with pride to have fulfilled the basic requirements to receive her diploma. She was certainly entitled to that glow, but let me tell you, we're talking basic. There was nothing extraordinary on that child's transcript.

She had never been a class officer and never had she joined any clubs. She had never acted in a class play, played a sport, or even sung in a chorus. I wondered if she had even the slightest regret about those missed opportunities and, further, how she would feel when the valedictorian made her speech. Would she be a little jealous? Probably not at all. Just as she was too cool for prom, she was too cool for school. But would a residum of ambition brush off on her and make her want to try harder to distinguish herself in college? I certainly hoped so. Every parent, relative, and friend gathered there in the growing humidity of that nasty, tacky gymnasium that smelled like thousands of dirty old sneakers wanted for these young people to go forth into the world and make something solid and good of themselves. We all wanted to brag about them and to have concrete reasons to be proud.

From the start of the day I could see that Belle was nervous. We had all assembled at Trip's for a graduation breakfast. She had been unable to eat and nearly drove us crazy blathering away like a moody flibbertigibbet. And me? I was harboring a quiet concern that Belle and Linnie's older Spanish boyfriends were going to show up at her party and cause a scene. No one had said whether or not they had been invited. So naturally the busybody in me had to ask to calm my own nerves.

"I'm so nauseous," Belle said. "I'll just drink a Coke. Are there any Cokes in the fridge?"

"She doesn't want pancakes?" Eric said, incredulous that anyone could resist the piles of steaming pancakes that Rusty continued to bring in from the kitchen.

"That's more for us," Amelia said. "Pass 'em over here!"

"Let her starve," Linnie said with typical compassion.

"Why don't you stick it, okay?" Belle said.

"Why don't you?"

"Nice mouth," Amelia observed.

"That's enough, girls!" Trip said, pushing a full forkful into his mouth.

I saw my opening and took it, using the voice of Aunt Demure.

"So, Belle? Linnie? Are Juan and Antonio joining us this afternoon?"

"Puhleese," Linnie said, eyes somewhere around the rafters, indicating I was really completely stupid to ask such a really completely stupid question. "I don't *think* so. We dumped them a week ago."

"Idiots," Belle said. "Seriously. They were total idiots."

"Oh," I said serenely, relieved beyond words and understandably hesitant to ask for the sordid details.

"Would someone kindly pass the sausage, please?" Chloe asked, as though she were a little princess asking for a crumpet.

Chloe had learned that good manners were always rewarded at the Wimbley tables, although lately I had witnessed her consumption of much more than her fair share of everything. The girl was a Hoover. But this was not the morning to remind little Chloe that if she didn't watch her caloric intake, she'd soon become a nasty glutton with a backside as broad as a barn.

"Gag me," Linnie said, and passed the platter to her.

"Be nice," Amelia told her.

"Yeah, pick on a beast your own age," Belle said.

I nodded in halfhearted approval, not that any of these girls had yet given a rat's little pink derriere about gaining my approval, halfhearted or otherwise.

It occurred to me then that beyond slumber parties, this was probably the first real party Belle had ever given. Or had given for her. I couldn't fault her for having some anxiety. My parties still made me a little nervous and it was a very important day after all.

Before we all climbed into our cars to drive to Walterboro, I took her aside. She was wearing a wrap sundress and flats that appeared to be new, and I imagined that Rusty had taken her shopping.

For the first time in months Belle was sporting only the smallest trace of Goth makeup—black lips and eyeliner. I had not told her to tone it down because it made her look like a Gypsy whore. Had Rusty? Or had she done this on her own? Incredible. Maybe she was finally getting my drift?

"You look lovely, Belle. I'm so proud of you," I said, wondering if she was missing her mother. "Are you all right? Do you have your cap and gown all straight?"

"Yep. It's already in the trunk all laid out in a garment bag. Millie pressed it for me when she came over this morning. She was here at like seven-thirty or something. She brought biscuits for us."

"Well, that was nice of her." I smiled, thinking I didn't remember seeing any biscuits. Trip and Chloe had probably eaten them all, right down to the last crumb. "That's good, then!"

"I guess, but then she made me put the stupid thing on, including the cap, and then she took a picture."

"Perfect! Don't you just love her?"

"Um, *not exactly*? I thought it was like major weird, okay? Showing up that early and all. Pretty *rude,* if you ask me."

"Honey, let's be nice today. Millie's family."

"Whatever. Did Dad put the speakers outside?"

"Yes, the speakers are out by the pool."

"Did anyone remember to pick up the cake?"

"Of course!"

"If Rusty screws this up I'll kill her. Watch. Dad will do something really stupid to embarrass me."

"Rusty could plan a party for the queen of England. I cannot vouch for your father."

"Yeah, sure. We'd better get going."

Kids. Appreciative of nothing.

Ah, Millie! Queen of all Baked Goods! Seeing to the details! That was Millie Smoak for you. Of course she wasn't family, but

I'd claim her blood over a lot of other people, present company included. Here's what Belle and maybe more especially Linnie had yet to grasp. In our world, women took care of everything, especially each other, and the art of making each other look good was something that gave us great joy and satisfaction. Lesson one of adulthood was putting the needs or even just the wishes of others before your own and then taking pleasure in making them come to pass. If Belle had an inkling of all Rusty had done to make this day perfect for her, she would be speechless. Wouldn't it be wonderful if by the end of this day, Belle had a new appreciation of Rusty? Rusty certainly deserved some huge accolades for her efforts.

I wondered then if we should have invited Millie to the graduation. Miss Sweetie and Miss Nancy were coming to the barbecue, although they claimed they could only stay for a little while. I was having a WWLD moment. Would Miss Lavinia have made Millie come? Never. Even with all of Mother's eccentricities and grandstanding, she would never have inflicted that kind of wretched invitation on anyone she liked. Graduation ceremonies were an endurance contest, like dance recitals with forty different numbers. You sat for hours, cramped and trapped in an itchy seat, waiting for your precious child to twirl across the stage for a whole whopping two minutes. Ta-da! Millie was smart to take a picture and then wave good-bye. The biscuits were a bonus. Mother would have approved of Millie's ingenuity.

Matthew, bless his heart, had graciously offered to attend but was visibly relieved to learn I couldn't wrangle another ticket, unfathomably highly coveted as they were, even if he was the president of the United States. Well, okay, probably if he was actually the president . . .

Ah, me. Here we are. Another heinous graduation. Three hundred kids. Ugh. I would survive this torturous morning by sending my brain somewhere else and that's exactly what I did. While the principal worked his way through the unfortunate but necessarily long list of announcements, introductions, and the Pledge of Allegiance, I daydreamed about Eric's future. Whatever career that Eric decided to pursue, I knew that he would be brilliant. Yes, he would. He would be rid of his older woman and he would be brilliant. My heart swelled with pride as I studied his profile. Thank you, God, for my gorgeous boy.

While the valedictorian waxed lyrical about how she intended to save the world, fix global warming, end world hunger, and cure cancer, encouraging her class to join her in that quest on whatever road they walked, I pretended I was skiing in the Alps. I was at the top of Four Roses, shushing down to the center of St. Moritz, just in time to grab some *Rösti* and *Weisswurst* for lunch and then to watch the Romanian team practice on the bobsled course while indulging in a hot mug of *Glühwein* to knock the chill off the afternoon. The plan was to snap out of my happy fog when Belle's name was called, just in time to see her collect her diploma. So that's what I did. I daydreamed and daydreamed and soon I was completely lost in another world.

As they began calling the graduates to the stage, I relived every minute detail of my last intimate encounter with Matthew. Every single inch of it, if you know what I mean. In retrospect, this was probably not the wisest indulgence, but there I was, legs in the air, screwing my brains out with him in my imagination, innocently unaware that back in the gym at my little niece's graduation, I was breathing like a marathon runner, sprinting the last few yards to a win. Without even realizing what I was doing, I undid another button of my blouse, swept my hair up with my hand, threw my head back, and was completely busted a split second before taking a ride on that fabulous tsunami of release. I was just about to holler "Woo! Yes! And oh my God!" at the top of my lungs when Chloe yanked hard on my skirt.

"Hey! Are you all right?" she asked, scared out of her mind.

"What?" *Where am I? Oh, no! Wait!* "Yes, of course! I'm fine!"

What was the matter with me? I was completely startled. And I nearly snorted in laughter. Ultimately, I was very grateful for the interruption. It would have been very unseemly for me to experience an operatic moment during this auspicious occasion, but, God in His heaven and all His beloved saints, I was this close to hitting the high notes of my aria. What a dangerous imagination I have! Naughty, naughty auntie! Poor Chloe! The child probably thought I was going into seizures.

"Are you sure, Aunt Caroline? Your face is all red."

"I'm fine, honey. It's just a little warm in here."

"Sure is. Momma used to say it's hotter than the hinges on the back door of hell."

Before I could correct her for speaking of her mother in the past tense or for repeating such an undignified thing in public, they called out Belle's name.

Isabelle Wimbley!

Praise everything holy for the arrival of the *W*s! Trip, Rusty, Eric, Amelia, and Linnie all whooped like raging lunatics. I clapped my hands politely, as I was still composing myself. And giggling to myself. Chloe looked up at me as if she couldn't decide whether to whoop or clap, and unable to make up her mind, she simply jumped up and down in her place for a few moments, which I have to say was perfectly adorable for a little girl to do. Even Chloe, who had red hair like a wolf. Poor thing.

Soon after I had regained my composure and Belle's official graduation had taken place, a crackling recording of "Pomp and Circumstance" poured forth from the speakers and all the graduates filed out. The spectators followed, happy as larks to be liberated from that nasty hellhole of a gym. I would surely have the sulfuric fumes of dirty sneakers coating the back of my throat for a month. Honestly, someone should notify the county health department.

As we were crossing the parking lot I saw a woman and a man

getting into a taxicab from Columbia, a sight rarely seen in this neck of the woods. I would have sworn the woman was Frances Mae wearing large sunglasses. If it was her, she was leaving, which made no sense to me. Maybe it wasn't her. I wondered if anyone else had noticed, but it didn't seem like they had. The parents and kids were too busy taking pictures of themselves to even wonder what a cab from Columbia was doing there.

"What?" Trip said, seeing the quizzical expression on my face.

"Oh, nothing," I said. "I just thought I saw someone, that's all."

"Oh. Hey! There's our girl now! Hey, Miss Graduate!" Trip called.

Belle was completely animated, hugging lots of different girls, presumably her friends, who were just as ebullient, yelling "woo-hoo!" And "yes, we did it!" Their gowns were unzipped and billowing around them in the warm breeze, revealing the clothes they'd chosen for the occasion. Most of the girls were wearing sundresses like Belle's and they all seemed so innocent to me. Young and innocent. Surely I had been that way once. They were smiling and talking a million miles a minute, posing for pictures with each other. They were calling out loudly that they would see each other back at our house in a little while. It seemed to me that the entire class planned to attend and it looked like our Belle was enjoying an unusual moment of popularity. I was doubly glad that the family was giving her a barbecue even if she was a skunk most of the time.

I was in the car with Eric and Amelia. All the others were driving home with Trip and Rusty. On the way back I just listened to my two and enjoyed the easy conversation between them.

"So now Belle's coming to Columbia like Sherman," Eric said.

"Let's hope not. I just hope she grows up a little before August," Amelia replied.

"So it's decided, then?" I asked.

"Yep. God, she was such a little bitch this morning."

"Language!" I said. "It was just nerves, hon."

"Yeah, probably. But you'd better tell her," Eric said. "College is no walk in the park, whatever that means."

"She'll find out on her own. No worries about that. I wonder what Dad got her?"

"I don't know. Hey, Mom? What did Uncle Trip get for Belle?"

An uncomfortable lump of panic presented itself in my throat. Unless Rusty had bought her something, the answer was probably nothing.

"Darlin'? I couldn't guess. But isn't a party like this enough?"

Silence.

And then, "Did we get her something?"

"Of course we did!" No, we didn't. "And, I'm sure Trip has something very special for her."

"Like what?" Amelia said.

"Well now, even if I knew I couldn't tell you, could I? Let's just let her be surprised. Don't you think?"

"Mom and Dad bought me diamond-stud earrings. Dad probably got the same thing for her."

"Whatever. Hey, do you mind if I play some music?" Eric had already plugged in his iPod. "It's Jimmy Buffett, Mom. Just for you."

"Thanks, baby."

The subject was changed, but I knew there was going to be a sinkhole in the day if I didn't produce a gift for Belle. How stupid of me! I felt a flush of guilt that I had not dealt with the issue. The truth was I had thought of it but had resisted going to Crogan's and shelling out the money for something beautiful for her because she was so freaking unpleasant to me. I thought I was standing on higher moral ground. Now I realized that all I was really doing was fanning the flames of her rebellion by not putting her insufferable attitude aside and rewarding her with a gift. Crap. (The usage of *crap* is different and permissible when thrown around silently in my head. I would never say it aloud, except in front of a few people, and only on occasion.) Okay. Fine. My Buddha Within would dig around in my jewelry drawer and see what I could find.

I turned right on Parker's Ferry Road and drove to the dead end and the gate for Tall Pines. Millie or Mr. Jenkins or both of them had attached big bouquets of blue and silver balloons to the gate. Balloons again. They reminded me of Mother and I smiled a melancholy smile.

"Well, if anyone misses the entrance they must be as blind as a bat," I said. "Do y'all want me to drop you off at Trip's?"

"May as well," Amelia said. "My car's there."

"Yeah. And Rusty could probably use a hand," Eric added.

Our wrought-iron gates always startled me with their originality. I used my remote and opened them. I never did discover who had made them, but whoever it was, was an artist. Wild turkeys and ducks decorated their borders and clusters of pine trees stood in the center of each one. When I was a girl the gates were embarrassing to me. Of all the things in my screwed-up life to be embarrassed about, why I chose the gates is anyone's guess, but there you have it.

The road up to our house from Parker's Ferry was a long and slow one because of the potholes in the packed dirt. It was time to repair it again. Along the way I passed under the umbrella of ancient live oaks that dripped with long sheets of Spanish moss. When I was little I used to run around with long pieces of it on my head, pretending to have Rapunzel's hair. Of course this gave me a head filled with chiggers. Millie would wash my scalp with kerosene to kill them while Mother reclined on her chaise, alternating between sipping straight bourbon and swearing a swoon was coming, too grossed out to even look at me. I would be made to take an oath on the family Bibles to never do it again, and of course, the very next week the chiggers would mysteriously reappear at bath time. That was my idea of a wild time. Boy, have things changed.

Years ago my daddy put in some duck ponds on the sides of the road, and the cypress trees he planted were now grown and had turned the water brackish, like black tea. Mother had supervised the planting of stands of palmettos, pampas grass, fuchsia azaleas, and white camellias and let them grow wild until it looked like Mother Nature was the gardener of our naturalized plantings. It was more spectacular than ever.

I pulled around to Rusty and Trip's house and Eric and Amelia got out of the car, slamming the doors. They must have seen me flinch at the noise.

"Sorry!" they said, and laughed.

I lowered my window.

"It's okay. I'm going to change clothes, you know, check on things, and I'll see y'all in a little bit," I said. "Tell Rusty if she needs anything to give me a shout, okay?"

"Will do!"

As soon as I pulled away, I dialed Rusty's cell.

"Hey, it's me. Where are you?"

"Just pulling into our road."

"Oh, okay. Don't say anything, but did you and Trip get something for Belle?"

"Of course! Didn't anyone notice the diamond studs in her ears?"

"No! Wonderful! Okay, I'm almost at my house. If you need anything, call me."

My car rolled to a stop, and I got out, crossed the yard, and opened the kitchen door. Before I could think of a thing, I was overwhelmed by the smell of the roses I had cut the day before. I went immediately through the kitchen to the dining room and on to the living room, half expecting their numbers to have tripled. But that was not the case. Everything was exactly as it had been when I left home in the morning. The fragrance had basically traveled from room to room as though I had sprayed the whole house with flowers. I wondered if the intensity of the fragrance was a sign. Was my Miss Lavinia saying hello? I wished it were so.

"Your rotten granddaughter graduated from high school this morning! You'd think she graduated from Harvard, the way she acted," I called out to the ethers as I climbed the stairs. "You sure didn't miss much!"

I began to rummage around my jewelry drawer. I could have easily put some cash or a check in an envelope, but that seemed too impersonal. If this had been a big party in New York, like a wedding or a Bar Mitzvah, there would have been a decorated box with a slit for envelopes sitting on a table. But down in the Lowcountry we were expected to show our affection for the honoree with something thoughtful and tangible. What did I have that was suitable for a girl her age? Not much.

I looked through all the little boxes and velvet sacks that held a lifetime of collections. Clunky earrings—no good. Ropes of cheap fake pearls à la Chanel—I wouldn't be caught dead in them now, so neither would she. Diamond tennis bracelet—yeah, sure, I was gonna give this child diamonds? I didn't think so. Finally, I came upon a silver Elsa Peretti heart on a chain from Tiffany. Elsa was unfortunately no relation to Rusty. Perfect. In the bottom of the blue suede bag were earrings to match. I couldn't remember when I got them, and I thought, well, actually, that's a good thing because then at least I'm not going to give up some treasure with all sorts of emotion attached to it. My mother came to mind again as I remembered her giving me a diamond pin in the shape of a bow the day I married Richard. I asked her who it had belonged to and she snapped back something like "How should I know? I bought it on Forty-seventh Street yesterday from a nice man named Corey Friedman." She had not wanted to waste an heirloom on a marriage of which she did not approve and I did not want to waste anything of personal value on my niece. There was a strain of cynicism in my DNA!

I put them on the dresser, deciding I would give them a wipe with a silver cleaning cloth to polish them up after I changed. I had a gift bag and some tissue in the kitchen I could use to make it look like I had thought of this long ago. Saved by a minor stroke of deceit.

What had I given Amelia? I remembered it had been a watch, now a perfectly useless gift for anyone under thirty in possession of a cell phone as we know. Was it important that the gifts to my nieces were of the same monetary value? Well, I supposed I was going to get the answer to that before the day was out. The Internet had become an easy way to help the busybodies verify almost anything in seconds. I wasn't about to fret over that either.

After I changed into black linen slacks and a crisp white shirt with *the pearls*, which was all very casual but still elegant, I went to my office for some stationery to write Belle a congratulatory note.

Dear Isabelle,

These earrings and necklace were given to me by my mother, your grandmother, on the occasion of my high school graduation from Ashley Hall so many years ago. I know she is with us today in spirit and that if she could, she would tell you how proud she is of you, as we all are. Take care of these little treasures, darling girl, and take care of yourself, too. We wish you every good thing that life has to offer! Congratulations!

With lots of love,
Aunt Caroline and Eric

I looked at the lies on the page and said out loud, "I'm going straight to hell."

Soon my golf cart was rolling across our property toward Trip's place with Belle's gift on the seat next to me. I was feeling pretty good about the world. I was glad that Belle's graduation had gone smoothly and even more relieved that it had ended without me tripping the light fantastic in front of everyone. I wondered again if that had been Frances Mae in the parking lot. Well, it didn't matter really. If she was coming home, she'd appear at some point, and if she wasn't, she wouldn't. Our clan had dealt with bigger and messier surprises. But she wasn't due back for two weeks. Yikes. In two weeks I'd have to hear her voice and look at her ugly face.

The early-afternoon sun was warm and there wasn't a single cloud in the sky. As I approached Trip's property I could already hear the voices of the kids from beyond the trees. What passed for music these days was blaring and I could smell the burgers on the grill. As they all came into view I was reassured again that we had all done the right thing to throw this shindig. The vibe in the air was happy.

Mr. Jenkins and Trip were cooking together and Millie was helping Rusty organize the buffet table. And there in their midst were Miss Sweetie and Miss Nancy stacking a tower of chocolate-covered strawberries, gossiping and laughing as they worked.

Cars were parked all over the lawn and kids were everywhere, coming in and out of the house, slamming the screen door, laughing and high-fiving each other, throwing each other into the pool. The girls shrieked as they hit the water and the boys chased their next victim. I stood and watched for a moment, sort of mesmerized by their energy. They were fully absorbed in their youthful rhapsody and even I was getting caught up in all the excitement.

Not much had changed since I was their age, except that what was considered decent for a girl's bathing suit seemed to have shrunk to next to nothing, leaving zero to the imagination. And these young men, not all but many of them, probably jocks, appeared to have muscles, rock-hard abs, and biceps with definition. I mean, it's certainly more than improper for me to remark on the virility of a male more than half my age, but between us? Truly, they were impossible not to notice. I wondered where their daddies were? I know, I know. Mea culpa.

Just as my thoughts were turning from borderline evil to full-blown fantasy for the second time that day, I spotted Matthew with three grinning young men in swimsuits, T-shirts, and sunglasses who I correctly assumed were our lifeguards for the afternoon. I worked my way toward them. No wedding rings on any of them. They seemed like they were in their early thirties. What were they saving themselves for? Matthew was wearing shorts and a knit shirt, looking pretty delectable himself.

"Hey, darlin'!" I gave him a hug. "Thanks for coming!" I said as he introduced me to each one of the guys.

"Tough duty," one of them said. "Glad we could help."

"Yeah, it was either young girls in skimpy bikinis or man the speed trap in Jacksonboro. Difficult decision for us," said another, grinning like the proverbial canary-swallowing cat.

"Yes, ma'am, the safety of our young people is our first priority." The third one said this with a straight face and then burst out laughing.

These three stooges were elbowing each other, pointing to various girls, and not the least bit concerned about their silly attitudes or the fact that in some cultures they were old enough to be the fathers of any of them.

"You think those things are real?" Moe said, remarking on a particularly well-endowed young woman. "I mean, whoa, momma!"

"Please tell me they're over twenty-one," Larry said.

"Sixteen is the age of consent," said Curly.

"All right, guys. That's enough," Matthew said, and then shook his head. "Men are dogs. I told them to just keep an eye on the kids, not to use X-ray vision."

"Like they need it? Come on. Let's see if we can help Rusty and Trip and say hello to Miss Sweetie and Miss Nancy. Can I get you something?"

"A glass of tea would be great," he said, and we navigated our way toward the buffet table.

"How about y'all?" I said, calling back to Matthew's guys.

They said they were fine, that they would help themselves when they got hungry or thirsty, not to worry about them.

"Look at these gorgeous strawberries! Wow! Thanks for bringing them!" I hugged Miss Sweetie and popped one in my mouth. "Tho good!"

"Wow! Did you make these?" Matthew asked, and helped himself to one.

"Not only did she make them, *mon cher,* she grew them!" Miss Nancy said, and wiggled her eyebrows at him like a flirty chanteuse. "I'm leaving for France tonight. Three glorious weeks! Anybody want to come along?"

"Miss Nancy is a big flirt," I said, and she smiled, not caring a bit. "Three weeks? Fabulous! Y'all know my friend Matthew Strickland, don't you?"

"Yes, yes! How are you?"

We chatted for a while and it was pretty clear that Mother's oldest and dearest friends were trying to decide if Matthew was a romantic interest or just an old classmate. Wasn't I my mother's daughter? Shouldn't they have known? Their pointed questions made me laugh.

"And so tell me, Matthew, how long have you and Caroline been, um, *friends?*"

"Not long enough," he said, thoroughly confusing them.

They liked him very much and said as we were leaving them, "He's darling, isn't he? Just darling!"

Belle's party seemed to be progressing just as I hoped it would. Belle was surrounded by a group of girls, whispering to each other, laughing, and then whispering again. It did me a lot of good to see her so happy. At that moment the mood all seemed so normal to me. I liked normal. Sometimes.

"Matthew? I want to go in the house to put Belle's gift someplace safe. Want to come with me?"

"Nah, I'm thinking about a burger, to tell you the truth. When I got here I wasn't even hungry, but you know how it is, you smell food and the next thing you know, you're starving. Can I get you one?"

"Sure, why not? No cheese! I'll be right back."

"Got it!"

I hurried up the back steps and crossed the back porch into the kitchen, looking around for a spot. There were some other gifts on the table, so I put our gift bag there with the others, sort of tucked away, in case there was a hooligan in the crowd with sticky fingers. You could never be too sure. And wouldn't you know it, just then a nice-looking young man came in through the back door. His bathing suit was dry, so I didn't have to give the "don't drip on the floor" lecture. I assumed he was looking for the bathroom, so I pointed in its direction.

"Down the hall on the left?"

"Right! Thanks!"

I watched his back and just then a girl came out of the powder room and he handed her a little sack that zipped to close, the kind of thing a woman might throw in a big purse to hold her powder and lipsticks. Well, if that's what they were used for, what was he doing with it? I smelled something fishy. Maybe it didn't have lipsticks and powder in it? I decided to follow the girl but to keep my distance. She was oblivious anyway. She sailed right past me and out the door, across the lawn, and down toward the dock. I left the house quickly in search of Matthew.

"Come with me," I said when I found him. "I think there's some nonsense going on."

I was right. As we made our way toward the dock, where six or seven kids were huddled, we hid behind one live-oak tree and then darted to another. One kid left and then two followed. I was sure that if anyone was watching us we looked as ridiculous as Inspector Clouseau in an old *Pink Panther* movie, on a mission to solve a crime. But one thing was for sure—we smelled weed.

When we were about thirty feet away, Matthew decided to take a good look and see who was left down there.

"You're not gonna like this," he whispered after taking a risky gander at the scene.

"What now?"

"Your little niece Linnie is down there blowing a doobie."

"Um, I don't think they say 'doobie' anymore. But let's go kick some butt anyway."

We walked toward their cloud of smoke and laughter and they never even saw us coming.

"Holy shit," one kid said when he saw us.

"Let's have the drugs, son," Matthew said.

Everything happened so fast. The kid with the joint threw it in the river and he was just about to toss the sack when Matthew caught his arm in midair and took it.

"I said, I'll take that," he said.

"He's a fucking cop," Linnie said. "Thanks to my lovely aunt, we're busted."

"Police brutality!" the same kid yelled.

"Thanks to *me*?" I said. "Did you get drugs from me? I don't *think* so, Linnie."

Matthew continued to hold the boy's arm in the air. "You don't know shit about brutality, you little asshole, so why don't you just shut the hell up while I decide whether or not to take y'all down to the station."

"Matthew!" I said, mildly shocked by his language. I pulled out my cell phone and called Trip.

The remaining kids tried to slip around us but Matthew blocked their way. "Stay right where you are," he warned, holding another guy by the arm.

"Take your hands off me, dude," a young man with a ponytail said. "I know my rights."

"Dude?" Matthew said. "Really? Dude?"

"I wouldn't call him dude if I were you." I waited for Trip to answer his cell.

"Who do you think you're calling?" Linnie said to me, very angry.

Who did *I* think I was calling? Did she really say that? To *me*?

"Like it's any of your business? I think the better question is, just *who* do you think you *are*?" I gave her the quadruple flaming eyeball and the Greenwich, Connecticut, jaw of steel. Trip answered right away. "Trip? Dockside, right now. Yep."

"Like what I do is any business of yours?" she replied.

That was when the reasonable Aunt Caroline became the living embodiment of the cumulative fury of every Wimbley who had so much as a drop of our blood in their veins. I was smoldering, white-hot mad, wildly furious in a way I had not been in years. My insides were quaking and I knew I was about to completely lose my temper on behalf of generations.

Trip appeared then, running down the hill, hell-bent for leather, probably thinking that one of the kids had jumped off the dock and cracked his head wide open. Rusty was right behind him.

"What's all this?" Trip demanded, out of breath. "Linnie? What's going on?"

Matthew held up the evidence—a baggie of pot and some rolling papers from the confines of a lady's cosmetic bag.

"Oh, Linnie!" Rusty said, so much more nicely than I would have. "How could you? Today of all days?"

"How could I? How could I? What! Are you kidding me? Did it bother you to ruin my family? You fucking whore!"

Trip lunged for her and I stepped in, giving Linnie that so-overdue and so-well-deserved slap right across her face. In that split second I knew Trip would have strangled Linnie and right in the moment I decided it would be better if I took care of her. My hand stung as though I had laid it across a hot burner on my stove.

"Ow!" She burst into tears. "Daddy! How can you stand by and let her—"

"Save your tears, Linnie," Trip said, still furious.

"What should we do here?" Matthew asked him. "Trip? This is your property. What do you want to do with these young reprobates? Should we throw them in the river and feed 'em to the gators? Not much meat on 'em, though."

"No. As attractive as that sounds, just guessing we'd probably never hear the end of it. So why don't you all go on home and never come back? How's that? Now. And, Linnie? Go to your room. I'll deal with you later."

The kids scattered like a handful of marbles tossed on a granite floor, all except Linnie.

"I really, really, really hate my life," she said, tears streaming down her face.

"Move it," Trip said.

"Well! You didn't set much of an example here today, did you?" I said.

"Wha-ev-vah!" she said, and stomped off the dock. "Honest to God!"

Linnie continued to curse loud enough for us to hear her until she reached the house. Rusty, Trip, Matthew, and I just stood there in a kind of stunned disbelief.

"Millie's not going to like this," I said. "Is there no end to Linnie's defiance?"

"She'll only know if you tell her," Matthew said.

"Pal? Millie Smoak knows all and sees all," Trip said. "Don't ask me how."

"I thought pot was supposed to mellow you out and make you think everything was funny," Rusty said.

"Linnie has issues," Trip said. "Her sense of humor is greatly impaired."

"Well, I think it's disgraceful," I said. "I would no more have smoked pot on my mother's dock than I would have jumped off the Cooper River Bridge."

Matthew was strangely silent.

"What are you thinking?" I said to him.

"Ah, honey. I think pot, while it's still illegal . . . well, it isn't the worst thing in the world. I see kids doing meth and much worse stuff than this. Heroin. You have no idea."

"Are you serious? This is no big deal?" I was shocked.

"May I say something?" Rusty said.

"Of course," Trip said.

"Number one, I really think her defiance is a cry for attention. It's so over-the-top that it's ridiculous, isn't it? And number two, she's probably very jealous of her sister today and was trying to look like a big shot with the older kids. I mean, the pot wasn't hers, right? Anyway, I wouldn't be so hard on her."

"She called you a whore, Rusty!" I said. "That's unforgivable!"

"Look, in her heart she knows I'm okay. She's just a kid, angry with the world. Come on, we're letting this juvenile drama ruin Belle's party, and besides, I'm hungry!"

Matthew nodded and looked at Trip, who was radiating love for Rusty's kind heart. I was still pissed off in purple, paisley, plaid, and lavender, as we say around here.

We began walking back to the party and Matthew looped his arm around my shoulder.

"Come on now," he said. "Let's lighten up. This is a party for your niece, right? It's a happy occasion."

"So everyone thinks I'm an old prune, huh?"

"No one called you old, Caroline."

I punched him in the arm, jokingly of course, and he slapped my backside. I really needed the balance he brought to my life. The question was, what did I bring to his?

15

The Unforeseen

THE HURRAH BROKE UP AROUND six o'clock when all the graduates were obliged to return to their homes for supper and other,
smaller family parties. All over Walterboro, marinated chicken and
rib eyes sizzled on smoky grills, steaming casseroles were being
pulled from hot ovens, prewashed salads were tossed, and celebra-
tory sheet cakes, personalized with congratulations by the nice lady
in the bakery at Wal-Mart, were being admired. I sighed in agreement with misty-eyed parents all around Colleton County, recount-
ing the day and saying how nice was that Wimbley barbecue, wasn't
it nice? While they talked about Tall Pines and what they thought
of all of us and all we had, they silently struggled to sort out the
confusing emotions that came with their child taking another next
step toward leaving the nest the same way we did. Family members

hugged each other, mothers and fathers expressing their worries in whispers about how their children would fare at universities farther away than a day's drive. What if Mary got sick? What if Johnny needed something? And what about those children not headed to college but to Iraq or Afghanistan? It made me quake with fear to think of Eric in uniform. I could already see the nightmares that would wake me up every night, drenched in sweat. No matter how hard I tried, I would be unable to erase the image of my only boy seriously injured. No, no. We were lucky, blessed beyond reason, to have our two and soon three children just under an hour away at the University of South Carolina. I was grateful to God and everything holy for that peace of mind. Every mother and father knows these things are true.

Matthew was on duty that night, so he left a little early, and the Wonder Boys, who collected a few phone numbers from some of the pretty girls, had been paid and gone on their way. Eric was outside cleaning the grill with Trip and Mr. Jenkins and putting all the foam noodles in the shed, placing the lounge chairs back where they belonged.

Rusty and I were still in the kitchen washing dishes and putting everything back in its place while Amelia and Belle dried what seemed like dozens of forks, knives, and spoons. Millie gathered up all the sopping-wet pool towels, wrung them out, and had the washing machine humming the soothing music of white noise as she folded another warm and sweet-smelling load right from the dryer.

Linnie was upstairs sleeping off the pot after hell rained all over her in the form of a very stern lecture from her father. I overheard it all from the hall outside her bedroom.

"Drugs are not okay, no way, no how!" he said. "I don't care if it's just pot and not meth or something worse. If you want the keys to your car back, you'd better turn yourself around immediately. No more sass! Do you hear me?"

"Yes, Daddy."

She sure sounded sarcastic to me.

"And I expect you to apologize to Rusty for what you said. Is that crystal clear?"

"I'm sorry, Daddy."

Really? How about not in a million years?

"Don't tell me, tell her! Now you stay here until you're fit company."

"Sorry, Daddy."

She didn't mean a word of it.

I scurried to the hall bathroom because I heard him coming. He was so mad he didn't even accept her apology. I surely didn't want to be caught eavesdropping! Not with him in *that* mood! And, I wasn't quite my mother yet, because let me tell you, she would have opened Linnie's door and added her two cents to Trip's! I didn't.

Chloe was napping, too, having thrown up for the second time in just days, but this time from overeating. A bunch of Belle's less enlightened classmates were the culprits behind her humiliation. Earlier in the afternoon, they kept giving her hot dogs and counting how many she could eat, egging her on. Then they started calling her Goat Girl, laughing and saying she'd eat any kind of garbage they put in front of her. Belle rose to the occasion and was furious with all of them and rightfully so, and told them to hit the road.

"I can't believe y'all can't be nice to my little sister? What kind of jerks are you?"

In a rare moment of big-sister love, she tried to impress on Chloe that she had to learn to think for herself and to learn to stand up for herself. So while poor misguided Chloe retched over a garbage can, Belle was heard pleading with her to grow up.

"Oh, Chloe, it's okay. Listen, those guys suck. We should have invited some kids your age. You can't be messing around with kids that much older than you, you know?"

"I want my momma! I'm sick!"

"I know, honey, so do I."

I had not loved hearing that, but then I had to remind myself that Belle had graduated from high school without her mother there and she was probably feeling bad about it.

"I worry about that kid," she said later on as we cleaned the kitchen. "What's going to happen to her when I'm not around to watch her back?"

Had our Belle grown a heart and a conscience that very day?

"I had the same worry about you," Amelia said, "but you managed."

"I'm just saying she can't count on Linnie like I used to count on you."

"Yeah, Linnie is like beyond beyond!" Amelia said. "And she doesn't have the greatest judgment about stuff either."

"Listen, it took forever, but I finally came to the conclusion that it ain't worth it to be a badass. I mean, what was I thinking all this year? Linnie will grow up eventually."

So, our Belle had decided to grow up, too? Praise God! Two down, two to go!

"She was just trying to impress the seniors," Rusty said.

"Humph," Millie said, and changed the subject. "Poor little Chloe was so upset. Make me angry to see how them older children pick on a little girl. Ain't right. You 'sposed to look out for the least. Says so in the Bible, 'eah?"

"I agree," I said.

Rusty chimed in with, "Well, there's some truth to all of what y'all say."

"Like what?" I asked.

"Well, like Belle says, it doesn't seem that Linnie is as concerned with Chloe's well-being as I'd like to see either. I don't know, I guess . . . look, Chloe is real sweet, but she's a goofy little girl, you know? She's lightning smart one minute and then in the next she's all silly and desperate to impress anyone who will give her two seconds of attention. She needs to learn how to say no. I mean, she'll grow past this awkward stage, I'm pretty sure about that. But right now she's kind of a mess. I mean, the worst thing is to grow up to be a pleaser. You all know what I'm saying?"

And as though the Council of Satan had orchestrated it, there stood Chloe in the doorway. She was embarrassed again, although unsure of exactly why. It wasn't that Rusty had really said any one thing that was unfairly critical of her; it was that Rusty had said anything at all. Rusty barely had the young highnesses' permission to speak to them much less voice opinions. Chloe started to wail and I thought, Oh Good Lord, here we go again! Please bring this crazy roller coaster of a day to an end.

Millie took Chloe by the hand. "You just a little girl and it's not your fault. Those big kids oughta be horsewhipped! Now come let Millie wash your face, 'eah?"

"Okay," Chloe said, and sniffed.

I had only raised one son but it occurred to me then that I could raise ten lovely sons, one hundred beautiful sons, for the time and energy spent to raise one half-assed daughter. My mother had probably felt the same way, God rest her soul.

Later that night, when it seemed that reasonable order had been restored in Rusty and Trip's house and in the world of all those girls, I was finally back at my house, sitting in the kitchen with Millie. Eric had stayed behind to play some games with the girls. Anybody playing video games that much couldn't be too deeply embroiled in a hot affair, I told myself. Millie and I were exhausted. I was sipping on what had to be my nineteenth glass of iced tea for the day, knowing I'd be up half the night from all the caffeine.

"So, how was the actual graduation?" Millie asked.

"Dreadful," I said. "As expected. They're all the same. But listen. Want to hear something very strange?"

"Tell it."

"I could have sworn I saw Frances Mae there. She was with a man. Right after the whole rigmarole was done and we were outside in the parking lot. This woman wearing big sunglasses climbed into a cab from Columbia. She looked just like her. Do you think she might have flown back just for the day? Is that even possible?"

"Chile? Anything is possible with that woman. Maybe she was there with a nurse or something. A bodyguard?"

"I'd bet anything that it was her. I mean it stands to reason. I wouldn't miss my child's graduation unless I was in ICU."

"Me either."

"Yeah, well, I'm embarrassed to say this, but I'm still hungry. What's the matter with me?"

"Me, too. I don't like no hot dogs. That ain't food. You want me to see what we got?"

"Why not? I think there's some leftover ravioli that Eric had yesterday."

"Humph. That ain't food either." She went to the refrigerator and began to forage, pulling plastic containers out and pushing them across the counter. "All this needs to be thrown out. What are we saving this for? A hurricane? And what was I thinking we was gonna do about dinner? I should have taken something out of the freezer."

"If I miss a meal I won't die from starvation. It's okay."

But Millie was already reorganizing the contents of the freezer and had pulled out two large containers of soup.

"Okra soup or split pea. Pick one."

"There are some chunks of ham in the okra soup, I hope? I need protein."

"Girl? You gone off your rocker? Show me some okra soup that ain't got no ham hock in it and that dishwater been make by a Yankee hand. Humph. Okra it is."

"Okra soup sounds dandy to me!" I got up and preheated the oven to four hundred degrees. "I'm making corn bread."

"You hear me complaining?"

"Nope." I took eggs and milk from the refrigerator and a bowl from the cabinet. "So how did you like Little Miss Linnie's behavior this afternoon? I knew she was up to no good. I could feel it in my bones."

"Humph. You need to rely on them bones more than you do, 'eah? Bones don't lie." She put the container in the microwave and set the timer.

"You're probably right. Did you hear that I gave her a good slap right across her face? It was only about a year overdue."

Millie stopped in her tracks and looked at me like I had lost my mind. "You did *what?*"

I took a deep breath. There was no way I was going to take any grief about slapping *that* foulmouthed child. "Look, Millie. I never slapped a child in my life who didn't deserve it, but this was too much. She was so out of control she called Rusty an *F*-ing whore."

"What? What are you telling me? Please don't tell me this."

"Yep. In front of her father. She was down on the dock smoking pot with some of her friends, or rather Belle's friends, and Matthew and I caught her." I told her the rest of the story. "Trip was in a midair lunge, on the way to snapping her neck in two. I stepped in between them, thinking a slap from me was the lesser of two evils. I mean, Millie? What would you have done?"

"Law. I don't like hitting and slapping. You know that, 'eah? Goes against everything I stand for. But maybe sometimes a chile needs something to shake 'em up. Specially that knucklehead."

"You can say that again. Listen, Trip was so angry with her I might have saved her life. But I'm sure she hates my guts now."

"Humph. Don't worry about that. I put all kinds of Bach Remedies in them biscuits and I guess it don't work on her." She took two soup bowls from the cabinet and two large spoons from the drawer. "Got a mind like two mules."

"Yeah, she sure does. Linnie is a big problem. Big problem."

"I'm not so sure."

"What do you mean?"

"That Linnie is just a young girl feeling her oats for the first time. By and by, she'll come around. You'll see." Millie sighed deeply and then said in a low voice, "No, she ain't the big problem."

"Well then, what is?" Millie sank into a kitchen chair and patted the table. She meant for me to sit with her for a minute. "Let me just get this mixed and in the oven."

"All right. Okay. Look. I gone tell you something now and iffin you repeat it? I'm coming after you with my long scissors to snip out your tongue, you 'eah me?"

I zipped my lip and crossed my heart. "What's going on?"

"This ain't no joke." Millie raised her chin in the air and set her jaw in a sorrowful and forbidding frown. "A blackbird got in my house this morning."

"Oh, no. Oh, Millie. Oh, no."

I stopped stirring my batter and looked at her. A cold chill came over me from the top of my head right down to the tips of my toes. Someone, some dark and fearsome thing, had walked over my own grave. I shivered again and as quickly as I could I sat in the chair opposite her.

In the Gullah culture of the Lowcountry, a bird in the house was a terrible, terrible omen. It meant imminent death, death that was unexpected, or one that would befall someone long before their time. Here was the warning to prepare ourselves for a catastrophe, and because we had been given this information, there might be a price for us to pay as well. A piece of favorite jewelry would go missing for a while or money would disappear from your bank account. Or maybe you would catch the flu. We needed to pray for protection. Millie always said this kind of thing was the work of the Ajogun, evil spirits that roamed the earth on a mission to destroy human lives. I felt weak and sick inside.

"Do you remember when your daddy passed? I had all them crows tapping on my windows?"

"I remember."

"And when Miss Lavinia went to glory? Birds came down the chimneys. I had to chase the devil with a broom to get them out of my house."

"I know it. I remember." I got up from nerves, needing to move to stop my own trembling. I poured the corn-bread batter into a pan and slid it into the oven. "What can we do, Millie?"

"I think it's time for me to do something big 'cause I got a bad feeling about this. Very bad. And I need you to help me."

"Millie?"

"What?"

"Who's the target?"

"I don't know. I gots to ask Oya."

Oya was Millie's favorite goddess of her African Ifa religion.

We ate our soup and corn bread in relative silence, pausing now and then to add a detail to the plan. First, we had to pray for protection. We would go to Millie's to begin all the old rituals. Then we had to keep praying. If a week or so went by and nothing horrible happened, we could hope it was just a crazy bird. But the odds on that weren't very good. Once the bird was in the house, that was it.

If you could be reluctant and anxious at the same time, that's exactly what we were. We did a hasty cleanup of the kitchen, grabbed a few things we needed, and seconds later we were out the door, on Millie's golf cart, and on our way to her house. I saw Millie pack a very small container of the soup and slip it into her pocket along with a spoon.

As we bumped along the yard I said, "That's for Daddy and Mother?"

"Yes, ma'am."

It was going to be a long night. Millie's profile was chiseled and resolute. My heart continued to palpitate, causing my breath to come in spurts. I was very fearful.

Millie's cottage was well tended by her and evidence of Mr. Jenkins's talents was everywhere, too. Her porch was in perfect repair, her shutters glistened from a recent coat of paint, and tiny pink and white flowers tumbled from her flower boxes among the cascading ferns. The cushions of her rockers and porch swing were covered in a tropical print of large green leaves and exotic fuchsia blooms. It was very inviting and welcoming and completely betrayed the serious nature of what went on behind her closed doors. We went inside.

"Wash your hands, too," she said as she thoroughly scrubbed her own.

Clean hands were an essential step in beginning the rituals for far more important reasons than cleanliness. In many cultures, water is the element that washes away sin, illness, and every kind of negative influence from the outside world. If you come into a friend's house from traveling or shopping, you wash your hands before you sit down to eat. If you come into Millie Smoak's house to convene with her African deities, you had better be sure your hands are clean *and* your heart *and* your mind. In my life I had seen more than enough proof—if you screwed with the deities, they'd screw with you. Millie's brand of religion was a two-way street. Washing hands was a small sign of respect.

Since my return to Tall Pines and my divorce from Richard, and most especially since my mother had gone on to her great reward, Millie and I had grown closer, particularly in matters relating to her spiritual practices. We talked about them all the time, referring to different spirits in the course of casual conversation as though we were talking about our good friends. I still wasn't sure what or who I believed in, among her pageant of spirits, but the results from her prayers, trances, potions, and so forth were astounding. I always said, when Millie prayed, Millie got answers. Truthfully, we didn't always get the answer we wanted, but we got an answer. Millie seemed unusually worried this time and so I was going to participate in her ceremony with all I had. My insides were roiling and I felt wobbly. What did the warning mean? Death for who? I strongly suspected that Millie already knew and I begged my God to protect my child. And then to protect us all.

First, Millie threw a long white garment over her clothes that resembled a priest's surplice. Next, she tied her red silk sash around her waist and opened the door to her residential place of worship.

What would have been a closet filled with old trench coats and umbrellas in the front hallway of most people's homes was an altar in Millie's. There were tiers of shelves like steps that ran from the floor almost to the ceiling, all draped in white cloth. On the shelves were gourds decorated with feathers, cowrie shells strung like necklaces, bowls of herbs, dried flowers tied with ribbons, pictures of my family that were so old the edges were curled with age, candles of various colors that represented different deities, a standing crucifix, and statues of different Christian and Catholic saints. Jesus, Mary, and Joseph were there in various configurations and Saint Anthony, of course, was alongside Saint Francis of Assisi and Saint Christopher—another holy triumvirate. In between them were small clay statues of Ori, Obatala, Eshu, Oshun, Ogun, Shango, and the rest of the sixteen angels, and of course, a larger one of Oya, her favorite.

When I was really little I had played house with them, pretending they were a family of dolls. Millie used to tell me stories about them all. Each one of the angels stood for a particular quality and their purpose was to remind us to always look for the highest potential and the godlike qualities in everything and everyone. Basically, it was the golden rule of treat others as you would like them to treat you. With respect. In general, that was a pretty good philosophy that would serve anyone well.

I knew that Millie considered herself to be a devout Christian, but she gave equal weight to the angels or the orisha of her Yoruban religion of Ifa, in which Millie still reigned as high priestess. For all my life, people came around looking for Millie's help to mend their broken hearts or to solve money problems, or for advice on finding a better job. Some people thought she could remove spells or *plateye* and that she could send the Hag to ride their enemies. I had no doubt she could do all those things and more because those same people came back time and again to see Millie Smoak. They brought her flowers, fresh fish, or a pecan pie but never money. Millie refused to take money, saying it was wrong and that her spirits would be offended if she did, that it was wrong to take money for helping people through the angels.

As a child, when I had trouble I would give that trouble over to Millie. She always made me feel better. More important, she made Trip and me feel loved when we probably weren't. She had been on hand for every important event of our lives, celebrating with us, mourning with us, and taking pride in all our accomplishments. And when we got too big for our britches and needed a good talking-to? Millie was the only one who could make us feel remorse and get us back on the right path. We cared what she thought of us. So my affection, our affection, for her was lifelong and profound.

For the very first time, Millie handed me a length of red silk and told me to tie it around my waist. I took this as an indication of the depth of her concern.

"And stand by to light the candles, too," she said in a low and serious voice.

Did accepting the silk and wearing it mean that I was now a member of the Church of Millie Smoak (population two) or what? By Millie's mood, I knew we needed all the help we could get, and the full support of Oya, the Wind, who could blow our worries away. I tied the sash around my waist as fast as I could. Whatever I could do to bring about protection and safety for our loved ones superseded any uncertainties or cynicism I felt.

She sprinkled some water on the floor and lit the red candle, designated for the god Eshu Elegba. She called out, *"Iba! Elegba esu lona!"* It had been a while since I had attended one of Millie's ceremonies but I remembered that Elegba was sort of the King of the Road into the spirit world. If you were trying to contact a female deity, it was best if you showed your respect for Elegba first. Then Millie went into a series of what might best be described as deep genuflections, except they were far more dramatic. Her right hip touched the floor, followed by her left shoulder, and then she reversed the process. This was to let the god know she was trying to contact a female and would he please tell the other male elders that she needed to gain entrance into their realm.

Next, she lit a candle for Oya the Wind, the great warrior, who, in addition to all her other powers, had psychic abilities. She picked up a small, carved box of frankincense and spooned some of it onto several bricks of charcoal along with wood chips of cedar and dried acacia leaves. She lit them carefully with an almost inverted black candle, fanned the smoke into the air with a swirling motion, like a conductor of an orchestra trying to rouse the strings to a full crescendo. Next she took two gourds from the altar and handed me one. She called out in Yoruban to Oya, knelt on her prie-dieu, and closed her eyes. Every so often she would raise her gourd and rattle it, and when she did, I gave mine a good shake. Soon she was lost in a trance, eyelids fluttering, bouncing her jaw up and down, nodding emphatically as though she were in conversation with someone I could not see. Strange as this may seem, I could sense a real change in the atmosphere of the room, like there was someone else there with us. Someone or something. The air became very heavy as though a storm were coming. Oya was also the goddess of storms.

I stood a few feet away, watching, waiting. Millie's brow became knitted in seriousness, and perspiration ran down the sides of her face. I had never seen her perspire before and it frightened me. Suddenly and inexplicably, I did not have a single bone to support me. I felt myself sliding down the wall to the floor, where I sat in a puddle of disorientation and confusion. There was something wrong with my vision. Everything was covered in a cloudy mist, as opaque as any fog that ever washed the Lowcountry. I could feel tremendous pressure in my ears and my heart was racing faster and faster. Millie was shaking her gourd and I could not respond. I closed my eyes and then there was nothing. The next thing I knew, Millie was shaking my shoulder.

"Wake up! Come on, Caroline! Let's wake up!"

"I'm up! What happened?" I scrambled to my feet and ran my hands through my hair. I must have been some sight.

"You okay?"

"Yes! I'm fine! What happened?"

"Humph. You tell me!" Millie grabbed my jaw, squinted hard, and looked in my eyes. "Humph," she said again. Then she felt my pulse. Deciding I was fine, she dropped my wrist. "You's fine. Just fainted. Too much action for you. Come on, we got to get going now!"

"Fine! Let's go!"

I untied the sash and handed it to her and she looped it around the neck of the hanger along with hers. I blew out the candles and she put a bowl over the charcoals to kill the last sputters of burning incense.

"We need rusty nails, sumac root, and red pepper. And basil.

Evil can't go where basil was. And some bay-laurel leaves. And goofer dust."

"But goofer dust is killing powder, Millie. Isn't it?"

The word *goofer* comes from *kufwa,* which is a Congolese term meaning "to kill" and it was used in dark rituals to literally snuff out the candles of an enemy.

"Not how I use 'em. You going against me?"

"What? Heavens no! Not in a million years."

Yeah, sure, like I thought I knew more than Millie about this kind of thing? Even after all the years of witnessing what she did, you could still put all I knew in a thimble.

"I'm spreading it on the road, to stop the evil from coming on our land. When it's put together with them nails, the sumac, and red pepper, it becomes powerful cunja for protection. You remember that?"

"I'll never forget it."

As you might guess, *cunja* was the bastardized version of *conjure,* like the Hatfields and the McCoys, who were always conjuring up something to fight about. Over time the verb became a noun and popular usage altered the definition to mean "tool." Millie knew every tool in her garden and shed.

"And we gone leave bay leaves and basil on all our doorsteps. Iffin that don't bring peace to our world, then I don't know what."

We left the house by her back door with a flashlight, a jar of red pepper, a small sack of dried bay leaves, and a fistful of rusty nails that Millie kept in a coffee can in her pantry. We went straight to her garden so that she could gather the herbs she needed, and when we had them all tucked into a brown paper sack, we got back on the golf cart, heading for the family chapel and to pay Miss Lavinia and my deceased father, Mr. Nevil, a late-night visit.

"You know why you fainted, don't you?"

"No. The last time I fainted was a million years ago."

"Well, we're fighting some powerful evil, Caroline. I needed your energy to reach Oya. I wasn't satisfied until I was sure I was in her presence and I borrowed a little juice from you. Only 'cause I had to."

"Nice." Could she really do that? Glom onto my grid like a poacher with Southern Carolina Electric and Gas? Apparently.

"I'm sorry but I'm getting on, you know. Pretty soon I need to be thinking 'bout retirement. Either you're taking over or all I know goes with me."

"Ah, Millie. Can we talk about this another time? I mean, what happened to your training with Eric? For the longest time, I thought that you had him on the hook."

It was true that I was fascinated by Ifa and all that Millie did, but did she really think a white woman, a less than devout Episcopalian who owned a plantation in South Carolina, could carry on the root work and spells that began with her ancestors in Nigeria and then the Caribbean hundreds of years ago? I had serious doubts. And I couldn't believe she didn't.

"Humph. Eric. Sweet boy. Had 'em and lost him. He got so interested in the world that he probably doesn't remember the first thing I taught him."

"Which was?"

"Iffin your nose be itching? Somebody gone fight with you."

I laughed then, remembering all those things Millie used to tell me when I was little—that you had better throw salt over your left shoulder on a new moon or else you'd see haints walking, or that if you dropped a fork, company was coming, or that a hat on the bed meant death, or that it was bad luck to bring fruit into the house in odd numbers. The exception, of course, was three. Three of anything was good. Trip and I had spent our childhoods looking for signs and full of wonder over the unseen world that existed all around us. And we found signs all the time because of the direction in which Millie had hurled our trajectories.

We passed the old icehouse and windmill, mere curiosities now, as they had not been used in decades. Next we went by the barns where we once kept our horses and the kennels where Trip's hunting dogs lived when they weren't on the end of his bed. Finally the greenhouse came into view, where Millie nursed her herbs and Mr. Jenkins babied his Meyer lemon trees all winter long. We made the turn on a tiny road paved with broken oyster shells and hard-packed dirt. The slim cross over the family's chapel came into view high on the crest of a bluff that reigned over the Edisto River. We were there. The small building's Romanesque dusky-gray silhouette loomed large against the dark blue sky. I had to admit it was eerie, like something from an old episode of *Dark Shadows*. Our small family graveyard stood off to the side, built up with brick coping and surrounded by wrought-iron pickets and low brick columns to create an enclosure. It had a special charm of its own.

When Trip and I were little, we played there like mad, absolutely convinced it was haunted, and even now I am certain it was and is. The creaking old chapel was our clubhouse until our mother ruined it with a renovation, restoring it to suit her purpose of making a supper club and concert hall for chamber ensembles. On her death I had changed it back into a chapel, supervising the reinstallation of the pews from their storage place in the barn after Mr. Jenkins refinished them. The stained-glass windows were repaired and polished to a sparkle. The heart-pine floors were waxed and waxed until you could nearly see your face in them. Everything received two fresh coats of paint. It was beautiful and I imagined it looked very much like it had generations ago.

At the far end of the chapel was a small riser that had served as the altar so many years ago. The original altar had been removed aeons ago and now a round table with intricate inlay stood in its place with a beautiful Chinese blue-and-white vase. As often as time allowed, I filled it with branches of crepe myrtle, magnolia leaves, and roses. Always roses when they were in bloom, because Mother had loved them so. Then, with Millie's advice and input from Miss Sweetie and Miss Nancy, we chose pictures of Mother by season and framed them in silver, changing them often. Crogan's found a silversmith for us who engraved a beautiful plaque with her name and dates, and on the first anniversary of her death, we affixed it to the wall at eye level, next to the niche where her picture stood behind a beveled-glass door, smiling out at us. Every time I looked at her picture I was struck by her electric verve. She seemed alive even on paper. Our stunningly pretty mother had an unmatched zest for life and love and people, and she was full of more beans than they had in Boston. God, I missed her so. I missed her every single day and night and I always would.

This was our shrine of remembrance for her and it certainly did the job. I loved to come here with flowers, to change her pictures or to buff her plaque. I'd take a seat in a pew to meditate and just think about life. As much as I loved to hang around the dock, I think I did so mainly because of its proximity to the house. The fact was that there was no spot on our property so imposing as the bluffs that held the crypts of my great-great-great-grandparents and every relative who had gone on before us. But the crypts occupied the prime real estate. My first ancestors to be laid to rest in this country were positioned to catch the breathtaking sunsets and the breezes from the river. They could smell the breath of Oya, who hummed to them, sweet songs with easy words to help them rest.

On many afternoons I had come here with Eric to share an apple and a story about our past. We would climb right on top of the enormous cement crypts and discuss the legacy of those brave soldiers from all the wars underneath the elaborate headstones or the babies in the tiny graves who had died from yellow fever or smallpox. When we ran out of facts, mindful of our southern heritage, we just made things up and entertained each other with whatever kind of fabrication we could invent.

But there was no fabricating anything that night. Millie and I were there for a specific reason. We rolled the golf cart to a stop and sat there for a few moments.

"I really should put some foundation lighting out here," I said. "It's as black as pitch."

"Yeah? How often you come out here at night?"

"Almost never."

"Well then, save your money. Come on. Let's go now."

"Well, you sure are snippy tonight!"

"Humph."

Millie, who was the greatest stoic I have ever known, was unusually nervous.

We approached the graveyard carefully, as the ground was very uneven. Millie and I held on to each other's arm as we climbed the three steps to the gate, and I reached forward to push it open. It was stuck and moving it required me to put my weight against it. The stalwart gate, was so furious for the disturbance that it howled and screeched like a thousand owls from hell as I pushed it open wide enough for us to pass through.

Great, I thought, they're coming to get us.

"I'll remind Mr. Jenkins to oil this thing," Millie said.

"Yeah," I said, "it needs it."

I wondered if an oiling would make the screech disappear. Around here, things had a way of howling when they felt like it. Inanimate objects were believed to have a spirit just as the warm-blooded creatures did. Part of the deceased continued to hover, meddling in your daily affairs when they saw a need or had an urge.

We tiptoed around to my father's grave, where Millie and I sat down on the brick wall surrounding it and read the headstone.

JAMES NEVIL WIMBLEY II

1927–1974

BELOVED HUSBAND AND FATHER

"Sunset and evening star,
And one clear call for me!
And may there be no moaning of the bar,
When I put out to sea."
—Tennyson

"Your daddy always did love Mr. Tennyson. He surely did. And he loved my cooking." Millie was choked up with emotion, or maybe her emotions, combined with worry and fatigue, were getting the better of her. The hour was growing late. She took a tissue from her pocket, blew her nose, and returned the tissue to the same pocket. She pulled a small conch shell from her other pocket and dug a little hole from the place on Daddy's grave we imagined would be over his heart and she emptied the okra soup there, covering it up and patting down the dirt. "All right, Mr. Nevil, I'm taking a little dirt for a good cause and I hope that's okay with you." Then she scooped up some dirt with the conch shell and dumped it in a baggie.

I could smell the river, plants rotting at their roots, fish decomposing, salt, and the smells of the water itself. Millie was drawn to it as I was, as surely as a magnet has to point north. We walked toward the old crypts together and stopped to have a look. Once we were out from under the umbrella shade of the live oaks, the light changed. The moonlight reflected on the water combined with all the stars made it seem like early evening. It was spectacular. Despite the great beauty all around us, Millie continued to fret.

"I think we might be too late, Caroline."

"Too late to protect ourselves? Don't you think Daddy is still looking out for us, too?"

"Yeah, I do. Of course I do. But sometimes, when the wheels are already set in motion, you can't stop 'em. You know that, don't you?"

"Yes. Can't we enlist all these cousins and aunts and uncles buried here?"

Millie looked at me and her face was forlorn and defeated. She knew something I did not and was not going to say it because we shared a superstition that verbalizing the terrible thought might bring it to pass. She turned back to the graveyard and held her arms open wide.

"O Heavenly Father! O Mother of the World! All of you risen in the light of the Lord, hear my prayers! Have mercy on us now and forever and keep us safe from harm! Keep all of us, family and friends, safe from harm! Amen! Amen!"

"Amen," I said with a sense of dread and hope, my feelings wavering toward dread.

Millie was obviously feeling very down, as though she believed that she had been unable to accomplish what she had set out to do. And beyond offering my company and moral support, I did not think that I had been particularly useful either.

We decided to go into the chapel for a moment, just to check on Mother's place. I used the flashlight, fumbling with my keys to unlock the door. We stepped inside and flipped the light switch that lit the brass chandelier that hung overhead in the middle of the chapel. It would not be right to come the whole way out here and not pay a little respect to Miss Lavinia. We were both surprised and unnerved to find her picture frame turned over behind the glass door. Maybe there had been a tremor or a strong wind, or maybe the arm on the back of the frame wasn't that sturdy. I opened the glass door, picked it up, and was surprised to see that the picture was gone.

"What in the world?" I said to Millie. "Who would take Mother's picture?"

"Humph. Door was locked. Nobody been in here since I came last week to sweep and dust. Maybe that picture done walk out of here all by she self."

"Oh, Millie! Honestly." How ridiculous, I thought. I took the frame, tucking it under my arm, intending to replace the picture with another.

"Time to go," she said. "Still got herbs to place and nails to drop and goofer dust to spread on the road."

We did all that with Millie muttering her prayers and then we walked away as though all our efforts were already tainted with futility. But we had done our best and we would have to wait and see what the morning and the forthcoming days would bring.

Millie dropped me off, and to be honest, I hardly remember locking up the house that night except that I peeked into Eric's room and he was there fast asleep, snoring like a cub. As long as Eric was there and sleeping, I could rest, too.

Then in the morning the phone rang very early. I reached one arm out from under my covers to answer it while my face was still buried in the mattress. It was Rusty.

"Hey! Do you still want to go down to Beaufort with me to get the puppy?"

After last night with Millie, I had completely forgotten that I had promised her I would go. I groaned and said, "Oh Lord, Rusty! I'm still sleeping. Can I beg off?"

"Sure! I'll call you when I get back! I'm off to change Chloe's life! It's Mother's Day, you know."

I smiled to myself and hung up, rolling back over to sleep. But you know how it is. The phone rings. You're startled and unfortunately reenter the world by speaking. You lie back on your pillows. Your mind starts racing and you're awake. That's it. You're as wide-awake as you can be, so you give in and get up, stretch, and look at the clock. It was only eight. On most days I would have already done ten sun salutations (all that was left of my once-vigorous yoga habits) to stretch out my bones, showered and dressed, and eight o'clock would find me in the kitchen reading the paper and drinking coffee. It was almost nine-thirty when I finally got downstairs, only to see Matthew's patrol car pulling up in the yard. I knew right then something was dreadfully wrong.

I opened the door and stood outside with my mug, watching him cross the lawn. Starched shirt, creased trousers, sunglasses, holster with gun . . . My stomach was rolling in distress and I struggled to stay steady and stave off the panic already rising in my blood.

"I came to you first," he said. "Ride over to Trip's with me."

"What is it, Matthew? What's happened?"

"There's been a terrible accident on Highway 17 . . ."

"Rusty?"

"Yes."

"Is she dead?" I inhaled in a gasp and my chest got so tight I could scarcely breathe.

"On impact. That's the only blessing. She never saw the eighteen-wheeler coming and I'm sure she never felt a thing. I'm so sorry."

"Oh, no!" I screamed.

Within seconds my face was soaking wet and I didn't even know I was crying.

Once the wheels are set in motion . . . Had not Millie used these exact words?

I left a note for Eric, took my cell phone, and left.

16

Rusty

Trip wasn't home. He was out fishing, which is what he did almost every Sunday morning. It was Trip's way of practicing religion—drop a hook in the water, thank God for all the treasures of the beautiful Edisto River, and be at peace for a little while with his dogs, Mo and Abe. The girls were still sleeping, as was my Eric, all of them like fallen redwoods. There would be plenty of time for them to hear the news. It would be just as horrible and incomprehensible an hour from now.

Matthew and I were in the kitchen, worried and shaken. There was nothing to do but wait.

"I'll make a fresh pot of coffee," I said, pouring the muddy contents of that morning's pot down the drain in the sink. It smelled of cinnamon.

Rusty had a cup of this, I thought, her last cup of coffee on this earth was laced with cinnamon. I started to cry again as I poured clean water into the well of the coffeemaker and wiped away my tears with the back of my hand.

"Rusty was the kind of girl who went that extra distance and tried to make everything just, well, special."

Matthew had no idea what I meant but he said, "Yes, she was."

I changed the filter, refilled it with ground beans, and pushed the start button.

"Can you call his cell?" Matthew asked gently.

"It usually doesn't work. Out on the river, I mean. No tower. But that depends on where he is on the river." I took my phone out and pressed four on speed dial and send. Almost immediately there was a recorded apology from his carrier. "There's no reception." I dropped my phone on the table and covered my face with my hands. "Oh God! Matthew! Why did this have to happen? She was so happy! They were so happy! This is going to tear Trip apart! I just know it! Oh God. They really loved each other, you know . . . ?" My voice trailed off and I was going to really lose it.

"Come here," he said.

He pulled me close to him, put his arms around me, and I just wept and sighed and wept and sighed. Finally I spoke again.

"Oh God! Don't you understand? This is going to kill him," I said.

"Ain't nothing killing nobody." It was Millie, standing there in the doorway. "It's Rusty, am I right?"

I nodded and Matthew gave her the details. For the first time in my life, Millie seemed old and a little shrunken. She had dark circles under her eyes. She probably had not slept a wink all night. She sank into a chair and listened, crying a little and wringing a tissue in her hands until it was just shreds of wet paper.

"Oh Lord," she said quietly. "This is so wrong. Just so wrong.

She was so young. So beautiful. I saw it coming and I couldn't stop it. Oh Lord! What has become of this world? I gots to call Mr. Jenkins. Call him right now."

Millie pulled herself up with considerable effort, went to the wall phone, and dialed Mr. Jenkins's cottage. Yes, I thought, Millie is bone weary from disappointment and sorrow.

All she said was, "Come to Trip's. Right now. We got terrible trouble." She hung up and said, "He'll be here directly."

"What time do you think Trip went out?" Matthew asked me.

"I don't know. Usually he goes out on high tide. Not that it matters. Trip could navigate his boat through pluff mud. He knows every sandbar in the river by name. When was high tide this morning?"

Matthew said, "Where's the tide clock?"

Trip had one in almost every room. I checked the one on the wall by the back door.

"Tide's going out. He'll probably be home soon. And then what? Then his life falls apart. Oh my God! What a terrible day this is! What are we going to do? Oh my God. Oh my God." I could feel myself starting to hyperventilate, something I had not done in ages.

Millie, who was still seated at the table, looked at me. "Caroline Wimbley? Get her a glass of water, Matthew, please? Caroline? You listen to me, 'eah? Time for you to put on some Lavinia. Right this minute! Your brother's going to need a lot of love this day."

"I know, Millie! I know. But this just breaks my heart, too! You know?"

"Yes, but I'm sorry, it don't matter. You gotta rise. Worry about your heart tomorrow."

I shuddered, considering the weight of her words.

The back door opened. "What's happened here?" Mr. Jenkins said, standing just inside the doorway. "Where's the chillrun?"

Millie was so upset she was struggling to calm herself, but at the sight of Mr. Jenkins, she burst into tears again. "Sleeping in they beds, Jenkins. It's Miss Rusty. Jenkins, it's Rusty who's gone. Gone home to God. Oh, merciful Lord!"

"What? Sweet Jesus my King! Say it ain't so!"

"It's so, Jenkins. It's so."

"She was killed in a terrible car accident," I said.

"Oh, no!" he said.

"Oh Lord above! My boy, Trip." Millie almost wailed. "His Rusty is gone, and oh, this house is gone be a house of sorrow now. A house of sorrow now!"

"I found this in the roses," Mr. Jenkins said quietly.

It was the crumpled picture of Mother.

"The roses at my house?" I asked. I felt a rush of goose bumps all over my arms.

"No, Miss Caroline," he said, as somber as could be. "It was in the roses from Miss Lavinia's garden that we transplanted here."

"Oh Lord! Miss Lavinia was coming to aide her child!" Millie said. "Oh Lord!"

Mr. Jenkins seemed to age in front of my eyes, as though with this discovery he had now seen it all. He kept staring at Millie from the doorway. Seeing the tenderness and the deep concern in his face, Millie began to really weep, letting it all go.

Old Mr. Jenkins hurried over to her, put his hand on her shoulder, took her other hand in his, and leaned down. "Come on now, my sweet Millie. Please don't cry. You'll break this old man's heart. Come on now." He reached into the back pocket of his trousers and produced a perfectly laundered handkerchief and handed it to her. "Come on, my girl. Let's pull ourselves together."

His sweet words confirmed the depth of their devotion to each other to me. In the midst of all our sorrow and pain, I had happened on an affirmation of their love. And I had learned that Mother was all around us, knew what was happening, and had tried to be a source of comfort. It only made me cry more. None of us were ready to stop crying and figure out how to deal with the truth. Even Matthew choked back tears.

Matthew put a mug of fresh coffee in front of each of us and the mugs sat growing cold. After a little while, I got up and went out to the porch to watch for any sign of Trip.

"Do you want to go down to the dock to wait?" Matthew said. "I can go with you."

"No, it's probably best if he ties up the boat. Matthew? Where did they take Rusty?"

"County morgue. Gonna have to identify her, I'm afraid."

"Oh, dear Lord. Is she, I mean, was she . . ."

"Not too gruesome. Her chest was crushed by the steering wheel and that caused her instant death."

"Oh, I just hate this."

"Of course. I do, too. She was a great lady."

"Yes. She really was. Do you know she was on her way to Beaufort to get a puppy for Chloe?"

"No. I didn't know that." He shook his head. "What a sin this is. What a terrible loss. I always say that road is a death trap."

"It's the worst. Makes me a nervous wreck to drive it."

"It's lethal. I think this is the sixth or seventh fatality on that road this year."

We waited and waited for what seemed like eternity. The girls were not stirring and there was no sign of Trip until at last I heard the motor of his boat in the distance. I waited until he was on the dock and tying the rope to the last cleat before I called to Millie and Mr. Jenkins.

"He's back," I said. "I'm gonna go meet him."

"Do you want us to come?" Matthew said.

"No, it's probably best if I go by myself. I won't be long."

I began walking down to the dock and Trip turned to see me. His dogs, Mo and Abe, began to run to me.

"Hey!" he said. "What's Strickland here for? Running you in for illegal bear hunts again?"

And then he saw my face. I'm sure it was puffy and red because whenever I cried that was what happened to me.

"What's wrong, Caroline? Tell me."

"Oh, Trip. I'm so sorry . . ."

"What? The girls? Are they all right? Tell me!"

"They're fine, Trip. It's Rusty. Oh, Trip, she was heading down to Beaufort to get that puppy for Chloe and there was an accident. A terrible accident."

"What are you saying? Is she hurt? Where is she?"

"Oh, Trip. I'm so sorry. Rusty is gone, Trip. She's dead. She got in a terrible accident with an eighteen-wheeler and she died right away. She didn't suffer, Trip. She never even knew what hit her."

"I don't believe it. I don't believe it! How can this be? No! It can't be!"

Trip was shouting then and his eyes were darting all around as though Rusty might hop out from a hiding place and this would just be some kind of a really bad joke. Some kind of cruel stunt. He began to shake, and no surprise, he broke down in tears.

"You're telling me the truth, aren't you? This is really so?"

"Yes, that's why Matthew is here." I sighed so hard and put my arm around his shoulder. "He heard it on the police radio and went immediately to the scene. It was too late, Trip. I'm so sorry."

"Oh my God," Trip said. "Oh my God."

The next hour was spent as it is usually spent when these kinds of horrific shocks and devastating losses occur, trying to make sense of something that makes no sense. "Why?" Trip said at least one hundred times, and all we could say was, "I don't know. This never should have happened. Why her? I don't know, Trip. This never should have happened."

Millie and Mr. Jenkins were in some kind of shock, particularly

Millie, who was so disappointed that her angel Oya had not been able to intervene—because, perhaps through her own negligence, her prayers had been offered too late. We told her to stop blaming herself.

"Millie? Listen to me. It might have been more horrible if you hadn't asked for mercy. Right? I was supposed to go with her. I could've died, too."

She looked up at me.

"Oh, sweet Jesus," Millie said, and hugged me with all her might. "Praise God you're safe! Praise God."

Mr. Jenkins was filled with grief, too. It was a terrible shock. "She was a fine woman," he said over and over.

"Yes, she was," we would reply.

Finally, after a period of time that seemed acceptable, I took the reins and began to figure out the details.

"Do you know if she had a will? I mean, what were her wishes?" I said to Trip.

"I have no clue about a will," Trip said. "But I know she meant to be cremated. And she has a brother, Owen. His number is probably in her red leather address book. On her desk."

"I'll find it," I said, and went upstairs to look. My legs felt like they weighed a thousand pounds apiece. "I'll call him."

I found it easily and then bumped into Amelia, who was just waking up and on her way to the bathroom.

"Mornin', Aunt Caroline. How're you?" She rubbed her eyes and looked at me. "Whoa! What's wrong?"

When I told her, she became terribly upset, talking fast and repeating herself.

"Wait! She can't . . . how did this . . . ? When did this happen? Where is she? Did they take her to the hospital? Where's Dad? What can I do? How did this happen again? Couldn't they *do* anything?"

We went into Belle and Linnie's room and Amelia brought Chloe in to tell them all. They were stunned and horrified. Chloe cried the hardest, with her head in my lap. Millie must've heard the commotion because she was there at the door and then in the middle of our grieving group with a box of tissues for all of us.

"I just can't believe it!" Amelia said.

"But who's gonna take care of *me now*?" Chloe said.

What was left of my heart shattered again.

"Don't you worry, baby," I said. "You still have your daddy. And Millie and I are right here."

Millie smiled at me then. So, okay, I may have seemed like I was suddenly willing to step in and take over, but that child's tears just ripped me to pieces. To be honest, I *was* stepping in. I wasn't leaving anybody's little girl hung out to dry. Not in my family. Even if she was Frances Mae's.

"Do you want me to call Eric, Aunt Caroline?" Amelia said.

"Yes, sweetheart. In a minute. Thanks. Just tell him to get up and dress himself."

"What? I mean, should I tell him what's happened?" Amelia's eyes grew large with the fear of delivering such an awful piece of news. "I've never been in this position before."

"No. Let his momma do that," Millie said. "How about I go pick him up on the golf cart?"

"That's probably best," I said.

"You come with me, Amelia," Millie said. "It will be easier for him iffin you're there, too."

"If you all want to tell him, it's all right," I said.

The girls asked a lot of questions, and not surprisingly, they wanted to know why she was on Highway 17 at that hour and on a Sunday to boot. When it was revealed that she was bringing home the puppy for Chloe as a surprise, I thought poor little Chloe was going to collapse.

"It's my fault!" she wailed.

"It ain't no such thing," Millie said. "Rusty's time came, honey, and that's all there is to it. We never know the hour when God's gonna call us home. That's why you have to be very good."

"Rusty was good," Chloe said, looking down at the floor. "I know I'm not supposed to, but I liked her."

"So did I," Amelia said, and hugged Chloe. "She was really good to us."

Belle said, "Gotta say, well, Chloe's right. Rusty was a nice person and she sure threw me a great party yesterday. She really did. I wish I had told her so but I didn't, and now it's too late for that. Holy crap. I mean, I wasn't like in love with her, but she sure was way too young to die. For real. God, I feel terrible."

Suddenly all eyes turned to Linnie, who was still under the covers, not saying much.

"What?" she said, looking very angry. "You want me to say how great she was? How much I wanted to be like her or something?"

"No, darling," I said very nicely. "I guess we're just wondering how you're feeling? I mean, do you want to talk about it?"

"What is there to say?" She made one of those awful noises that start in the depth of your throat and convey extreme frustration, and she slammed her fists into her mattress. "We're the Wimbleys, right? Nothing but one freaking trauma after another! Why can't I just have a normal family? You know what I mean? Does anybody here know what normal is?"

The room was quiet then. I did not point out that the responsibility for a fair chunk of the *abnormal* in her own personal life could be laid at her own feet. Even Chloe realized then how self-centered her sister Linnie was and she was uncomfortable for her.

"Gosh, Linnie!" Chloe said. "Aren't you going to miss her? Even a little?"

Linnie simply glared at her.

"This isn't about you, Linnie," I said, using the quiet and extremely polite voice of matriarchal authority. "It's about Rusty losing her life. Your daddy is going to be very sad for a long time and he's going to need his girls to rally and to help him get through this. And I'm gonna be sad, too." They looked at me and nodded. All of them except Linnie. "All right now," I said. "You girls get dressed and pull up your beds, okay? This is going to be a difficult day, so let's get going."

"Okay," they said.

When Millie and I were alone in Rusty's office, where I decided to make the call to her brother, Millie said, "Miss Lavinia is smiling at you, Caroline. She would say you handled that very well."

"Thanks. I guess." I sighed hard and started looking through Rusty's address book. "My father used to say that the first rule of power is to use the least amount necessary to get the job done."

Millie sighed. "Then Mr. Nevil would be proud, too. I'm going down to get breakfast started. Still gotta eat."

"Okay." I found Owen's number. "I'm just gonna make this call and I'll be there."

I made the call to Owen Peretti, who was completely floored by the news.

"Oh God! Oh, no! What can I do?"

"Well, Trip is going to go down to the morgue to identify . . ."

Owen said he was getting on the next plane. Rusty was the only family he had. He would call us back with his flight information and could he stay with us? Was there room?

"Owen? The one thing we've got here is room. You can stay with me or Trip. We'll figure that one out when you get here."

I hung up and sat at Rusty's desk for a few minutes. I shook the mouse of her computer and the Web site for the breeder came into view. I clicked on the toolbar for the contact information and directions and printed it. I checked her recent e-mail, and sure enough, there was a thread of correspondence with the breeder. Rusty had planned to buy Chloe a female cocker spaniel puppy. Twelve weeks old. There was a jpeg attached to one of the e-mails with a picture. The puppy, like all puppies, was absolutely adorable. I was unsure of what to do but the breeder had to be called. So did a lot of other people—Miss Sweetie, Miss Nancy, Rusty's old students. I decided I would coach Amelia and enlist her help to go through Rusty's contacts, and notify them as soon as we had a plan. And there were Trip's associates to consider as well. He had a list, too.

I went downstairs and everyone was gathered around the table eating scrambled eggs, grits, and bacon. Even Matthew was chipping in, buttering a pile of toast. Everyone was there except my brother.

"Hey, Mom," Eric said, and got up to give me a hug. "I can't believe . . ."

"Yeah, me either," I said. "You okay?"

"Yeah. I'm okay. Just sucks, that's all. I guess I should say 'Happy Mother's Day' but, man, this is so awful."

"Yes, it is." I kissed Eric on his forehead. "We'll celebrate double next year. Where's Trip?"

"Feeding the dogs," Millie said.

"Right," I said, knowing better. "I'll be back in a few. I'm taking the golf cart."

The dogs were indeed devouring big dishes of kibble down at the kennels but Trip was nowhere in sight. I knew where he was and minutes later I found him. He was on my dock, leaning over the rail, trying to gather himself together.

"How's it going?" I asked, patting him on the shoulder.

"Like shit," he said.

"Brilliant summation," I said, hoping attorney humor might help him a bit.

"Yeah. Thanks." He shook his head. "Jesus, Caroline. You know what? I still don't believe it. I mean, I know once I see her in the morgue I will, but right now? It just doesn't seem real. We just had coffee together a couple of hours ago and boom! Now she's dead?"

"I know. It's completely surreal. I spoke to her brother, Owen. He's coming."

"Good. How'd he take the news?"

"Same as the rest of us. Terrible. Rusty was his only family."

"Oh Lord. Poor guy. I hardly knew him. To tell you the truth, they didn't talk much."

"They'll talk a lot less now." Gallows humor.

"Man, is that the truth? So, now what?"

"Now we take a deep breath, go to Charleston, do the ID, arrange for a funeral home to collect her body, and do what we have to do."

"McAlister-Smith's?"

"Yeah, either them or Stuhr's. They're both top-notch. I know someone at McAlister's."

"Then McAlister's it is. Should we call them?"

"I'll make the call," I said. "They're going to want to know if we want to have a memorial service there."

"No, let's do it here or the chapel. I think the chapel. What do you think? Too small?"

"No, that's perfect. If it's a big crowd, I'll get a tent. We can have a reception afterward at the house. My house. I have better parking. McAlister's will help us compose something for the newspapers. Do you want to run it in *The State,* too?"

"Why not? Should we call that reverend? What was his name? Charles Moore? Someone should officiate. God, I haven't been to church in so long he'll probably hang up the phone when he hears my name."

"Honey, when he hears your name he'll see dollar signs. Not to worry. Just write him a check."

"How can you joke at a time like this?" He said this and looked at me as though I had no shame.

Well, I stared back at him and said, "Who's joking?"

"How much do you think is appropriate? I mean, what's the number?"

"Just tell him what's happened and you'd also like to make a contribution to the church as Mother used to do. You know, does he have a special need?"

"Wait! I remember that guy! He'll say he needs a new roof!"

I couldn't help but giggle then. Reverend Moore did know how to work the wallets of his flock, especially the ones who had some major long green in them. But here was Trip, once again, playing the role of El Cheapo.

"Trip?"

"I know. I know. Don't worry. I'll do the right thing."

"We should get going," I said.

We walked back toward the golf cart together. He put his arm around me and squeezed my shoulder.

"Hey, Caroline?"

"What?"

"Thanks."

"Oh, you're welcome. You'd do the same for me."

"Yes, I would. I mean it. Thanks."

A plan of sorts was made. Amelia and Millie would make the immediate phone calls and I would go down to Charleston with Trip and Matthew. Matthew took the rest of the day off to be with us.

By late in the day, when we got back from Charleston, which, by the way, was the most emotional . . . it will be a while before I can talk about it, but by the time we returned, the reality of our tragedy was beginning to sink in. There were a dozen or more cars at Trip's and it looked like there was a party going on. There was. But a pretty somber one.

One of Trip's clients greeted us at the door.

"Hey, Trip. Sorry about your loss, man. Terrible." This unidentified scruffy-looking man, who was on his way out, stopped, shook Trip's hand like he was pumping water from a well. Then he said, "I brought you some kind of a pound cake from the wife. She said you'd need it and it sure looks like you do. And I brought you about five pounds of fish. All cleaned and ready to release into the grease. Lotta folks in there. Let me know when you have the, um, details, okay? I left my number with your girl."

"Thanks," Trip said. "Thanks a lot."

"Bad news travels like wildfire, doesn't it?" Matthew said.

"It sure looks like it," I said. "I need a glass of wine."

"Me, too," Matthew said.

"Who the heck was that, Trip?"

"One of my regulars," he said. "I'm taking all comers these days."

"That was Joe Maloney, town rabble-rouser," Matthew said. "I lock him up, your brother here gets him out. Part of our revolving-door policy down at the hoosegow."

"Good grief," I said.

The porch was bulging with people who were having a glass of tea, or something stronger, as the cocktail hour was nigh, after all. Trip disappeared into the crowd and Matthew and I made our way toward the kitchen. I saw the older girls and was pleased to see that they were all dressed nicely and that even Eric had put on a dress shirt. I squeezed his arm.

"Where's Chloe?" I asked.

He shrugged his shoulders and continued talking to his cousins. For as bad as the situation was, it did me a lot of good to see Eric and his cousins sticking together. I went upstairs to put away my purse, and on the way back, I checked Chloe's room. She was right there on the floor playing with a baby doll with her back to the door. She did not see me or hear me coming and I heard her talking to the doll in a very angry voice.

"You're ugly! You're stupid! And, you're bad! Yes, you are! And I'm going to cut you up in little pieces and feed you to the chickens! Oh, cry all you want, but you killed the queen and now you have to die!"

She picked the doll up by its feet and slammed its head on the floor over and over.

Now, I'm no shrink and we know pretty much how I feel about them since my ex-husband is one, but I think it was obvious that Chloe was acting out. She still thought she was to blame for Rusty's death. Had Linnie told her that? Probably.

"Chloe?"

She stopped and turned to me. She didn't say a word.

"May I come in?"

She nodded.

I went into her room and knelt down right beside her.

"Sweetheart? Can I hold your baby?" She let the doll drop and I picked her up, cradling her in my arms as though she were the most precious baby in all the world. "Look, Chloe! She's just a baby! Babies don't hurt anyone on purpose and they're too young to take out grown-up anger on, aren't they?"

"Yeah. So?"

"You're still my little baby niece and you're still your momma's baby and you always will be. Don't you know that?"

"Yeah."

"Well, we're not going to let anyone hurt our baby because babies can do no wrong. You're only in the second grade, for heaven's sake! Second graders are just too innocent to plot and scheme and carry out something terrible enough to die for. Aren't they?"

"Yeah."

"What happened today is not your fault in any way, shape, or form. Do you believe that?"

"No."

"All right, then. Tell me. Why in the world would you think that?"

"Because in my heart I know that if I hadn't wanted that puppy? Rusty wouldna died."

"Baby, maybe not or maybe she would've. The point is that Rusty was a whole big grown-up and she made that decision to go to Beaufort on her own. You didn't push her into her car! You didn't even know she was going, for heaven's sake!" I was going nowhere fast with this mule-headed child. It was time to change tactics and just pull out the big guns. "Look. You believe in God, don't you?"

"Yeah."

"Well, didn't they tell you in Sunday school that God knows everything, even the number of the hairs on your head?"

"Yeah."

"So then it follows that He also knows when it's your time to go to heaven. Look, sweetheart. Rusty died doing a good thing. She wasn't on her way to rob a bank or to set somebody's house on fire."

"I don't get it. What's the point?"

I was thoroughly exasperated, so I stood up and handed her back the baby doll.

"*The point?* I'll tell you the point! The point is that *if* it was your fault, I would tell you. *Believe* me. I would tell you. In fact, you'd be hearing it from *everyone*. You're not hearing it from *anyone*. So it's not your fault. Get it now? Okay. So. So, now I'm going downstairs to get a glass of wine and to thank all the nice people who are coming to express their regrets over this family's great sorrow. I would advise you to do the same."

She giggled.

"What's so funny?" I asked.

"I don't drink, Aunt Caroline! I'm too little."

The lovely, sweet Aunt Caroline, the one who lived her life inspired at every moment by His Holiness the Dalai Lama—that one? Yeah, well, she'd had it with little girls who thought they were smart enough to raise themselves and didn't need or believe the opinions of their elders. I left the room and went downstairs, straight to Millie's side.

One look at me and she read my mind.

"That chile gone be okay. Don't worry so."

"I know."

"How'd it go down in the Holy City?" she asked. She was cutting pimento-cheese sandwiches into fourths and putting them on a tray. "Terrible?"

"About the worst thing I've ever seen. Ranks right up there with seeing Mother dead. Except worse somehow."

"Oh, Law. I expect it was," she said, shaking her head. "Oh, Caroline, I'm so sorry you had to see that. And your brother."

"Thanks. Let me help you with that," I said, and she stepped aside.

"Thanks. Miss Sweetie brought the biggest strawberry shortcake I ever did see. It's out in the dining room. And we got five hams already. Jenkins is over there slicing 'em up to beat the band. And Trip's friends done bring enough fish to relive the Bible story where they multiplied the food? Yes, ma'am. That's in Mark."

"Chapter nine!" Mr. Jenkins called from halfway across the crowded room.

Millie was startled. I had to smile at her surprise. She looked back at me with that spark in her eye that I love so much.

"Ever since he got them hearing aids? He can hear a dollar drop clean across town," she whispered.

"I heard that!" Mr. Jenkins said.

"Humph," said Millie, and I just shook my head, smiling, really smiling.

Somehow, we were going to get through this horrible tragedy. And somehow, we were going to be fine.

17

Spirits Fly

I WOKE UP THE NEXT morning still thinking about my dreams, which were confusing and fragmented. I hated those kinds of dreams because they were disturbing and left me feeling unsettled. Then, as I reconnected with the world, I remembered that Rusty was dead. No wonder I had passed the night in fits. And no wonder I would begin the day in a bad mood. I would have given anything to turn the clock back forty-eight hours. Maybe Millie and I could have figured out how to save Rusty. But maybe Millie's prayers had saved me. I did not know. I simply did not know and neither did my bones.

There were a thousand details to see to in order to put together Rusty's memorial service and there were some *situations,* too, that were sticky matters of etiquette. For example, we could not say in the obituary that Rusty was survived by Trip and the girls because in actuality he was still married to Frances Mae. Awkward. So how would Trip's friends and associates know he had lost Rusty? And what would Frances Mae say when she heard?

I decided to add something to the obituary to clarify the point without fueling the tongues of all of Charleston and Walterboro to propel their wag fest. After all, we knew people talked about us. Sometimes Mother would say she damn well hoped they did. But in truth, our challenge had always been to give them as little as possible to work with.

I mentally drafted the addendum while taking a fast shower:

Friends and colleagues of Ruth "Rusty" Peretti are invited to join the family of Caroline Wimbley Levine and James "Trip" Nevil Wimbley III at the chapel on the grounds of Tall Pines Plantation for a memorial service this Saturday at one o'clock in the afternoon and then immediately afterward for refreshments at her home. For directions and contact information please e-mail info@mcalister-smith.com or call them a. . .

Yes, I decided, that's what I would do. Or something like that. So then, I thought, how many people would show up? Would we need a caterer? Valet parking? Flowers? Rentals? I got up, threw myself together, and hurried downstairs.

It was only seven-thirty and Millie was already in the kitchen, taking inventory of the boxes of glasses we used to serve large numbers of people. They were spread all over the counters. She was planning Saturday's event and both of us would rather have fallen on the swords of Sherman and Grant than use plastic goblets, even the really good kind that looks like cut glass.

"Morning!" I said. "Coffee?"

"I already had two cups. Moses. That mess gimme the shakes. And these glasses are dusty. Woo! They are dusty, dirty!"

I poured coffee into a mug for myself and added a dash of cream. If Matthew liked it, maybe I would, too.

"I'm trying to get Rusty's memorial service organized in my brain and I'm thinking we need to get Trip over here. Did he bring the morning newspapers yet?"

"I ain't seen hide nor hair of him yet this day. Maybe be best for you to go over there and see what's going on. I'd better run these things in the dishwasher, 'eah?"

"Yeah, I guess. Can't hurt." I looked at Millie's face. "What's the matter, Millie? You look worried."

"I'm always worried. I think we're gonna have a hard time with Trip, Caroline. Never saw a man so broke up like he was last night. Can you imagine what it was like to go to that bed without her at his side? Every widow and widower I ever did know say that first night? Terrible."

"Yeah. Must've been awful."

Millie was right. Last night, after everyone left, Trip had parked himself in his favorite armchair and wept openly with his face in his hands and his elbows on his knees. He just couldn't reconcile himself to her death and he couldn't get over seeing her on a slab at the morgue. He was absolutely inconsolable and I remembered wishing that he would come around or hoping he would. Trip was not usually so emotional and always seemed to take things in stride, better than I did anyway.

"I expect it was. I keep wondering, if your mother was alive, what would she do?"

"She'd guilt him into action in about two seconds, right? If that didn't work, she'd drag him out of bed and into a shower."

"Humph. You are right." Millie laughed a little then and shook her head. "Yes, ma'am, she would. Ain't nobody *ever* who could lay on the guilt like Lavinia Boswell Wimbley! Nobody, no, ma'am!"

"Hmm, look, it wouldn't be unusual for him to take a day or two off. Who would blame him? I mean, she was the love of his life."

"Yes, she was, but them girls ain't gonna be no kinda source of comfort for him, 'eah?"

What was Millie trying to tell me?

"Okay," I said, "who's Miss Lavinia now? You give me the guilt and I go give it to him. I'll be back in a little bit. Maybe I'll go make them all breakfast or something."

"See? Now, that's a good sister!"

"Whatever," I said, and blew her a kiss.

I picked up the papers at our gate in my SUV and drove the distance to Trip's because it was faster than the golf cart and I didn't feel like a hike. The day was so beautiful and clear. It was confounding and even infuriating to me how the world could go on spinning in light of our tragedy. Shouldn't it have paused for a moment? Shouldn't there be a sign that Rusty made it to heaven and that she was all right? Like the sun sending fantastic streams of light through the clouds? There was no sign. Nothing but a cosmic silence so loud I ached to think of it.

Trip's house was quiet. I just let myself in because he never locked his doors. He kept our granddaddy's old Parker Reliable next to the bed in case of unwanted visitors and everybody knew it. I walked all around the rooms and found Chloe in the den, sitting on the floor eating a bowl of dry Cheerios and watching reruns of *The Sopranos*. It bothered me that she had access to adult programming. Not appropriate for this viewing audience, I thought. Trip probably didn't even know how to work the television, much less turn on parental blocks. I would handle this just as my mother would.

"Morning, honey! Whatcha watching?"

"Hey!" She didn't even look up at me, she was so enthralled with the television. "I don't know, but you know what? The family on this program? I mean, their kids are really messed up! You *can't believe* the bad words . . ."

"Um, maybe you should be watching something else? Like *Sesame Street*? Or *SpongeBob*? Or *anything* else in the world except this?"

"I'll change it when they have a commercial."

"No," I said, "we'll change it right now and we'll find you something better. Young ladies shouldn't have to be exposed to foul language. Especially before breakfast." I smiled at her and she gave me a dirty look that compressed her features in a most unattractive way. Arching my eyebrow I thought, With your little rubber face, you could go join a carnival, bless your heart. I picked up the remote and clicked through the channels until I found something animated, with dancing ponies, rainbows, and princesses. "Perfect. Is your daddy up?"

"I don't know," she said, and was immediately sucked into the new program. "I didn't hear him yet."

Witness the almighty power of television, I thought. She would've glued herself to *Nova* or *Gilligan's Island* with the same intensity, which was why adults needed to supervise what kids watched. There was so much wrong with the world. So much.

"Your sisters?"

"They'll be up in time for supper," she said.

"Uh-huh," I said. "Okay, well, I'm going to go and rouse your father and then I might make some French toast, if you're interested."

She bobbed her head and I wondered if she had heard a word I said.

When I got upstairs, Trip's bedroom door was closed. I knocked on it lightly.

"Come in," he said.

I opened the door and his back was to me. He was in his pajama bottoms and a T-shirt, looking out the window.

"Hey," I said, "thought you might like some company this morning." When he turned around to face me, I had to stifle a gasp. His eyes were nearly swollen shut from what I imagined was continuous weeping. He had the shadow of Samson's beard growing on his face and neck and his hair was sticking up all over the place.

"Wow. You look good."

"Right. Thanks," he said. "Who gives a shit?"

"Well, you'll scare the hell out of the children, that's all."

"Children? Maybe Chloe's a child, but the others certainly are not. Want to hear what Linnie said last night after you left?"

I really didn't *want* to hear it but I was going to.

"I'm sitting in the den bawling like a baby and Chloe says, 'What's wrong, Daddy?' Miss Linnie gives me a drive-by and says, 'Daddy's whore is dead, Chloe. Haven't you heard?'"

"Please tell me you're lying or exaggerating or something!"

"No. I am not. This is who my daughter is. I don't even know what Amelia and Belle think. They haven't said *one word*. You know, you'd think they'd say *something,* wouldn't you? Like, 'Gee, Daddy this must be so awful for you.' Something! Anything!"

"Trip? I'm no shrink but I think Linnie is just full of teenage anger. Period. I mean, her mother has brutally disappointed her over and over again. Your relationship with Rusty never got any support from Frances Mae, so she must have some very confusing feelings about it. As for Belle and Amelia, I think they just don't *know* what to say. Seeing you so upset probably reinforces the fact that you don't love their mother."

Trip was quiet for a moment and then he said something that really got to the heart of the matter.

"Let me ask you something, Caroline, and you don't have to answer me now, but do you think my relationship with Rusty was wrong?"

"I don't need time to consider that. Remember I've been a witness to Frances Mae's outrageous behavior for years. No. It was not wrong. Your marriage to Frances Mae had more than its share of complications and every person in this country is entitled to the pursuit of happiness, aren't we? You're not supposed to be made miserable and just suck it up for your whole life. Frances Mae drove you to drink and gamble and ultimately straight to Rusty's arms. She wasn't the right wife for you. She made you into your worst self. Rusty made you happy. What else do you want to know?"

"Even though we have four children together?"

"That's the complicated part. But divorce happens every single day. Now, why don't you get a shower or something and I'll rustle us up some breakfast. I got the papers this morning, but let's not make that a habit, okay?"

I closed his door and hoped that my supporting him would help him let go of some of his pall. At least somewhat. I worried about him until I heard the water running in his shower. Trip *was* flat-out devastated. I didn't blame him one bit, but I had never seen him like this. Ever. Except when Daddy died.

But guess what? I was devastated, too. Rusty had been my best friend for the past ten years and I loved her like I would have loved a sister. But, as Millie pointed out to me, this was no time for my self-indulgence of grief. The fact was, the moment we had to act was now, not later next week. We had to plan a proper send-off—no, a beautiful *glorious* send-off for Rusty, and he needed to be a part of it. I set up his coffeemaker and pressed the start button.

That little Linnie was going to hear it from me. Wait till I tell Millie, I thought.

I looked around in Trip's refrigerator to see what there was, and once again, I was reminded of Rusty. Needless to say, the refrigerator was bulging with packages of sliced ham, just as the freezer was filled with more fish than we could eat in six months. But in between all those baggies and packages wrapped in aluminum foil, there was plenty of everything healthy that a family should eat—low-fat yogurt, fresh-squeezed organic orange juice, organic eggs, and skim milk. In the bread drawer under the counter there was a loaf of whole-grain white bread, a bag of low-salt rice cakes, and an unopened bag of Oreos, Rusty's favorite guilty pleasure. It was true, or at least it seemed to be so, that modifying the girls' diets had calmed them down considerably. It had not made them less belligerent or defiant, but at least they were less frenetic in their day-to-day evil pursuits. Every victory with them was small, slow to come, and hard-won. Rusty had possessed the patience of Job. I did not. And then Frances Mae crossed my mind. Her rehab was almost over and then what? Couldn't she just stay out of the picture until we adjusted to this? But would Trip ever adjust? Probably not, if the looks of him that morning meant anything.

I took a pad of paper and a pen from the shelf by the phone and sat down at the kitchen table to make a list. Call Reverend Moore, clarify the obituary, call Miss Sweetie to think through food and flowers, clean up the whole chapel area, replace Mother's picture . . . finally, Trip appeared in the doorway, clean shaven and dressed in khakis, a knit shirt, and Top-Siders, pretty much his uniform. He looked better.

"And here he is! Good morning, sweet brother of mine. You want coffee?"

I poured a mug and handed it to him. "This is only because you are a grief-stricken wretch. Do you want French toast or waffles?" Of course I had hoped that a sassy jab would get a smile out of him, but it did not.

"I don't want anything. But thanks."

"Well, look, I'm cooking for Chloe, and you probably never ate dinner last night. So I'm ignoring your polite refusal and making you French toast anyway."

"I gotta feed my dogs."

"Fine. Go feed your dogs. Breakfast will be on the table in fifteen minutes."

I got out his biggest frying pan and filled it with strips of bacon and turned up the gas. Then I made the batter for French toast with eggs, milk, vanilla, a pinch of salt, and a generous sprinkle of cinnamon in tribute to Rusty. I set the table for three, thinking if the other girls wanted something to eat, whenever it was they deigned to lift their lazy backsides out of the sack, I'd make them something then. Or they could make a ham sandwich.

Soon the traveling smells of cooking bacon brought Chloe in from the den, and when Trip came back inside, he lingered in the kitchen, scanning the morning papers and sighing like an old woman, until I finally was able to coax him into taking a plate of food. I sat with him and Chloe and we began to eat. Trip's sadness permeated the air all around us, hanging like smog. He would take a bite, swallow, and then clear his throat as though the act of swallowing was almost too much for him.

"More juice?" I asked.

"No, I'm good. This is delicious, Caroline. Thanks."

He was never that complimentary. "Yes, it is and you're welcome." I smiled at Chloe, hoping she would catch my sense of humor, but her face was just as sullen as Trip's. Great, I thought. Today is going to be like dragging giant fish through pluff mud with a gaff.

"Daddy?" Chloe said.

"Hmm?"

"Are we ever going to be a family again?"

Oh, fine, I thought. It was *Les Misérables,* Wimbley style, Act 99.

"We are a family, Chloe. What do you mean?"

"I mean, are we going to live here now? And what happens when Momma comes back? Do we have to go back to the other house and live with her? And is she ever coming back?"

"Of course, she's coming back in just days, week after next I think, and when she does we'll have to see how it plays out."

In two weeks? I thought. Oh, great.

"Honey," I said, "I think what your daddy is saying is that you don't have to worry because the grown-ups are going to do whatever is in your best interest. All right?"

She nodded and shoved a huge forkful of food into her mouth. I was reminded that I wanted to discuss gluttony with her, too, but sadly, this wasn't the appropriate moment. "Now. Would anyone like anything else? More coffee, Trip?" I dabbed the sides of my mouth carefully with my napkin and placed it on the table. I was channeling Lavinia again.

"No. Thanks."

"So, are you going into the office today?"

"No, I thought since Owen's arriving around two, that I would pick him up in Charleston and then—"

"Good thought. I could use your help and his with planning the memorial service."

"May I please be excused, Aunt Caroline?"

"Of course you may." All hail the spirit of Emily Post. "Just put your dishes in the sink, okay?"

"Sure!" There was a terrible clank as Chloe dropped the dishes in the sink and they banged against the porcelain. Another issue to be discussed. "Thank you for breakfast," she said, and skipped out of the room. I sighed and my inner bitch retreated for a moment.

"She can be such a precious child, Trip."

"Yeah, right. You think those manners are for real?"

"Trip? Darlin'? It's a far better thing to be a disingenuous little twit than it is to tell your elders to stuff it. I much prefer insincerity to vulgarity. Don't you?"

"I suppose." Finally he cracked a smile of amusement, but it faded in his next breath. "So what's up for today?"

I gave him the litany of tasks and he said, "Look, why don't I clean up the kitchen and you call that crazy sumbitch? I can't take him today."

"Reverend Moore?"

He nodded.

"Deal. But, Trip?"

"What?"

"He speaks well of you."

I giggled then but Trip looked at me as though this was not the time for humor of any sort. And it would never be again.

I pitched camp at the desk in Trip's den and began making phone calls. I reached Reverend Moore's voice mail.

"Reverend Moore? This is Caroline Wimbley Levine calling. We have had a tragic loss in our family and I'm hoping you are available to conduct a memorial service at our chapel this Saturday? Please call me back at . . ."

I had barely replaced the receiver in its cradle when the phone rang. It was the good reverend himself. Did he screen his calls? Well, clergy got their share of crazies, so I couldn't be critical if he did.

"Ms. Levine? How wonderful to hear your voice! It's been such a long time! I don't mean that as a criticism. No, no! Never! I'm so sorry for your loss. Please tell me how I may be of help to your wonderful family. I think of your beautiful mother every day. Every day."

Our man of the cloth was taking insincere to new heights. I rolled my eyes without the benefit of an audience and gave him the particulars. He was genuinely shocked and saddened to hear that this had been the most unlucky fate of our Rusty, he said. He actually had known her and had nothing but the nicest things to say.

"These things are sometimes unfathomable to me," he said, "and I am forced to remind myself that the Bible says in Romans, Chapter 8:28, that all things work together for the good of God."

"Yes," I said, thinking, Is he kidding or what? No matter what I had said to Chloe, I always had a hard time believing that a young person's death was ever God's will. Maybe he was massaging the interpretation? "So, then, will we see you on Saturday?"

"Of course! Now, would you like to choose music and will there be family members who would perhaps like to offer a reading from the Bible?"

I told him that I would get back to him about those things and I thanked him. So he wasn't Thomas Aquinas. He meant well, I thought.

I called Miss Sweetie next.

"I still can hardly believe what has happened, Caroline. How's Trip doing?"

"I can't either. Trip? Well, to tell you the truth, I don't think he's doing so well. He is really, really sad. I mean, to the point of barely functioning."

"Well, maybe he just needs a day or two. You know, it's a lot to process. His whole life is turned upside down again. Thank goodness he has you, Caroline."

"Well, I hope you're right," I said. "Rusty's brother is flying in today. Owen. Trip's driving down to Charleston to pick him up. Maybe I'll go with him because we also have to stop by McAlister's to pick out memorial cards and to finalize the obituary."

"Oh, my dear! It's all so, so terribly sad. And, now tell me, how are the girls doing? Do you think it might be a good diversion for them to spend a day with me and learn about the strawberry business?"

"Miss Sweetie? That's a splendid idea! I mean, we have to find something for these girls to do this summer or we'll all lose our minds. But today? They're still sleeping and I'm very concerned about getting Saturday organized."

"Well, then, just tell me what I can do . . ."

She generously offered to provide all the desserts, little bites that people could pick up without cutlery.

"You don't want to be picking up forks from all over your yard for the next six months, do you? People are well meaning but way out, you know. You'll be finding forks in the azaleas come Christmas!"

"No doubt. You know, maybe I could send the older girls over to you to help you bake for Saturday? What do you think?"

"Definitely! I just hired a woman named Lynn Brook from the school system—she teaches first grade, I think. Anyway, she's marvelous and she's heading up our new internship program this summer. Oh! Did I tell you that Bobby Mack called?"

"No, you didn't. And I will ask the girls about that. Let's see what they think. What did Bobby Mack say?"

"Well, I knew you had your hands full and all with the graduation and everything, so I sent him a case of that strawberry-pomegranate jam last week? He loved it! He's using it on ribs and roasts and everything in sight and he's taking the whole inventory off our hands! Isn't that the best news?"

"Yes! That's great! Does he know about Rusty? He liked her so much. We used to have dinner, just the four of us, all the time."

"Don't worry, Caroline. I'll be sure he knows. Is there anyone else you'd like me to call?"

"No. Gosh, you know what? I don't know. I'm having trouble thinking all this through. I just hope we don't forget anyone . . ."

When we hung up I went looking for Trip and couldn't find him anywhere. Chloe was back in the den in front of the television.

"Don't you think you've watched enough television for a while, honey? You're going to ruin your eyes."

She looked up at me and crossed her eyes as hard as she could and then broke into a fit of giggles. I was not amused.

"Humph. You'd better be careful, they'll get stuck like that. If you see your father, please tell him I'm looking for him."

Maybe he was out on the river or who knew? I decided I would go pull up his bed and get his towels to throw in the wash. His door was closed. I opened it a few inches and saw the outline of his body under the covers. He had gone back to bed. This was not good. I closed the door and wondered what to do about it and decided to leave him alone for a while. Maybe he hadn't slept well and just wanted to catch a nap before driving to Charleston. That was probably it. But a little voice inside my head that sounded an awful lot like Miss Lavinia said, *The man's grieving. Let him have his time of grief. But don't leave him to his own devices for too long.*

It was true. What if Trip took his comfort in the company of Jack Daniel's and went on a bender? That was just about the last thing we needed.

It was barely ten o'clock. I decided to go back to my house and see how Millie was progressing. She was still in the kitchen.

"How'd it go?" she asked.

"I'm not sure I did anyone a lick of good."

I told Millie everything that had happened and she said, "Humph. That Linnie needs somebody to tan her hide."

"You can say that again. Wait! I thought you didn't approve of that!"

"I'm making an exception. Know what? You'd bess go down to Charleston with your brother and you drive the car. He sounds like he might be too distracted. You know, we don't need another tragedy around here."

What had she seen in her head now?

"Yeah, that's what I was thinking, too. I'm kind of worried about him, Millie. I've never seen him like this. And those girls are lying in bed, good for nothing, and Chloe is watching television too much . . ."

"We gone pray for him, Caroline, we gone pray like mad this time."

"Well, we sure have a lot to do before Saturday. I guess I can use Mother's roses for flowers. The gardens are in bloom but I don't want to strip them bare, you know?"

"I think there will be plenty. Now, if Miss Sweetie gone do all the sweets, then I gone do all the savories. I'll make ham biscuits and pickled shrimp, and iffin that Bobby Mack can send us a pork shoulder, I can make shredded-pork sandwiches on soft rolls. How's that sound?"

"That sounds perfect. I'll help you. I think all that plus a few cases of champagne and white wine and we're on our way."

"And booze, of course. Better check to see what we've got."

"I'll do it," I said, and made a mental note.

"I just talked to Jenkins. He's been down to the chapel since the crack of dawn, cleaning, cleaning. Raking the ground to get rid of twigs and to level it a little bit. He's got two men with him putting the 'amen job' on all the brass fittings and so on. And he says he's got them stained-glass windows so clean you can count the hairs on Saint Peter's head. You got to get me another picture of Miss Lavinia, you know."

"It's on my list."

"Good. Now, where'd I put those silver party trays? You know they gots to be all blue with tarnish. Ain't used 'em since Christmas . . ."

Millie was thoroughly occupied in a conversation with herself. I went upstairs with the intention of waking Eric. On the way home I'd had the thought that perhaps a few hours fishing with Trip might do them both a lot of good.

My mind returned to the plans. Should I rent a piano for the chapel? Impossible. What about a chamber group? Or just a harp? Given the logistics, violins and flute or cello were probably better than trying to push and pull a harp up that hill. I had to make more calls. And I needed chairs but how many?

"Eric?" I said softly, and opened his door. He was on the phone.

"Who are you talking to?" I mouthed.

"Dad," he whispered to me, covering the mouth of the phone with his hand. "I'm talking to Dad. What? Oh, sure . . . he wants to talk to you."

Oh, great, I thought. Just what I need. *Paging Ms. Levine! Dr. Pathetic on line one!*

"Sure," I said evenly, and took the receiver. "Richard?"

"Caroline! What a shock this is! Terrible! Simply terrible! How's Trip managing?"

"Not so well right now, but you know, the wound is still fresh."

"Yes, of course. Well, I imagine it must have been rather a trauma to pay a visit to the morgue. Vile business, all that. Body pulled out of a cubby in a wall on a stainless-steel tray like an unbaked loaf of bread. I'm sure she had no color. Was she very cut up? Very bloody? Dear God! Must've been awful for you, too."

"It wasn't great. I'd rather have been at a Bob Ellis shoe sale, that's for sure." Did he actually want the gory details? "These things are more explicit on *Law & Order,* I'd say."

"Well, do you have Trip's number? I'd like to give him a call. You know, offer my condolences."

"Sure," I said, and gave it to him. "So, you're well?"

"I'm okay, I suppose. You know, still putting one foot in front of the other and making it from Monday to Monday. You?"

"Well, that's good. Me? Oh, I'm fine. Just this horrible loss . . . it's a lot to cope with. You know, Frances Mae is away . . ."

"Oh? Where is she?"

"Um, she's receiving a little counseling out in California on the virtues of sobriety."

"Again?"

"Yes."

"Oh, my! Was this precipitated by her usual theatrics?"

"You don't want to know." Did he really think I was going to tell him everything as though we were two old friends gossiping over the hedgerow? I didn't think so. Why did he set my nerves on edge? The mere sound of his voice was enough to get me going. "Anyway, we have her four girls, and now with Rusty gone, I imagine a lot of their care will fall to me. They're not going to be too happy about that."

"Ah! I can see it all now! You are gearing up for a hot Lowcountry summer?"

"Oh, Richard . . . you're such an ass."

"Thank you, my dear. And you are still my treasure."

"Thank you," I said. Suddenly I wanted to beat a hole in the wall with the receiver of the telephone while he was still on the line, crack his skull via Verizon.

"Well, let me call him and see if I can help him get through this."

"Great. That would be great. Thanks. Take care."

I handed the phone back to Eric, smiled like Miss Lavinia, and left him to finish his conversation with his father. My ex-husband. Whom I had been completely freaking insane to marry.

I spent the rest of the morning doing all the things that needed to be done. It was Millie who pointed out that McAlister-Smith's would be glad to come out here on Saturday and oversee the service.

"They got chairs, tents, something to put down in case the ground is wet, and everything else you need. It's what they do, 'eah?"

"Yes, but I don't want those ugly metal chairs, you know? I want something elegant, you know, like ballroom chairs? Is that too over-the-top?"

"Not to me." Millie stopped, put her hands on her hips, and looked at me. "What are you trying to do here? Control the whole world? Girl? They can probably get ballroom chairs for you. Ask them! Then it's one less thing for you to worry about. They can get them dropped off, placed in position, picked up. You don't need all this fool mess to be worrying about!" Then she dropped her hands and smiled. "Sorry. I just . . ."

"You're right, Millie. You are actually one hundred percent right. I'll ask them."

"Good! Now, do you remember where we put up the punch bowl? I've been looking high and low . . ."

I e-mailed the addition for Rusty's obituary after a conversation with one of McAlister-Smith's directors, who was very, very helpful. Yes, they could acquire all the walnut-finished ballroom chairs with tan leather seats that we needed. And of course, they would put up a twenty-by-twenty tent just in case of foul weather. And did we want a guest book? A podium to hold it? Pens? Everything was decided by phone, fax, and e-mail, even the urn, and I was so relieved. The last place I wanted to take Trip was to the funeral home. It would be bad enough for him on Saturday when they delivered Rusty's ashes to the chapel.

Two o'clock came around faster than I thought it would and the next thing I knew I was driving with Trip to the airport to pick up Owen.

"Let's take my car," I said.

"Why?"

"Because I'm the oldest and you have to do what I say. Besides, I need gas."

"Fine," he said, and climbed in.

We drove to the end of Parker's Ferry Road and turned right onto Highway 17. Trip was silent. I thought, Well, okay, he'll talk when he wants to, but the silence went on for so long it became very unsettling.

"So, Trip?"

"What?"

"Feel like talking?"

"What is there to say? I never loved anyone in my life like I loved Rusty, and I lost her. In the space of a few seconds she was here on earth and then she was gone. Poof! Just like that. If one person tells me it was God's will, I'm gonna hammer them."

"I sure don't think it was God's will. Not for a second. And I don't think it's karma either."

"Explain it to me, then, because I just keep telling myself it doesn't make any sense. It makes no sense at all."

"It depends on your view of the world, you see?" I gave him a quick glance and he was looking out the window. "Look, we're going to start with some very basic Western Christian assumptions, okay?"

"Such as?"

"There's God and there's the devil. There's heaven and there's hell. Are we okay with that?"

"Whatever. Okay."

"Okay. So, there's God's work on the grand scale—nature, humanity, and all the good stuff on earth and in the heavens."

"Where are we going here?"

"Hang with me for a few minutes, Mr. ADHD. So? Ever since we were little children, we were told that we're here to love and serve God, right?"

"Yep."

"Then there's free will. This *tragedy* is where free will comes in and the devil gets fat. Free will is the enemy here. Say you're driving an eighteen-wheeler and you get a text from your girlfriend's friend to say she saw your woman cheating on you in a bar last night."

"Lovely."

"Right? So you're pissed, so pissed that you want to text your girlfriend and tell her to kiss it, right?"

"Yep."

"So you know you're not supposed to text while driving, but some little devil in your head gives you a poke in the brain and says, 'Oh, go ahead,' and so you do. You hit the send button and run across your lane into oncoming traffic and kill somebody. Not exactly God's will."

"Look, I don't believe any of that shit."

"I'm not asking you to. I'm just saying it's a way of explaining it. In the cosmic sense. It's a little win for the bad guys when somebody innocent gets taken out before their time. Anything that can make you rant and rave against God is good for them."

"Do you really believe that crap?"

"Sometimes I do and then at other times I don't know what I believe. But I know this much: I'd sure rather believe there's something out there that can save us from ourselves than to believe that everything is just random."

"Yeah, me, too."

"Gimme your paw, you sorrowful son of a bitch." I held my hand out to him and he took it. I gave him a good squeeze and said, "I ain't leaving you, Trip. Ever."

"Thanks," he said, and squeezed my hand back.

18

Carry Me Home

OWEN WAS STAYING WITH TRIP for the simple reason that he preferred to be in the house where his sister had lived. Perfectly understandable, even though Trip was running out of beds. But Owen wanted to look at Rusty's things and envision her there, to remember how her life was. I thought that was awfully sweet, really. I mean, let's be honest; sensitive, sentimental straight men are on the endangered-species list. He wanted to get to know Trip and even his young hellions he had heard so much about.

The unfortunate thing about this arrangement was that Trip was not up to the job of playing the gracious host. In fact, he was so bereft that he had canceled all of his appointments for this week and the next. Taking two weeks off seemed dangerous and excessive to me, but I was keeping my big mouth shut about that. He was such a pitiful mess, I found myself running back and forth to his house to preside over meals and everything else. I didn't mind. It was only for a few more days and I thought Trip managed his emotions a little better with people around to whom he felt marginally accountable for keeping that upper lip stiff. And if I hadn't learned anything else from Miss Lavinia, I had learned that in times of sorrow sometimes it was best to *pretend* that everything was going to be all right. It made terrible things somewhat easier to endure. So I showed up for every meal to at least try to make the girls feel that life was still happening and that things were close to normal, given the facts.

To our relief and great surprise, Amelia, Belle (who had dropped her Goth getup almost completely), and Eric helped at every turn. Linnie was still smarting from her run-in with me and with her father at the cookout and she probably suspected there was another round of recrimination to come. I wasn't done with her yet. No, ma'am. So she was actively engaged in making herself scarce, which was fine with me. And needless to say, Chloe's interest in the goings-on was only apparent when the goings-on held some benefit for her—the delivery of a cake, for example. Otherwise, our little Chloe was to be found playing games on the computer or watching television ad nauseam. The binoculars I had brought her held absolutely no interest for her. After the memorial service, I had every intention of having a serious talk with Trip about both girls, and I would be happy, I thought, to try to knock some sense into their heads at no charge. Well, I wouldn't be literally happy about it, because what masochistic fool would relish mixing it up with those two truculent beanbags? Worse, any guidelines we put down would require our own vigilance to see that they were carried out. Would Trip be a reliable partner in the taming of Linnie and the grooming of Chloe? There was ample room for serious doubt. Every time I thought about myself as the agent for this Olympic-level metamorphosis, I found myself releasing a deep sigh, knowing it would be I alone, not Trip, who would shoulder the burden. But somebody had to be the grown-up. For a split second, I actually wished Frances Mae was back, but only for a split second. And she would be back in the wink of an eye. Had I had any success with the girls?

Meanwhile, the older three were washing glasses and dishes, taking phone messages, and answering the door to accept deliveries of flowers, all sorts of food, and of course directing a seemingly endless stream of visitors. Trip and Owen held court in Trip's study while the rest of us scurried around like squirrels trying to maintain orderly chaos. The smaller flower arrangements we kept in the house and the large sprays and baskets were sent down to the chapel via Mr. Jenkins's golf cart, with Millie at his side holding the flowers steady. It seemed like I wouldn't need mother's flowers after all.

And the food was distributed to all of our freezers, with Millie making the call on what we could eat now, use for Saturday's reception, and what was unworthy of our table.

"You all ain't eating this mess," she said, inspecting a casserole. "Beef stew, my big fat foot! Smells like possum."

"Ew, ew, ew!" said Amelia and Belle.

"Lemme see," Eric said, and gave it a whiff. "Grooooooss." He made a gagging sound that sounded like "bluugh" and Chloe giggled.

Into the garbage it went.

It was Wednesday night and I was sitting across the table from Owen and Trip after a huge dinner of fried chicken and creamy potato salad, compliments of one of Trip's clients' wife or aunt or somebody. I had completely lost track of who was bringing what and I was grateful then that Amelia was keeping a list. There would be a hundred notes to write and a truckload of platters and bowls to return. Writing the thank-you notes could be another teachable moment. I could show the girls how to use a fountain pen and how to write the notes in two perfect succinct sentences that would cover all we needed to say. And if they balked about thanking people for their kindness at the time of Rusty's death because she was their daddy's lover, I would remind them that they ate the darn chickens, fish, casseroles, and cakes, had they not? I was ready for them.

Forgive me for pointing this out, but Owen was just adorable. You could see that his hair, now shot with gray at the temples, had once been the same color as Rusty's. Since his arrival, he had been especially kind to Trip, saying that he was so grateful to him for taking care of his sister, and no, he would not be taking her ashes back home with him, that he felt Rusty's remains belonged with Trip because this was where her heart and soul would always be. When we came back from Charleston, they took a long walk all over the property and then a ride in the boat to inspect the majesty of the Edisto up close. We talked about Rusty's love of the Lowcountry over dinner, a dinner that was punctuated with long gaps in the conversation as the realities of Rusty's death choked us up again and again.

"This is a beautiful place," Owen said. "The river is really spectacular. I had expected rushing water, but it's smooth like glass for as far as the eye can see."

Trip perked up slightly. "That's right. And, what's interesting is the saline balance. Sometimes when there's a bit of a drought, it's freshwater. But after a big rain, it turns brackish."

"I've never heard of that but then I'm unfamiliar with rivers. But if you want to know how to housebreak a puppy? I'm your man."

"I'll bet so," I said, and was reminded about Rusty's death once again.

"Well, down here it's critical to know this stuff. Back in the day when our ancestors grew rice here, somebody had to really understand when it was safe to flood the fields. Well, that was all a long time ago . . ." Trip faded out, back to the Land of Despair.

"Salt water kills rice plants," I offered, thinking that as a veterinarian from Chicago, Owen probably had no idea what flooding the fields had to do with growing rice unless he vacationed in Vietnam.

"Owen? Do you care for peach pie? Or would you like chocolate cake, pound cake, or some of that very scary molded Jell-O congealed fruit salad?"

"My goodness! So many choices!"

"Owen? This is how we do things in the Lowcountry, darlin'. And it shows you that Rusty was loved by a lot of people. Me included. And so is Trip, much to my utter and complete surprise."

"Thank you, Caroline," Trip said, and sighed for the billionth time.

"No charge." I smiled at Owen. "I'm kidding, of course."

"I know that. I think peach pie, right?"

"The smart money is on the peach pie," I said, wondering what he looked like in the shower.

I know, I know. It's disgusting to have those kinds of thoughts in a time of grief, but they just popped into my head uninvited all the time. Maybe it was how I kept myself functioning, especially when there was something so painful hanging in front of my face. But oh God, seriously? I wanted the night to end so that the next day could come and go, too. I wanted it to be Sunday and for the memorial service to be over with and done. It was going to be awfully hard for Trip and for Owen, too. And for me.

Later, after we said good night to Trip and Owen, and Eric and I were back at our house, in the kitchen having a bedtime snack, I was talking to Eric about that very topic. He had not had much experience with death, beyond my mother's and some grandparents of a few of his friends.

"So what's wrong, Mom?" He dipped his chocolate-chip cookie into a glass of milk, let it hang there until it was about to dissolve, and quickly ate it. I was amazed it didn't splatter all over the table. "I think everything is going along the best it can, I mean, considering. Don't you?"

"Oh, it is, except for Linnie's smoldering rage and Chloe attaching herself to anything with an LCD screen for hours on end. I just keep thinking about Saturday. I mean, can you imagine what it's going to be like for Trip to see an urn with Rusty's ashes in it? I just think he's going to go to pieces; that's all."

"Worse than he already is?"

"Maybe. I don't know."

"Hey, nobody's said anything about it to me, but do y'all think old Aunt Fan is doing the happy dance or what?"

"Eric! Merciful God! What a terrible thing to say! Anyway, how would she even find out?"

"Internet? Maybe one of the girls called her?"

"Well, as far as I know, she can't take calls, but she probably could get a message. Who knows? Listen, I actually had a weak moment today when I wished she was back. Then I got over it. But I'll tell you, I am very worried about Trip. I've never seen him like this."

"Yeah, he's pretty out of it."

"Before I forget, I want to thank you for all you've been doing. You and your cousins—well, two of them anyway—you've all been a big help."

"No worries. But, man, it sure is a lot of work to have somebody die, isn't it?"

"Yes, it is. Wears you out."

"Mom?"

"Yeah, baby?"

"I'm thinking of spending the summer in Columbia taking some summer school classes. Is that okay with you?"

I knew this wasn't about summer school. This was about that woman Erica, the cradle robber. But if I objected, wouldn't that make him want her more? I was so beat from all that was going on. I didn't have the strength to argue and I thought it was best to think it through.

"I don't know, sweetheart. Let's talk about it tomorrow."

Eric rinsed his glass, put it in the dishwasher, gave me a kiss on the cheek, and went upstairs.

"No worries," he said, over his shoulder. "We can talk tomorrow."

I was feeling empty and blue and decided to call Matthew.

"Hey! How's it going?" he said. "Rusty's brother get in okay?"

"Yeah, he's a doll. And he looks like her, which is strange, to say the least. What are you doing? You still working?"

"Yeah, but I'm done at ten. Want some company?"

"Yeah. I do. Maybe for a little while. You know, I haven't seen you since Sunday."

"I figured you were up to your neck."

"I am."

"Then I'll see you in half an hour."

"Great," I said, and pressed the end button.

Well, there it was. I missed Matthew. And I needed him. That was kind of a surprise to me, but it was true. When the world went to bed for the night, I went to bed alone. Well, *usually*. When Eric was home, I was a freaking cloistered nun. But now that fate had ripped through the fabric of our world and snatched Rusty away, I realized there was no one to console me. Oh, Millie had her eye on me just like Miss Sweetie did, and even Eric showed concern for how I was doing. But they weren't a substitute for having a relationship with someone who was really mine. And I was really his. I wondered then if I had it in my character to make that kind of commitment again, and I'm sorry to say that at that moment I thought I might just be out of juice. Or maybe I was so traumatized by Richard that I was still terrified. And every time I looked at Trip, I was reminded of the dangers of loving someone too much.

I was upstairs in my bedroom, the room formerly known as Lavinia's boudoir, running a brush through my hair and checking my makeup. Maybe it was time for me to bring Mother's big statue of Shiva down from the attic and reinstall her. Mother had used her arms to hold handbags, but maybe a daily dose of Shiva would remind me to be strong and to keep my wits about me. I had once been a pretty serious student of Eastern religions, sort of a Zen-style minimalist, halfway vegetarian and an unflappable yoga-girl, but all of that alternative curiosity had gone by the boards as I tried to retool myself to fit back in the Lowcountry groove. Gosh, now that I've spelled it out, it doesn't seem like I was terribly committed to any of it, does it? Well anyway, no more "downward dog" for me.

These days found me surrounded by generations of opulence and excess, praising the tasty attributes of the almighty pig at meals, giving serious office space to Millie's magic, and getting it on with the county sheriff every chance I had. And, because I was the last player standing on the ball field, I had all but assumed the temporary oversight and care of Frances Mae's girls. Well, my situation with the girls couldn't last forever. And Millie was a huge help.

I gave my wrists and throat a spritz of Joy thinking if Matthew knew what my perfume cost he would pass out cold on the ground. But men didn't have to know everything, did they?

I decided to wait for him outside on the veranda. The night was clear and beautiful and the air carried the loamy smells of the earth, pine, and the river. I hoped the weather held through the weekend. There was nothing more maudlin than a soggy funeral. Through the trees I could see the lights from Millie's cottage. She was still awake. Lord knows, she had the stamina of ten women. I wondered if she was praying for Trip and I hoped she was. Poor Trip. His heart was so low that his spirit was literally dragging.

"Lavinia? If you can hear me, you had better do something more for your boy besides getting yourself tangled up in the roses!"

I had replaced her picture in the chapel with one of her and Daddy taken on their wedding day. Daddy was wearing a Panama hat and Mother was all decked out in her "going away" ensemble. She had always told me that her suit was made by Dior and that Rich's in Atlanta had ordered extra fabric to custom-make a little pillbox hat with a veil to match it. They looked very chic. She was so young and smiling so happily, on Daddy's arm, looking like a million dollars. Mother had loved her clothes with the same passion that she loved everything else.

Maybe that was a weird picture to have chosen. I suppose I just thought it was sort of symbolic, you know, that Rusty was to have been Trip's bride by the spring of next year, and here she was now, going away. But I had made the calculated guess that no one would make that connection except perhaps Millie. God, Rusty's death was so damn unfair. And I missed my mother then, missed her something fierce. I was fighting off a bad case of the blues.

Matthew's headlights were coming up the road and I stood so that he would see me. He rolled to a stop and got out. He wasn't in his patrol car and he wasn't in uniform. It was clear he had dressed to see me because he had just shaved and I could smell a trace of his cologne right before he reached me. He smelled like citrus and strangely like sugar as well. Edible, okay? I know, I know. Eric was upstairs and I had a friend's life to lay to rest. It was futile to flex the muscles in the southern quadrant.

"Hey," I said. "You look nice."

"Thanks," he said, staring into my eyes, "so do you. New dress?"

"Matthew? I'm wearing pants."

"Right."

Some pretty animated smooching and moderate groping ensued and I was feeling better already. There was no better medicine in the world than a good-looking good-natured man who wanted to throw you down.

"Eric here?" he said.

"Yeah."

"Damn," he said.

"Matthew? He's gonna be here until August, unless he goes to summer school so he can shack up with that baby thief."

"Nice. I'll pay his tuition."

"Very funny. Are you sure you don't live with your momma?"

Since Matthew and I had begun fooling around, I realized that I had never been to his house.

"No, I do not live with my momma, but my house is very modest."

"You always say that like you live in a tree or something. What? A rusted-out trailer? So fix it up or move. There's nothing longer than a Lowcountry summer and I'm too old to do it in the hayloft."

He laughed quietly. "What's wrong with a hayloft? I think they can be pretty romantic!"

"Oh, sure!"

"Come on, let's get a glass of wine and I want to hear everything that's happened since I saw you last. God, you look good to me."

"Thanks," I said. "So do you." I had already told him that, but compliments are one of those things that are okay to repeat.

He grabbed me by the arm as I was reaching out to open the door, stepped in front of me, opened it, and held it for me.

"Just how long do you think we're going to carry on this way?" he said.

"Until you get tired of me?"

"Uh-huh," he said. "Not happening."

He was alluding to that unpopular topic of commitment. Unpopular with me, that is. "Let's not think about that tonight, darlin'," I said as he followed me to the kitchen. "We still need to send Rusty off to heaven and get Trip back on his feet."

"You're right, but at some point . . ."

"I know. We'll discuss it. I promise."

I could feel his frustration with me in the tone of his voice. I mean, droves of women were out there on the prowl like big hungry cats, desperately looking to sink their claws into a husband, any kind of man, as though the acquisition of a man would solve all their problems.

"So Trip's having a rough time?"

"Terrible."

"Tell me what's happening with him."

"Oh, Matthew, just to look at him breaks my heart."

"Poor guy . . ."

We talked and talked until the bottle was empty, I was out of words, and finally, as propriety dictated, and with certain reluctance, I pushed him out of the house. Rats, I said to myself as he drove out of sight. This was certainly a night I would have loved him to stay. I crawled into my bed thinking he was the sweetest man on earth and Lawsamercy, and he sure did have some beautiful lips.

By God's grace we got to Friday. Rusty's obituary ran yesterday and today. I was absolutely astonished and sickened that a whole life, especially the entire life of someone so vibrant, could be reduced to a couple of paragraphs. It was very depressing. But on a happier note, it was amazing how many of her old students from Walterboro and Trip's clients and colleagues had called and asked for directions. I expected we would have a crowd, a sprinkling of sightseers included, because our plantation was rarely open to the public. Matthew had promised to dispatch a few plainclothes officers just to be sure some thugs didn't try to make a fast getaway with the family silver. Millie and I were in my kitchen discussing it and she thought a discreet security detail was an excellent idea.

"You can't never be too sure, 'eah?"

"Oh God, I hate to think like that," I said. "Always suspicious . . ."

"Don't be calling on God less you in prayer. How many times I gots to tell you that?"

"Sorry," I said.

"Hush. Now, what are we doing about dinner?"

"Anything except ham. I never thought I'd say this, but I'm tired of it."

"Me, too. We all gone start oinking soon. Then fish it is. Let's cook right here. That kitchen they got over there ain't no kinda kitchen."

"I agree. Too small."

"Humph. Like a little bitty tuna can is what. Maybe Eric and Amelia want to make hush puppies?"

"Why not? I'll make a salad and cut up some lemons."

"Do you see me blocking your way? Humph."

"I'm ignoring that. We can eat in the dining room. The temperature is perfect and I don't feel like dealing with the no-see-ums at sunset."

No-see-ums rivaled the mosquito for the position of state bird. They were all but invisible ferocious little bugs that would devour you like piranhas. Well, almost. My daddy used to call them "flying jaws."

Millie and I still had some energy to tease each other, but we were weary from all the meals we had put on the table since Sunday. Cooking for nine or ten people three times a day is exhausting. Even though friends and neighbors brought lots of dishes already cooked, they still had to be warmed, the table had to be set, side dishes had to be prepared, and then, when the meal was ended, it had to be cleaned up. "Well, it will all be over after tomorrow."

"Humph. That's when it starts all over again, girl. That's when the true loneliness sets in on your brother and the struggle to go on begins. All them people gone come and keep him busy telling stories while they eat and drink and then that's it! Gone! They all goes back to they own life, leaving him all alone. It's always like that." She looked in the freezer and took out two large plastic bags of fish fillets. "I hope this is flounder."

"Me, too."

"That's the way of the world."

"You're right but he's got his girls, at least. Amelia and Belle have been great. And at some point I imagine he'll want to go back to the office. He's got to."

"I surely hope so. Well, let's get them kids on the phone to come over here and help us old women make another meal. I'm gone get a big pot of grits going, too. When that Mr. Owen sees the grits, I want you to take a picture of his face, 'eah?"

"Got it! Wait! Who you calling old?" She cut me her eye and I had to laugh. I might not have been that old, but by that evening I felt every single one of my years. I called Eric, who was at Trip's playing with his dogs and talking with his cousins.

"We'll be right there," he promised.

Over the next hour, there was a flurry of elbows and chatter as dinner came together. Our meal waited on the buffet in Mother's silver serving dishes, piping hot and ready to go. Millie left the house to take a generous plate to Mr. Jenkins, which I knew really meant she was going to enjoy her dinner with him. They weren't fooling anybody. I poured myself a well-deserved glass of wine and Trip seated me in my chair. I had just snapped my napkin open and pulled it across my lap when I heard an unfamiliar car arriving.

"Eric? Be a darling and go see who that is, will you? Millie's out. Tell them we've just sat down to dinner, all right?"

"Sure," he said.

I paused, waiting for him to return. I felt like Mother when she refused to raise her fork to begin the meal until she was good and ready, using her position as a weapon while Trip and I squirmed in hunger. But the truth was that a signal to begin a meal together was a good habit to have. It kept a meal from turning into a free-for-all.

The kitchen door swung open and there was Eric with the most peculiar expression on his face.

"What is it, sweetheart?"

"Guess who's coming to dinner?"

He stood aside and my ex-husband, Richard Levine, entered the room.

"I should've called, I know . . ."

I stood, and Richard, with his most continental flourish, came quickly to my side, took my hands, and kissed me on both cheeks.

"Richard!"

"Yes, it's me, darling. Do you have room for one more or shall I wait in the kitchen by the stove with a sandwich? God, you look magnificent! How can you look so well under these dreadful circumstances? Trip! Please! Don't get up."

Trip got up anyway and came to shake Richard's hand, but Richard pulled him into an embrace as though Trip were his long-lost brother.

"Richard . . ." Trip said.

"I'm so terribly, terribly sorry about Rusty. You poor devil!" Then he scanned the rest of the table, smiling like Saint Nicholas, and turned back to me. "Do we have any scotch in the house?"

We? That was a very proprietary thing for him to say. We, indeed.

"Yes, I'm sure *we* do. Eric, why don't you get another table setting for your father and I'll pour him a cocktail."

"No! Please! You sit! I've invaded your home at the most inopportune moment of the day! I insist!" He held my chair for me and I took my seat again. He leaned down and whispered, "Does the liquor still reside in the cabinet under the toaster in the kitchen?"

"Yes. It's there."

"I'll be right back! Please! Everyone! Why don't you begin."

He was giving us permission to begin our meal? Every last person at the table was slack-jawed and I am certain my face was bright red.

"Yes," I said, recovering, "let's do begin. Fish and grits are no good cold. Trip? Why don't you help the girls . . ."

What a memory Richard had! Did he lie awake in bed in New York thinking about my liquor cabinet? Or was I so predictable that he knew I would manage Tall Pines exactly the way my mother had right down to where the booze was? And what nerve! I was so surprised to see him that I hadn't had the presence of mind to get angry about him barging into my home. But a little inner voice, the same one that sounded like my dear Lavinia, told me that I would have that opportunity before the night was out. Yes, I would.

So that's how dinner went, with Richard seated on my right, having pushed his chair in next to mine, asking me all about the strawberry business and every other thing he had no right to know. After his third scotch he began squeezing my knee under the table, which I kept swatting away, while he continued telling everyone how beautiful I was. Loudly. The older girls were snickering and who could blame them? Even Trip and especially Owen were thoroughly amused. But Eric and I were understandably mortified.

"Can I call you Uncle Richard?" Chloe said.

"Of course," he said. "Although Caroline and I are divorced, which I guess might make me your ex-uncle Richard."

"Does that make me your ex-niece, too?" Chloe said.

"Hush up, Chloe," Amelia said, then turned to Richard. "She's a chatterbox sometimes."

Amelia was the only one of Trip's girls with any grace.

"You can't tell me to hush up! You're not the boss of me!" We just looked at Chloe and hoped she'd take the cue anyway, but her awkward questions continued. "So is that why you never ever sent me a Christmas present?"

Richard laughed in a way that can only be described as a blustering guffaw, which caused Trip and then Owen to laugh also.

"Chloe!" Trip said.

"That's enough, Chloe," I said.

"So, what do you think of Aunt Caroline's looks?" Linnie the devil incarnate said.

"Why, she's ravishing! I thought I said that before."

"About one thousand times!" Chloe said, giggling like a fool.

More snickers filled the air as Linnie goaded him and Chloe pestered him to the point that his patience began to wear thin.

"So, why did you and Aunt Caroline get divorced?" Chloe said.

Amelia stood up.

"That's it! Chloe? Come with me!"

"Why? What did I do?"

Everyone at the table fell silent as we watched the big sister take the baby of the family in hand. Amelia led her into the kitchen, probably read her the riot act, and a minute or two later brought a much more subdued Chloe back to finish her meal.

Richard squeezed my thigh and I was so startled that I jumped.

"Cut it out, Richard," I whispered, and pushed his hand away again.

If you knew anything about the history of my relationship with Richard, you'd know that I was pretty sensitive about activities carried out with hands under the table. One of the reasons he and I separated and ultimately divorced stemmed from a terrible incident where I found him with his ex-wife, Lois, in a restaurant. She was, please pardon the expression, um, how to put this? Okay, she was doing something to his you-know-what with her right hand under a linen napkin. Yep. And I caught them. Never mind the location of his traveling left hand, okay? I threw a glass of champagne in her face, called her a very unladylike name, dumped a pitcher of ice water on Richard's withering willie, and suggested the sham of our marriage was over. After a whole lot of psychobabble from him on how I was too pedestrian to understand his needs and that it was just sex with Lois and not love and that he loved me even though he was coming home reeking of her stupid perfume . . . I finally said, you know what, Richard? Like my daddy used to say? This is some bodacious bullshit. Infidelity was infidelity, any old way you wanted to dress it up and slice it. Immediately following was a sunny dressing-down from him on how using bad language was so déclassé. I decided on the spot it was time to dump his sorry ass. That was ten years ago. I thought I had all but completely expunged him from my life except on the big issues with Eric, but here he was, desecrating Tall Pines with his drunk-ass presence and my knee with his drunk-ass hand, all under the guise of sympathy for Trip, with whom he had rarely shared a serious word in twenty years. Who was he kidding?

I heard the kitchen door open and close. Millie had returned to supervise the restoration of order.

"Excuse me for a moment, won't you?"

Trip did the bounce, which is the act of lifting his bottom several inches from the seat without fully rising to acknowledge that a lady was leaving the table, as my father did for my mother in their day. Owen followed suit, and Richard, who saw no reason to do anything except pour another scotch, remained firmly planted in his chair because Brits only rose for the queen of continents. I hurried to the kitchen.

"What?" Millie said when she looked at me, and then she knew without me saying a word. "What? No! That man is here? Do I need to call Jenkins and tell him to get the pitchfork and chase him clean back to New York City?"

"Millie? Be cool. He's Eric's father. And he's drunk. I think. But he's staying. In the guest room. There's not much we can do without making a terrible scene. I won't have Rusty's service marred by the asinine antics of my ex-husband."

"I'm gone tell him hello. You stay put." She went toward the swinging door to the dining room.

"I'll do no such thing." I was right behind her.

"Well! Do Lord! Looky who's here! It's my old friend Dr. Levine!"

Richard hurried to his feet. He wasn't unsteady in the slightest. I would have fallen right on my face with that much liquor in me.

"Mrs. Smoak! You are as pretty as ever! How are you, my darling?" He took her hand and kissed the back of it. "Don't you ever age?"

I saw her smile and get suckered in as he regaled her with his litany of lovely but completely shallow compliments. In the next instant, she got ahold of herself and her jaw went back to steel. "No, you are right. I don't age. Thank you for acknowledging that."

"Ah!" Richard said, not to be brushed off so easily. "Still the charmer, I see! Well, that's good." Then he quickly took his seat with his back to her.

He was the biggest boor on earth.

"Does anyone care for seconds?" I asked.

Everyone shook their heads.

"Pie might be good," said Chloe.

"You don't need pie. Dinner was great, Aunt Caroline," Amelia said, taking her plate to the kitchen.

"Yeah, especially the entertainment," Belle said, following her.

"I'm saying nothing," Linnie put in, and scooted by, giving me the hand that said "talk to the hand."

I'd had it.

"That's probably best for everyone," I said. The little snipe.

Linnie stopped, came back, and leaned down to whisper to me: "Nice husband, Aunt Caroline. You may think my momma is trash, but this guy is the biggest fucking asshole I ever saw."

"You're right, Linnie. Thank you."

"What was that?" Trip said.

"She said she thinks you're doing remarkably well tonight."

"Well, thanks, Linnie," Trip said. "Getting together like this with my family is good for all of us."

Richard raised his glass to Trip in agreement and continued to try to dominate the evening.

"So, Owen! It's Owen, isn't it? Tell me all about yourself, old man! And, Trip? Why don't we all go in the den and let the others clean up? I want to hear how you're really feeling about this god-awful tragedy."

Trip got up, I took his plate, and I walked to Richard's side.

"Richard?" I whispered. "Go easy on Trip, okay?"

"My God, you're a beautiful creature," he whispered back. "Have I ever told you that?"

"Kiss my ass, Richard," I whispered.

"Love to!" I heard him say, and my skin crawled.

What had I ever seen in him? I mean, seriously! He always was an arrogant ass, but now he was a balding, paunchy, drunken, sexist, really unattractive arrogant ass, with those dreaded liver spots on the back of his hands and wiry hair growing in his big stupid ears. All my alarms began sounding in my brain. *Danger!* Richard was not being so ridiculously flirtatious with me for nothing and he had not come here because of Rusty. There was another reason and I was going to find out what that reason was. So far, all I knew was that his chances of seducing me were zero. Zip. Zilch. Nada. It was time to turn on the frost.

The men disappeared to my father's den and I went to the kitchen with the others. Eric looked at up me when I came in, shaking his head. I could see he was distressed.

"Come here," I said, and we stepped away from the others. "You okay, baby?"

"No. I am like totally pissed. I mean, like what's up with Dad showing up like this?"

"I am just as clueless as you are, sweetie."

"I mean, I haven't heard from him in months. I make one lousy phone call to him to tell him about Rusty because I thought I should, and boom! He drops in like he was just in the neighborhood? And he's flirting with you like that? I mean, do you want him to flirt with you like that?"

"Absolutely not."

"I didn't think you did. So, what's he doing here?"

"I guess we'll find out. But why are you so angry?"

"Didn't you see the way he was acting? Completely bizarre!"

"Yeah, pretty strange."

"He's my father, you know? And he embarrasses me."

"Baby, he doesn't embarrass you or me. He embarrasses himself."

"Whatever. He's such a total jerk."

"Don't say that. He can't help himself."

"I'd lock my door tonight, if I were you."

"Don't worry, Eric. I'm a big girl and I can handle it. Come on, let's get these dishes."

I hoped there would be nothing to handle.

The kitchen was finally clean and I had managed to avoid any other confrontation with Linnie, who I think I surprised by agreeing with her assessment of Richard. But what could I say? She was right. She shouldn't have said it, of course, but she was right. At least we agreed about something. Just as I folded my dish towel over the rack to dry, Trip came into the kitchen. He looked like he was a thousand years old.

"I'm exhausted," he said. "Richard wears me out."

Trip's eyes were bloodshot, his shoulders were slumped, and everything about him spelled sadness. I hoped that Richard had come out of his stupor long enough to do Trip some good.

"You poor thing. Why don't you take your girls and Owen home and get some rest. Is Richard sleeping yet?"

In our family, *sleeping* was a well-worn euphemism for "passed out."

"No," he said incredulously. "Any *normal* person would be."

"He's not normal."

Trip gave me a sliver of a grin. "I'll say. It's incredible how stupid people seem when they're drunk and you're sober. Hey, FYI, I got the dirt on Prince Harry."

"Spill it. Spill it this instant."

"He got kicked out of MIT for plagiarism, moved to San Francisco, developed a drug habit, and was last seen panhandling on the streets in the Haight."

"*What?*"

"You heard me. Good one, right?" Now he was grinning. Trip

knew about Richard's low opinion of Eric versus Harry's superiority and that his cruel comparisons had eroded any affection I ever felt for him. "*And* Richard and Lois are all washed up."

"Oh, sure. He used to tell me that all the time."

"No, this time it's for real. She married a nice Jewish dentist named Herb and she's moving back out to the Five Towns on Long Island. Hewlett, I think."

"Holy crap! Herb? Who names their kid Herb?" *Crap* is the perfect word.

"I saved the best for last."

"Let's have it." I cringed. I knew I wasn't going to like what I was about to hear.

"Steel yourself, sister. He asked me if I thought he had a chance with you."

"Oh. No."

"Yeah. He wants you back."

19

Glory Rising

W<small>HEN</small> I <small>WOKE UP, THE</small> house was unusually quiet. Yes, I had locked my door last night, and no, praise everything holy, I have no recollection of Richard tapping on it like some idiotic little mouse seeking shelter from the storm. I simply assumed he found his way to the guest room or that he had fallen asleep downstairs and stayed there. I mean, if he didn't have better sense than to arrive at my house uninvited and unannounced with a suitcase, to proceed to get roaring drunk, and to monopolize the evening's conversation and mortify us all? He could sleep in his cheap rental car for all I cared. I looked up at the ceiling and thought, Mother? What would you do if you were me? I could almost hear her giggle. I knew immediately that she was telling me to find some humor in the *situation* and at the same time not to relinquish control for a single second.

I got up and dressed for the service, knowing that once the day was under way, there would be no time to come back to my room and change. I wore a simple black linen sheath and flats. And of course, Mother's South Sea pearls. I took a large-brimmed black straw hat from the closet in case I wound up in the sun and I put lots of tissues in my little black bag with my lipstick and, yes, reading glasses.

Millie was already in the kitchen kneading dough for biscuits.

"Good morning!" I said.

"Humph," she replied.

"Millie? It's not even eight o'clock! Isn't it a little early to start harumphing?"

"I'm harumphing because *somebody's* ex-husband is passed out facedown on the floor of the living room with a liquor bottle in he hand that he clutching for dear life, smack-dab in the middle of your poor dead momma's Aubusson. *That's* why I'm harumphing. Miss Lavinia be spinning in she grave, that's what."

"Really? Grave spinning seems to be a family specialty lately. Let's leave him there and see if he has the decency to feel awkward about it." I poured myself a mug of coffee.

"Doubt it."

"Me, too. But you have to say, Mother's rug sure has taken a beating from the in-laws, hasn't it?"

"What? Oh Law! Girl? You bad today, 'eah?"

Millie started to laugh, and then I began to laugh, until we both had tears streaming down our faces, remembering. I was referring to the epic, pyrotechnic catfight I'd had with Frances Mae when she was nine months pregnant with Chloe and not playing well with others. I was home from New York for a visit and Trip brought his entire clan for dinner. Afterward the little girls gave us a ballet performance, during which Linnie knocked a Waterford bowl from its spot on a table and sent it crashing to the floor. Mother made some unfortunate remark about how it came directly from the hands of

Robert E. Lee and was irreplaceable—this was a complete lie—and she went on to say that she would deduct it from Trip's inheritance. I knew she was joking, but Frances Mae did not. Well, let me tell you, Frances Mae had a meltdown about the size of Three Mile Island, screaming it was robbery not to reward her for her overactive reproductive system—my words, not hers. Then she made the fatal mistake of calling my son a moron and retarded and I said some pretty terrible things to her including "get out of my house," which was the clincher. Frances Mae had always believed, for absolutely no good reason at all, that when Mother went to her great reward, she and Trip would inherit all of Tall Pines and its contents and she would reign. So when I told her to get her ugly, mean, redneck, stupid, trashy fat ass out of *my* house, she peed on Mother's rug. Yes! Peed! Then she blamed me for making her lose control of her bladder. I ask you this. Would Lavinia Boswell Wimbley have given this house to someone who peed on a priceless Aubusson that had once covered the floor at Versailles in Marie Antoinette's bedroom? Never! Maybe I should say "nevah!" Oh, all right, Mother bought the rug at Stark Carpet in New York after I was born, but it was pretty enough for Marie Antoinette, okay?

Millie and I finally stopped laughing.

"Oh, mercy! I needed that! Whew! Do you want coffee?"

"No, chile. I already had mine."

"Oh, goodness! Well, I guess I should go and get the old bastard off the floor and send him to the showers before his son sees him like that. What do you think?"

"Tha's up to you, but it's probably the nice thing to do. Take him some aspirin, too, and water. He's gone have the broken-bone fever all day long."

In the Lowcountry, broken-bone fever was what you had when every bone in your body ached like they were broken, for no apparent reason.

"You're right." I filled a glass with water and grabbed the bottle of aspirin from the drawer where I kept Band-Aids and disinfectant, bug spray and safety pins, rubber bands and spare change. "One of these days I'm going to have to sort out this drawer. I'll be right back."

I got to the living room and there he was in all his glory, arms and legs akimbo, flat on the floor like a skinny octopus wearing a navy Brooks Brothers blazer, snoring like something from the forest primeval. One leg of his trousers was up around his knee and his argyle kneesock was pushed down around his ankle. If I had to guess, I'd say he had an itch, tried to scratch it, and fell asleep in the process. Lord! When was the last time his legs had seen the sun? Ew. He couldn't have been very comfortable. And shame on me, I wished I had a camera.

"Richard?"

No answer.

"Richard?"

"Wha . . . ?"

"Oh, dear, Richard. Now what's all this? We have bedrooms, you know."

"Leave me in peace, woman. My head's spinning."

"O-kaaay. Your call! I'll leave the aspirin and water right here, and when Eric gets up for Rusty's memorial service, which is in just a couple of hours, and sees you here like a derelict, you can explain it to him. How's that?"

"Good. That's good."

"The whole family will be here at ten."

No answer.

Within seconds, he was snoring again like a grizzly.

Well, as much as the wicked part of me would have loved to let him just completely humiliate himself in front of the entire world, I could not. I would not have this day be remembered for the wrong reasons. I had a vision of the waitstaff we had engaged stepping over him with trays of pickled shrimp and smoked salmon on toast points. No, no.

"Richard! Get up this very instant and go get a shower!"

I knew my voice was leaning toward shrill, and if there was one thing I despised, it was a woman with a shrill voice. But it was effective. He rolled over and opened his eyes, and blinded by the light of day, he shielded his face with his hand.

"Where am I?"

"You are currently regaining consciousness on my living-room floor, where you spent the night. You cannot remain here, as there are several hundred people arriving in the next couple of hours to send the sainted soul of Rusty Peretti to heaven's gates. So! Get up, go upstairs, and take a shower or I'm calling my brother to make you."

He stared at me as though he had lost all understanding of the English language, but finally he rolled on his side and pushed himself up into a sitting position. I helped him to his feet.

"I feel like bloody hell," he said, staggering from the room.

"I'm sure you do. Your things are in the green room, Richard. For God's sake, pull yourself together."

"I'm too old for this," he said.

"I've been telling you for years to grow up," I said. I doubted that he heard me.

It wasn't long before Trip, Owen, and the girls came through the kitchen door.

"Mornin'," Trip said, and gave me a kiss on the cheek. "Y'all are good to do this for us again."

"I know," I said. "It's true. So, how are you holding up?"

"I'm okay, I guess."

He was not okay and I knew it. His mood was very dark. Morbid, almost.

"Owen? Y'all help yourselves to coffee if you want and I'll get everyone else together."

Eric appeared, showered, shaved, and wearing a coat and tie.

"Oh! You're here! Sweetheart? Go get your father and tell him breakfast is almost ready, please?"

"Sure." He turned on his heel.

Somewhere in the middle of the hullabaloo last night, Millie had promised them all breakfast because Owen was in love with Millie's grits.

"I had no idea they could be so delicious!" he said to her. "I am completely shocked!"

"Well, they are," she said, smiling. "Come back tomorrow and we'll have 'em with eggs!"

She had indeed produced another pot of yellow grits, along with dozens of steaming scrambled eggs, sausage patties from Bobby Mack, and two cookie sheets of biscuits. And of course, Miss Sweetie's strawberry jam. We assembled around the table and Richard was still not there.

"Well, I don't think we should wait for him, but, Eric, why don't you go tell him that—"

Suddenly Richard was in the doorway.

"Sorry," he said, and took his seat. He looked awful.

We passed the platters and bowls all around the table until everyone had served themselves. I lifted my fork and the meal began. Even though the food was absolutely delicious, I couldn't help but notice that Trip was pushing his eggs around on his plate, not really eating. I didn't blame him. I wasn't that hungry either. But Eric and the girls, especially Chloe, were shoveling in the biscuits as fast as they could, rivaling Owen, who ate for two men, buttering his biscuits and spreading jam all over them. He closed his eyes while he ate. He was experiencing some kind of culinary rhapsody. I thought he was awfully chipper for someone on the way to his sister's memorial service, but then everyone handled grief in their own way.

"I think this was the most wonderful breakfast I have ever had in my entire life," Owen said. "And you make this jelly?"

"Jam," I said, smiling. "My partner does. You'll meet her today. I'll send you a case."

God, he was as cute as a bug. Because I was under the watchful eye of Richard and in the presence of children, I suppressed a medium-size urge to fly around the table and wipe the crumbs away from Owen's heart-shaped mouth. Shameful, I suppose, but it's just how it was. Don't I get points for resisting the urge?

Right after breakfast, the girls were in the kitchen with Owen, all of them helping Millie assemble ham biscuits. Rosario was there, too, cutting rounds of ham with Millie's special biscuit cutter.

"I still don't know why we didn't hire a caterer," Millie said. "I must think I'm a young girl! Mr. Owen? Check that pantry for a bottle of Mrs. Sassard's artichoke relish, will you?"

"Artichoke relish? Ahem. Mrs. Smoak, we can handle this." Owen placed the quart bottle on the counter next to Millie. "Don't worry."

We had no sooner taken the last plate to the kitchen than the doorbell started ringing. I stood there opening and closing it as I directed waiters, musicians, the funeral director from McAlister-Smith to where they should go. Mr. Jenkins and Eric had commandeered our golf carts, taking people down to the chapel, where the tent and chairs were being set up.

Trip was by my side. Richard had excused himself on the pretense of helping Eric and trying to squeeze in a little quality time with his son. What on earth they had to talk about was beyond me. I had not told Eric what I had learned about his half brother Harry's troubles and I wondered if Richard would. Come to think of it, Richard was so bombed last night he probably forgot that he had told Trip anything, including the part about taking another shot with me. But honestly, after his behavior, did he really think I would be interested? As I understood it, he wasn't leaving until Sunday, so he still had twenty-four hours to give me nightmares for the next ten years.

Miss Sweetie was the next to arrive. Her delivery truck was right behind her and she waved the driver toward the back of the house. I gave her a hug as she came into the foyer.

"Good morning, Caroline! Come here, Trip, and let this old lady give you a hug. You poor thing."

She hugged Trip as though he were her own child, saying how sorry she was and that Rusty was such a wonderful girl. Trip choked up from tears and I was not surprised. I fished out a tissue from my pocket and handed it to him.

"What a terrible day this is. If your mother was alive, I know it would break her heart, too. She held Rusty in such high esteem. Oh, dear me! I miss Lavinia so!"

"Me, too," I said, choking up a little myself. "Every minute of every day."

"And with Nancy gone off to Gay Paree for so long, I can't even get a bridge game together for four! Isn't that awful?" Miss Sweetie blotted her eyes with a tissue. I had not noticed that she was teary, too. We were some trio.

"When is she coming home?" Trip said.

"Not until the end of June, but, darlin', I spoke to her just last night and she sends you all her love. She's just sick in her heart that she can't be here for you."

"Well, thank you and please send her my love, too," Trip said, and I thought, Well, that's pretty sweet coming from him.

"Oh, Miss Sweetie," I said, "thanks so much for all you did. All the muffins and everything . . ."

"And I brought two hundred cucumber-and-dill finger sandwiches! And chicken salad. But oh, shoo, it was nothing. Now I'd better get out to the kitchen and help Millie. I hope that fool delivery boy of mine brought everything I told him to bring. I gave him a list but he probably never looked at it!"

I smiled then, thinking that this was why Miss Sweetie would live to be a hundred—because every day had a busy agenda.

The valet parking company arrived and a dozen uniformed drivers stood at attention at the head of our driveway, ready to take the keys of our guests and shuttle them down to the chapel. The funeral home had smartly arranged for eight brand-spanking-new golf carts to move those who were aged, infirm, or wearing the wrong shoes back and forth between the chapel and the house.

At least we had been lucky with the weather. It was a beautiful day, the skies were as clear as they could be, and blue, so blue! We stepped back and closed the front door as guests began arriving. We would greet them after the service. Matthew slipped inside the house and gave me a kiss on the cheek and he shook Trip's hand soundly. He was wearing a dark suit, white shirt, with a red silk foulard tie, and he looked like a different person.

"Matthew? I don't think I've ever seen you in a suit. You look gorgeous!"

"Well, thanks! Y'all doing okay? Do you want me to stay with you or go on down there?"

"We're good. Go on to the chapel. We'll be along in a few minutes."

He looked at me funny for a moment and then shook his head.

"Okay. I'll see you down there," he said.

"Why'd you run him off?" Trip asked. "I thought he was your main squeeze."

"He is, sort of, but everyone here doesn't need to know it, do they?"

Trip gave me an odd look then. Had I told Matthew I would meet up with him in the chapel because I didn't want everyone to think I was in a committed relationship with him? Or was I in a committed relationship with an officer of the law, someone allegedly below our social status? Wouldn't it have been ultrabizarre to have Matthew on one side of me and Richard on the other?

"I can be in love with anyone I want, Trip Wimbley. And I can marry anyone I want, too!"

"I'm sure you can, but what in the hell are you talking about?"

"You didn't say anything?"

"No. What's the matter with you? Hearing voices, Sybil?"

"I'm fine."

No, I wasn't. I wasn't fine either. I was worried that I had inadvertently insulted Matthew and my body temperature skyrocketed.

"Caroline! You're as red as a beet! Are you . . . ?"

"Menopausal?"

"Yeah!"

"No! Absolutely not! Bite your damn tongue, Trip! How old do you think I am?"

"Hey? I'm just saying . . . it's no big deal, you know? If you are?"

"Well, I'm not!"

The funeral director was on the front steps, handing out programs with a map showing where the chapel was located on our property and offering people the option of a ride. It was getting to be time to go. The last person to arrive was Reverend Moore.

He came through the door looking very serious, holding his vestments high in a long hanging bag.

"Good morning, sir." He shook Trip's hand.

"Good morning, Reverend Moore," Trip said. "Thank you for coming."

"It's an honor," Reverend Moore said. "Truly it is."

I could almost hear Trip thinking *Ka-ching!* Honored? The bill for Reverend Moore's services had probably just gone up another hundred dollars.

Trip shot his eye at me and I knew I was right. Sometimes we could hear each other think.

"And, Miss Caroline?" He was ogling me like I was a Bluffton oyster on a half shell.

"Good morning, Reverend Moore."

"Call me Charlie, please." He leaned his head to one side and smiled so wide I could count his dimples. He probably thought that posture made him seem boyish. It did. I had never noticed his dimples before.

"Charlie," I said, and grinned.

I knew I was supposed to be serious today but this man was so silly! Okay, look, if I was interested in Charlie, you would have already heard about it. Charlie was not my type but I couldn't tell you why. He was handsome enough. He was smart enough. And I suspected he probably had a reasonably decent sense of humor. I guess fate had just not brought us together. And then I realized the real reason was that I was the *last* person cut out to be the spouse of any kind of clergyman.

I wanted to say, *I'm so wrong for you, Charlie, you can't even imagine!* Instead I said, "You can change in the powder room. It's a quarter to one."

"Thanks," he said, and disappeared down the hall.

We made our way down to the chapel in a kind of a procession. Trip, Owen, and Charlie were in the lead, the girls were huddled in the next golf cart, and Richard, Eric, and I brought up the rear. I knew Millie and Mr. Jenkins would be along and that work would stop until we returned.

I had to say McAlister-Smith had transformed our ancient chapel that sometimes seemed so dark and depressing into a warm and welcoming place of worship. The doors were flung wide open, anchored by enormous baskets of flowers. The front windows were raised so that even if you were sitting outside, or way back under the oaks where we stood, ready to make our way as a family up the long aisle, you could still see the whole way to the table—the table where

Rusty's ashes sat in a beautiful urn, surrounded by hundreds and hundreds of flowers.

The guests rose as we passed, following Reverend Moore, up the steps and into the chapel to seats reserved for us. I didn't see Matthew anywhere and I worried then that he had left.

On the altar's right side were our four musicians, three violinists and a cellist, all of them from the Southcoast Symphony in Charleston, led by Dawn Durst, the Canadian virtuoso who had played all over the world to rave reviews. I couldn't tell you exactly what they were playing, but I was grateful that it was not a mournful dirge. I had wisely left the musical selection to Ms. Durst.

I sat next to Eric and Richard was on his other side. The girls, to our relief, had not made a fuss about attending the service or sitting with their father or acknowledging his grief. I suspected they still harbored some measure of guilt for how badly they had treated Rusty. I hoped they were giving that serious thought because Amelia and Belle, but most especially Linnie, needed to develop adult consciences. And even though I knew they wished their family was still intact, they recognized the depth of their father's grief and finally felt some sympathy for him. And poor Chloe; she sat in her pew crying and crying asking everyone how they got Rusty into the urn. When Belle and Linnie told her, she cried even harder. I guess the details of cremation were pretty gruesome news for a child to hear. Poor kid.

Poor Trip. He was right in front of me. I leaned forward and put my hand on his shoulder, letting it rest there for a few minutes. He reached his hand up and patted mine.

It was a lovely service. Reverend Moore led us in prayer and quoted the Bible many times as he gave a short eulogy, talking about how we could take comfort that Rusty was in heaven with God, where she belonged. I worried that Trip might get up and give him a good pop in his jaw. He did not. But it was Owen who gave the more personal eulogy, talking about all the support Rusty gave him when he struggled in school with undiagnosed dyslexia and a string of other learning-style differences. He swore that it was her generosity of spirit, her patience, and her love that allowed him to put his fear of failure aside and try other methods for studying until they found the right compensating skills, ones that led to success for him and a career teaching learning-disabled children for her.

"Rusty found a home here in the Lowcountry of South Carolina and, I confess, this *is* the most unbelievably beautiful place in America."

That one remark endeared him to us for all of eternity.

"And, she found a loving home with the Wimbleys. She adored you, Trip . . ."

I saw my brother's shoulders begin to convulse and I knew he was weeping. I put my hand on his shoulder again and Richard reached over and offered him his handkerchief. Richard wasn't *completely* good for nothing after all. What do you know?

Suddenly I noticed that Millie and Mr. Jenkins were standing to the side of us in their choir robes! I should've known Millie wasn't going to let us have some painful, dreary service. This was precisely why we loved her so. Millie knew how to provide the right balance. When Owen was finished and stepped down, she and Mr. Jenkins went to the platform and stepped up. Millie spoke to Dawn Durst.

"Can you gimme a E flat on that thing?"

"Yes, ma'am?" she said, and played an E flat.

Millie hummed until she was in perfect pitch with the note. Then Mr. Jenkins took out his harmonica and began to play, Millie singing the verse and Mr. Jenkins pausing to sing the refrain. They gave us an old-fashioned gospel-music rendition of "Free at Last" with incredible optimism and rocked the house. One by one, we stood and clapped until everyone, inside and outside, was on their feet clapping and singing along.

Way down yonder in the graveyard walk
I thank God I'm free at last!
Me and my Jesus going to meet and talk
I thank God I'm free at last!

They sang every verse they knew twice and slowed down at the end for Mr. Jenkins to let his harmonica wail with joyous strains of hope and promise.

"We done sent Miss Rusty to Gawd today!" he said, speaking out loudly to the congregation, who clapped some more. "Yes, we did!"

"Hush! I told you, no talking!" Millie whispered loud enough for us to hear. "You agreed!"

"Humph. At my age? I says what I want!"

No matter how sad we may have been, we all had a smile on our faces. It was the perfect end to the perfect service. Reverend Moore gave a general blessing to everyone and we began to file out, shaking hands with many old friends as we went. We went slowly so that Millie and Mr. Jenkins would have time to get home before us and put all the staff on notice.

On the way back to the house, as we rolled along the uneven ground, I was thinking about Rusty and how good she had been for Eric and all the other young faces I saw in the crowd who were probably touched by her as well.

"She was a heckuva gal," I said.

"She sure was," Eric said. "I'll miss her."

"I could use a little hair of the dog," Richard said.

Eric looked at me with uncertainty. His generation used other terms to describe the cure for a hangover, which was another cocktail, of course.

"A dwinky," I said. "Daddy's a little green around the gills."

"Ah," said Eric. "Hung."

"Yes," I said. "Be extra nice to him."

"Thank you," Richard said.

I wondered if Richard was simply too ill to pursue his intentions or had he changed his mind? There had not been a grab or a feel from him all day. He was awfully subdued.

As we stepped off our golf carts, waiters were there to offer us a choice of wine or champagne and told us there was a full bar on the veranda. We were hardly inside the house before we were offered sandwiches and all sorts of other delicacies. Richard, who had rushed ahead of us, had found the bar and procured a scotch, popping hors d'oeuvres in his mouth along the way, nodding his surprise and approval at each one.

"This is pretty swanky fare for the boonies, darling. However did you pull it off?"

"This is not the boonies, Richard. What's the matter with you?"

"Sorry," he said, but the elevation of his eyebrows said, *Yes, it is.*

He was not sorry one bit. From the very first second that the scotch hit his bloodstream, the old Richard, the insufferable one I didn't like anymore? Yeah, that one was back.

I looked across the crowded room and thought I saw Josh Welton, Eric's old tutor and my former, um, we had a brief, um, unbelievably smoking-hot night or two years ago. Yes, it was him, Dreadlock Man, Dr. Kama Sutra, Lama Tantric Yoga, and he was coming toward me. I had not seen him in aeons. I wondered what he was up to and hoped it might be, well, *me,* but then I remembered why I really, really didn't like him. Nonetheless, I sucked in my stomach and corrected my posture.

"Caroline!" he said. "How are you?" He took both of my hands in his and kissed them. "You look amazing!"

"Well, thanks. How's life?"

"Dull," he said. "My love life is the Sahara."

"Whoa. Don't tell me you're at a funeral trolling for action."

"No, I'm here because I thought the world of Rusty Peretti. But if you want to have dinner next week, I'm around."

"We'll see."

"You're not still mad at me, are you?"

"Now, why in the world would I be mad with you, Josh?"

"Because I probably wasn't as sensitive as I could have been when your mother passed away. I apologize again."

"Oh, Josh. Listen, I'm not mad at anybody. It's bad karma to hold a grudge." There had to be at least one hundred people in the living room, dining room, and hall, never mind all the people on the veranda. I could hardly hear him and I certainly didn't want anyone else to hear me, so I leaned in. "Here's what I think, Josh. You're a great guy. You're a fascinating guy. But you know what? You're a little prick. Not as big of a prick as my ex-husband, but a prick all the same. Excuse me."

"Wait a minute. That's not nice, Caroline."

"No. It's not. Let me put it another way. You know the old story about the scorpion and the turtle?"

"Help me."

"Okay. The scorpion and the turtle come to a river and the scorpion says, 'Listen, Mr. Turtle, I can't swim and I need a ride across this river. Can you help me?' Well, the turtle knows scorpions can't swim but he also knows that the scorpion will sting him and that sting will kill him and they'll both drown, so he points that out. The scorpion says, 'Oh, no, no! I won't sting you! I swear!' So reluctantly, the turtle lets the scorpion get on his back. They get about halfway across the river, and sure enough, the scorpion stings the turtle. As the turtle is dying he says, 'Why'd you do that? Now we're both gonna die!' And the scorpion says, 'Because I'm a scorpion and I couldn't help myself.' "

"And that's why you won't see me? Because I'm a scorpion?"

I glanced to the other side of the room and could've sworn I saw Bobby Mack. He was headed my way, too, looking fully recovered, robust, much thinner, and ready to take on the devil. Fine by me, because for some reason, I was *full* of the devil.

"No, you're a prick, but there's not much difference to me. Both pricks and scorpions hurt people and really don't care. And that's not an opinion. It's a statement of fact. Now I gotta go see a man about a pig. Excuse me."

I could hear Miss Lavinia gasp the whole way from heaven, but then I heard her laugh. It was her all right. I had waited ten years to tell Josh that some things were simply unforgivable. He shouldn't have been a scorpion when I was mourning Miss Lavinia.

Bobby Mack was standing right in front of me.

"Darlin', baby boy! Look at you! You look absolutely grand! The picture of health! How are you doing?"

I just adored Bobby Mack and I always would.

He hugged me like the ferocious old papa bear he was and said, "Caroline? I'm coming back! For a time I thought it was lights-out for me, but it's not! I'm just so happy to be alive! Now tell me, how're you all doing with this terrible, terrible loss? Rusty was a fine woman. Oh my God. What an awful shock!"

"Horrible. This is just unbelievable, isn't it? We're all so sad."

"How's Trip?"

"Trip is totally devastated."

"Poor bastard. I sent him twenty pounds of baby backs. I hope he enjoyed them."

"I know you did. That was so sweet of you. We're serving them today."

"That's not my ribs on the table over there with all that nasty rub on them, is it?"

"I'm afraid so," I said. "Owen, Rusty's brother, fixed them last night—some midwestern secret barbecue rub."

"What?" Bobby Mack's color was rising along with his voice. "I didn't even recognize them! Why, it's sacrilege!"

Jesus H. Christ! Don't have a stroke! Please! Not at my house!

"Darlin'! Come on now!" I linked my arm through his and navigated him away from the platters. "I'm inclined to agree, but you know, sweetums, not everyone understands how to treat a pig like we do. And it's her brother, you know? He wanted to do something. Tough day for him, too, and all. Don't say anything, okay?"

He made a concerted effort to calm his breathing and threw his hands in the air. "No, no! I won't say a word. But on my soul, it's a terrible crime."

"I know, baby," I said.

As soon as I walked away, Matthew appeared out of thin air and was standing by my side.

"Where were you? I couldn't find you!"

"You had your hands full. But I was there. Beautiful service," he said, "but it's awfully crowded in here. Want to step outside?"

We got a drink at the bar and walked away from the house. Something was bothering him.

"What's wrong?" I said.

"Look, this may not be the time or place to bring this up, but I just want to ask you a question."

"Sure! What's up?"

"Do you think Chloe still wants a puppy?"

"What? That child needs one something terrible!"

"Well, I've got one in my car. That cocker spaniel she was supposed to get? She's in a crate with food and a collar and a leash . . . ?"

I stood back and stared at him. It was the last thing I expected.

"I saw the paperwork lying around in Trip's kitchen, so I called the breeder and she drove her up here. The puppy's had all her shots and all that stuff. What?"

I threw my arms around his neck and hugged him as hard as I could.

"Oh, Matthew! I think I love you, Matthew! I really do think I do!"

"Well, this is excellent news," he said, and hugged me back.

20

Reckoning Days

THE OLD FOLKS IN THE Lowcountry used to say that if we lived long enough we'd see everything. They may or may not have been wrong, but I sure have seen a lot of things happen that I never thought would come to pass. Let's start with the convoluted, self-serving reasons for Richard's visit.

It was the Saturday night after the memorial, the valet service and waiters were gone, the rentals had been picked up, and the kitchen was almost back to normal. Some generous soul had thought to bring us a stuffed and roasted turkey, which was a wonderful diversion from all the ham. Millie and I made gravy and mashed potatoes, so we had hot turkey sandwiches for everyone. Comfort food. Chloe was out-of-her-mind thrilled with her new puppy, who she promptly named Missy. Eric and all his cousins played with Missy until it was time for supper. Seeing Eric then, playing like a kid? It was hard to envision him cavorting with Erica the Pedophile.

"Too bad Matthew couldn't stay, Caroline. He's really a helluva guy. I told him so, too," Trip said. "He sure made Chloe happy."

"Yeah, he's amazing. He had to go to restore law and order out at a social club. I always worry when he has to answer a call like that."

Owen said, "Well, from what I've seen of him, I think he can take care of himself just fine."

Owen was leaving in the morning to fly back to Chicago.

"I hope so and, Owen?" I said, thinking about how much he really did remind me of Rusty. "We have all really enjoyed the chance to know you a little better. I hope you'll come back and see us, 'eah?"

"Terrible way to get to know anybody but I'll do that. Promise."

"Yep. I'll take you fishing, on the Edisto. Make a Lowcountry boy out of you," Trip said.

"That sounds like a deal," Owen said. "This is so strange, but I feel like I've known you guys all my life."

"That's what happens when the chemistry is just right," I said, hoping Trip wouldn't tell him how many chemistry experiments I had conducted, i.e., pheromone romps! But all silly jokes aside, I believed then that a visit from Owen might make us all miss Rusty a little less. I really did.

We shared a casual kitchen supper and then Trip, Owen, and the girls got themselves together to go back to their house. Chloe stood by the door with Missy curled up in a ball in her arms.

"I love her, Aunt Caroline."

I looked down at Chloe and thought, You know what? She's not a *bad* little girl, she's just really ugly. Maybe we can fix some of it and maybe she'll grow out of some of it, and in the meanwhile she's got a new puppy to love. Not so terrible.

"That's good, sweetheart. You take very good care of her, okay?"

"Oh, I will!"

I knew she would. I planted a kiss on her cheek and she hugged me with her free arm.

They were so tired. We were *all* so tired. Eric had disappeared upstairs to his room, probably to call his babysitter. Even Millie made an early departure. I had just closed the door behind them all and turned on the dishwasher. Richard was still sitting at the kitchen table and it was obvious to me he was hanging around to unburden himself of some serious something.

"Can I get you anything, Richard?" I spoke with that tone of voice that really meant *last call at the bar*. My intention was to escape to my room and sleep for ten years or so.

"No, thank you." He swirled the scotch and ice around in his tumbler. "I want to talk to you, Caroline. Can you sit with me for a minute?"

"Of course," I said.

There was no apparent reason I should say no at that moment, so I sat. I may have thought he was a skank and I may have praised heaven a thousand times in the last twenty-four hours that I divorced him, but those were not good enough reasons to be inhospitable. He was, after all was said and done, Eric's father.

"Would you like a glass of wine, my dear?"

I loved the way he offered me a glass of wine in my own house.

"No, thanks. I'm actually going to turn in, in a few minutes. It's been a long, terrible week and I've really had it."

I rested my chin on the heel of my hand and my elbow on the table, giving him my full attention. Let's get this over with, I thought.

"I'm sure. Well, I wanted to say some things to you and you don't need to answer me now. Just muse on them and we can talk next week or whenever you want to. I've been doing a lot of thinking . . ."

"Maybe I'll have that glass of wine anyway," I said. He started to get up and I said, "No, no! I'll get it. You talk, I'll pour." I got up and went to the cabinet for a goblet.

"There's a sauvignon blanc on the door of the fridge," he said. "It's open."

"Great." I helped myself and took my seat once again. Had he inventoried every last drop of alcohol in the house? "So what's going on, Richard?"

"Well, a number of things. At long last, Lois and I are completely finished with each other. We broke up after Harry was expelled from MIT for plagiarism."

"Oh, Richard! I'm sorry." I tried to sound sincere. It was a struggle.

"And then Lois married Herb. Herb the dentist from the Five Towns on Long Island."

"Good grief. I wouldn't name a dog Herb."

"Me either. Silly name."

So, he didn't remember he had already told Trip all of this or maybe he thought Trip had not told me? Either he was really that snockered or he was so arrogant he didn't think my only brother would share that kind of newsy gossip with me? The former was pitiful, because it seemed Trip and I both married people who drank way too much. And the latter was pathetic proof that Richard had scant understanding of the love and trust a brother and a sister could share. And he was a psychiatrist. He took money from people to help them solve their personal issues. How ironic is that?

"Well, I'm sorry for your trouble, Richard."

"That's not all . . ."

I waited for him to tell me about Harry's drug problems and about him living on the streets, and he did. After I heard way more about Harry than I wanted to know, he got up, picked up the wine bottle, and refilled my glass.

"That's just awful, Richard. I know you had such high hopes for him."

"Yes. Yes, I did."

"Look. Life is long. Sometimes, anyway." I was thinking of Rusty then, who was robbed of decades. "He may come around. He's a smart boy."

"Not so smart actually. No common sense. And not a grain of kindness in him either."

I began reliving the past, remembering what a little son of a bitch—an accurate description of his mother's personality and of Harry's demeanor—he had been to Eric when they were just little boys. He was heinous to Eric, and Richard always took Harry's side.

"Yeah, he was a tough nut."

"So, you don't hate me, then?"

"Heavens no! Why would I hate you?"

"Because I always held Harry in such high esteem over Eric."

"Well, Richard, there's the difference between us. I knew you were just plain wrong. I always focused on Eric's character and potential, not his ability to mainstream in some stupid private school where the faculty is so underpaid and ridiculous they wouldn't recognize a gifted child if he bit them square in the face. And Harry? Even when he was six years old, I wouldn't have left Harry with a small animal, a small child, or a pack of matches for more than five minutes."

"In retrospect, that was probably a wise call. I bet on the wrong horse and lost."

"It would appear so. At least for right now. But you never had to make the bet, Richard."

"You're right. And that's the thing, isn't it? I never had to make the bet at all. I should have loved them equally. And intellectually I did, but for some reason I could never show it."

"Probably because *emotionally* some men like to take competition to dangerous levels. That edgy thing you were always after, even with Lois. Whether it was sex or anything else. Do you know how often I watched you place the value of a win over everything? Between your sons, Richard! You made them compete for your affection. It was so hateful."

"So you do hate me."

"Not at all. I feel a little sorry for you. You can never capture what you could have had with Eric and I don't think you can ever repair the damage done by all the rejection. I wish you could but I don't know how you could."

"Dear God, Caroline, why don't you just stab me to death?"

"Look, Richard, I don't want to hurt you, but where were you during the past decade? Am I just supposed to overlook all the heartbreak you caused our son? The silence on his birthdays? The visits that never materialized? All the broken promises? I'm just stating the facts, Richard. I mean, I still can't figure out why you're here now."

"Caroline. Why am I here, why am I here? I am here, Caroline, because you were right and I was so desperately wrong, and because I am so, so dreadfully sorry for everything. I mean everything. And I thought this might be a chance to patch things up. You know, give it another go. Because, Caroline, you have something I'd give my last dime to have."

"Really? What's that?"

"A family, Caroline. A good, solid, sensible, and wonderful family. I have nothing except the remnants of my relationship with you and with Eric. You have a wonderful brother. You've turned my son into a spectacular young man. And I think you know how I feel about you, Caroline."

"Is there any more wine in that bottle?"

He poured the rest of it out for me.

"Thanks," I said. "Okay, Richard. There's something I have to tell you."

"What is it?"

"Do you know that very nice man who was at the service today? The one who brought Chloe her puppy?"

"Yes, the young man? The policeman?"

"He's my age actually and he's the sheriff of Colleton County."

"A thousand pardons." Richard arched an eyebrow. I could read his mind. So he couldn't tell the difference between a busboy and a waiter? Weren't they basically the same thing? "What about him?"

"I'm in love with him, Richard, and I think I'm going to marry him."

Just then, the old cuckoo clock on the wall that we brought home from Switzerland when I was a girl, the one that hadn't made a peep in years? Well, it went nuts, cuckooing and chiming at least twenty times.

Richard howled with laughter.

I said, "That'll be enough out of you, Miss Lavinia!"

"I think your mother disapproves," he said.

"Tough noogies," I said. "I'm gonna marry him anyway."

"Does your young man *know* this?"

"No."

"So, there's no hope for us, I suppose." I shook my head and he strummed his fingers on the table. "I figured as much. Well, what about Eric? Do you think he has room in his heart for an old foolish man who's filled with regret?"

"You'll have to take that up with him. I hope he does, but, Richard, if you ever let him down again . . ."

"You'll have me arrested?"

"Yeah, I'll have you arrested. Now I'm going to bed. I'll see you in the morning."

That grandiose proclamation had been two weeks ago, but it had a short shelf life. Eric had yet to hear from his father. No one was surprised because long ago we had resigned ourselves to having very low expectations when it came to anything that had to do with Richard. Who was it who said the road to hell was paved with good intentions? Well, he or she was a very smart cookie.

During these two weeks, many interesting things and many good things have happened as we made an effort to restore normalcy to our lives. *Southern Living* magazine had confirmed the date for their shoot and I was very excited about that. I'd been pinching and pruning all the beds in the garden like they were up for an award.

But, I'm sorry to say, Eric had an awful disappointment. Well, sorry and relieved. He went back to Columbia a week before classes started to attend summer school. He said he wanted to get a tough biology requirement out of the way and that to do it in an abbreviated semester when it was his only subject would be so much better, or so he tried to convince me. He was staying at a "friend's" apartment and I knew good and well he was playing house with Erica. Like we say in the Lowcountry, I might have fallen off the turnip truck, but it wasn't yesterday. And I also knew some mischief was afoot because whenever he called me, I could hear traffic, which meant he just happened to be outside. Gee. Did I perhaps think he was trying to call me without a crying baby in the background?

But it only took five days of this subterfuge and suddenly he was back in my house with all his belongings. Something had gone dreadfully wrong. Without a word to me or anyone, Amelia, who was staying home for the summer to help with the girls or at least until Frances Mae resurfaced, rode up to Columbia, picked him up, and brought him home.

I was in the kitchen with Millie, who was mixing up dough for chocolate-chip cookies, discussing Trip's worsening depression, when we watched them pull up in the yard.

Amelia didn't even come inside. She just helped Eric unload his duffel bags to the back steps. I knew instinctively that she was trying to avoid confrontation. We'd all had plenty of that to last a lifetime or maybe two. But I wasn't going to confront anyone. I was thrilled to pieces to have my boy back at Tall Pines! And I was really grateful that I had stayed out of his romance and let it implode on its own.

"Darlin'! You're home!" I gave him the biggest hug. "What's going on?"

"I don't want to talk about it," he said, passing through the room en route to his. He stopped, sighed, and turned to face me. "I mean, I'll talk about it but just not now. Okay? Hey, Millie."

"Uh-huh," Millie said, and watched him pass.

The swinging door closed behind him.

"What do you think?" I asked her.

"I think Trip just got himself the fishing buddy he sorely needs."

"Think he broke up with that woman?"

Yes, I had confided in Millie. Who else did I have to talk to? Matthew? Oh, sure. Men like Matthew just love to talk about young people's love affairs. So, I had spilled the beans to Millie. She probably knew anyway. Who was I kidding?

"Excuse me, but am I baking his favorite cookies or what?"

Of course! See what I mean? Millie knew he was coming.

"Why didn't you tell me?"

"Because you'd start wringing your hands and worrying about him until he got here and I don't need no more trouble to contend with for a while, iffin that's all right with you. We still got a full plate with your brother, 'eah?"

I looked her in the face and thought I was so mad with her that I was going to stamp my feet, just the way my mother used to do. But then I realized she was absolutely right. If I had expected anything was wrong in Eric's world, I would have been a complete wreck, fretting more than I was fretting about him being *with* Erica, whom I fully intended to murder or not, depending on the depth of Eric's despair.

"Don't you know I haven't had a decent night's sleep since he left?"

"Don't you think it's time to let him grow up? There's young men dying in Afghanistan and you're worried about this kinda fool?"

She had me.

"Well, what am I supposed to say to that?"

"Nothing, 'cause you know I'm right. You needs to take a big *chill pill,* like them girls say, and let him come to you. He will, by and by."

She *was always* right and I just hated her for it then.

But on to other issues, Millie and I were deeply concerned about Trip. He was so broken and morose. He wasn't shaving. He wasn't working. His appetite was terrible and he wasn't even *fishing,* for heaven's sake. I also suspected he wasn't sleeping during the night. But he sure was sleeping in his clothes on the sofa in his den, all day long. And, perhaps worst of all, he wasn't bringing me the morning papers. I'm just kidding about that, okay? I had to wonder, was he even aware that Frances Mae was in the wings?

"Oh, fine. Millie, I think Trip's mourning has gone on long enough, don't you? I mean, he's got to shake himself out of this horrible wallowing misery and get back to work. I think I'm going to have another talk with him this afternoon."

"Yeah? What you gone say?"

"I'm going to tell him that Rusty would not want him to act like this. That's what. And I'm going to send Eric over there, too. Maybe Trip can make himself useful and give Eric some advice on women or something. Maybe Eric can get him to go out in the boat."

"Right time for Frances Mae to come home," Millie said, dropping spoonfuls of dough on the cookie sheet.

"What? Excuse me, but didn't you just say we had enough trouble to contend with for a while? And I know it's time, but what makes you think it's the *right* time for her to come back?"

"'Cause I been working my roots to bring her home."

"What? Why in the world would you do that?"

Millie turned around to me and put her hands on her hips. I was about to get a lecture.

"Because it's enough! You can't keep on running back and forth to Trip's house. You need to get your own life back, too. And them girls ain't got the supervision they needs and you can't give it to them nohow. And they don't need to be living with his misery all the day long and then all through the night, too. He crying for his dead lover all over the house and they don't need to hear all that. It's too confusing for them. Children need they own, even if she is Frances Mae. She's the evil that they know and it's always better to stay with the evil that you know." She slipped the cookie sheet into the hot oven and closed the door with a slam.

"Wait a minute, Millie. Are you gonna stand there and tell me that the girls are better off with Frances Mae? I mean, haven't you seen a vast improvement in Amelia? And Belle? I'll admit, Linnie is something of a challenge, but she has a job! Even Chloe has straightened up. And all the girls are eating better, are they not? They're not as wired."

"Caroline? You ain't they momma and that ain't *never* gone come to pass nohow, 'eah? They daddy ain't worth two cents right now. I don't know how long he plans to carry on like this and that's his business. I'm just saying, it's time for Frances Mae to come home and see about her girls. You see about your boy and she needs to see about her girls. Amen."

"Amen, huh? Well, fine. I'm going over there right now and taking that chili we made for them."

"Humph. Chili. Chili ain't gone change the fact that it's time for her to come home."

I took the plastic container out of the refrigerator and picked up my purse.

"I'll be on my cell."

I let the door close in what might be called an adult slam, just loud enough to show I meant business, too. I got in the golf cart and pressed the gas pedal to the floor, charging across the yard at perhaps five miles an hour. Not a very dramatic getaway, I'll admit, but it was the best I could do. Millie was telling me that I had failed to transform the girls and she was right. I had failed. And they were wearing me out.

Well, as soon as Trip's house came into view, my heart took a lurch to my throat. Frances Mae's SUV was in the yard. Oh, please, Lord! Not today! I had not had the time to figure out how I would deal with her.

Amelia and Belle were outside watching Chloe swim. Amelia waved to me and I waved back. I knew then why Amelia had not come into the house. Millie and I would've seen Frances Mae's return all over her face. And Belle wouldn't squeal if she knew. Linnie had started a new job that week, working in Miss Sweetie's test kitchen. Believe it or not, she was reasonably happy. I know, that's a hard one to swallow, but even Miss Sweetie said Linnie was a natural for the food industry.

I went right into the house. There, in the kitchen, wiping down the counters with a spray bottle and a roll of paper towels, was the odious Frances Mae.

"Don't you know how to knock on a door?" she said.

"Well, look who's here." I put the chili on the table. "Where's my brother?" The Loathsome One. I had to say, she'd lost a lot of her baby fat. She actually looked pretty good for someone with lips like tires.

"Trying to get some rest. We'd appreciate it if you'd lower your voice."

"We?" I said. "Who is this *we?*" What did she mean?

"Boy, for somebody who thinks she's so smart, you sure do have a bad memory."

"Come on, Frances Mae, pull your claws in. I just walked in the door with a meal for your children. Can't you say thank you?"

"We don't need *nothing* from you, thank you."

"Really? Fine. What's going on?"

"Well? First, I hear that Rusty's dead and I thought, 'Wow, that's too bad.' Linnie sent me a message, which is how I found out, in case you want to know."

"Yeah, I'll bet the news about killed you."

"Look, Caroline, you know how I felt about her, but I *never* wished anybody dead. Not even *you.*"

She was lying through her teeth, according to my bones.

"Oh, thanks. Thanks a lot. I really believe *that.*"

"I couldn't care less what you believe or not, okay? And then my time was just about up in my program anyway, so I started making my plans to come back. So, I get back here to my house in Walterboro two days ago and call my girls to see if they're still alive and they say they are *so, so* glad I'm back because everything is *terrible!*"

"What's so terrible?" Not one of them had said a word to me! Not one word! The treachery!

"That their daddy can't even hardly speak more than two words. Talking to him is like talking to a *goll-dang zombie!* And he's laying around all day——"

"Chickens lay eggs, Frances Mae. People *lie* in bed."

"Oh, my! You're *right!* Thank you, Queen of Nothing, for correcting my English."

I just stared at her. She was so disgustingly vulgar. I felt like I must have been running a fever of about 110 degrees.

"I mean, Caroline, if I learned anything in California this time, it's that sometimes people really *do* need professional help! If you love Trip so daggum much, why couldn't you see how depressed he is and do something about it?"

"Of course I saw! We all did!"

"So you made him a pot of chili. Isn't that precious? Chili's a big help. Whoop-de-do! I made arrangements through Promises for a good therapist and we start seeing her tomorrow."

"Well, that's good! *You'll* probably need one for the rest of your pitiful life!"

"Oh, go blow it out your ass, missy! I ain't got time for you."

Who did she think she was talking to? Dismissing me like that?

"Frances Mae? Why don't you / . . . why don't you just go blow it out of yours?"

"Ooooh! Scaaary!"

"Let me tell you something, you ungrateful piece of rubbish. I made a pot of chili, but I also made three meals a day for your girls for the *whole time* you've been gone. *And* I saw to it that Belle had a wonderful graduation party for her entire class. *And* I listened to your girls when they needed to talk, corrected them when they needed it, and I dried an ocean of their tears. *And* I cleaned your filthy dirty house in Walterboro. You've got *some* nerve to come back here with this kind of attitude. You ought to be on your *knees* thanking me instead of acting like *this*. Just *who* do you think you are?"

"I'm Trip's wife, honey, and I'm back. Just like I said I would be. I'm back for my family *and* Trip. Trip and I stayed up all night talking. I'm taking my family back. I put the house in Walterboro on the market yesterday and I'm moved in here as of today—well, as soon as the truck arrives. So, Caroline? This *is my* house and *you're* no longer needed. So, why don't you just trot your bony ass right back out the door?"

"This is *not* your house! This is my *brother's* house! And I don't believe a word you're saying!"

"You can believe whatever you want! It don't make no never mind to me! And, you dumb bitch, fifty percent of every single thing he owns is mine anyway! You really *are* stupid, aren't you?"

"Millie knew you were coming. I should've warned my brother."

"Honey? It was *Millie* who told me to get back here and rescue my family!"

What? WHAT DID SHE SAY?

"Okay, *that's* it. You listen to me, Frances Mae *Litchfield*! You can tell your lies to everyone else, but don't you ever, *ever* lie to me about Millie Smoak!"

She got really quiet and looked at me. Then she had the crust, the freaking *audacity,* to actually smile at me.

"Then why don't you just go ask her, Caroline?"

I was beyond furious then. There was probably a cloud of steam all around me.

"I will! *Right now!*"

I turned around and marched out of the door and then I stopped and went back inside, where she was still standing. Quintuple hairy eyeball billowing smoke and shooting fire doesn't begin to describe the look I gave her. I picked up the chili and left.

Okay, it was probably childish to take the chili back, but bump her! Seriously! And I didn't believe a word about Millie talking to her! Millie would've told me! I couldn't make my stupid golf cart go fast enough. I began to perspire. What if Millie *had* talked to her? Why wouldn't she have *told* me? Did Millie just let me walk into a nest of snakes? No! Millie wouldn't do that to me! There had to be an explanation!

I pulled up to the door and hopped out. I looked at the house and said to myself, Okay, calm down! Calm down! You're going to give yourself a heart attack and have to give up sex forever. Millie Smoak has never betrayed you in your whole life. There is a reasonable explanation for all of this. And Frances Mae was getting back together with Trip? Over my dead body.

"Millie?" I called out as soon as I opened the door. "Millie? Where are you?" I threw the underappreciated container of whoop-de-do chili on the counter. "Millie?"

"I'm right here, coming as fast as I can! What's the matter?" She came through the swinging door and stopped. "What in the world is *wrong* with you now?"

I looked at her right in her eyes and said, "Is it possible you knew Frances Mae was back and that she has moved into Trip's house and she put the house in Walterboro on the market and that it appears that they are reconciling? Is it possible you knew all this and *didn't* tell me?"

"She did? They are? Oh, my glory! I gots to sit down."

"Come on, Millie, what happened?"

She looked awfully sheepish and was quiet for a few minutes, obviously trying to gather her thoughts. She would start to speak and then stop. Millie was nervous. Millie was the very last person in the world besides Eric I ever wanted to have words with and I knew I had to let her off the hook.

"Millie? If you did know all this, I'm sure you had your reasons for not telling me. I just got caught off guard, and well, I think I called her a liar. And some other things." I sank into a chair next to hers.

Millie smiled at me, reached over, and patted the back of my hand.

"Caroline? Listen, that fool called the house two days ago crying and carrying on. Just the sound of her voice makes me hoppin' mad. She says she needs to know how Trip is doing and I say, 'You listen to me, he's in a terrible situation and I think it's high time you came and took care of your girls.' That's all! She just hung up on me. I didn't know she was *here*! I didn't know they was back together! What's *the matter* with your brother? He can't live without somebody waiting on him hand and foot every minute of the day?"

"Apparently not!"

"If I knew all that, I most *definitely* would've tell it to you right away! I kept meaning to tell you that she called but I kept forgetting! My memory is getting worse and worse. Oh Lawsa!"

"Oh, Millie. Come on. It's okay. It really is. Lord, I can't bear that vile woman! She's worse than ever and now she's back in our lives? Oh, Millie! What are we gonna do?"

"Caroline? Chile? You know I love you like a daughter, don't you?"

"Yeah, but?"

"Then you listen up. You gots to stop sticking your nose where it don't belong! I know you been trying to take care of your brother and his children and we all been trying! But that crazy woman is still his wife, and iffin he wants to throw a parade in her honor on Highway 17 the whole way down to Charleston, there ain't a single thing you can do about it. You 'eah me? Stay out of this."

"Merciful Mother of God. You're right, of course. I'm so glad my mother didn't live to see this."

"Me, too."

A few hours passed and it was time to eat again. My life was so managed by periodically squelching the hunger of everyone around me, it was just ridiculous. But as we all know, meals serve other purposes, too. Eric finally came down to the kitchen looking for some lunch.

"Feel like a tomato sandwich?" I said, holding a tomato up for him to see. "These came from Millie's garden. First ones of the season."

"Sure. Wanna eat outside?"

"Why not? You wipe off the glass and knock the pollen off the cushions and I'll meet you out there in a few minutes."

Soon we were sitting across from each other drinking iced tea, devouring our lunch, and talking about the news flash of Frances Mae's return.

"So, that was my morning," I said.

"Holy crap," he said.

"Eric! Well, actually, to be honest, I was thinking something much worse in my head."

"For once in my life, would you please tell me exactly what you were thinking?"

"Okay. How's this? I was thinking I wish she would kiss my ass in Macy's window and then fall off the Empire State Building and go straight to hell."

"Wow, Mom. Cool."

"And, I want you to think about this. I know you broke up with Erica and you probably feel awful . . ."

"Her baby daddy came back."

"Oh! Baby daddy? Oh! You mean the child's birth father?"

"Yep."

"Well! That's actually probably a *good* thing. Maybe? I mean, the child needs his father, right?"

"Who knows that better than I do?"

"Um, actually, I know it, *too,* remember? And so does Uncle Trip."

"Right. Anyway, it's probably better this way."

"Listen, Eric, I'm gonna tell you something about love and I want you to remember it." He looked up at me. His gorgeous eyes were so sad and I died a thousand times. "Love is the most wonderful miracle in the world. Don't ever apologize for loving someone. Our ability to love someone else is still the greatest gift God ever gave us."

"Yeah, it might just be. But right now love's not making me happy. It's making me feel pretty miserable."

"And your uncle Trip is miserable, and I've been miserable, and guess what? You'll fall in love again and get your heart broken about one hundred times before you find the girl you want to settle down with. So cheer up, there's a lot more misery in store for you but there's also a lot more happiness. All part of life's great adventure."

"Yeah," he said, and cracked a grin. "I guess."

"I'll kill her if you want me to."

"Oh, Mom!"

"Really! It would be my pleasure."

"Mom! Stop!"

After lunch the phone rang. It was Trip. He sounded halfway

human again. Well, more like he had just crawled out of a box in the basement of his brain, but at least he was alive.

"It appears that my family owes you a large apology and we'd like to offer that by way of dinner tonight. Will you and Eric join us?"

I bristled. I wasn't exactly ready for round two with the Evil One.

"Thanks for the invitation, Trip, but I have plans with Matthew."

"Bring him. Seven o'clock." And he hung up.

Matthew said he'd absolutely love to come. He wouldn't miss watching Frances Mae in action for all the illegal drug money in the country. Great. Now I had to go make nice with the Viper.

Matthew was at my house at seven and rapped on the kitchen door. Eric and I were there, futzing around, turning off lights, checking to be sure the stove was off, and doing the usual rituals we always did before we left the house.

"Hey, Eric! How's it going?"

"Good? You?" They shook hands.

"Good. Y'all ready for a little fun?"

"I'm not happy about this, you know," I said.

"Look at it this way, Mom! It's just a normal family get-together!"

"Yeah, sure," I said, and then I thought of something. "You know what, Eric? I can't believe one of those girls didn't tell you about Frances Mae? I mean, you drove all the way back from Columbia and Amelia didn't say *anything*?"

"Well, first of all, blood's thicker than water, and second, I think I moaned and complained about my own *situation* the whole way home."

Boy, I sure was suspicious.

We drove over in Matthew's car and walked right in the back door and into the kitchen. If Frances Mae thought I was going to ring a doorbell in my own brother's house, she could kiss it in Macy's window every day until the Mayan calendar ran out and the Apocalypse came.

"Hey!" Amelia said when she saw us. "How're y'all?"

"Been better," Eric said.

"Oh, come on to the table. Everything's ready."

There was no cocktail hour in a house where no one drank.

"Hi," Frances Mae said, without making eye contact.

"Hi, Frances Mae. Trip?" I said. "Where would you like us to sit?"

Trip shot a look to Frances Mae. I could hear Frances Mae's filthy mind thinking she'd like to give me the finger and tell me to sit on it and spin. I really could. But in the interest of harmony, I kept that news to myself.

"Anywhere you'd like," she said.

"Sit by me!" Chloe said. "Did you see Missy? She can shake hands! I taught her!"

"Show me after dinner, darlin'." I smiled at her as Matthew held my chair.

Matthew sat next to me and Eric took a chair across from us after all the "ladies," using the term with high hopes for the future, had been seated.

Trip offered a short blessing because dinner was getting cold and Frances Mae and her girls began passing food around the table, helping themselves to spaghetti with Bolognese sauce, salad, and garlic bread. I was so uncomfortable I thought I would never be able to eat, but I managed to take a few bites.

"So!" Trip said. "When's *Southern Living* coming, Caroline?"

"Tomorrow."

"Why are they coming here?" Amelia asked.

"To take pictures of my roses," I said.

Conversation was strained and then Frances Mae lost it one more time.

"Well, la-di-da for you. So, Caroline? What's all this nonsense I hear about you trying to turn my girls into debutantes?"

Trip's eyes shot her a glare.

"I told Mom about the party in December, Aunt Caroline," Amelia explained. "I hope that's okay."

"There ain't gonna be no party, Amelia. It ain't necessary, and besides, we don't do that kind of thing in *my* family."

Amelia was instantly crestfallen. I realized she had become pretty excited about the party despite her own worries and that she had decided to trust me to make it happen. Why would Frances Mae want to deny her a party anyway? Because it made her happy to deny me the pleasure of doing something for her daughter that might mean she had a relationship with her aunt? How sick is that?

"Frances Mae?" I said her name as nicely as I could. "Why don't you and I discuss this another time? Hmm?"

"Caroline? I don't think so. You think you always know what's best, don't you? How come you didn't do something about your moron nineteen-year-old son shacking up with a twenty-eight-year-old grown woman with an illegitimate baby? Tell me that."

"That's it!" I slammed my napkin on the table and stood. "What is the matter with you, Frances Mae? Are you so filled with hatred and anger and jealousy that you can't show any appreciation for anything? And are you so mean-spirited that you would try to humiliate my son in front of his cousins, his uncle, and my friend? Let's go, guys. We're out of here."

Eric stood. His face was flushed. Matthew stood as well.

Trip said, "Caroline! Come on! Sit down!"

"I don't want to be a part of this, Trip. I'm sorry, but I can't bear this kind of behavior. Good night. And Frances Mae? One other thing."

"What?" she snarled at me. She actually *snarled*!

"I liked you better drunk. At least you were nice some of the time. You know what? I didn't say a thing about how I found out about your daughters screwing the gardeners when we found their underwear in the bushes, or did I say a word about Linnie doing drugs? No, I did not. You should see your ugly, nasty face. My poor brother."

Somehow I found the wherewithal to make a reasonably dignified exit from the table, out the back door, and out of their lives, or so I hoped.

The next morning when I woke up, figuring that Trip had not done so, I went to get the papers. On the way back to the house I noticed that all the color from my roses was gone. I stopped my car and got out, began walking and then running toward the bushes. I could not believe my eyes. The heads of every single rose in my mother's garden had been cut off at the top and they were all lying on the ground.

21

Make War Not Love

I JUST WANT TO KNOW who did this, Trip. I want you to find out who did this *immediately* and I want there to be *serious* consequences." I was shaking with anger and outrage. Of course, I completely knew in my bones and in my heart and soul that it was Frances Mae. "This is *beyond* defacing private property. This is the work of someone who needs a *goddamn exorcism*."

I had called Trip and told him to come immediately. I think I was screaming my head off. When he showed up in the rose garden, he was honestly and absolutely aghast. Mother's roses were an utter shambles. And Trip looked terrible, as bad as I have ever seen him.

"This is some horseshit." He pulled out his cell and called his house. "Frances Mae? Get the girls together and get over to Caroline's on the double." Pause. "I don't give a good goddamn what you're doing. I said,

Now!" Pause. "Put the puppy in her crate." Pause. "Fine, leave Chloe home. But *move it!*" He closed his phone. "Caroline? Go in the house and put on a pot of coffee. Stay there until I come get you."

I didn't budge.

"Please?"

"I'm calling Matthew."

"For what?"

"I want the person who did this to be arrested. And then I get to call *Southern Living* magazine and cancel, right?"

"Oh, great. That's right," Trip said. "I can't *take* much more."

I got back in my car and moved it up to the house. When I got inside, Millie was there, making waffles.

"Morning!" she said, in a chipper voice, completely unaware of last night's dinner theater or this morning's massacre.

"Morning," I said.

I slammed the newspapers on the table and pulled out my cell phone to call Matthew. He answered right away.

"Matthew? Are you on duty?"

"What's wrong? Yeah, I'm on duty."

"You are? Good! I want you to come over here right now and bring handcuffs!"

"What's wrong, Caroline?"

I choked up with tears of rage.

"Answer me when I ask you a question, please," he said.

"Okay, just gimme a second here." I cleared my throat. "Somebody came on my property last night and cut the heads off of all my roses! There are hundreds of blooms lying on the ground! And, not that it matters to anyone but me, my gardens were going to be in a big feature article in *Southern Living!*" I started to cry. "I want her locked up! I want her out of my life, Matthew! I can't stand this! I don't live like this!"

"I'll be right there," he said, and ended the call.

I collapsed into a chair at the table and Millie put a box of tissues in front of me.

"Tell me what's going on 'eah. Stop crying and tell me."

"Oh, Millie! I just can't stand her another second! I can't stand her! You can't believe . . . oh God!"

I cried and cried, and in between my bursts of tears I got the whole story out, the horrible exchange of insults from last night and the condition of the roses, too. It wasn't just the roses I was crying over. It was everything.

"*Why* would she do such a thing? *Why?*"

"I don't know, honey. That's a angry woman, though. You know, chile, when she starts running her mouth like last night, you need to just excuse yourself. Don't take her on, Caroline, 'cause she don't care what she says and who she hurts. But you know, you shouldn't tell on her girls. You were making such nice progress with them and now it's all undone."

"I wasn't going to just sit there and let her humiliate my son, Millie. You wouldn't either."

The door swung open and Eric came in.

"Holy crap, Mom! What's wrong *now?*"

"Somebody done took all the heads from the roses and ruined your momma's garden. She thinks it was your aunt and she's very upset."

"She *can't* come here and do whatever she wants and just say these *terrible* things! She *can't!*" I was so discombobulated my words came out in a jumble, but I knew Eric and Millie understood what I meant.

Millie stood over me and rubbed my back in little circles, trying to calm me down.

"Mom? Can I say something?"

I nodded and looked at him. I'd defend my boy against an army of Frances Maes if I had to.

"My auntie Fan is a crackpot and whatever she says about me is totally irrelevant to me. Even her girls know she's a nut bag. Who cares? Uncle Trip will kick her butt and she'll be okay for a while and then something else will set her off and we'll be going at it with her again! It's who she *is*! She's the family *lunatic*! So, don't waste your time getting all worked up over a crazy person. She can't help it. You know?"

"Boy?" Millie said. "When did you get so smart?"

I blew my nose. He was right.

"We were almost rid of her and now she's back, and oh Lord! She's so *awful*!" I said.

"Nope. She's crazy first and then she's awful, Mom."

"Mean as the devil, too," Millie added.

"Yeah, that about sums it up," Eric said. "One, crazy; two, awful; and last, mean."

"Well, we're finally in agreement," I said.

"So, am I getting fed around here?" he asked.

"I'm making you pecan waffles," Millie said, and went back to stirring her batter. "Why don't you set the table? You know, help the ladies out?"

"Sure." Eric looked out the window. "But for how many? We got company."

I got up and looked out through the glass panes in the door. There they all were—Frances Mae, three of her girls, Trip, and Matthew.

"Oh, please. I'm all done with them for a while. They're too much!"

Frances Mae's arms were flailing in the air, fingers were being pointed, and the girls looked very serious. But I noticed something very curious.

"Why is Linnie smiling?" I said.

Millie stood next to me to have a look.

"Humph. Maybe she had a hand in it, too," Millie said.

"I wouldn't put it past her, y'all. She's not right in the head either," Eric said. "Besides, you *did* blow her away last night, Mom."

"Yeah, I guess I did."

"What you saying now?" Millie said.

I had left some facts out when I gave Millie the rundown of all that happened last night. So I told her everything. Millie's third eye was pretty accurate, but it didn't always pick up all the details.

"What?" Millie said. "Girl? You something else now, 'eah? Something else."

I kept staring out of the window in the back door. At last the conversation grew less animated and it seemed that Matthew was finished listening. Then he was coming toward my door, so I opened it and stood aside.

"Morning, Mrs. Smoak. Morning, Eric. Caroline? Do y'all think this First Responder might be able to impose on your hospitality for a cup of coffee?"

Millie immediately filled a mug for him and handed him the carton of half-and-half.

"You mean, you're *not* going to arrest her?" I was incredulous.

"Have you had your breakfast, Officer Strickland?" Millie said. "I'm making pecan waffles and there's plenty."

"Why, I really shouldn't, but all right, if it's no trouble, that is. Thank you."

He sat at the kitchen table and removed his sunglasses, hooking one arm of them through the breast pocket of his starched uniform shirt.

"The waffle is really awesome," Eric said, swirling a bite around in his syrup.

Matthew smiled at Millie and I wanted to kill them all for being so nonchalant about this terrible travesty. I mean, I *know* no one died and not one person was physically wounded, but Frances Mae couldn't be allowed to just decapitate an entire garden of roses with no consequences! It was maddening! What was the *matter* with them? *All* of them?

"So, when you all are finished thinking about your stomachs," I said, "does anyone want to tell me what happened out there?"

Matthew took a sip of his coffee and looked at me.

"Trip has her under control. I don't think you'll see anything like that happen again. Ever."

"Really? What makes you so sure about that?"

"Because he told her that this kind of behavior is a deal breaker."

"*What* deal?" My heart was beating so fast it scared me. "What *deal*?"

"I'm gonna let your brother tell you and he's coming inside in a few minutes," Matthew said. "In the meanwhile, Mrs. Smoak, this is the most delicious waffle I think I've ever had."

I got up and looked outside the door again. Frances Mae and the girls were driving away and Trip was walking toward the door.

"Matthew! You have to give me more than this! *What deal?*"

"Just hang on for a couple of minutes, Caroline."

The back door opened and Trip came sailing in as though all was well, except for the fact that he looked more haggard and spent than he had just an hour ago. He sat down at the table and Millie placed a mug of coffee in front of him.

"What's that I smell?" he said. "Wow. Waffles."

"I just put one on for you," Millie said. "Be done in a jiffy. Caroline? You want one?"

I shook my head no.

"So?" I said.

"So, it's like this. She didn't do it, Caroline."

"Oh, baloney," I said.

"Look. If she had done it, there'd be a million little scratches on her from the thorns. Her arms are as clean as a whistle. So are the girls' arms. Not one scratch on any of them."

"That's impossible," I said.

"Listen, Frances Mae was just as horrified as you were."

"Oh, please." All I could think was Frances Mae was the world's greatest liar now and forever. "She cares about my garden, Trip, come on."

"No, she doesn't give two shits about your garden and she doesn't know the first thing about gardening either. Besides, she doesn't even own clippers. So, you have to ask yourself, who and why, right?"

The conversation continued for a long while until I finally came to accept the possibility that Frances Mae had, in fact, not tried to murder my roses.

"I have an idea of who *might* have done it," Eric said. "I mean, it's a long shot, but I might be right."

"Who, Eric?" Matthew said.

"Yeah! Who do *you* know who would do such a thing?" Trip asked.

"Humph," Millie said under her breath. "That chile's smarter than everybody in this room all added up together."

"Yeah, right. Mom? Does cutting off all the flowers kill the bushes?"

"Why no, it doesn't. Most of my bushes in bloom now are hybrids. They bloom all summer. Why? Why do you ask that?"

"Because I didn't know that and Uncle Trip and Officer Strickland don't know that. So who would?"

"Someone who raises hybrids or someone who sells them?" I said. "A landscaper?"

"Yeah, a landscaper who wanted to impress a girl, but didn't really want to do permanent damage? And a niece who wanted to screw up her aunt's shot at fame with her garden? Which would explain why Linnie was smirking?"

"Oh God, Eric!"

"Miss Caroline! What'd I tell you about calling on God except in prayer?" Millie said.

"Who says I'm not praying? Trip? Remember those two boys who Belle and Linnie were seeing? Have they been coming around?"

"How the hell would I know?" Trip said. "Things have been a little crazed lately, you know."

I wanted to say, *Bubba, you are so Dickens's* Bleak House, *you don't even know it.* And next I could read Millie's mind as she thought, You see? He's admitting he don't know what's up with those kids and *that's* why it's a good thing Frances Mae is back!

"What do you want to do, Trip?" Matthew said, wiping his mouth and putting his napkin on the table. "Pick 'em up for questioning?"

"Let me talk to Frances Mae and Linnie first and I'll give you a call later. What do you say, Caroline? They're your bushes, not mine."

"I say, see what you can find out," I said.

"I gotta get going, Caroline," Matthew said. "I'll call y'all later. Hey, Eric?"

"Yeah?"

"If you're right?" Matthew said. "You ought to think about a career with the CIA or the FBI."

"Cool." Eric nodded and took his empty plate to Millie. "I'm going up to my room, Mom. I gotta get a shower and then I'm going to hang out with Amelia."

"Sure," I said. When he was gone I looked at Trip. "Whaddaya know? The day has arrived when I don't have to bribe him to take a bath."

"Humph. That's a wonderful boy, 'eah? All right now," Millie said, and closed the door of the dishwasher. "I'm gonna go pay my sweet Mr. Jenkins a visit and tell him to move his bones! We needs to clean up the rose garden. Y'all need to be alone for a little bit to chew the fat."

"There's a lot to chew on, Millie," I said.

"Humph. You're telling me? You know, I can use all them petals for my root work." Millie winked at us and went to the door. "Make up some sachet for all the closets, too! Mix 'em up with some lavender?"

"Keeps the moths at bay, right?"

"That's right. See? You're learning!"

"Learning? Sometimes I wonder if I ever learn a thing," I said. "I'll be along shortly." I knew my day would be spent restoring the garden, pinching back the tiny heads so the bushes would produce the largest blooms. With any luck, they would all be flowering in two weeks. Maybe *Southern Living* would come back then.

Trip smiled, sort of, and then said, "Look, Caroline. I don't blame you for thinking it was Frances Mae. I thought she did it, too, especially after all the brouhaha at dinner last night. And after what she did to those poor innocent billboards, I knew she didn't have a problem with a certain amount of vandalism. Believe it or not, she doesn't fault you for thinking it was her."

"Well, that's mighty *F*-ing nice of her," I said.

"Yeah, I know. And we're *gonna* get to the bottom of this. If Linnie's the cause for this? She'll be digging onions in Georgia by next week."

"Yeah, sure. You're really Mr. Tough Love with her."

"No, I'm not Mr. Tough Love with any of my kids. Never have been. That's why I need Frances Mae, Caroline. And those girls need her. They got Litchfield blood and there isn't anyone who can keep them in line except another Litchfield."

"Send them back to Walterboro."

"Yeah, I'm sure you'd like that and I wouldn't blame you for that either. But we're gonna try something different this time because the girls need two parents. This is a chance to see if we——Frances Mae and I, that is——to see if we can straighten them out, get them into good colleges and into the world to make something out of themselves."

"Wait a minute. I'm not buying this. Sorry, Trip. Sorry." Rusty had only been dead for a few weeks. Wasn't this like, I don't know, too soon to have another woman in his life?

"Look, I told Frances Mae in no uncertain terms. I said, 'Listen, Caroline's my sister and she's my family. I'm not going to have y'all fighting like two cats in a bag every time I turn around.' I told her,

Caroline, I mean I laid down the law. If she wants to be with me, she is to be polite to you. You are my only sister, I love you very much, and I have lived here for the last ten years because of your generosity. She needs to think about that and be grateful."

"When hell freezes. She wouldn't show an ounce of gratitude to me if her very life depended on it."

"Well, she will now."

"We'll see about that. Look, I don't want to fight with her, Trip. It's just that I can't stand her because she's *so* offensive and rude. You heard what she said about Eric last night, didn't you? She's horrible!"

"Yeah, and then we all heard what you said about my girls. Not nice, sister."

"Excuse me, but you said nothing to stop Frances Mae and she started it in the first place!"

"Um, two wrongs don't make a right, do they?"

"Oh, Trip. This is just all so wrong."

"I'm not saying this isn't a little screwed up, but this is the solution I have chosen for the time being because I believe it's in the best interest of my girls. Not *my* best interest, but my *girls'* best interest. I would be really grateful if you would support me in this because it's taking all the strength I have to try and work this out."

"Tell me why you're really doing this, Trip. Gimme the real reason, okay?"

"The real reason? Okay, here it is. I saw Chloe scream with joy when Frances Mae showed up. I saw Linnie, Belle, and Amelia run to their mother and throw their arms around her and they cried tears of happiness. Real tears. Spontaneous tears. Caroline, do you know how powerful that is? And then they *begged* me, *they all begged me* to try again. You may think I'm weak and you may think it's the wrong decision, but if you were in my position? I would have loved to see you just try to say no."

"She's going to drive you out of your mind, Trip."

"Maybe," he said, and smiled. "But it will get me back to work, if nothing else."

"See? You can't live with her and you know it. Honest to God, Trip. She is the crassest and most disgusting woman I have ever known." I looked at him then and he seemed angry. "Sorry, but she is."

"Caroline? This is where I draw the line with you, okay? I just asked you for your support. You're going to have to stop making derogatory remarks about Frances Mae."

"Sorry," I said. I wasn't sorry one damn teensy bit and he could see it on my face.

"Look, you can think whatever you want. Just don't say it, okay? Please?"

Was I capable of not criticizing Frances Mae after all these years of feeding my one and only indulgence? It was seriously doubtful. And it was equally doubtful that Frances Mae would be able to control her tongue either.

"You can tell Frances Mae I'm calling a truce for the moment. If she behaves herself, so will I."

"I'll tell her."

"Trip? Does letting Frances Mae back into your life have anything to do with Rusty dying?"

"Only in that I know I've had the love of my life and lost her and that I will never feel that way about a woman again. So, what the hell? I may as well try and right some wrongs, you know, be a better parent?"

"Are you viewing this as some kind of penance? You can't be serious! And what are you going to do when Chloe goes to college in ten years? Are you really going to spend the rest of your life with Frances Mae?"

"Who knows, but do you know the line in that old song, 'It's cheaper to keep her?' "

"Oh! Trip! Come on!"

"Caroline, I'm doing this because it's the right thing to do."

I was incredulous.

"It's your life, Trip."

"Yes, it is. Now, I'm going home to have a serious chat with your namesake, Miss Linnie." He stood up and tucked in his shirt. "Thank you for breakfast."

"Anytime," I said, and closed the door behind him, wondering if he was telling me the truth. Maybe I was being gullible to consider believing he was taking Frances Mae back for the right reasons, but I just wasn't sure. I wasn't sure about many things.

I made my phone calls for the morning, including one to the magazine. The editor said no problem, they'd check back with me in ten days to see if I had any blooming roses to shoot.

"You're very kind," I said. "Thank you for being so understanding."

"Believe it or not, Ms. Levine, this has happened before, but it was another rosarian who did it out of jealousy."

"Good grief!" I said.

"Yes, ma'am! It's a crazy world out there."

I wanted to say, *Listen, baby, I could tell you stories that would curl your hair.* But I didn't. I thanked the woman on the other end of the phone again and hung up.

I spent the rest of the morning assessing the damage to my poor roses and cleaning up the ground and the bushes with Millie and Mr. Jenkins. We filled a dozen brown paper bags with rose heads and another dozen with clippings.

"See this, y'all?" I called them to have a look. Every cut mark was made by clippers, not scissors. And they were made on a slant, just as a professional or someone who knew about roses would do. The more I thought about it, the more I was convinced that this had been done by a landscaper.

"You're right, Caroline. Don't you think so, Mr. Jenkins?"

Mr. Jenkins looked at Millie, glowing with affection.

"Mrs. Smoak? I think you're so pretty in the sunshine, I could give you a kiss right here and now!"

He moved toward her and she jumped back.

"Oh! Stop, you old fool! Go on now!" Millie said, and dissolved into a fit of giggles. "Don't listen to him, Caroline! He's crazy as a bedbug!"

"Oh, let him kiss you, Millie!"

"That's right! I could go any minute from natural causes!" he said.

"He's a devil, 'eah?" Millie said.

I wondered for a brief moment how successful he was in the bedroom. I know. I'm gross.

Finally, when the sun was directly overhead and frying my scalp, I admitted to myself that it was too hot to work. I went back to the house for lunch and made a tomato sandwich just like the one I had yesterday. If anybody wants to know what they eat in heaven? Tell them vine-ripened tomatoes with a liberal smear of mayonnaise on white bread, salted and peppered. Wash it down with a big glass of sweet tea over ice and a sprig of mint. Food just doesn't get any better than that. Pork included.

Right after one, Matthew called.

"Want to have dinner? I've got some steaks."

"Sure. Why not?"

"How's seven?"

"Perfect. The bugs will be gone and we can eat on the veranda."

"Any news on the Rose Murderer?"

"Not so far. I think we all know what happened, though."

"Yeah. My money's on Eric's theory. What a smart kid."

"Thanks, darlin'!"

I was so glad to know Matthew would be there to end the day. I checked the pantry. I had potatoes to bake and somewhere there was a bottle of red wine. I had not seen Eric all day and I just assumed he was coming home for supper, so I set the table for three.

Later on in the afternoon, Eric drifted in wearing swim trunks and a T-shirt with flip-flops. He was turning a golden brown and the hair on his arms was bleached white. He and his cousins had probably spent the whole day by the pool, listening to music and ragging on the older generation. I remembered those days of small acts of rage against the establishment with a special fondness. I sighed hard then thinking about the world Eric and Trip's girls would eventually enter, one by one. It would be unknown to me, to Trip, to all of us. Advances in medicine, technology, communications, and all the other fields that seem to prop up the world will be as familiar to them as their own names and all these advances will render us, the elders, dinosaurs. What a thought.

The first place he went was the refrigerator as though that's where we hid the money.

"We got anything to drink?"

"There's a pitcher of tea right in front of you. So, how are the girls?" I asked.

"Do you mean, did Linnie confess?"

"No, right?"

"Right."

"Well, it will all be made clear in due time," I said.

"Or not," Eric said. "I mean, Mom, even if that guy Antonio did it, why would Linnie tell you? I'm gonna go wash off all the sweat. We sat by the pool for like hours."

As I dressed for dinner I thought about what Eric had said about Linnie. Why would she admit it, even if she knew? He was right.

It was a perfectly gorgeous Lowcountry evening. Although the sun had already slipped into its sleeping place, the sky was streaked with the most beautiful colors—dark peach that bled into red the color of rubies and slivers of purple, like regal stripes on the robes of a queen. It was impossible not to stare until it all disappeared and night overtook the day.

About half an hour earlier, while there was plenty of light, Eric and Matthew decided to take a walk down by the river. Matthew wanted to talk and Eric wanted to show him some new gadget, a depth finder, I think, that Trip had gotten for his boat. I was fussing around with the table, making sure I had everything that we needed out there for dinner. No, I had thought of it all and I was pretty pleased with myself. Since Millie wasn't around—she and Mr. Jenkins actually went to the movies together to see some animated film about penguins—I was on my own to test my domestic and culinary mettle. To tell you the truth, I don't know why I was always so insecure about my abilities in the kitchen. Maybe it was because I wanted to be a great cook, not just a capable one.

The grill was ready and I looked up to see Eric and Matthew ambling along the path, returning for dinner. I liked the sight of them together. They were good company for each other and I especially liked the way Matthew treated Eric. He made him feel whole. Come to think of it, he made me feel pretty much the same way. Whole. I felt something wobble in my throat. Nerves, I guess. I was in love with the man and not sure what to do about it.

I was struggling with the corkscrew, pushing the cork farther and farther into the neck of the bottle, except for the chunk that I pulled out when the cork broke into two pieces.

"I'm such a spaz!" I said. "Help!" I called to them.

"You want me to open that bottle of wine?" Matthew called out. "Hang on for a minute!"

I threw my arms up in surrender. He rushed up and took the whole mess away from me and removed the rest of the cork easily. Eric went into the house.

"Wow," I said.

"You do realize this is the second time I've rescued you today?"

"And I hope the service comes with a fee," I said, whispering. Oh, you bad girl.

"It does." He wiggled his eyebrows at me like the landlord in the old Dudley Do-Right cartoons. "But it might be hard to deal with."

Really? How hard?

"Then charge me double," I said, and giggled.

"What are y'all whispering about?" Eric came back out of the house, popping the top on a can of soda. "Aw, God, Mom! Are y'all being gross?"

"What? Eric! You shock me! Mother's never gross!" I said, and laughed.

"Your mother is a paragon of virtue, son! A paragon!"

"Well, I don't know if I'd go so far . . ."

We were at the table soon, and if I may say so myself, the steak was the best I'd had in ages. We were having a wonderful time, gobbling up the meal, dissecting Frances Mae's return, under an oath that our cat talk would stay among us and never be repeated, when lo and behold! As though we were calling to them across the breezes, here came Trip, Frances Mae, and Linnie.

I stood to greet them and then Matthew and Eric stood, too.

"Hey!" I said. "Did y'all have supper?" Note: The last thing I wanted was to share my dinner with Frances Mae. Or that little snit, Linnie.

"We're all set," Trip said.

Linnie's attitude was showing and Frances Mae didn't look too happy to be in my company either.

"Well?" Trip said.

"Fine! I came to say I'm sorry, Caroline," Frances Mae said. "I want us to get along and I know I make it complicated to do that, so that's what I wanted to say." She looked from face to face and then to Trip, who nodded in approval. "Okay. I said it."

I shrugged my shoulders and thought, Okay, for Trip's sake, I'll lie through my teeth.

"I'm sorry, too, Frances Mae. We're family, you know? It would be nice for us to get along better than we have in the past."

I didn't mean a word of it and we all knew it. I was about as sincere as she was. If she made one false move for the rest of her life, I'd let her have it.

"And Linnie wants to tell you something, too, Caroline," the old bag said.

"You tell her, Mom!"

Frances Mae reached over and yanked a handful of Linnie's hair so hard I thought it would come right out of her head. Linnie yelped, I gasped, and Trip's eyes opened wide as if to say, *See? This is why we need old F.M. at home!*

"OW!"

"Tell her, girl or there's plenty more where that came from." Linnie said nothing. Frances Mae took another handful of her hair and was about to obliterate the child's best asset when she finally spoke.

"All right! Quit it! I'll tell her! Aunt Caroline? I'm sorry for what happened to your roses. I didn't have nothing to do with it, though. It was that stupid Antonio I used to hook up with? Remember I told you back when Belle graduated that we both broke up with those guys? Well, we did. But Antonio didn't want no part of that. Oh, no. He just wouldn't accept that we was finished. He kept calling and calling and sometimes I would talk to him because you know what? I was sorta scared not to. I mean, I didn't want him to think I hated him, I just didn't want to be with him anymore."

"And?" Frances Mae said, very excitedly as though she was in a hurry to leave, which I hoped she was. "Finish your story!"

"Fine! But back off, okay?"

Frances Mae stepped back and gave Linnie a good slap across her face. "You don't *ever* tell me to back off, do you hear me?"

"I'm sorry, Momma," Linnie said, rubbing her cheek.

"Fresh mouth," Frances Mae said, and her face turned scarlet. Even she had enough sense to know it was iffy at best to whack the shit out of your teenage daughter in front of others.

"In our house this is behavior modification therapy," Trip said with the smile of a saint.

"Hey! Whatever works," I said with a newly found sense of benevolence toward Frances Mae.

While Frances Mae's method of discipline had yet to synchronize with the "proper time and place" theory of when to deliver the whack, the slap, or the yank, I had to admire the swiftness of her delivery and the heft behind it. Frankly, at that moment, I was so happy to be relieved of the responsibility of those girls, Linnie in particular. What the hell was I thinking when I thought she could be tamed?

"That's right," Frances Mae said. "So, missy?"

"Okay, so," Linnie said, trying to gather her thoughts again. "Anyway, Antonio isn't so easy to get rid of, you know? He just—"

"Oh, hell's bells, girl, I'll finish the story," Frances Mae spat. "Otherwise we'll be here all night! So, Caroline, when the girls saw what happened this morning, they were all talking about it, except my Linnie here. I *knew* she knew something she wasn't telling, so I took her aside, and after I screamed at her for an hour, she finally told me what she thought. So I said, gimme your phone. I called this Antonio, who just happened to be on speed dial even though my Linnie here claims to have lost interest in him, and I said, 'You listen to me, boy. You leave my daughter alone, do you hear me? She don't want no part of you! And we know you came over here last night and we know what you did. Shame on you! We can send you to jail if we want to, do you understand?' And he's all like sí, sí, señora and I'm like, 'Well, my sister-in-law is gonna deal with that part but if I ever see you coming around here again, I'm gonna blow your brains out and tell the cops I thought you was a robber! Do you need help to understand this?' And he says, no, no, señora. Anyway, you can have at him, Caroline. Here's his number."

She handed me a piece of paper with a phone number on it. I looked at it and then I looked at her in wonder.

"Frances Mae? That was brilliant!" I said, and meant it. "What you did, I mean! Where do you get the courage? What if he comes back here to slit your throat?"

"Let him try," Trip said.

Frances Mae actually smiled. "I'm her mother, right? I'm just defending my kid, that's all. I told you I was coming back to get my family and get them straight and I'm doing it."

"Well, okay, then!" I said. I mean, listen, I didn't like this woman, never had, never would, but I had to admire her spunk. "Would y'all like to stay for some pie?"

"No, we gotta be getting along, but thanks. See y'all later."

And then I saw the strangest thing happen. Trip got in between Frances Mae and Linnie and put his arms around both of them and gave them a squeeze. They rested their heads on his shoulders. I was breathless. He loved them. My eyes weren't lying. My brother, the same man who could terrify an entire courtroom packed to the rafters, preferred to let Frances Mae be in charge of the family. And she was the drill sergeant who was up to the task. He wanted his family intact, too. And, wonder of the world, the son of a bitch still had it going on for Frances Mae Litchfield.

"Did you see that?" I said.

"Yep," Matthew said.

"Think I should file charges against Antonio?"

"Nope," Matthew said, "let him garden for you all summer at no charge. I'll work it out."

I was so in love with Matthew then I thought I might faint.

"Hey! Wait!" Eric called out to them, and they stopped, turning back to face us. "Mom? Is it okay if I go over there to play Halo?"

"Of course!" I said.

"Can I come with you?" he called out to the others.

"Come on, boy!" Trip called back, and waved him over.

We watched, Matthew and I, as Eric ran to join them.

"He doesn't need my permission to do that. He's almost twenty."

"Funny, that's the same thing he told me."

"What?"

"That I didn't need his permission."

"To do what?" What was he talking about?

"Ask you to marry me. Not that I really did, but you know, he's your son and all and I wanted him to be a part of everything. And I gotta tell you, I love that kid. Love him to death. Anyway, I asked Trip's permission, and he said, please marry her, for God's sake. I thought that was pretty funny."

My jaw dropped.

"Apparently, Trip thinks since I'm here all the time saving you from one thing or another that you probably really do need me."

"I do! I do need you!"

"Good! That's settled! And I think the thought of your ex-husband showing up really scares him, especially if you're in the house alone. He said that old dude *is* a very scary guy. I have to agree with that."

"He is."

"And I don't want you running around with other guys. It makes me really crazy."

"It does?"

"Yes, of *course* it does. I want to kill them in cold blood. Except for Bobby Mack. I liked him well enough. So, there it is. What do you think about all that?"

"I think, I think . . . I don't know what I think! I mean, Matthew! Are you sure you want *me*? I mean, you see what my family is like!"

"What? Caroline? I have been in love with you all my life. Your family doesn't scare me. In fact, I know more about your family than I do about my own! So, is it yes? Wait! I almost forgot. Come with me!"

He grabbed my hand and started running.

"Where are we going? Matthew, slow down!"

Dusk was long gone, night was settling in, and the moon was on the rise. We were heading for the dock, running like two fools on the slick grass, slipping and sliding. He was going to kiss me in the moonlight and I was going to tell him how much I loved him. I would tell him over and over until he told me he believed me.

When we got there he said, "Whew, I'm winded!"

"Me, too!"

"Okay," he said. "You stand right there. No, wait. You sit. I have this all rehearsed in my mind and I don't want to blow it. I mean, how many times in your life do you do this? Right?"

"Right!" I said, and nodded like a bobble-head doll.

I sat on the old bench. It was so quiet then, just us and the sound of the Edisto lapping against the pilings and my heart pounding against my ribs. He reached in his pocket, pulled out a ring, and dropped to one knee.

"I love you, Caroline. Say you'll marry me and make me the happiest man in the world."

"Dear, sweet Matthew, put the ring on my finger and make me the happiest woman alive!"

It was a large, round white diamond solitaire, so brilliant, in fact, that it took my breath away. It flashed its significance even in the dark.

"Matthew! It's beautiful!"

"It was my mother's ring. I know that if she had lived long enough to know you, that she'd want you to have it."

I started to cry and I was embarrassed because he probably thought I cried too much, but it made me think of my own mother.

Miss Lavinia was probably standing on our dock with his mother, somewhere in the shadows, watching this moment when their children declared their love for each other. What would my mother say to me? I wondered, and then I knew. She would say that she was proud, proud of me living my own life, an authentic life, that I was bold and she loved that I was bold. She had been bold once and wasn't this act of commitment to Matthew me truly living up to her reputation? I was going to marry again and this time I was going to marry for love.

Matthew handed me his handkerchief. I just loved men who carried handkerchiefs, but I think I may have told you that before.

"Don't cry, baby. I'm going to take care of you for the rest of your life."

I looked at him straight in the eyes. His eyes were brimming with tears, too.

"And I'm going to take care of you."

"Oh my God! I am so filled with relief! Let's tell Jenkins to clean the chapel for an August wedding. Is August okay with you?"

"I love August! August is just perfect. Oh my God, Matthew! I thought you'd never ask me to marry you! Now that you have, I think I never thought I could be this happy again."

As always, the Edisto River heard my heart and our promises to each other and carried them down to the bluffs. Someday the bluffs would call for us when it was our time and we would join our ancestors to celebrate the lives we had so cherished. But not yet. I had learned that much. That time is short. We watched the moon climb and the first stars of night as they began to twinkle and dance. He pulled me close to him and wrapped his arms around me.

"It's all going to be all right, Caroline. It's all going to be all right."

Epilogue

THE MORNING OF OUR WEDDING Trip got it in his head that he wanted to take Matthew and me out for a round of clays. As I dressed, I had to laugh because shooting clays had been one of my favorite pastimes after my return to Tall Pines, right up until my birthday this year when my world turned on its ear. Eric, Trip, and I would challenge each other and blast clays to bits, laughing and carrying on, having the time of our lives. I also remember thinking back then that my life was a terrible bore, that I desperately needed to buy a condo in Charleston, volunteer for the symphony or the Gibbes Museum, something to break the monotony of my dreary, humdrum existence. Humdrum? If I'd had to endure any more than I'd dealt with this past summer I would have had a nervous breakdown and perhaps spend the rest of my days like a dithering idiot, medicated to the eyeballs and licking the walls of my attic, which is where true southerners kept their addled relatives.

It was just before eight and why I told Trip I'd do this when my wedding was just hours away? Well, darlin'? That was anybody's guess. Maybe he was feeling nostalgic and sentimental. Or maybe it was one of the few things he could do without Frances Mae hanging on his heels harping about one thing or another, which he must have enjoyed at some level or why would he tolerate it? They got a good offer for their house in Walterboro and closed on the sale two weeks ago. Some nagging thing in me kept worrying that if their marriage blew up again, where would she go? Or maybe it was just that selling that house made her move to Tall Pines that much more permanent, which was enough to rattle every nerve the rest of us had, including Millie's and Mr. Jenkins's.

Ah, Frances Mae! Not the ideal in-law, to be sure, but I had to give her credit for a few things. Her children were certainly happier with her back and they were much better behaved. And she appeared to be mellowing. Just last week I was down in the chapel thinking of how I wanted everything to look for the ceremony, where flowers would go and so forth. I was sitting in a pew on the left side and she came in and sat in a pew on the other side.

"Hey, Caroline. How're you?"

"Good. You?"

"Good. Millie said she thought I'd find you here."

"Millie was right. What's going on?"

"Well, I've been doing a lot of thinking lately and I decided that maybe I was wrong about a few things."

"Like what?"

"Well, you know you said you wanted to give Amelia a party because she was coming of age and I went off on you and said forget it?"

"Yep. I remember." You ungrateful stupid hillbilly from hell, I thought. Did you ever in your life do anything for anyone else just to be nice?

"Well, here's the thing. Now I'm thinking something like that might be good for Amelia. She's all gawky and awkward, you know? And I ain't ever seen her with a boy. Not even once. Do you think we could find her a boy?"

Was she enlisting my help? Was she asking me to help her make Amelia more graceful? Had some force of nature kidnapped the twelve million devils from my sister-in-law's soul? I could not have been more surprised at her change of heart.

"Frances Mae? If you want to have that party for her, I'd be thrilled to organize it. Of course we'll find her a boy, an appropriate boy, just for her. Someone's who's smart and nice like she is."

"Really?"

"Absolutely! And, I'll take her to New York as I had promised and I'll buy her the prettiest dress in the whole town! I'll do it!"

"That's wonderful! You know I was just so nervous when I got back from California. A deb ball just seemed awful snotty to me."

Some would argue that that was the point, but I didn't feel like insulting her just then. Maybe I had mellowed, too.

"It doesn't have to be, Frances Mae. Ours would just be a dinner dance for friends and family."

"Well, if it's a family thing, you know, a tradition? Then I need to try to make myself comfortable with that."

"It's not that big of a deal, really." The poor thing was so insecure.

"There's just one other thing."

"What's that?"

"Can I come to New York, too? I ain't never seen a big city, except the Los Angeles airport when I went out there to, you know, get my mind right? I've always wanted to take a ride on the Staten Island Ferry so's I could see the Statue of Liberty."

Okay, this is where my heart stopped and I got a cold sweat. If I said no, we'd regress back to the way things used to be. If I said yes? Oh, how bad could it be? Maybe she'd get on the ferry and jump. One could always hope.

So, ever the optimist, I said, "Why not? Let me just get married and then we'll plan the whole thing! It'll be fun."

Who was I kidding?

"Hey, Frances Mae? Did I spot you at Belle's graduation? Is that possible?"

"Yep." She pulled out her cell phone and showed me the pictures she took. "I had to sneak in with one of them male nurses because my treatment wasn't over and I had to go back. Look at this one." It was a snapshot of Frances Mae and Belle. Belle was beaming. Belle had never said a word.

"What? She didn't tell a soul!"

"Caroline? Don't ever underestimate my relationships with my girls. We're tighter than ticks on a yard dog's ass."

"Right," I said, and thought, Well, aren't you the lyrical one?

So, I was slipping on my olive cotton twill trousers and a sleeve-less white cotton turtleneck to go shoot clays with Matthew and Trip, thinking about traipsing around Manhattan with Frances Mae and Amelia while Eric was having lunch with his father at the 21 Club or some old-establishment watering hole. It would be some trip all right.

In a few hours I was going to be Caroline Strickland. I was taking his name because I didn't want there to be any confusion about my commitment to Matthew. I slipped on my shoes, and at the last second, I grabbed one of Mother's old Hermès scarves, the one with the olive-and-brown birds all over it and tied it around my neck, just like she used to do. I hurried down the stairs with enough time to spare for a cup of coffee. I was to meet Trip and Matthew in the barn.

"Here come the bride!" Millie sang out as I pushed through the kitchen door.

"Yep, here she is! We got any coffee?"

"Yes, ma'am! I'll pour you a cup since it's such a big day and all."

"Thanks!"

"Now, where're you headed this morning?"

"Shooting clays with Trip and Matthew." I took the mug from her and gave it a splash of cream. "I'll be back by noon."

"Going out shooting a gun on the day you get married? What kinda fool is that? You'd better be careful, you 'eah me? And be back in this house by noon, no messing around."

"Oh! Why? Millie! What? Did you see something?" Oh God, all we needed was a disaster!

"What? No chile! Your hairdresser called. She'll be here at twelve noon sharp! So don't be dragging your heels! You don't want to be late for your own wedding!"

I took several big gulps of the coffee and poured the rest down the drain, rinsing out the mug.

"Don't worry! They can't start without me! I'll be back!"

It was hot, but a perfect day to change my life. The Lowcountry-blue sky without a cloud, a breeze laced with pinesap and flowers, the Edisto placid and soothing.

Trip and Matthew waited in the distance, their cars parked outside the barn. I was on the golf cart, the one that would be festooned later on that day with white bunting and satin ribbons with roses tied up in the knots. We had not invited so many people, it was really just us, Miss Sweetie and Miss Nancy, and a few friends from Jacksonboro and Charleston, maybe thirty guests in all. As a gift, Bobby Mack was catering a barbecue dinner for all of us. He and I had remained good friends and Matthew was determined to learn the fine points of roasting a pig from him. Matthew said he didn't want me to run away and leave him for a pork belly. Ah, Matthew. I hope you won't give up your day job to do stand-up.

When Matthew asked Eric to be his best man, I asked Amelia to be my maid of honor. This was cause for great excitement for Amelia. I was determined still to take that child under my wing and it appeared that Frances Mae was going to let me, as long as I didn't turn her into a snob. I had no such intention. I just wanted to spoil her with attention and affection like I wished someone would have done for me. Surely there could be no harm in that as long as I didn't come between her and her mother.

So we had our morning of sporting clays, built by my parents just before my father's death. And I was reminded of them at every one of the eighteen courses. I wished for my mother something mad. I wanted her to see the beautiful man I was to marry in just a few hours and to get a sense of how extraordinary he was. They had only known each other in passing but I knew that Matthew had my mother's eye.

Mr. Jenkins had positioned the trap houses so that, just like in the old days, we would be surprised to discover the direction of the clay bird's flight. Matthew shot extremely well for a beginner, joking that it was all his years of experience in chasing drug dealers that helped, but it was easy to see he'd be able beat us all very shortly. He asked Trip why he had never made it a hunt club and Trip said, well, he didn't know why and maybe that was a good idea. It would certainly help toward paying the maintenance. I told them their man talk was boring, the humidity was rising, and I was ready to go home. After all, I had a date with the man of my dreams and I wanted my hair to look good. I kissed Matthew on the cheek and then I gave Trip a smooch, too. Nothing could ruin my good mood.

I had two new dresses for the occasion and still could not decide what to wear. Anna Abbot, my hairdresser and friend for ages, was there with me in the bedroom. My hair was up in Velcro rollers and my makeup was done. I showed her the ivory one and she said it would make me look washed out. Then I held the pastel-pink one next to my face and she said the color made me look like a goddess. Well, I guess that decided that! "Goddess works," I joked, and put it on.

It was nearly three and time to go. Trip knocked on my bedroom door and I told him to come in. He reminded me that he had given me away when I married Richard but that he intended to do a better job this time. "This one's gonna stick," he said, and we laughed, knowing it would. Yes, it would. Matthew would be a spectacular husband and I would be the best wife I knew how to be.

As I left the house, Millie hugged me with all her strength and wished me good luck. Mr. Jenkins took my hands and told me he intended to marry Millie as soon as she would sign the marriage license. She said he shouldn't go around telling tales and he just winked at me.

Trip, Amelia, and I climbed on the golf cart. Amelia told me she thought I looked beautiful and I told her she did, too. In minutes I was there, standing in the doorway of my family's chapel on Trip's arm, wearing pastel pink, feeling the penny Millie had slipped in my shoe, with the handkerchief every bride in our family for the last hundred years or more carried tucked in my flowers, and holding an armful of Mother's roses that smelled so sweet. Amelia went before me. She had never looked as lovely as she did that day. She walked gracefully to the end of the chapel and turned to face me. Little Chloe was there with Missy, who wore a big satin bow on her collar for the occasion. I spotted Frances Mae, Linnie, and Belle. Susan and Simon Rifkin were there, Jack Taylor and his wife, Mimi, the pound-cake queen, and the Misses Sweetie and Nancy and Bobby Mack. Millie kept blotting her eyes and Mr. Jenkins patted her arm. The congregation was a mosaic of my life and Matthew's. I couldn't wait to see how it would grow and spread.

The musicians were playing Vivaldi and all our friends rose from their seats and turned to face me. Matthew and Eric waited, smiling at the other end of the aisle, standing to the left of Reverend Moore. I thought of Miss Lavinia, for as much as I loved Matthew, and I did with all my heart, I missed my mother so desperately. To our great surprise, all the lights in the chapel flickered, there was a clap of thunder, and from nowhere came a brief summer shower that smelled so green and clean, lasting just long enough to cool the air. Water. The symbol of new life, being born again, and it was water that filled the mighty Edisto. Maybe Mother had sent that shower, something to let me know it was good and right to marry Matthew. I'd never know until I met her on the bluffs.

"Mother always had to have the last word," I said.

"You're right. Well, they're all waiting, Caroline. Shall we do this or do you want to make a break for it?" Trip said.

I suppressed a giggle. "No. Let's marry me off one more time."

I went into the chapel, smiling, with a full heart and without a worry in the world.

Acknowledgments

THE ACE BASIN IN THE Lowcountry of South Carolina is first and foremost a magical place. Life seems to roll along in an unhurried way, belying the incredible surprises her powerful spirit will show if you only learn how to look for the signs. I want to thank the following people whose amazing inspiration, patience, and generosity of spirit to share their interpretation of the signs left me filled with wonder and enriched this story in innumerable ways. First and foremost, my sister and brother-in-law, Lynn and Scott Bagnal of Edisto Beach, South Carolina. This book would be a snore without y'all. I love y'all with all I've got. Special hugs to Roger Pinckney of Daufuskie Island, South Carolina, whose wonderful book, *Blue Roots,* sparked my own memories of haints and hags, spells and cunja, and clarified many details I had almost forgotten. Anyone who considers themselves or aspires to be Geechee in their soul should rush right out, buy that book, and savor it. To Michael Hickman of Jacksonboro, South Carolina, many, many thanks. I am still remembering with gratitude that steaming hot afternoon you drove me down Parker's Ferry Road to the old plantation that would become the inspiration for the location of Tall Pines. Well, Michael? Tall Pines lives on! Special thanks once again to Frank and Nina Burke of Ravenwood plantation for the crash course on sporting clays and all their wonderful stories about authentic plantation living in the twenty-first century. The devil is always in the details and much of what you shared with me is littered through these pages, performing tiny exorcisms. I hope!

Special thanks to my friend of many decades, Charlie Moore of Mount Pleasant, South Carolina, for once again taking up the cloth to portray the Reverend Charles Moore. Charlie Moore was and is still one of the funniest, smartest, coolest men to have ever lived and I am sending you a big smooch, my friend. The dweeb he plays in these pages bears no resemblance beyond height and gender to Charlie's intellect, character, or sex appeal.

To my agent and great friend, Larry Kirshbaum, a true prince and the most charming and elegant gentleman in the whole darn city of New York, with enormous gratitude for his excellent counsel and humor. To my wonderful editor, Carrie Feron, for her good humor and incredible insights and understanding, I am giving you three curtseys, plus a bow, and a scrape and blowing you many kisses of appreciation from the other side of the Hudson.

And to the entire William Morrow and Avon team: Brian Murray, Michael Morrison, Liate Stehlik, Adrienne Di Pietro, Tessa Woodward, Lynn Grady, Tavia Kowalchuk, Seale Ballenger, Ben Bruton, Greg Shutack, Shawn Nichols, Debbie Steir, Frank Albanese, Virginia Stanley, Bobby Brinson, Jamie Brickhouse, Rachael Brennan, Michael Brennan, Carl Lennertz, Carla Parker, Michael Morris, Michael Spradliln, Brian Grogan, Gabe Barillas, and Deb Murphy, thank you one and all for all the miracles you bring about every day, for your amazing and generous support. Y'all make me want to dance!

To my writer friends in New Jersey and South Carolina who prop me up from time to time with your amazing humor and generous compassion: Pamela Redmond Satran, Mary Jane Clark, Laurie Albanese, Debbie Galant, Deborah Davis, Benilde Little, Christina Baker Kline, Liza Dawson, Jack Alterman, Marjory Wentworth, Jenny Sanford, Josephine Humphreys, Barbara Haggerty, Mary Alice Monroe, Pat Conroy, and his long-suffering wife, Cassandra King Conroy, I love y'all like a crazy woman! And if I left anyone out, I'll buy you a glass of wine at Station Twenty-Two Restaurant on the island or at Halcyon in the 'burbs.

To my dear friend Buzzy Porter, Buzz Man, Wonderful One— I'm missing you! Is there Chick-Fil-A in our future? And special thanks to Giovanni Castilla for bringing an international flavor to these pages.

To Debbie Zammit, my stalwart and dearest friend of so many years. It's a little scary who keeps me on track, who is so meticulous that I look organized, and so funny and crazy, what can I say? Thanks for another year of fabulous tuna salad and for making me laugh until it hurts. Love ya, love ya!

To Ann Del Mastro, Mary Allen, George Zur, and Kevin Sherry—the Franks adore you all and deeply appreciate all you do to keep us afloat. To Penn Sicre for your friendship and faith. To my fabulous cousin Charles "Comar" Blanchard of Mount Pleasant, South Carolina, for reasons too numerous to cite. Love you all!

To the real people who appear in these pages besides Charlie Moore, Oscar Rosen, Nancy Poole, and Lynn Brook, if they act out of character, and I'm just guessing that they will, don't blame them. It's just the writer having some fun and their antics in no way reflect the character of these law-abiding, tax-paying, mighty-fine folks.

To booksellers across the land, and I mean every single one of them, I thank you from the bottom of my heart, especially Patty Morrison of Barnes & Noble, Charleston, South Carolina, who has led the launch of *nine* books and with whom I have eaten more cookies than either of us will ever admit; Larry Morey and every single sainted soul from Barnes & Noble in Mount Pleasant, South Carolina; Jennifer McCurry and all her brilliant staff at Waldenbooks in downtown Charleston; Margot Sage-El of Watchung Booksellers in Montclair, New Jersey; Frazer Dobson and Sally Brewster of Park Road Books in Charlotte, North Carolina; and everybody hold the phone for Jacquie Lee of Books a Million! Holy moly. What can I say? Jacquie, you are the greatest! You all are the greatest! My whole family is in your debt and all the Franks thank y'all from the depths of our gizzards!

To my wonderful husband, Peter, and our two glorious children, Victoria and William, I love y'all with all my heart and I thank you for your endless patience and support. I am so proud to own the bragging rights because with everything you do and just because of who you are, you make my heart swell in gratitude.

Finally, to my readers to whom I owe the greatest debt of all. I am sending you the most sincere and profound thanks for reading my stories, sending along so many nice e-mails, for being my Facebook friends, for coming out to book signings in the rain and all kinds of crazy weather. You are why I continue to try to write a book every year. I hope someday you'll find yourself in the Lowcountry's ACE Basin and get some of Millie's magic for yourself.

I love you all and thank you all. Yes, I do, 'eah?

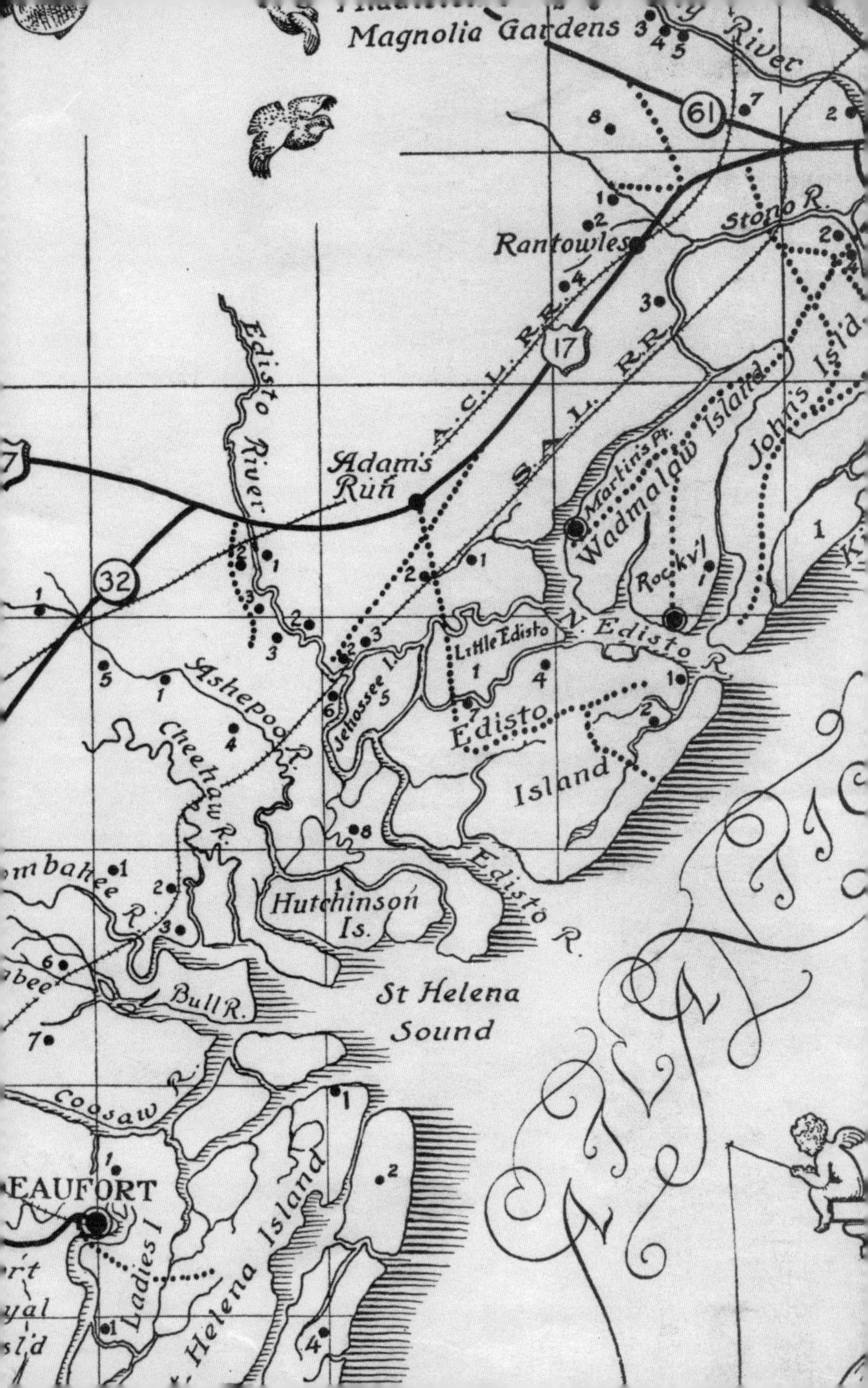

Magnolia Gardens
River
61
Rantowles
Stono R.
A.C.L. R.R.
S.A.L. R.R.
17
Edisto River
Adam's Run
32
Martin's Pt.
Wadmalaw Island
Johns Isl'd
Rockv'l
N. Edisto R.
Little Edisto
Ashepoo R.
Jehossee I.
Edisto
Island
Cheehaw R.
Combahee R.
Hutchinson Is.
Edisto R.
Bull R.
St Helena Sound
Coosaw R.
BEAUFORT
Ladies I
St. Helena Island
Port Royal Isl'd